Dedicated young surgeon Paul Abbott had begun a new life after escaping with the beautiful quadroon woman Micaela. But the Civil War soon separated them, taking Paul to the frustrating army hospital where he was appalled at the army's callous disregard of human life.

Micaela was left alone. And the dark and evil Léon Jacquard, who had been her owner, vowed revenge for her leaving him. He set into motion a dangerous plan that included kidnapping, rape—and death. Now it would take nothing short of a miracle to reunite Paul and Micaela. . . .

Mitchell Caine

WORSHIP THE WIND

FAWCETT GOLD MEDAL • NEW YORK

WORSHIP THE WIND

Produced by Lyle Kenyon Engel

© 1979 Book Creations, Inc. and Mitchell Caine

Published by Fawcett Gold Medal Books, a unit of CBS Publications, the Consumer Publishing Division of CBS Inc.

ISBN 0-449-14178-0

Printed in the United States of America

10 9 8 7 6 5 4 3 2 1

For Ren, the girl that I married

"Battle is the ultimate to which the whole life's labor of an officer should be directed. He may live to the age of retirement without seeing a battle. Still, he must always be getting ready for it exactly as if he knew the hour of the day it is to break upon him, and then, whether it come late or early, he must be willing to fight—he must fight!"

General Charles F. Smith, Commandant of Cadets at West Point, in speech during graduation ceremonies, 1843.

". . . the fascination of a great battle wholly overcomes all prudential considerations. There is nothing on earth approaching it in sublimity. . . . Personal danger is forgotten until the danger is over."

Sylvanus Cadwallader, war correspondent with General Grant during the Civil War.

Prologue

i

On the eve of battle, the general slept badly. His swollen leg was still bothering him, but his conscience troubled him far worse. Before retiring, despite solemn promises to Julia, he had again indulged in a few drinks with his officers. Fortunately his devoted chief of staff had extricated him before he had lost all control and reason.

Alcohol was his curse and damnation; it had darkened his past with failures and ridicule. Corroded his sleep with nightmares.

Another such slip at a crucial moment could result in the needless slaughter of thousands of men under his command.

It could also result in his commission being stripped away, and he would be right back where he had been before the war started:

On the street again, without friends or money. Despised. A hopeless failure. His last chance for redemption utterly shattered. . . .

ii

Rolling out of bed, he hobbled across to where his rumpled uniform had been carelessly flung over a chair. Slight of build, round-shouldered, slovenly in manner and even in uniform somewhat scrubby in appearance, he looked anything but a warrior. Nor was he temperamentally suited to the profession of killing. Death sickened him. He agonized over pain, whether suffered by a man or beast. He detested the sight of blood; even the sight of red meat nauseated him.

Only by a fluke of circumstances had fate lifted him, virtually overnight, from obscurity to the exalted status of a general.

Dressed, he limped downstairs just as the last stars were dissolving like sand in a gentle and widening bowl of gray.

Chief of Staff John Rawlins was already up and sorting mail that had arrived via mail steamer from Cairo during the night. He was a frail-looking man of about thirty with thick black hair and a beard contrasting sharply with an abnormal pallor. But for all his sickly appearance he seemed always to be breathing fire and fury. His burning black eyes were fueled by several obsessions. One was his crusading hatred of slavery. Just as bitterly he detested strong drink.

But most passionately of all he was convinced that his general was a military genius—yet one who could never fulfill his destiny to its noblest dimensions without the kind of protection and devoted help that only he, John Rawlins, could provide.

"Heard you moving around down here, Rawlins. Up earlier than usual, aren't you?"

The chief of staff allowed himself a tight smile of respect mingled with reproach. "Yes sir. Lot of extra chores to handle today." His reference was to previous orders to move headquarters upriver today, right after breakfast, and the brunt of such responsibilities always fell on him.

"Is everything set to go?"

"Yes sir." The question had been superfluous. Prior to any move Rawlins never failed to kick all the aides awake amply ahead of time. All files and other headquarters paraphernalia were already packed and stowed on the general's steamer. The horses had been saddled and put aboard. The captain was under orders to keep steam up and be ready to push off at a moment's notice.

"By the way, any message from Buell?"

"Yes sir." Rawlins produced the dispatch that had been delivered by courier during the night. "He expects to arrive with his troops before noon."

"Good." The general smiled. "That's all we're waiting for before we launch our attack and start whipping the hell out of the rebs. . . ."

At that moment the steward's assistant appeared to announce that breakfast was on the table. The general started away. His limp was very pronounced. Rawlins called after him:

"You're obviously in great pain, sir. Shall I get a doctor to have another look at your ankle?"

The general paused. His bad leg dated back to several nights ago when his horse had slipped in the mud and fallen during a heavy downpour, pinning his leg underneath. One of the regimental surgeons had cut off the boot, applied hot and cold dressings, then a soothing balm of wet leaves and ointment—something he had learned from the Indians, the doctor had said. It had done wonders in lessening the pain.

"When we get to the landing will be soon enough, Rawlins. And try to get the same doctor who treated me the first time. What was his name?"

"Abbott, sir. Paul Abbott."

"That's the one. A good man." The general had the

greatest respect for the medical profession as a whole but harbored grave doubts about the skills of the average army doctor. He had a memory flash of Paul Abbott's steady gray eyes, the speed of his deft fingers, his calm, sure air of competence. "It might be a good idea to have Dr. Abbott transferred to the headquarters medical service."

The chief of staff allowed himself one of his rare grins. "That has already been done, sir."

iii

At the breakfast table, the general's coffee cup was raised halfway to his mouth when the first thunderous crash of cannon came rolling down the river.

He held the cup suspended while his trained ears made their instant assessment. The heavy detonations, coming from about twelve miles upriver, were continuous. This was no ordinary skirmishing action between enemy patrols. Big guns had been unlimbered: twenty-four-pounder howitzers; a battery of ten-pounder Parrotts; a howling medley of six-pounder Napoleons. Not his artillery.

General Ulysses S. Grant put down his cup untouched and stood up.

"Gentlemen," he said to the staff officers around the table, "I fear the enemy has got the jump on us. Let us be off. . . ."

Book One

SHILOH

"*I swear by Apollo, the physician, and Asklepios, Hygieia, and Panacea and all the gods and goddesses . . . that I will keep this oath. . . .*

"*I will follow that system of regimen which, according to my ability and judgment, I consider to be for the benefit of my patients, and abstain from whatever is deleterious. . . .*

"*With purity and with holiness I will pass my life and practice my art . . . for the benefit of the sick and will abstain from every voluntary act of mischief and wrongdoing to women, men, and slaves. Whatever, in connection with my professional practice or not, I see or hear in the lives of people which should not be discussed abroad, I will not divulge, believing such things should be kept quiet and secret.*

"*While I continue to keep this Oath inviolate, may it be granted to me to enjoy life and the practice of my art, respected by all men in all times. But should I trespass on and violate this Oath, may the reverse befall me!*"

From the Hippocratic Oath, c. 460–370 B.C.

One

Bloody Sunday

i

The long roll on the drum began with the suddenness of lightning out of a blue sky and continued with the greatest rapidity. On and on.

Throughout the Federal encampment of weathered white army tents crowded amid the lightly timbered woods as far as the eye could reach, all soldiers stopped whatever they were doing, momentarily frozen in place like statues. Some were hunkered around campfires frying salt pork, boiling coffee or just loafing. Others were shaving in front of mirrors attached to trees. The more industrious were polishing their rifles with ashes from dead fires. A few were off in the bushes performing their natural morning functions and a sprinkling of laggards still snored on the hard ground inside their tents, for murky dawn was still cloaked behind a heavy mist.

The ribbon of fast staccato sounds kept unrolling, sending prickles up the spines of veterans, jabbing at the nerves of raw new troops.

Grab your weapons and fall into battle formation! Double-quick, double-quick! was the throbbing message.

A mounted picket came galloping through the camp. The tails of his blue jacket flapped in the breeze; his canteen banged rhythmically against a thigh. A musket slung from his shoulder bounced to the fast three-beat gait of his foam-flecked horse.

"They're a-comin'—" he shouted. "Swarmin' outta the woods like ants—!"

The rolling boom of artillery and a distant spatter of musketry fire accompanied his words.

As the men scrambled for their rifles, varied emotions were reflected on their faces: astonishment, disbelief, chagrin, the pallor of fright; but most of all, an upwelling of rage—

For the past week or so they had been recovering from their ordeal on the jam-packed and unsanitary river transports, where almost to a man they had endured bouts of the ague, dysentery or typhoid. Many had died. But ashore and resting up in the warmth of a Tennessee springtime, breathing in the tangy scent of peaceful pines and the sweetness of peach blossoms they had felt as safe and happy as at a picnic back home. They spent their days swimming in the streams, playing poker, writing letters, practicing their marksmanship on squirrels and stumps. During daylight a calliope on one of the steamboats brayed out patriotic ditties; regimental bands played lusty marches each evening. It was like being on a holiday. Even the outlying pickets had become chummy with their counterpart rebel pickets stationed only a few hundred feet away. They had called out friendly gibes at each other, and often under the cover of darkness had joined each other around campfires to exchange tobacco and a swallow or two of whiskey, and gab.

All the while, smug and complacent with the belief that the great Union army—whenever the officers got around to giving the orders—could easily overrun and wipe out the whole derned cowardly rebel army quick as a wink. The hull Yankee army was primed and ready, eager to lick 'em good and end the hull derned war. What were the godderned generals waiting fer?

But this—it was a lowdown dirty trick for the rebs to jump a man before he hardly had time to get awake and take his morning crap!

How come old Useless Sam Grant wasn't looking out for them?

Amid the grouchings were expressions of joyful excitement from some of the recruits.

"I'm ready fer 'em!" cried a young private from the 71st Ohio Volunteers, his boyish face wreathed in gleeful anticipation. "I been waitin' fer a chance to blast at 'em. It sure beats jist shootin' at stumps." He was literally trembling with eagerness. Soon he would be facing the enemy, fighting bravely. A hero. Soon he would *really* have something to write home about.

A lanky Iowan veteran looked at him in disgust. "You dumb little shit—you'll be the first one to show 'em your ass." Gripping his rifle in a relaxed way with one hand, the fingers of his other automatically checking his ammunition supply in the box at his belt, he bent low and hustled off toward the sound of firing.

Bullets began whistling overhead, nipping off twigs and leaves. Company commanders were bellowing orders; bugles were sounding. A shell screamed overhead, slashing through treetops. It landed near a tent, exploding redly, plowing up gobs of earth and a shower of pine needles.

And now above the swelling din of attack could be heard the spine-chilling rebel yell screeching from thousands of throats.

Someone cried, "Gawd—here they come!"

ii

In a hospital tent about a mile back, Captain Paul Abbott listened with incredulity to the continuous roar and thunder of battle. Mingled with the booming of heavy field siege artillery were the cadence of drums and furious musketry fire that from a distance sounded like a million maniacs beating empty barrels with hammers. Reverberating through the muggy morning air, all of it sounded ominously close.

A rasping voice caught his attention:

"Gentlemen, before the casualties start arriving, I believe it incumbent on me to clarify the situation here, and the procedures I shall expect you to follow—"

The speaker was Chief Surgeon Avery Britton, a lean man of about fifty with a weathered, wrinkled face, grizzled hair and a peppery temperament. Above his eyes, of palest blue, the forehead was creased with perpetual scowl lines that seemed to deepen as his arrogant glance slashed around at the other seven doctors in the tent. Britton had served his entire professional life in the regular army, now holding the rank of major, and keenly felt his superiority over his colleagues, who were only volunteers from civilian life holding temporary commissions as mere captains.

"First of all," he went on, "I must remind you that we're seriously short of medical supplies—"

They all knew. Supplies had been depleted by sickness on the river transports. Typhoid, pneumonia, malaria, dysentery, bilious putrid fevers and smallpox had swept through the troops, crowded a thousand to each boat. So many had died that they soon ran out of coffin wood and started pulling out wall panels. Finally they just wrapped the dead in sheets or any old rags they could find. It was estimated that a third of Grant's great Army of the Tennessee had either died or was too immobilized by illness to fight by the time they reached the battle zone at Pittsburg Landing.

"Now among our shortages—" The chief surgeon began reading from a sheet of paper the various items in shortest supply. Bandages, fresh dressings, ligatures, tourniquets, sponges; no beds, bedding, hospital clothing or articles of diet for the sick at all; only a minimal stock of the proper medicines; only ten ounces of tartar emetic—

A gust of laughter interrupted.

"That's sure one medication we don't need here," commented one doctor.

Whether from polluted drinking water or a natural effect of the standard diet of hardtack and salt pork, virtually every man in the army had suffered, or was suffering, the form of camp diarrhea known as the "Tennessee quickstep." Despite General Grant's stern orders that privies must be used, many a private had rushed into the nearest bushes to find himself almost elbow to elbow with a red-faced officer trying to maintain his dignity while squatting to relieve the urgent call of nature.

Unamused, Britton continued: "Some of our shortages can be directly attributed to a number of our own medical staff who have drawn medicine, special foods for the sick and whiskey—particularly whiskey—in a most profuse and extravagant manner for private purposes. . . ."

There was an abashed silence. A shell went whooshing, whistling overhead and some of the doctors glanced up uneasily, unconsciously ducking their heads a bit.

"How about anesthetics?" someone asked.

"As already noted, the whiskey supply is very low; so is the opium; and there's only a limited supply of mandrake."

"Don't we have any ether or chloroform?" asked another listener, whose name was Saul Simon. He was a slim young man with a mass of dark ringlets that fell to his ears and gentle dark eyes.

"The army has not yet seen fit to authorize such newfangled nostrums, Simon."

"Newfangled! Ether, chloroform, as well as nitrous oxide have been in use now for over fifteen years!"

Britton frowned. "Such matters are up to Congress to decide. Congress keeps a tight control over every detail in the army, and they've divided their membership into hundreds of committees for that purpose. Their medical commission, unfortunately, is considered among the least important of them all."

"But in the case of badly wounded men," Saul Simon persisted, "how can we deaden the pain for them after our present supply of opiates runs out?"

"Simon, you've only been in the service a few weeks. You've never experienced warfare, or you wouldn't ask such a stupid question. Barring the arrival of fresh supplies soon—highly unlikely—we'll simply use what army surgeons have always used—speed. In the case of amputations, we'll make the agony as brief as possible."

"That's . . . barbarous! I call it a damned shame when a man gets injured while risking his life to preserve the Union and can't be assured of the finest treatment known to the medical profession."

"Everything about war is a damned shame, Simon. Always has been and isn't likely ever to change. Humans being the ornery fools they are," he added, then turned to glare around at the others.

"While on the subject of amputations, I want to stress that I want no time wasted on wounded extremities. In other words, if it is estimated that it will take more time to clean up a ragged injury to a limb than it would to amputate—then amputate! It's cleaner, faster, takes less nursing attention afterward and is less apt to gangrene."

Paul Abbott, who had been leaning against his rough board operating table, stationed next to Saul Simon's, and listening to the chief surgeon with fuming annoyance, was now startled into a response:

"Do you really mean to say, Major Britton, that a quick amputation is more desirable than spending a little extra time trying to save a limb by medical means?"

"That's exactly what I mean, Abbott. What's best for the army as a whole always takes precedence over what's best for the individual. We've got an army of over thirty thousand men out there—"

He paused to listen to the increased volume of enemy shells that were now screaming through the air alarmingly close, to explode only a few hundred yards away. They howled, shrieked, whistled and sometimes seemed to groan in flight. Paul feared that any moment one of

18

them would land just right and demolish the tent and all in it.

Unperturbed, Britton continued: "As I was saying, over thirty thousand men out there—and only thirty doctors in the whole army to take care of them. If the fighting stays as hot as it sounds now, before long a hundred doctors wouldn't be enough—"

The front flaps of the large tent suddenly swished aside as a burly soldier holding up the front end of a stretcher entered. The wounded man on the stretcher, a lad of about eighteen, was sobbing softly.

"Whar' ya want 'im dumped?"

Britton glanced around. The early morning sun slanting against the canvas cast a murky yellow glow down over the rough wooden operating tables around which the surgeons and their assistants, crowded close in the limited space, nervously waited.

"I'll take him," he decided, jerking a thumb at his own table, beside which stood a wrought-iron brazier over which simmered a pot of boiling oil.

Even as he spoke, the tent flaps were being jostled by another stretcher entering, and crowding close behind still another.

"Whar'll we put this one?"

"Put him on any of the tables that are empty," snapped the chief surgeon, helping with the placement of his own patient on his table, face down because the wound was in the back.

"Thar's a hull mess of 'em out thar'," said one of the stretcher bearers. "Hunderts of 'em on the ground ever'-whar' yeh look. Ain't gonna be 'nough room fer 'em in here. . . ."

Britton, bending over his young patient, let out a snort of disgust. "Minié ball in the back!"

". . . Mother . . . Mother," the boy was sobbing, half in delirium. "War'n't my fault, I swear. The colonel ordered us . . . tol' us to run an' save ourselves. . . ."

"He was with Appler's division," confirmed the stretcher bearer. "Saw Appler with my own eyes runnin' like a goddamn rabbit to the rear, shoutin' his fuckin' head off.

The 71st Ohio broke an' ran too, an' Prentiss's batt'ry is took—"

"That's a thunderin' lie!" angrily interjected one of the wounded just arriving. "Prentiss an' his hull brigade is still out there fightin' off the hull rebel army. I was right there beside Prentiss when I got it."

By now the influx of battle victims was creating a traffic jam as they were brought into the tent. Most came on stretchers; some were clumsily carried by arms and legs by two or three soldiers.

Leaving his sobbing patient unattended, Britton came over to help with the distribution of the newly arrived.

"Now here's a leg that'll have to come off right away," he said, looking down at a white-faced soldier who lay sideways on a stretcher, clutching bloodstained hands at a bent leg while trying to suppress moans convulsively choking from his throat. A torn trouser leg revealed a crimson mess of mangled flesh. Bright red blood pulsed out with each heartbeat.

"Don't give him much chance, though," he added bluntly—army surgeons had no need for bedside manners. "Looks like he was nicked by a six-pounder cannonball and it got an artery. He's already lost too much blood."

Paul Abbott, who was helping, had quickly produced a tourniquet and was applying it to stanch the flow of blood.

"Let me take him," he said. "I think I can save the leg."

The chief surgeon snorted. "I've already warned about wasting time, Abbott. I know how you like to fuss over cases with all those crazy theories about infection you claim you got from those foreign loonies, Lister and Pasteur."

"I resent that statement, Major Britton," said Paul, busy adjusting the tension of the tourniquet.

"Resent it all you want, but the fact is, any case you handle, I could handle twice as fast. I'll wager on that."

"And I'll wager," Paul snapped back, "that the sur-

20

vival rate of patients I handle is more than twice as high as that of your patients."

Britton's face mottled a furious red. "I was an army surgeon while you were still in short britches, Abbott! In the Mexican and Indian wars I was in situations where casualties were brought in by the wagonload—all screaming for help and me the only surgeon. If I dawdled over any one of them trying to save a leg—like you can afford to do in civilian life—the rest would be dead before I got to them. Speed, speed, *speed* is what counts. I can get a leg off in thirty seconds, an arm in twenty."

"We're wasting time, Major, so why don't I just take this man and—"

"This one is for Simon," the chief surgeon said brusquely, and motioned the stretcher bearers to Simon's table.

Saul Simon's face blanched. "Major . . . I-I've had no training as a surgeon. I had only two years of medical school and began practice just as a doctor of medicine. I . . . I don't know how to do an amputation."

"Well, you'll never find a better medical school than war," said Britton with a kind of gleeful mildness. "Here, I'll show you how it's done—"

He signaled to one of his assistants. "Bring over the oil!"

Paul, meanwhile, as he helped lift another of the battle victims to his own table, listened to the chief surgeon in a growing fury of frustration. He could well visualize the tableau ahead—the grating bone and flesh saw, the screaming patient firmly held down by medical assistants, then the boiling oil to sear the bleeding stump—

He wondered if young Simon could take it. Since the young physician's arrival a few weeks ago, Paul had become quite friendly with him, and had known at once that Saul Simon, while gifted with medical intuition, a talent for diagnosis and the proper use of medications, was never cut out to be a surgeon. His sensitivity made him shrink from the pain of others. In all innocence he had volunteered his talents to the Federal medical service—never dreaming that he would be assigned to battlefront surgery.

". . . here, take a good long pull from this bottle," Britton was saying to the terrified patient.

"I—I don't drink strong spirits."

"Well, get it down some other way then, and you won't scream so loud. . . . One of you men hold his mouth open, and—"

The patient began coughing, choking, gagging as the liquor spilled from his mouth.

"Now keep in mind, Simon, that speed is a surgeon's greatest asset. In taking off a leg, all you have to watch for is to keep a flap of muscles from the back of the limb—that's to cushion the bone ends so if the fellow pulls through he can be fitted with a peg leg. Any dunce of a carpenter could do it. Now watch—"

As the soft, pulpy rasping of the saw biting into live flesh began, a quivering shriek burst from the patient. Rending screams crescendoed to a tormented climax—then sliced off into silence as, mercifully, the patient passed out.

The sawing continued steadily, inexorably. . . .

A flurry of stumbling movement brushed against Paul. It was Simon rushing past, bent forward. He barely made it through the tent opening before the vomit came gushing up out of his throat.

iii

It had been almost a year ago to the day that Paul Abbott had broken out of jail in Louisiana to escape a lynch mob. He had been falsely accused of aiding runaway slaves. His escape had been effected by Micaela Delacroix, a clever and beautiful octoroon who had risked her own life to save his.

With Micaela and a boatload of slaves he had fled north. In Washington, where there were no laws against such mixing, the two married. Paul volunteered his services to the Army Medical Corps. He was granted a leave of absence before beginning service; there followed several weeks of married happiness that were marred only by Paul's sadness at having been forced to leave behind his infant son, Carson, left motherless by the death of Paul's first wife, Sylphide.

A consolation was that he need have no worries about Carson's welfare, for he had been left in the care of the child's uncle, Etienne Troyonne, a rich Creole planter and a devoted friend of Paul's. Mail still got through between the warring North and South by means of neutral ships, and the most recent letter from Etienne, arriving only yesterday, had reassured him that his young son was in good health and happy.

The frequent letters from Micaela were less reassuring. Their infant daughter, Rill, whom Paul had never seen, had been born a few months ago. Micaela and the baby lived in a rented cottage outside Washington with two former slaves. One was the black girl Aurora, who had been Paul's former wife's maid; the other was her husband, an African-born giant named Zambullah. Zambullah, raised a warrior, yearned to join the battle against his former slave masters but was denied service in the Federal army because of his color. He remained behind to look after the two wives and tend the fields of the small farm. Also living with them was Bessie Barnwell, the widow who owned the cottage.

Although Micaela's letters were full of homey little details about Rill and their daily life, Paul read between the lines an indefinable restlessness. He could never quite forget that Micaela had been the mistress of a wealthy planter, Léon Jacquard. She had been accustomed to luxury and excitement. Still only twenty-four, she had a vital, exuberant nature, a love of adventure. He did not question that she loved him as deeply as ever, but sensed that she was chafing under the restraints of a life as a wife and mother in a humble cottage.

Often he wondered if their hasty marriage had not been

23

a mistake. The sedate and respectable life of a doctor's wife was hardly suited to her lively spirit.

Another of his many mistakes, he was beginning to think, was his transfer from the convalescent hospital at Camp Griffen, where first he had been assigned. There he had been appalled and disgusted by the miserable quality of the medical service; by the frequency of wounded soldiers arriving from the battlefront suffering more from inept medical attention than from their original wounds. They suffered from clumsy and unnecessary amputations; infections and gangrene were so far advanced that many of them soon died. Convinced that he could do more at the front lines where skilled medical attentions were most urgently needed, he had requested, and received, a transfer to the front.

And had landed in the Army of the Tennessee at Shiloh—where conditions for giving good medical treatment were even worse.

Adding to his despondency was the news that his Southern friend, the sensitive Etienne, would soon be fighting on the other side. Etienne had written:

My Dear Paul,

Your last letter, the most agreeable proof that you still hold me in fond remembrance, arrived two weeks ago and I would have answered much sooner except for events of great moment in my usually staid life that have left me quite destitute of free time and energy.

But before I reveal them, let me first hasten to inform you about a subject most dear to both our hearts—your son Carson. A healthier and happier child would be hard to find. If there is any fault to be found, it is probably that he is in danger of being spoiled by all the affection lavished on him. The house servants adore him—he is of such a sweet and gentle nature—and my love for him could not be greater if he were my own son. It is one of the few gratifications of my life to know that at least one other person exists in whom some of my blood flows, even though distantly as a cousin whose mother was your wife and my dear cousin.

Indeed, it is this very love for Carson that has given the impetus for a great change in my life. It has been perhaps the obvious and natural outgrowth of my concern for the child entrusted to my care. The truth is I am but a poor substitute for a father, and a black mammy is hardly the best mother substitute for a white child. In short, I have endeavored to rectify the lack by taking the great step that, until recently, I thought to be inconceivable; I have taken a wife.

Her maiden name is Narcisse Duplessis, and a sweeter, kinder person would be difficult to imagine other than your dear departed wife. Narcisse is much like her, which should give you a fairly clear idea of the beautiful, admirable lady who henceforth shall take over the role of mother to your son.

My other bit of news is simply that I have accepted a colonelcy in the Confederate cavalry and soon will be engaged in active warfare against the North.

My entry into this terrible conflict that has torn our country asunder is the most painful step I have ever taken. One of the more dreadful aspects of it is the thought that you who have proven to be a dear friend will be numbered among my enemies. I, who once prided myself on being a philosopher, can find no philosophy to justify this. But I have no choice. I cannot deny my allegiance to the South, I can only consider it a tragedy, and I hope and pray that this madness which pervades the country will be dissipated soon, and that the mingling blood of brothers will cease to flow.

By the same token you are performing what you deem to be, and rightly so, your duty to your northern allegiance. Yet with no animosity in your heart, I am sure, as I have none in mine. With this thought, my dear Paul, I will end.

Your loving friend,
Etienne

The letter had scarcely lifted Paul's spirits. The thought that a bullet fired by the gentle Etienne might well find its mark in one of the suffering men who were streaming into the hospital tents—or the reverse, that Etienne himself might fall wounded or dead—was saddening.

Where was Etienne now, he wondered?

Two

Etienne

i

At Les Cyprès, a farewell party was in progress. Every window of the great white house sparkled with candlelight. Music, fast and gay, filled the enormous living room. The air was sweet with the scents of jasmine and magnolia, mingling inside with fine perfumes from Paris and a trace here and there of expensive cigar smoke.

Since it was still early, a few guests were still alighting from carriages or saddle horses that filled the wide curving driveway. Many of the guests had already arrived by steamboat all the way from New Orleans, to be met at the private quay by coaches that would deliver them to the house.

Sieur Etienne Troyonne, one of the most respected figures in Louisiana, was going off to war and the party was in his honor.

Narcisse Duplessis Troyonne, Etienne's bride of barely a fortnight, sat on a velvet sofa languidly fanning herself.

None would have suspected that behind her composed manner and proper smile she was in a terrible fret, revealed only by the tapping of a slender pale blue slipper.

Narcisse, at twenty-three, was nearly as beautiful as flesh and blood ever becomes. She had a glorious wealth of champagne-pale hair, tidily netted below the ears, flawless creamy skin and wide-set eyes of brilliant turquoise. Heavy earbobs with long golden fringes hung almost to the shoulders of an exquisite pale blue satin gown overlaid with ivory lace.

And therein lay much of her exasperation. Narcisse demanded nothing less than perfection in her appearance and dress. Her rich gown with all its flounces and ruffles had been especially created for this evening by her own dressmaker—with one horrid lack. The Valenciennes lace trimming ordered from New Orleans had failed to arrive—thanks to the abominable Yankee blockade— and her dressmaker had been forced to substitute ordinary mull muslin lace. No man would ever notice or care, to be sure, but such details would be noted and remembered by every lady present.

All day she had been in a rage of disappointment about it, and now to top it off, Etienne, who earlier had ridden off to handle a small business matter before the guests started arriving, had not yet returned. How could he be so negligent!

Where was Etienne?

As if echoing her silent question, Madame Marie Louise de Menière, seated nearby in a big Empire chair, leaned close to ask, "And where is your adorable husband, my dear? Armand and I are so fond of him and would be terribly disappointed if we failed to see him— especially at his farewell party."

Narcisse repeated the lame excuse she had given to so many others, that Etienne had doubtless been unexpectedly detained by business affairs but would surely be here soon. Oh, it was so humiliating! So embarrassing to be alone to welcome so many guests, whose names she scarcely knew or remembered! His absence was wrecking her whole evening. That and the horrid mull muslin trim!

Madame de Menière laughed. "Ah, but you are so very young and so newly married, and not a Creole. . . . You have yet to learn Creole gentlemen have no true concept of time."

Narcisse, who had been reared in Richmond, was inordinately proud of her French parentage and considered herself superior to the tight little Creole ethnic groups of Louisiana who derived from heaven only knew how many alien racial mixtures. At the time she had first met Etienne at a reception for Jefferson Davis, President of the Confederacy, she had felt a slight sense of lowering herself by being duly civil to his flattering attentions. She soon discovered, however, by discreet questionings, that he was on intimate terms with the President, who owned an extensive plantation in Mississippi not too many miles away on the opposite side of the river from Etienne's Louisiana plantation. And that Etienne was a relatively wealthy man. A bachelor. Narcisse's father, before dying, had lost his fortune in railroad bonds, bank stock and Western notes of hand. None of her many suitors who had gone off to the war, some of them already casualties, had been as rich as Etienne appeared to be. And being reduced to genteel poverty, with only her beauty and a deplorable scarcity of eligible men to pick from, Narcisse had swiftly made her decision and used her considerable charms with such success that their engagement was announced soon after.

Josie Gourdin, a full-bosomed, wholesome-looking, freckled young redhead seated across from Madame Marie Louise, spoke up: "Being myself an outsider and married to one of your Creole gentlemen, I can only assure Narcisse that it's a futile hope to ever expect to fully understand a Creole male."

"Not true," Marie Louise said stiffly. "I understand my Armand perfectly."

"But you are a Creole, Marie Louise. All the doors of the Creole inner sanctums are open to you. Such is not

29

the case with Narcisse and myself. I have the added handicap of being one of those detested, so-called 'American' women, the daughter of a cotton merchant from the North. At the time that my brave Claude bestowed on me the greatest of all honors that can be vested on grateful womanhood—the offer of marriage—it was considered almost sacrilege for a Creole gentleman of good station to so lower himself. It was only after two or three years of marriage that I began to be received in Creole society."

"Tut, tut," Marie Louise said indulgently. "You should not take offense that we wish to preserve our culture. Times are changing, and of course men are always a law unto themselves. More and more these days our men are seeking to marry outside of their race." She shook her head, adding, "It is sad."

"Why sad, madame? Are Creoles not already a mixture of various alien bloods?"

"Creoles are like good soup," Marie Louise said solemnly. "You must have the right amount of just the right ingredients, and suddenly—*voilà! Complet, accompli!* All *parfait!* Nothing can improve perfection, but if one wrong ingredient is mixed in—*hélas!*" She made a grimace of distaste.

Josie laughed merrily; Narcisse fumed. Such arrogance! The incredible conceit and pride of the Creoles were beyond her comprehension. She had expected to be accepted as an honored, if not superior, addition to Creole circles. They actually *looked down on her*.

Josie and Marie Louise were now engaged in bantering repartee. The thick-skinned Yankee woman had stooped to buttering the older woman up, Narcisse thought resentfully. Bored, she barely listened. She knew she should be mingling with the guests but was too angry at Etienne and his Creole world to care much what they thought of her manners. She could be arrogant, too!

She looked over at the little orchestra led by Ammon, who was Etienne's coal-black *ci-devant* coachman. Recently a beautiful mulatto named Céleste, who looked almost white, had married him. People were shocked.

Even slaves had asked, how could she marry that horrid black man? Céleste's answer: "You see, I inherited the taste of my white father. My mother was coal-black." Narcisse found nothing humorous about it but Etienne had laughed uproariously and as a wedding present had elevated Ammon to be his body servant—a gentleman's gentleman, the highest level any slave could hope to reach.

Sitting in solemn dignity, his face scrunched up blissfully over his bow, Ammon was beating out the time with one foot so forcefully that the whole floor seemed to shake. Narcisse was suddenly aware that her own foot was delicately tapping in unison. The music was lively and she was dying to dance but knew it would be highly improper. Not only because of her husband's absence but because there were so many women present and so few men. The best and bravest had gone off to war. The only ones here tonight were either too old to fight, or uniformed officers on leave. It was said there were scarcely six men in the whole county young enough to interest a woman. All the others were *hors de combat,* the cripples and the drunks, the only corps of reserves —alcoholized patriots.

Idly she listened to snatches of the conversation buzzing around her:

". . . *that terrible* New York Herald *thinks we are shaking in our shoes—but we are as jolly as larks despite all they're trying to do to us.*"

". . . *why don't those infernal abolitionists leave us alone if they hate us so much? We want to separate from them—to be rid of the Yankees forever at any price— but they won't let us go—*"

"*Why? For profit of course. We get all the opprobrium for slavery while they, with the tariff they burdened us with before the war and stealing our cotton now, get all the profits of slavery.*"

"*Leave it to the Yankees to squeeze every penny out of every situation by hook or crook.*"

". . . *Lincoln and his hordes may kill us and lay waste to our lands for a while—but conquer us? Never!*"

There was a sudden cessation of talk, and then the brief silence was filled by an authoritative male voice:

"Ladies and gentlemen, I have an announcement that I know you are all waiting to hear. . . ."

Narcisse saw that a uniformed man stood just inside the door and had been holding up both arms for attention. He continued:

"I have it by telegraphic dispatch from Shiloh that Johnston and Beauregard are driving the damned Yankees right into the Tennessee River, killing them by the thousands. By tomorrow the battle will be over and it will go down as one of the most resounding victories of the whole war!"

The room exploded into clapping and cheers. And now the polite boredom had lifted throughout the room. Idle chatter was gone. Something electric was crackling through the air and voices began bragging emphatically:

"One Southerner can lick twenty Yankees anytime!"

"Well, they wanted war—we'll make them sick of it!"

"We'll teach them a lesson they won't soon forget!"

"States' rights, by God! Maybe they'll understand now that they can't take that away from us!"

Having recognized the military bearer of the welcome news as the very distinguished Commodore Barton, Narcisse had risen and started moving through the room to welcome him. She felt a hand on her arm.

"That *man*—" It was Madame Marie Louise hissing in her ear. "The one with the commodore—he is Léon Jacquard!"

Narcisse looked at Marie Louise in puzzlement. "Is he somebody important?"

"Hah! Armand would never allow him into our home, and I dare say if Etienne were here he would eject him forthwith. My dear, he is not received anywhere along the river. I can't imagine what he is doing in the company of the commodore."

"But why? He looks well-mannered and presentable enough."

"His reputation is unsavory. He came from Santo Domingo, where it is said he murdered and robbed to gain his riches. His grand plantation near here burned down. He was wounded by slaves and barely escaped with his life. I am surprised you haven't heard of it because of the scandal that involved the Yankee doctor who owns the plantation. . . ."

Narcisse was suddenly chilled. "What are you saying, Madame Marie Louise?"

"Have you not heard of Dr. Paul Abbott?"

"Of course—his son is living here as Etienne's ward, but certainly you are mistaken to think he has any claim on the plantation."

"Ah, I am sorry I spoke. If Etienne has not told you of it—"

"But I must know—" Narcisse was so agitated she gripped one of the older woman's plump arms with trembling fingers as if to shake her. "You must tell me—you *must*—!"

Madame Marie Louise shrugged. "Well, since it is common knowledge, I am betraying no secrets to tell you what I know and have heard. . . . When Pierre Gayarre, the original owner of Les Cyprès died, the plantation was left to his cousin, Sylphide Beauvais. Soon after—it is said by sly means—this Yankee doctor won her heart and they were married. She died giving birth to Dr. Abbott's child, who now lives here. It is also rumored that her death may not have been altogether accidental, since she had willed her entire estate to this impecunious Yankee and there were no other doctors present who might have saved her, and—"

"Please, *please*—I don't wish to hear any more," Narcisse pleaded in a tense whisper. She had already heard too much, and knew that Marie Louise was telling the truth. Why hadn't Etienne told her? She had heard that Creole men generally kept their wives ignorant of financial matters, considering it purely a male domain. And of course she could never be presumptuous or crass enough to ask how much money and property he had. Plainly he had access to a great deal of money and she simply had assumed that he owned Les Cyprès—the finest plantation she had ever seen—and that should he be killed in the war,

God forbid, or after he died of old age, she would become its mistress and owner.

"But don't you wish to hear of the scandal?" Marie Louise persisted.

From long practice, Narcisse had quickly restored her mask of cool composure. "But of course," she said lightly, "I love scandal. . . ."

"Dr. Abbott, who was secretly helping slaves run away from their masters, was also secretly carrying on an affair with Monsieur Jacquard's octoroon mistress. He was caught and put in jail for his crimes but the octoroon helped him escape and they absconded to the North together, where it is rumored—" Her voice faded away as she saw Commodore Barton and Jacquard approaching.

"Ah, ladies. . . ." The commodore's wide smile included Marie Louise, but was mostly for Narcisse as he gave a courtly little bow. "My deepest apologies for being so tardy."

Narcisse curtsied low before his splendid array of epaulets, aiguillettes, ribbons of valor and rows of buttons shining like fresh-minted gold coins in the glow of chandeliers, as did Madame Marie Louise.

"Even without the glad tidings you brought," said Narcisse with her most brilliant smile, "you would be welcome whenever you came, Commodore."

"I have other glad tidings, but first I wish to present the brave patriot I have taken the liberty of bringing along as my personal guest, Monsieur Léon Jacquard, mesdames—"

As he continued with the formal introductions, Narcisse was uncomfortably aware of Jacquard's burning dark eyes fixed on her intently. A chill slithered down her spine. It was not from the terrible red scar running along one temple, only partially hidden by the mass of black hair that hung to his broad shoulders. Nor was his face forbidding, for he was attractive enough in a savage sort of way with a sinister dark mustache above the white gleam of teeth in his swarthy face. And certainly his attire was proper, and plainly expensive. But for all his fine clothes and polished manners, he seemed as raw and rough

as a timber wolf stalking through the room. As she curtsied, he bowed low, and taking her hand kissed it lightly
—but holding it a bit too long until she drew it away, again
feeling a chill.

Madame Marie Louise did not curtsy, but merely ac-
knowledged the introduction with an almost imperceptible
nod of her head, to which Jacquard responded with a bow
and an amused smile.

"And what are the other glad tidings?" Marie Louise
asked the commodore.

"Monsieur Jacquard only yesterday with his single ship
took three prizes at sea, and by a feat of great cleverness
and great risk of life brought them in safely past the
Yankee blockade during the night. One was laden with
palm oil, one with salt and fruit, one with grain."

"Are you then a privateer, monsieur?" said Narcisse.

"The best in the whole South!" the commodore interjected enthusiastically. "But I much fear his exploits must
soon end, as the blockade grows more formidable by the
day. The Yankees are gaining so much strength on the
river that even New Orleans may soon be threatened."

"How terrible!" exclaimed Narcisse. "Already New Orleans is so destitute of supplies because of the blockade,
ladies find it difficult to purchase simple articles of dress."

Jacquard laughed. "If Madame Troyonne has any need
of any female furbelows—such as Valenciennes lace, perhaps?—I am sure I could arrange to satisfy your desires. . . ."

Again she felt that slithering chill—plus a needle of
shock. So he had noticed even that! What sharp eyes he
had! How incredible that a *man* should notice, and what
a boor he was to let her know! He was frightening. She
hoped her face was not turning pink from the warmth she
felt flaming in her cheeks. With an effort she recovered her
composure.

"Your generosity is overwhelming, monsieur, but during this period of shortages I think I can manage quite
well without, thank you. And now I must beg you all to
excuse me, as I must speak to the servants. . . ."

She hastened away. What a terrible evening it was turning out to be! All because Etienne was not here to perform his duties as the host. The whole party was out of hand. The guests were being left to float about on their own. It would all reflect on her shortcomings as a hostess. The first chance she had alone she knew she would just burst out and cry. She didn't know how much longer she could take it.

Where was Etienne!

ii

Etienne Troyonne looked very much out of place. Resplendent in his well-tailored new gray officer's uniform, he sat alone at a corner table in Cantwell's Tavern sipping moodily at a glass of warmish rum and water. Flies buzzed and made darting circles past his head. The tavern was thick with the stench of stale booze, stale smoke, unwashed spittoons and mansweat. Loud voices filled the room. Most of the men there wore ill-fitting, butternut-dyed brownish uniforms.

A slim mulatto girl, quite pretty, carrying a tray of empty glasses and a musty wet rag for mopping up tabletops, paused near him.

"Massa ready fo' 'nother drink?"

Etienne shook his head.

She smiled provocatively. "Massa like anythin' else?"

He appraised her carefully. At the bar, some of the soldiers were glancing in his direction. The bartender muttered something in a low voice, and after that their expressions were filled with the scorn they felt for a gentleman of quality who would lower himself to their own worst level.

"Yo' look down, massa. I-uns do anythin' to fo' sho' makes yo' feel real good."

The taut lines of his finely chiseled pale face softened, indicating a warmth and sensitivity that belied the aristocratic arrogance of his habitual expression. He had burn-

36

ing dark eyes, shadowed by heavy black brows that had a slightly satanic upward twist toward the temples, and black hair worn a bit longer than the current style, curling at the ends. It gave him somewhat the look of an artist or poet—an impression enhanced by his slender, almost delicate build and the slimness of his well-formed hands. For a man approaching forty, he was still handsome.

A thoughtful pursing of his thin lips was the only indication of the inner tug-of-war that was raging between the two sides of his nature: the "right" side that was needling him, shaming him, urging him to rise up and return to his beautiful new wife, to the going-away party she had planned for him, and the "wrong" side that periodically ruled his life, clamoring at him to go upstairs and ease the torment—

He gave her a kindly, almost apologetic smile. "Maybe another time. But for now, please tell Manda to go upstairs. . . ."

And thinking: *She's too pretty. Her skin is too light.*

He wanted the darkest of the dark: to wallow in it; to lose himself in eternal blackness. . . .

The mulatto flounced away, indignant.

Along the bar eyes laden with contempt followed Etienne as he headed for the stairway.

iii

Manda was coal-black and no longer young. She lay back on a cot and its lumpy mattress with the flickering rays of an oil lamp playing soft highlights over the contours of heavy pendulous breasts, the curve of wide fertile hips that had delivered at least a half-dozen mulatto babies into the world and a comely face capped with frizzy black hair salted with gray. The light added luminosity to large mournful eyes laden with the cosmic sadness of ages as she looked up at Etienne.

Totally submissive and waiting.

37

His visits to Manda—for he had known her and come back to her again and again over a period of years—always smote him with self-reproach. She was a whore not by choice but because she was a slave, subject to any abasement her owner cared to inflict. Even though the Black Code forbade the use of slaves for prostitution, no complaints had ever been lodged against the tavern by any white person, and certainly not by any black ones.

The shamefulness of it was one reason he had never violated any of his own plantation slave women. His own slaves were utterly dependent on him for protection, food, shelter, their very lives. His conscience would never allow him to abuse the trust invested in him by the grace of God.

Thus he had descended to the depths of Cantwell's rationalizing that the Cantwell whores were already degraded beyond redemption. It relieved him to a degree of any sense of blame.

Moreover, the sordid atmosphere of the tavern was an important element in the gratification of his dark cravings.

Etienne's erotic impulses were not simple. They evolved out of a complex balancing of guilt-laden sensuality, depraved fantasies and compulsive attraction to darkest sin against the reluctance of the fastidious and highly moral side of his nature—until those irresistible cravings, like a slowly fermenting brew of evil ingredients, built up to a point that overwhelmed all resistance. After which he was freed to embrace his pleasures; reveling, groveling in them. . . .

Such sexual intensities could only be aroused by thoughts of black women.

Never had he been able to think of raw sexuality in connection with a female of his own race—at least not the proper kind of lady that a gentleman would care to marry. With such exemplary creatures he could equate only purity and all the finest feminine virtues; such an image had been fostered in his childhood by his chaste, flawless mother, whose memory he cherished as one of God's highest angels. He sincerely believed that no real lady could possibly degrade herself by engaging in such animalstic antics as were required by the sex act, except for the ole purpose of procreation.

He had delicately managed to convey this to Narcisse before their marriage, quite honestly letting her know that his primary need for a wife was to provide a mother's love for his nephew, Carson, to properly oversee the running of the household and to handle social obligations. Narcisse had been in wholehearted agreement, assuring him that she desired nothing more than to be a devoted helpmeet to him and a loving mother to Carson, whom she adored.

"I ready anytime yo' is, massa."

He unbuttoned the jacket of his uniform and looked down at her on the foul mattress. Idly he wondered how many hundreds of bodies had rolled and writhed and humped together on it: the black submissive female and a male white beast in rut; both beaded with sour sweat and locked together in their unholy union of lust, cruelty and hate.

Raucous laughter carried up from the bar downstairs, and snatches of a popular ballad bellowed out in a doleful, off-key voice. It was a tale of a sad miner singing about his sweetheart Sally, who had sent him to dig for gold in California, promising that she would marry him when he returned. He returned with the gold and found her already married. To a new lover with red hair. Other drunken voices joined in the refrain:

> "Enuf' ter make a feller swear
> Sally with a baby,
> An' a baby with red hair!"

The cot complained as she rolled her weight on it.

"Jus' yo' tell me how yo' lak it, massa, an' I pleasure yo'. . . ."

She parted her thighs slightly, just enough to show the red wet gleam of vulva nestled amid the curling pelvic hairs.

A sharp thrill shivered up his spine. He had a sudden

39

remembrance of the first time he had ever had a glimpse of that most secret part of female anatomy:

A black slave girl in a dark corner of the sugar mill lying on a pile of dried cane stalks, her rough Osnaburg cotton dress hiked up around her thighs. . . . His father trousers down, on his knees between the girl's spread legs. In horrible fascination he had watched the powerful, steady thrusts of his father's haunches, heard his pleasurable gruntings, the soft plaintive sobbings of the girl. . .

He had fled, the scene forever branded in memory. Hating and detesting his father ever after.

But also seared to the core with crazy, pounding excitation whenever he envisioned that lewd black nakedness.

He hung his jacket on a nail on the wall; then began unbelting his trousers. . . .

iv

Afterward, he lay against the mammalian softness. Sated. Feeling perspiration still trickling down his back, beading his forehead. In his flushed but quiescent state, his senses were heightened to the cloying, sweetish-sour odor of their lovemaking, the feel of her slick-damp skin; around them the aura of taint, rot, the effluvia of sin that seemed to permeate the very walls of the dismal, bare-floored room.

Normally he would be preparing to leave as soon as his sexual tensions had been relieved, but this evening he was reluctant to withdraw from the maternal warmth, the tenderness of soft flesh. His face was pillowed against her breasts, a nipple pressing against a cheek.

His memory flashed back to the long-forgotten black mammy who had first nursed and cuddled him with her boundless love—

"Massa, h'ain't yo' got 'nuff yet? Yo' want mo'?"

"No, Manda. . . . I just want to lie here for a while. . . ."

Why? In an unusual reflective state so soon after sex, his head was full of vague, unanswered questions. Why, for example, had he come here tonight—on this of all evenings?

Because I wanted to see her once again, dammit! It's that simple. Tomorrow I'm leaving for war, and this could be the very last chance to see her again.

But she was just a whore. He knew it hadn't been only a need for sex that had drawn him. Sex was obtainable anywhere. It was something else. . . .

To assuage pangs of guilt, perhaps? For years I have used her, whenever the urge was strong, for my own vile gratifications. Treating her hardly like a human but like some creature completely at my mercy.

But that was true of all slaves, all whores. It was more than that. . . .

My sense of responsibility? Sympathy? Concern for her future? She is already getting too old to attract many customers.

That was part of it. He had, as a matter of fact, stuffed his wallet with bills, intending to give her a lavish parting present. But he knew at heart that it was far more than that. . . .

Why am I so afraid to face it? What is so shameful about it? During the years of knowing her so intimately, in the biblical sense, the closeness of the flesh has evolved into spheres of the spirit. Closeness—

In a flash his formless feelings suddenly crystallized.

A closeness I feel for no other human being. A kind of love.

In trying to sort out the right words, he began lamely: "Manda, I shall possibly never see you again, as tomorrow I leave for service in the Confederate army. . . ."

"Yo' g'wine fight agin' Linkum's army?"

Not answering, he looked into the mournful eyes, bottomless with the cynical grief of abandonment, and suddenly the urge became overwhelming: to give expression to pure affection.

Embracing her tenderly, his thin mouth hungrily sought her heavy lips—

Her reaction was instantaneous. Like a tigress she twisted and rolled away from beneath him, eyes now blazing with fury and scorn. Countless men had used her body in the vilest way, but none had attempted to kiss her. She had been born into the Ebo tribe, where to kiss while making love was the greatest of abominations. Bad enough for even an Ebo to do it.

But for a white man to touch her lips with his—

"Yo' git outta here, white man!"

Astonished and dismayed, Etienne groped his way to his jacket on the wall. Got out the wallet.

"But Manda, I was only trying to show you—I mean, I want to help you all I can because—" Hastily he opened the wallet and took out the thick sheaf of bills inside. Extended them.

"For you, Manda—"

Suspiciously she accepted the bills, examined them with glowering eyes.

"Dis 'federate money. . . ."

"Yes, almost a thousand dollars. Enough to buy your freedom."

"When Linkum's army git here, I be free anyway, an dat 'federate money won't even buy a pisspot!"

With a savage swing of her arm she flung a fluttering cloud of green and pink bills in his face.

"But Manda—"

"Now I give yo' somethin' to remember me by—"

She reached down beside the bed and got the chamber pot and with another wild swing sent the pot and all its contents of stale urine in a drenching shower all over him.

V

When Narcisse awoke, the sun was already slanting golden light through a narrow opening between the heavy brocade drapes. Her sleep had been fitful, her dreams terrible, frightening.

All because of Etienne!

The party had been a disaster. According to Creole custom, many of the guests—except those who had arrived and left by chartered steamboat—would have stayed overnight instead of enduring long rides home by coach or saddle in darkness. All the bedrooms had been prepared; extra cots and bedding were available; even mattresses were ready for use on the floor in case there was an overflow.

Yet not a single guest had elected to stay. Everybody had been effusively polite about it, and expressed great concern about the host's absence, but in truth she had not tried very hard to induce them to stay. It would only have prolonged the humiliation.

Thank God all of them had departed before Etienne's return—his fine uniform filthy with mud and swamp water. Due to an unwonted delay in handling a vital business matter, he explained, he had tried to hasten back by a shortcut through the marsh, where his horse had slipped in the mud and thrown him into the putrid waters. He had deliberately hidden out in the stables until all guests were gone before venturing into the house by the servants' entrance. Wrapped in a horse blanket, he had removed his uniform and left it soaking in a tub of water.

Sitting up in the great four-poster bed, she reached for the bellpull and gave it an angry little yank to summon a servant. Then settling back into silken pillows propped against the silk-padded headboard, she turned her thoughts to an examination of the *real* reason why her fuming aggravations of the previous night still vexed her.

It wasn't really because of Etienne's absence, his soiled new uniform or that silly mull muslin lace.

The real reason was all around her:

Her gaze swept around the luxurious room, which was a strange combination of masculine strength and soft delicate femininity—the masculine exemplified in the heavy oaken paneling and muscular beamed ceiling, yet still overpowered by the femininity of satins and silk brocades in soft muted tones, by graceful chairs of carved rosewood, the carved mahogany armoire, by this very bed in which she lay, with its bedposts carved in the typical Creole pineapple pattern, and over it a lofty *ciel*, or canopy, lined with blue satin and draped in a sunburst design, caught in the center by a gold ornament. At the foot of the bed was a *lit de repos*, a reclining couch; here and there a few graceful stands and tables of Italian marble.

It was the most sumptuous bedroom she had ever known, and since Etienne preferred the privacy of his own bedroom, it was all her own.

Or so she had thought. . . .

If Madame Marie Louise de Meniére had been telling the truth last evening, this beautiful mansion, the whole plantation, wasn't Etienne's property after all; she wasn't its true mistress.

It belonged to that Yankee doctor, Paul Abbott.

Why hadn't Etienne told her?

It would be crass of her, of course, make her appear like a scheming fortune hunter, to ask Etienne about it. But she had to know! What if he was not as rich as he seemed to be after all? What if, like her own father, he had lost everything in bad investments?

Old Le Barone, the family attorney, would know. He was a sweet old gentleman with a weakness for the ladies. She was sure he would recognize her right to know the true state of Etienne's financial affairs. She would visit him, she decided, as soon as Etienne left.

But for the time being she would hide her displeasure and do her duty as a proper loving wife.

There was a light knock on the door and moments later fat black Aimée entered pushing a serving cart on which was a vase of flowers and a steaming array of silver service containing her breakfast, prepared in accordance with instructions given to the chef on the previous evening: rich black coffee, hot chocolate, melon, fruit, brioche still warm from the oven, butter pats, marmalade, and in a chafing dish, *omelette à la Angelopolis*. Narcisse was a light eater but she loved to be served in abundance.

"Is Master Troyonne up yet?"

Aimée's cheerful face grinned toothily. "Law, yes! He been rompin' 'round wid Marse Carse lak he a li'l boy hisself. Dem two sho' have fun!"

"What about his uniform?"

"Ammon, he stay up all night gittin' it clean—law what a mess! Now it jest lak new. Wouldn't be right to go fightin' Linkum's army in a dirty uniform."

vi

When finally the moment of parting came, Etienne embraced her briefly, giving her a chaste kiss on the cheek.

"I have made all provisions for your comfort and peace of mind, my dear. You won't have to concern yourself with plantation matters as they will be handled by the plantation manager and his overseers. Ammon will be in charge of the house servants. Should you require anything I may have overlooked, or have need for additional funds in your bank account, state your wishes to Le Barone and he will provide what you desire. And should anything happen to me—"

"Oh my dear Etienne—I beg you not to talk of such a thing! I can't bear the thought that—" She bowed her head and let the tears that she could summon so easily grow in her eyes. He patted her shoulder tenderly.

"We must be realistic, my dear. Soldiers are frequently wounded or killed in battle, and should the worst happen to me, at least I can die secure in the knowledge that I have left Carson with the best possible kind of mother to look after him. Meanwhile, be of good heart, and I will write often—"

A choking sob escaped from young Carson, who had been standing a few feet away listening.

Etienne turned at once and knelt to embrace the youngster. "You mustn't cry, Carson. I'll take good care of myself, I promise, and I want you to be a brave little man

45

while I'm away and look after your Auntie Narcisse. And you remember to be good and obedient to her at all times."

"Yes, Uncle 'Tienne."

Watching, Narcisse was strangely perturbed. Etienne plainly felt far greater warmth toward his nephew than he did for her. And Carson plainly felt just as deeply for his uncle. She'd tried hard to win the lad over with gifts and affection, but never had he responded. He was a sturdy, nice-looking youngster with a wavy shock of dark brown hair, but there was something odd about him. He rarely smiled, and there was a curious intentness in his steady blue-gray eyes that she found unnerving.

Etienne gave Carson a final embrace, then abruptly stood up and turned toward the two young officers who stood near the door waiting. They were a captain and a lieutenant who were to be his courtesy escort.

"*Allons*, gentlemen," he called to them. "*En avant—*"

Without a backward glance he strode toward the waiting officers and the three of them went out.

Carson, meanwhile, went scampering up the stairs, a fresh torrent of tears streaming down his face. Upstairs he started sobbing.

Narcisse waited until she could hear the hoofbeats of horses fading into the distance, then with a determined air briskly walked upstairs. Carson was in his room lying face down on the bed, his shoulders quivering.

"Carson!" she said sharply. "Stop that blubbering!"

The small boy made no sign that he had heard.

Striding over, she caught him by his shirt collar, pulled him to a sitting position. He looked at her with frightened eyes, startled into silence; a trembling seized him as he started crying again.

"Now you listen to me, you sniveling brat—" On sudden impulse she slapped him furiously across the face. The impact knocked him backward on the bed, left the palm of her hand stinging.

For a moment even Narcisse was shocked. Why had she struck him so hard? The red imprint of her hand was vivid on his pale, tear-streaked face as he stared up at her with stricken eyes.

Her voice softened. "I only did that for your own good, Carson. You simply must be made to understand right from the beginning that I will not allow any more crying. It's not at all manly. Furthermore, from now on you will be expected at all times to do exactly what I say or I shall be forced to punish you till you learn obedience."

She forced a tight smile and sat on the bed beside him. "Now let us make up and be friends. . . ."

The gray-blue eyes blazed at her. The little mouth tightened with gritted teeth. Jumping off the bed he scampered off to a corner of the room and stood there, silent, looking with hatred at her.

"Very well, then," she said rising. "For the rest of the day you shall have to remain confined to your room and go without your meals."

She left the room, those eyes burning holes in her back.

Three

"My Tree in the Rain"

"During the night rain fell in torrents and our troops were exposed to the storm without shelter. I made my headquarters under a tree a few hundred yards from the riverbank. My ankle was so much swollen from the fall from my horse the Friday night preceding, and the bruise was so painful, that I could get no rest. The drenching rain would have precluded the possibility of sleep without this additional cause. Sometime after midnight, growing restive under the storm and the continuous pain, I moved back to the log house under the bank. This had been taken as a hospital, and all night wounded men were being brought in, their wounds dressed, a leg or arm amputated as the case might require, and everything being done to save life or alleviate suffering. The sight was more unendurable than encountering the enemy's fire, and I returned to my tree in the rain."

General U. S. Grant, Shiloh, 1862.

i

Looking at the hundreds upon hundreds of recumbent shapes of human wretchedness, Paul Abbott felt such a mingling of sickness, futility and anger as to make him forever hate the name of war.

They lay in haphazard rows on the ground, some covered with bits of gum cloth or soiled blankets; some half naked, parts of their bloodied uniforms stripped back to expose mangled limbs or raw wounds streaming with blood that darkened the ground around them. Some gave no sign of life; others spasmodically groaned, sobbed, plaintively called for help as their lives drained away. Many were already dead.

From all sides came the cry for *"Water, water, water. . . ."*

And none to be had except the polluted water that had caused so much diarrhea; nobody even to bring it to them, as the overworked doctors and their assistants were racing to keep up with the wounded already crowding the hospital tents.

Thousands more of the wounded and dead lay scattered across the three-mile triangle of wooded high banks along the Tennessee River where Grant's army had been loosely bivouacked. The few who could crawl stood a chance of making it back to the rear of the battle lines; most would remain writhing in pain and pleading for help that would never come.

Moans and appeals from the wounded were all but drowned out by the hellish thunder of sounds: the continuous racket of rifle fire; heavy cannonading of artillery; bellowed commands, oaths, screams; the banshee shriek of shells overhead. Over the woods and fields hung a pall of heavy black smoke; the sulphurous breath of gunpowder stung the eyes and nose. All was tainted with the smell of blood.

It was early evening and the battle had been raging without cessation since dawn. The Union army had been driven back over a mile by the jubilant, jeering rebels. The hospital tents, too close to the withering gunfire, had been hastily struck and moved back almost to the riverbanks, thereby losing an appalling number of patients. With too few horse-drawn ambulances to move the wounded, most of them had to be loaded like cordwood into empty ammunition wagons, which had no springs. In the hurried, jolting retreat over bumpy ground, many had not survived.

So severe was the shortage of space to shelter and treat the mounting number of casualties, General Grant had turned over his headquarters in a log house near the riverbank for hospital use. It was the best he could do, but far from enough.

Paul, accompanied by Saul Simon, had just emerged from the log house to sort out those of the suffering men most in need of immediate attention. His stomach rumbled from hunger—there had been no time to eat. His muscles ached from continuous, tense activity: cutting, sponging, suturing, tying, bandaging. . . . Even his bones ached; everything about him ached: his head, his spirit, his heart. . . .

Paul's and Simon's job was to divide the wounded into three categories: those who could be saved only by immediate treatment; those who could, if necessary, wait for treatment; and those whom nothing could save. It was a gruesome and cruel task.

As the two doctors started along one row, a clamor rose up around them: hoarse voices beseeching, pleading, vying for their attention—

"Doc, I been waitin' nigh three hours already . . . my guts is hangin' out in the dirt crawlin' with ants. Can'tcha do somethin' about it afore I—"

"Git me a gun, fer God's sake an'—" The speaker began coughing, gagging, coming up with vomit that slopped over his chest. *"E-either shoot me or lemme git my hands on one so I kin do it myself."*

". . . gotta have water . . . jist gotta have water. . . ."

"Iffen yeh could jist git me a swaller or two of whiskey, I could hang on a mite longer . . . jist 'nough ter wet m' tongue. . . ."

"Please . . . git this damn laig chopped off!"

One was muttering, *"It grows dark, Mother . . . growing darker . . . very dark. . . ."* Invariably, "mother" was uppermost in the thoughts of dying young soldiers.

Quickly Paul selected several cases and signaled to the

stretcher bearers to move them inside. Those already dead would be moved to the close-packed lines of corpses awaiting the burial squad. There would be no coffins; they would be buried as they were in trenches four feet deep, lying side by side, faces up and hands—if they had any—crossed over their chests. Makeshift wooden crosses marking their names would be stuck in the ground at their heads.

"They're the lucky ones," Saul Simon said as he watched one of the bodies being carried away.

His voice made Paul look at him sharply. Simon's face was tense and sweating, unnaturally pale.

"Are you feeling all right, Saul?"

Simon grimaced. "How could I possibly—how could *anybody*—feel all right amid all this—"

"I feel as wretched and hopeless about it as you do. All we can do is grit our teeth and do the best we can."

"There's no more 'best' left in me, Paul. I've tried—I've tried hard to do what Britton demands, but it's no good. I feel worse than a butcher. There's no way we can help most of these poor devils. Working against the slaughtering machine out there is like shoveling against the tide. I don't know how much longer I can stand it. . . ."

Paul saw that the man was close to the breaking point. The delicate sensitivity of Saul's superior brain had no defense against this horror.

"Here's another one for yeh—"

Two soldiers, walking stiff-legged from the weight, came up clumsily carrying a silent young battle victim. One leg, mangled above the knee, hung uselessly; blood was streaming from a chest wound. The newness of his blood-soaked uniform marked him as one of the recruits. One glance was enough to tell Paul that the lad belonged in the third category—those to be left to die since the costly amount of time that would have to be expended in probably futile efforts to save him might better be reserved for others more likely to survive.

Yet Paul hesitated. The smooth boyish face, grimed and blood-smeared, wrenched with agony, reflected a strange kind of stoicism. He looked up at the medical insignia on Paul's uniform but said not a word. There was no moaning, no pleading for help. Either he knew that surely he would die, or had implicit faith in God and the medical service.

An odd silence had fallen over some of the other men as they looked at the lad, as if suddenly ashamed of their own complainings.

The man who had begged to have his leg chopped off said huskily, "Why that kid ain't hardly as old as my oldest kid back home. He kin have my place—"

"Mine too," said another. "I wouldn't feel right iffen I went afore him."

"You take 'im an' fix 'im up, Doc. That pore kid shouldn't've been sent out to git kilt afore he's even had a whang at livin'."

Paul signaled to the two carrying the boy to follow him to the log building. Saul Simon tagged along behind.

They passed piles of the dead. They lay in grotesque poses, some headless, some disemboweled, others cut in two. Just outside of the log building was a heap of amputated limbs flung there by the surgeons' assistants. Gory arms, legs, feet; a clenched fist upthrust at an odd angle. The burial squad, far behind in their work, was busily loading the grisly remains into a wagon.

Entering, Paul was again assailed by the warm sickly stench of blood and death, the oily fumes of lanterns hung from nails in the walls for better lighting, the retching vomit of terror, moanings and screaming, the meaty, crunching, methodical sounds of surgical saws cutting through flesh and bone.

The single large room was so crowded with patients, doctors and their assistants, it was difficult to find passage. Nearly every spot upon which a man could lie was occupied: every tabletop, on boxes, under tables and in every other possible area on the blood-pooled floor. Footing was so precarious on the slippery surface that some of the doctors had wrapped bandages around their boots for better traction.

And this is where it all ends for the best of them, he thought bitterly. *In this ghastly charnel house.*

Some could manage to evade service and grow rich from the wars. It was only the finest and bravest, the poor and the fools who fought out of sincere dedication to their country who ended up in the operating rooms. Heroes.

It was about the same as sentencing them before the execution squad.

ii

Bending over the now-lax body of his young patient, Paul pressed one thumb hard against the long saphenous vein inside the thigh—effectively stopping the welling of blood. His other hand took a pulse reading from the radial artery. The pulse was weak, thready.

Meanwhile blood was still escaping from the wound in the chest.

An average adult body contained but five to six quarts of blood. A sudden loss of one third of that blood was usually fatal; in the case of slower bleeding, as much as two thirds of the blood volume could be lost over a twenty-four-hour period before death occurred. The big majority of battlefield deaths resulted from sheer loss of blood.

It was a facet of medicine that had long frustrated, yet engrossed Paul. How many countless thousands of lives might be saved by simple transfusions of healthy human blood to dying patients!

Yet it had never been a proven procedure. Transfusions had been tried many times, with sheep's blood as well as human blood. Almost invariably the patients died. In the very rare cases where the patient survived it was debatable whether it was because of or in spite of transfusions.

Paul had become fascinated with blood as a medical student in Edinburgh. There he had done autopsies on patients who had died after unsuccessful attempts to save them with blood transfusions. He had been startled to discover that the consistency of the patient's blood had been strangely changed by clumps of the blood cells adhering together, which in itself would quickly bring on death. Agglutination was the medical term for the phenomenon. It was his first inkling that all human blood was not alike, as most medical men still believed.

When later he had an opportunity to experiment with blood samples from scores of slaves, his first suspicions were confirmed—plus an exciting new discovery. Whereas most blood samples agglutinized when mixed, a few times he found that blood taken from two different individuals mixed together without agglutinating.

He had been elated, convinced that he had hit upon the basic secret for successful blood transfusions. It was only a matter of finding compatible blood.

But thus far he had found no opportunity to prove his theory. . . .

Nor would he have such a chance now, he thought as he looked down on his young patient, whose paleness, sweating face, weak rapid pulse and rapid respiration indicated that the blood loss had been severe. How much he had lost, or how long he had been bleeding, or if it was already too late to try to save him, there was no way of knowing.

No way except to plunge ahead with all possible speed and stop the blood flow. His thoughts raced—

. . . *a tourniquet to the leg temporarily—an orderly can hold it to the proper tension—while seeking the bullet embedded somewhere in the thoracic cavity . . . no way of knowing what veins or arteries might be severed within that complex inner maze of membranous tissues, bone, the arterial network; how much internal bleeding might be going on . . . whether the bullet could even be extracted without bringing on hemorrhage. . . .*

Only by cutting boldly like an explorer entering the unseen geography of hidden, forbidden areas of the body could he hope to find out. The only important matter of the moment was to try to save a life. It was always the ultimate challenge toward which his whole life had been directed, the constant battle against death. It was more than just a test of his surgical skills; it involved what many of his colleagues would have considered weakness, an emotional component that was the whole essence of his dedication to his profession—a reverence for the body and a deep sense of humbleness when confronted with the helpless innocence of any stricken human or beast on the threshold of death. Yet, brutal procedures were often necessary.

For Paul, surgery was always an awesome thing to undertake; something at once murderous, painful, healing —and full of love.

Soon he had the tourniquet applied, an assistant holding it. He picked up the scalpel—

"Blast you, Abbott—!" It was Chief Surgeon Britton glowering at him. "This man shouldn't have been brought in here. It's a hopeless case."

"I'll decide that for myself, Major."

"So *you'll* decide, will you?" Britton raged on. "And what will you decide about that mess above the knee—or are you too blind to see? In that location you can't even amputate."

Britton was right. Under the primitive battlefront hospital conditions it would be plain murder to attempt to amputate above the knee. The big arteries couldn't be cauterized nor could they be tied off soon enough to prevent blood gushing out that would bring on exsanguinating death.

"But I don't propose to amputate," Paul said coolly.

"You're an utter fool, Abbott! I've already given orders about how things are to be handled around here and you're deliberately disobeying. Now get this man out of here and go to work on some of the others!"

It was one of the few times in Paul's life that he came close to completely losing his temper. His smoke-gray eyes glinted as he straightened, but he managed to keep his voice under control:

"Kindly get the hell away from here, Britton," he said in a tense, quiet voice, "or I'll be court-martialed for assaulting a superior officer."

Britton's face reddened. He breathed heavily for a few moments, then got his own temper under control.

56

"All right, Abbott, carry on—but this isn't the end of the matter, you can be sure of that. . . ."

iii

After dark the rain began. It grew into a heavy downpour, with lightning and rolling crashes of thunder hardly distinguishable from the booming of cannon and red flames streaking from the massed artillery. Outside the log house and hospital tents long lines of casualties lay uncovered in mud and pools of water with torrents of rain slashing down at them like punishing flails from heaven—or hell.

Inside the log house Paul and his colleagues labored at their gruesome tasks, racing against time, against death—

Cut, clamp, sponge, tie, cut. . . .

Paul had done all possible for the young fellow he had brought in earlier. He had extracted a minié ball from the left side of the rib cage where it had been stopped by a rib. Fortunately the bleeding was minimal. Had it been a bayonet wound, the lad would have long since been dead. Clean incised wounds from sharp objects such as knives or broken glass bled profusely whereas puncture wounds from bullets or other blunt penetrating objects left torn, uneven edges and tended to bleed more sluggishly.

The big danger of such ragged wounds was that they contained more infective matter, had more crushed tissues. They contaminated quickly and soon gangrened—the wounded soldier's death sentence.

In the case of the mangled leg, Paul had carefully cleaned out the foreign matter, excised the crushed and torn tissues and tied off several veins and arteries. Since his personal supply of a highly effective antisepsis solution of his own formulation—carbolic acid and alcohol—was used up, he had substituted cleansing both the leg and chest wounds with soapy water, alcohol and copious flushings of salt water. Because of the serious damage to the tissues, suturing was not possible. The open gory cavity

57

in the thigh was finally dressed with compresses and bandages.

Throughout the debridement of living flesh without anesthesia—a harsh, painful procedure that could make the strongest scream or pass out—the lad had kept his eyes squeezed shut. The pale sweating face was wrenched with agony. His lips moved—but not once making a sound.

Paul had asked, "Are you all right, son? Are you able to speak?"

"Yes." His voice was barely audible.

"Are you in much pain?"

"No more'n the others, I reckon."

"What's your name?"

"Jody . . . Jody McNally."

"You're a brave lad, Jody. Do you believe in prayer?"

"I been doin' that right along. Whatever the Lord wants of me, I'm ready. . . ."

"Well, you just keep on with those prayers and we'll give the Lord all the help we can."

Afterward, he found an unoccupied corner where he had Jody placed on an old blanket so he could keep watch on his condition. Normally each patient, once the surgeons had finished with him, would be laid outside among others under the pouring rain to await transport to the river landing. Jody was too precariously balanced on the borderline of death to risk moving.

Now, as he continued working with furious but delicate speed on patient after patient, he was fighting against a growing numbness, a sense of slowly sinking into a mental grayness of utter exhaustion. His eyes smarted and watered from the oily smoke of lanterns, from the strain of the poor lighting. His head ached from the thick cloying stench of blood; from the heat generated by so many bodies, the boiling iron kettle over the fireplace, the brazier of simmering oil. He was lame all over. His stomach was sickish from lack of food and endless cups of black coffee. Except for a few brief respites he had been continuously at work since dawn. It was now approaching midnight.

All that kept him going was the knowledge of the

steadily increasing backlog of the wounded outside under the driving rain.

Some of the other surgeons had resorted to private bottles of medical whiskey. Tiredness, the booze and their general disgust was having its effect in louder talk, less restraint in expressing opinions:

"How'n hell does Washington 'spect ush carry on," said one tipsy surgeon, "without 'nough doctors, not 'nough tents, not 'nough medical supplies—"

"You mean not enough whiskey, don't you, Roscoe?" cut in one of the others.

There was a ripple of laughter.

"Roscoe's right," said another. "Except it isn't Washington should be blamed as much as our drunken general who doesn't get off his arse long enough to properly take care of his men. Except for his goddamn drinking the damn secessionists wouldn't have got the jump on us in the first place."

"Maybe that's why the quartermaster is out of booze," joked another.

"You're damn right thash why," said Roscoe, taking a swig from his bottle.

"Attention, everyone—!" roared Britton.

In the sudden silence, eyes turned toward the chief surgeon, who was now standing at attention facing the door. An officer with a cigar in his mouth and rain dribbling from his slouch hat and cape had just entered.

"At ease, gentlemen . . ." said General Grant, glancing around.

"Good God, General," said Britton. "You're drenched to the skin!"

The general took the cigar out of his mouth and smiled at it. "At least I've managed to keep my cigar dry."

"We can't have you coming down with pneumonia, sir. I recommend that you get in dry clothes and stay out of the rain. We can clear a place for you in here and fix up a cot so you can get a rest."

"That won't be necessary, Major. I've got a whole army out there in the rain without any shelter over their heads.

If they can stand it, I expect I can." He started toward the operating tables. "I only came in to see how you're getting along."

"As well as can be expected, sir, considering that we've run through most of our medical supplies. Is there any hope of more supplies arriving soon?"

"Not soon enough, I'm afraid. Of course, the only man who has the answer to that is General Halleck in Washington. . . ."

Grant stopped to stare down at one of the bloodied amputation cases being bandaged. Paul, nearby, noticed a grim tightening of the general's mouth, a muscle twitching in a cheek. The general suddenly turned away and started for the door. Britton followed.

"As I said, General, it would be no trouble to fix up a place for you here—"

Grant turned and said soberly, "I'll confess I did have that in mind, Major. But the truth is, I find the sight of all these poor devils more unendurable than facing enemy fire. I think I'll get back under my tree in the rain."

After he went out, one of the surgeons said scathingly, "The bastard doesn't give a damn about our shortages."

"Shut your rotten mouth!" Britton had whirled toward the speaker. His silvery hair was askew, his face mottled with rage.

"I've overlooked all the treasonable talk coming from you damned volunteer doctors up until now, on the grounds of your ignorance about the regular army and in consideration of the conditions you're working under. But one more disparaging word from any of you against our commanding officer and I swear I'll have you cashiered out in disgrace!"

He glared around at the silent doctors for a moment, then continued: "What I'm about to say might be considered just as treasonable, but I'm too fed up with hearing all these false rumors about the general when I happen to know different. . . .

"The facts are, way back on the troop transports weeks ago the general sent urgent telegraphic messages to Washington for more medical supplies. Washington replied, asking for itemized requisitions. That was done. After a long delay the requisitions were sent back by General Halleck with the notation they were not made out properly. Well, they were made out again—properly, we hope —and again forwarded to Washington. And we're still waiting. . . . Now that's the way the regular army works, gentlemen. Any questions?"

Saul Simon spoke up. "Isn't General Halleck behind the talk in Washington that General Grant should be removed for shipping casualties to the convalescent hospitals without adequate medical attention?"

"I see you're up on your reading, Simon. General Halleck has personally censured General Grant for not taking better care of his wounded."

There was shamed silence.

"And now I'll ask one last question," said Britton. "Has any one of you personally seen General Grant touch a drop of liquor or ever appear intoxicated in the slightest?"

Again silence.

"Now get back to work."

iv

Shortly after midnight the door slammed open and an officer wearing the single star of a brigadier general strode in.

"I understand this is General Grant's headquarters. Where is he?"

"He's somewhere out there under a tree, sir," said Britton with great politeness.

The general's eyebrows arched; anger glinted in his eyes. "Aren't you being a bit insubordinate, Major?"

"That is certainly not my intention, sir. I am only repeating what General Grant himself told us when he left here earlier. He didn't tell us what tree."

"Well, I'll find him. But while I'm here I'd better alert you to make preparations to move."

Britton looked astonished. "Good God, General—we can't move!"

"You have no choice. We've been pressed back on all sides by the enemy. The engagements have ended for to-night, but at the first crack of dawn we're expecting them to launch an all-out attack to push us into the river. I suggest you make ready to move immediately to avoid the congestion when all of our troops are in retreat." He turned to leave.

Paul called out after him: "But what are we to do with the casualties, sir? The hospital ship and all available transports are already loaded. The ambulances and wagons moving the wounded to the landing can no longer find any room to put them. We've got hundreds more lying out in the rain waiting for treatment—"

"This is war, Captain. If necessary, leave them behind and hope the enemy will be charitable."

"But sir, we can't possibly—"

Ignoring him, the general swung around and went out. Paul started after him.

"Abbott—" Britton snapped at him. "You heard the orders!"

"I heard them but I, for one, don't propose to obey them!"

He slammed out.

V

Rain whipped down in torrents. Except for an occasional spattering, the musketry fire had ceased but shells still screamed overhead, crashing through boughs of trees, jarring the ground. On all sides the wet blackness was frequently exploded with giant flashes of red, orange or white, like monster fireflies gone crazy.

One of the bursts of illumination revealed General Grant under a large tree nearby leaning against the trunk.

Paul slogged toward him through mud and wet grass. "General Grant—"

Another blinding flash disclosed the general holding a pocket watch near his face. His glance darted at Paul.

"Hold it for just another minute or two, Captain. . . ."

Mystified, Paul waited. After what seemed like several minutes in the drenching darkness, a heavy detonation from the direction of the river suddenly shook the ground with such force that he could feel it through his boots. It was accompanied by the ascending howl of a shell that arched high over the woodlands to finally burst in a distant sector, sending another shock wave and an eerie flash of light through the countryside.

Grant chuckled. "Right on the dot! You see, Captain, Gwin has opened fire from our naval boats. He promised to throw heavy shells every ten minutes with five-second, ten-second and fifteen-second fuses, along with an occasional shrapnel from the howitzers. That's to keep the rebs from getting any sleep tonight. What can I do for you, Captain Abbott?"

"General Grant, the medical service has been ordered to retreat to the river, taking with us only as many casualties as we can and leaving the others behind. I must respectfully refuse to obey such an order and request that I be permitted to stay behind with the wounded men."

The red tip of the general's cigar glowed bright; then, "Don't worry about it, Abbott. Just before you arrived I spoke to the general who issued the order, apparently under a false impression of our situation, and I corrected his thinking. Unfortunately I have too many nervous generals under my command, but I think with a little more seasoning most of them will learn that the only way to win a battle is not to run, but to stand tight and fight."

The tip of his cigar glowed alternately bright and faint as he puffed slowly before adding:

"We've been in the devil's own hornet's nest today and have taken quite a beating. But tomorrow we'll lick the hell out of 'em."

vi

When he returned to the log house, Saul Simon came striding to meet him. Paul was struck by the change in the youthful doctor's appearance. His neat attire of yesterday was in disarray; spatterings of dried blood caked his jacket and trousers. His normally cheerful face was creased with new lines of strain, worry, shock; the large brown eyes were eloquent with inner torment. One day amid so much blood and death had added years to his age.

"Paul . . . I think your young patient is getting worse. You better have a look at him. . . ."

Paul knelt beside the lad. His eyes were wide, shining strangely, and his breath was coming in irregular gasps, first deep, then shallow. The pale face shone with sweat.

"Jody, can you hear me? Can you speak?"

Jody's lips began moving.

"Joreen—" he gasped above his choking intake of air. "Jor—" He stopped from lack of breath.

I've done all I can, Paul thought. He doubted that the boy would last the night.

Four

Joreen

i

Joreen awoke with a start. Her sleep had been nightmarish, filled with horrifying visions: violence, death, blood. Blood everywhere. A pain-wrenched face calling her name.

The face was Jody, her twin brother. . . .

Sitting up in bed she tried to calm her thudding heart. Still, the terrible dream lingered so vividly she could still hear the shouting and cursing of men grappling in battle; the gunfire, the hard drumming of the hoofs of horses whipped into furious action.

All that day she had been troubled by a terrible certainty. There had been no rational basis for it. Her brother's letters told of nothing but how dull and humdrum it was to be a recruit far from battle, of his yearning for action, of his impatience with generals who didn't want to fight.

Yet she knew that the forebodings that had lain so

heavily on her spirits today were more than sisterly worries. She and her twin brother had an unusual affinity for each other. In childhood they had discovered that they always knew exactly what the other one was thinking or feeling. This strange faculty had been proven many times. Once Jody had fallen from his horse and broken an ankle miles from the farm. She had known at once, and mounting one of the plowhorses she had ridden unerringly in the right direction to find him.

So vivid had been the nightmare, she fancied she could still hear men shouting, the trampling of hoofs.

Suddenly she felt a cold shiver of alarm. The sounds were *not* an echo of her bad dream, but coming from outside—

Springing from bed, she hastened to a window and peered out into the darkness.

She peered down into a scene of wild agitation in the barnyard. Torches flared above the heads of about a dozen riders who were circling around the farm animals: two old plowhorses, three cows, a fat old sow with her litter of squealing piglets. From inside the barn came the frantic squawking of chickens being chased. One of the intruders emerged from the barn carrying two flapping hens. Stuffing one under an arm, he deftly caught the other by the head and swung it in a circle, breaking its neck; then did the same with the other.

They were all in gray and butternut uniforms. Rebels!

As the terrified, churning animals began pouring out through the open gate, the bone-chilling rebel yell broke out: *"Eee-yi-yay . . . Eee-yi-yay!"*

Anger overcame her fright. Those animals were their whole subsistence; without the two old plowhorses they couldn't even keep the small farm going. Unmindful that her attire was only a thin cotton nightgown, she rushed out into the narrow upstairs hallway.

Her father, carrying a flickering candle in one hand and a rifle in the other, was just emerging from the bedroom. His gray hair stuck up in wild tufts above a gaunt face and eyes that shone like blue fire. In his worn nightshirt with his scrawny legs and knobby bare feet, he looked as ancient as the firelock musket he clutched. He scowled at her.

"Joreen—what're you doin' up?"

"I saw them rebs messin' around in the barnyard, Pa. I was jest goin' down to git my gun. . . ." Her own gun, a small-bore musket mostly used for hunting squirrels and rabbits, was kept in a corner kitchen closet.

"Ain't nothin' for a female to tangle up with. It's one of them derned secesh foragin' parties. Now you git back to your room an' stay there while I go drive them away." He hustled toward the stairway.

"Don't go out there alone, Pa! There's too many of them, an' they got guns—"

"Any scum that'll come skulkin' around to steal from an honest man in the dark of night is cowards. I'll send them skedaddlin' with a shot or two—" He went clumping down the stairs.

She waited a few moments and then started down after him, feeling her way through the darkness with one hand on a wall while sliding her bare feet over the rough board steps.

Her father had already gone outside when she reached the kitchen. Fumbling through the darkness, she found the lantern and the box of Red Devil sulphur matches. As she was lighting the lantern, she could hear her father's wrathful shouting:

". . . godderned thieves git offa my property an' leave my stock be, afore I—!"

Two sharp pistol reports cut off his words.

Chilled by an icy stab of apprehension, she rushed to the door and yanked it open. Straining her eyes into the darkness, she saw only milling horses and the precious livestock being herded away. One of the riders, in the uniform of a Confederate officer, detached himself from the group and rode toward her, holstering a gun as he approached.

Soon the horse loomed in front of her. Its rider doffed his hat in mock courtesy, smiling grimly.

"Miss McNally, I regret to inform you—"

"Steen Saxton!" Her astonishment was mingled with

hope. Steen Saxton was the son of their rich neighboring farmer, Calvin Saxton, who owned over eight hundred acres of the best farmland. It had been well known that the Saxtons were pro-secessionist, as were many others who lived along this southern Illinois border area, and quite a few of the young men of such families had crossed over into Kentucky to join the Confederate army.

But certainly, despite having opposing views toward slavery and secession from the Union, Steen Saxton would not have wished any harm to come to his humble farm neighbor.

"What were those shots?" she went on. "Where's my father?"

He dismounted. "As I started telling you, Miss McNally, I am heading a foraging party to bring back food supplies for our forces. Unfortunately, your father was rash enough to try to interfere—"

In the pale moonlight ahead she saw the recumbent body in a flannel nightshirt sprawled flat on the ground, face down.

"Pa, Pa—" She started forward but Saxton caught her roughly by the arm.

"There's no help you can give him now. . . . He took two shots in the head."

She gave a cry of pain. "You murdered him!"

"We're at war," he said harshly. "The damned Federals are doing the same and worse all along the Mississippi. If your father hadn't been so foolish—"

She flew at him, hands clawing toward his face. "You vile traitor, you rotten killer—!"

With a slashing swing of a powerful arm he knocked her arms aside; his other hand dealt her a slap across the face that sent her reeling back. His handsome face hardened.

"Now you make it easier for me to avail myself of some of the sweeter fruits of war—"

With a sudden lunge he caught her in both arms and flung her over one shoulder. She began kicking and screaming, but there were none to hear. The last of the other rebels had ridden away with the livestock and the nearest farm was two miles away.

He carried her into the kitchen, closed the door behind them and dumped her on the floor. The sensual lips beneath his finely chiseled nose curled into a leer and his hard blue eyes glinted as his gaze roved boldly over her thinly clad body.

She exploded into a frenzied effort to escape. The hands of her pinioned arms tried to claw at him. Her bare feet kicked at him, doing no damage except hurt to her toes. When he brought his arrogant lips down to force their will against hers, her teeth snapped at them with enough success to taste blood.

He gave a hoarse yelp, jerking his head back; then laughed. "Fight all you want, little hellcat—it's more exciting that way."

The hand under her nightgown was bolder, forcing its way between her thighs. . . . His torso was a heavy pressure against her, an engulfing, overwhelming weight that was bearing her down. And now he was nibbling savagely at her lips.

Oh God . . . he's going to rape me. . . .

"Please, please . . ." she moaned as steely fingers twisted through her hair, bending her head back until the oppressive weight tilted her off balance. The two tumbled back heavily with a jarring, numbing impact. Through the swirling haze of pain and terror, she heard the clanking of his scabbard against the floor, saw that he was unbuckling his trousers, rolling them down.

Then hands were pulling, tearing at her nightgown . . . a hideous nightmare . . . hot breath panting in her face, wet lips moving against hers. . . .

In a final spurt of defiance her teeth snapped at him, caught his nose. He yowled in pain, slapped at her head so viciously that a brilliant burst of light showered somewhere in her head and momentarily she was dazed.

"Damned hellcat—try that again and I'll break your neck!"

Then a silent scream of anguish shot through her body like a stab of lightning. . . .

ii

Lying limp, she came slowly out of the grayness that encompassed her.

It was over. He had risen to his knees, a smile on his sweat-glistening face. Lazily, somewhat clumsily, he began to haul his trousers up.

With catlike speed she leaped up and gripped the handle of the saber in the dangling scabbard.

"Hey you—!" He grabbed for the saber, screamed and let his hand drop away. It was crimson with blood.

"Damn your slutty soul!" he howled, staring in stupefaction at his blood-streaming hand. Face mottled with rage, he started to rise but was hampered by the trousers half down to his knees. "By God, I'll kill you now, you . . ."

The words ended in a great sucking in of breath followed by a gurgling in his throat while his unbelieving gaze dropped to the shining steel protruding from his belly. As he looked she withdrew the blade and thrust it in again and again.

The silly look of astonishment was still on his face as he sank down and slumped softly forward. Blood from his mouth ran rich and dark over the floorboards.

iii

An hour later Joreen stared into the kitchen mirror and felt a strange prickling sensation race up her spine. The scissors were still in her hand; on the floor lay the fluffy mess of pale straw-colored locks she had lopped off.

She was looking at Jody—at the same face, the same hair, cut exactly as she had so often cut it for her brother.

And the same clothes, for she had dressed in old garments Jody had left behind.

Before leaving, she paused a few moments to stare down at Saxton's motionless body. The bloodied saber lay beside him. She felt no remorse, only a cold, hardened determination; this was the enemy.

Outside, the first hint of dawn was tinting the eastern sky as she mounted the late Captain Saxton's fine black steed. She carried no personal effects with her except her father's old firelock musket. And ammunition.

She drove spurless heels into the horse. As the spirited animal bounded off, she thought she heard the distant drumming of horse hoofs approaching from the direction of Saxton's woods. Quite likely it would be Steen Saxton's men coming to see why their leader had not returned.

She smiled thinly. Thank God she could ride and knew the country well, and Saxton's horse was probably the finest and fastest in his company.

If they wanted to give chase let them try.

iv

The morning sun was barely slanting its rays over the rooftops when Joreen rode into Cairo. As the stolen black stallion slowed to a walk on the main street of Cairo, the sudden assault on her senses of the hustle-bustle of the town absorbed all her attention.

She had never seen any place larger than small crossroads hamlets; she gazed around in awe. Even this early the streets and barrooms were filled with crowds of men, mostly soldiers, who seemed not to know what to do with themselves. On every corner the raucous voices of vendors of food and trinkets hawked their wares. Along the nearby wharves, river steamers and other vessels were crowded three rows deep. All seemed to be competing in a discordant medley of whistlings and tootings; steam spat out from the sides of wheelers to release boiler pressures.

Stimulating as it all was to her fresh young eyes and ears, she soon became aware of another strange new sensation. It came with the realization that none of the men gave her more than a glance as she rode past. There was none of the close scrutiny to be expected from street loafers in even the smallest of villages, no vulgar comments about her female attractions or lack of them, none of the usual lewd invitations directed at unprotected young ladies.

Dressed as a man she had for the first time in her life stepped boldly into the freedom and heady independence of masculinity—and had been accepted! Accepted as just another farm lad scarcely worth noticing. Their only interest was in the splendid horse she rode.

The unease she first felt riding into this totally male world began to give way to a glorious exaltation.

But young males were not free from heckling.

"Hey kid—whatcher doin' on a man's hoss?"

"Tell yeh what, young feller—I'll give you two silver dollars an' a pers'nal introduction to the purtiest whore in town for that hoss."

"Hell, he don't own a hoss like that—he's just the stablehand."

Ignoring such gibes, she rode on toward the Cairo Hotel, where Jody had gone to enlist.

As she neared the hotel, a drunken soldier with a very red nose and a bottle in one hand wobbled directly into her path to catch at her horse's bridle.

"Sir—take your hands off my horse!"

"I ain't a-hurtin' yer hoss . . . jesh offerin' 'im a friendly li'l drink." He lifted the bottle to the horse's mouth.

In a flare of anger, Joreen jerked a foot out of the stirrup and kicked at the man's hand, bringing a squawk of surprise and causing the liquor to slosh over. The man swayed backward a few steps, letting his jaw drop open in mock astonishment.

"Guesh I gosh the wrong end've the critter," he said, shaking his head contritely, "but I reckon thash kin be fixed—"

Before she realized what was happening, the besotted

72

soldier lifted the horse's tail and jammed the neck of the bottle into the animal's rectum, tilting it high.

Guffaws broke out as the powerful beast, stung by the burning liquor in a sensitive area, reared up suddenly, almost unseating Joreen, who quickly threw her weight forward and stretching both arms past the animal's neck, hauled down on the reins. It had little effect except to change his tactics. Head lowered, whinnying and snorting, eyes rolling, the horse now began a series of stiff-legged jumps; then went into such wild bucking and twisting that Joreen felt dizzy from the hard pounding against the base of her spine and wondered how long her neck could endure such wrenching jerks and twists.

She hung on grimly, legs clamped with all the strength she could muster against the animal's sides. She was a self-taught rider but she had no doubt that she could conquer the plunging beast. He was just bigger and could buck harder than any other she had known. It made her mad. Snatching off the old black felt slouch hat of Jody's that she wore, she began whopping it vigorously against the horse's rump.

"Stop it, you ornery cuss, or I'll beat yer derned hide off!" she yelled, whacking the hat first against one side and then the other, keeping the reins taut with her other hand.

Surprisingly the animal quickly calmed down. Tossing his head a few times, whisking his glossy tail, he pawed at the ground with one hoof and then stood still.

The crowd burst into applause.

"That's what I call right smart ridin'!" vouchsafed one of the onlookers, and there was a chorus of agreement.

A slender officer emerged from the crowd. "A magnificent display of horsemanship," he said in a smooth voice. Walking up, he took the animal's bridle and rubbed its nose in an easy way. He smiled up at Joreen.

"With such spirit, young man, you must be looking for a glorious career in the army."

For a moment Joreen couldn't find her tongue; not so much because the young officer had so unerringly divined her purpose, but because he was the handsomest man she had ever seen or imagined. He had silky blond hair that fell in ringlets below his ears, languid blue eyes, a fine straight nose and a wisp of mustache above very red and well-shaped lips. His complexion was like milk and pink roses. She never thought anybody, especially a man, could ever be so pretty.

"Uh . . . why yes sirree. I come here exactly for that. I want to join up an' fight."

"Splendid! What a stroke of luck for both of us! It just happens that I am an enlistment officer and my office is right here in the hotel. Come with me and we'll get you properly signed up. . . ."

Luck indeed! If all officers were as pleasant as this one, she was sure going to like the army. But all Joreen said as she dismounted was: "Is there someplace I could git some hay an' water for my horse?"

"Spoken like a true soldier! The first thought is always for the faithful steed that bravely carries you into battle. What is his name, by the way?"

Joreen hadn't really thought about it. She blurted out the first name that came to mind. "T-Thunder."

"Capital—such a fitting name for a war steed! Now we'll see that Thunder is taken care of at once." Turning, he clapped his hands smartly and called to a scrawny young soldier:

"Prentiss—see that this noble animal is stabled and fed. Give it the best of attention for my young friend here. Move smart now!"

"Yes sir," said the young soldier, lazily moving over to take the reins.

And to Joreen: "Just follow me, young man, and you'll soon be a proud, happy soldier. . . ."

Following, Joreen was half in a dream state. How kind he was! So gentle and concerned about her horse. His voice was so soft, so smooth; his movements so graceful. He made her feel like a bumpkin. Hardly thinking about it, she essayed a more ladylike, dainty way of walking—quite unlike her usual boyish stride—until she remembered that she was supposed to be a man.

She changed to a kind of bold swagger that she feared

74

might not be too convincing, but nobody bothered to notice. The lobby of the Cairo Hotel was so crowded with military uniforms of all ranks that it was hard to find passage between them. The air was thick with loud talk, smoke, heat and flies.

"In here—" said the lieutenant, opening the door to a bleak little room with no furniture but a small desk and two chairs. He indicated a chair.

"My office isn't very fancy," he said apologetically as he seated himself behind the desk. "In truth, I have far better accommodations in camp. Here, the generals get all the best rooms. This hotel was General Grant's headquarters, you know, up until a few months ago when he moved South. But enough of the trivia and on to the matter at hand—"

He leaned across the desk, resting on his elbows, slender hands clasped, and gave Joreen his nicest smile. "How old are you, lad?"

"Eighteen," she lied.

"Perfect! And what is your name?"

"J-Jory Jones," she said hesitantly. "Jory" was the nickname her brother had always called her by; she gave the false last name for fear of being blamed for the murder of the secessionist officer who had raped her.

"A charming name." The young officer smiled, his exquisite eyebrows tilting. "And you certainly come from a most patriotic—and should I say prolific?—family. You'd be surprised at how many of your valiant relatives —or at least those using the name 'Jones'—have volunteered for service in the Federal army."

He laughed softly when she flushed. "Frankly, most enlistment officers would find it hard to believe you're any more than sixteen, possibly seventeen. Normally we're quite strict about that—there are so many youngsters lying about their ages and names to get into the service of their country, but when a smart-looking lad like you comes along, especially with such a fine horse as well—there's a shortage of good horses, you know. Sheridan's taken almost everything he could lay his hands on for his regiment. As I was saying, in your case I'm willing to relax the rules—stretch them a bit, to be more exact—which is all to your advantage. You have no idea how lucky you are to come along at just the right moment to be accepted into our distinguished cavalry group—"

"Cavalry! But I came to join up with the infantry."

The officer looked horrified. "Infantry? Good God, young man, you can't realize what you're saying! The infantry is only for the roughest, crudest sort of men. It's all dirt, marching, sleeping in mud and walking into hailstorms of minié balls. Why most of our Illinois infantry contingents are at this very moment down in Shiloh getting mowed down like a hayfield under Confederate fire."

With an effort she suppressed her sudden new surge of alarm. Jody was at Shiloh! Her dire premonitions that he was in great danger were all too true. Perhaps he was already wounded, or worse—

"My brother's in the infantry in Grant's army, and I want to be where he is. I ain't afraid of bullets. All I want is a chance to fight them secesh devils."

"Ah! How fortunate for you that you came along at just the right moment! You see, if you simply volunteered in the infantry, you'd have no say about where you'd be sent. But our cavalry has already been assigned to support Grant's army, and if you enlist with us, you'll be going down into Tennessee where you'll get a chance to see your brother."

"Well," she said dubiously, "I don't know—"

"This must be your lucky day, young man! Normally I wouldn't consider accepting the enlistment of such a young stripling, but our group is being held up only for lack of a full complement of men and horses. We prefer, of course, the kind of spirited blades who can afford to bring not only their own horses but buy their own uniforms and weapons—" The officer made a gesture of good will. "But since you already have a fine horse and since we have many generous and wealthy backers willing to supply the items that our Federal government is not able to provide for our stalwart cavalrymen, the rest will be no problem. Once you have joined us, lad, we will be able to leave immediately to join Grant's army. How about it?"

Joreen was convinced. "I'm ready. I'll join up with you."

Oddly, the young officer frowned as if suddenly dubious. "Perhaps I haven't made it fully clear to you that in the cavalry you're not volunteering simply for an interlude of excitement, adventure and leisure. It's a hard rough life—"

"I know that. All I want is a chance to fight them secessionists!"

"Splendid! That's exactly the right attitude. However—" The young officer rose from behind the small desk and began pacing back and forth. The spurs on his black boots jingled as he walked. His hands were clasped behind his strong, straight young figure. He was about twenty-two, Joreen guessed, and a more handsome man she had never seen.

"In view of my responsibility to enlist only the highest caliber of recruits, I feel constrained to ask a few personal questions. Is it possible that your main reason for wanting to enlist is only to impress your girl friend? You do have a girl, don't you?"

Joreen shook her head vehemently. "No sirree! I don't have a girl."

The young officer smiled. "I can see you're even a smarter lad than I thought. Nothing can wreck a young man's chances of getting ahead in the world faster than getting moony over some pretty but empty-headed girl. Now there's one last thing I need to know—"

He swung around and with hands clasped behind him stared down at her with his bright blue eyes seeming to probe deep into her. Joreen's heart skipped a few beats under the hynotic gaze.

"First, let me explain that I am in particular need of a personal orderly—one who is as intelligent and willing a young soldier as I believe you to be, one whom I can slowly train and teach all the things you will need to know. Primarily it involves a willingness to obey orders, no matter what they may be. . . ."

"Oh, I'm willing to do anything you ask of me. I want to work hard and learn everything I can."

"Excellent! With that kind of attitude I'm sure you'll

soon discover that working as my orderly is a most fortunate assignment to have, one that many young cavalrymen would be most happy to get. You understand that I am in a position to grant various small favors to make the hard life of a cavalryman much, much easier. . . ."

"Oh, I ain't afraid of hard work—I've worked hard all my life, and I like work. I'm not afraid to fight—"

The lieutenant laughed. "A most laudable state of mind." He walked over close and clapped a hand on her shoulder, squeezed it slightly. "I was speaking of something else, something we might call 'esprit de corps'—or you might term it the camaraderie that develops between men thrown into a common cause."

The bright blue eyes were close to Joreen's. Her heart began to beat faster. "You do understand what I'm implying, don't you, lad?"

She was vaguely confused. She understood his words well enough but he seemed to be implying more.

"You'll never have to worry about me," she said stoutly. "I'll do my part."

"And as I said, you must learn how to take orders, my boy. You'll have to take orders you don't always want to take. You'll have to do what any officer orders you to do— whether you like it or not—at the pain of severe punishment if you refuse."

"I understand that."

The lieutenant's eyes had half lidded over. He still stood close in front of her. She felt disturbingly that his gaze was moving to her smallish breasts, which she was sure were not discernible under her loose shirt, continuing down her torso, and then seemed to rest at that most private part of her pelvic region. His red lips parted.

"I'm sure we'll have no problems," he said softly. "There's something about you . . . I sense we may be . . . kindred spirits. I'm confident that we shall get along very well indeed. . . ."

He suddenly straightened and went back to the desk. "Now I think we can get down to business. You're everything I'd been hoping for in a recruit—young, enthusiastic, very personable, satisfying in every way. So let's get on with it. . . ."

Pulling open a desk drawer he extracted papers, dipped a quill into the inkwell and began writing.

Within five minutes all the forms had been properly filled out with Joreen's signature and she had been sworn in.

"All right, Jory," he said, handing her a copy of the enlistment agreement. "You are now a private in the Federal cavalry."

She took the precious paper with trembling fingers.

"I sure thank you for making me a soldier."

Instantly the officer's face turned cold and hard.

"From this instant, soldier," he snapped, "you'll never again address me without saying 'sir' and showing proper respect for my official title, which is Lieutenant Sheldon Verlandigham."

"Why yes, I didn't mean—"

"Sir!" the lieutenant thundered at her.

"Why yes—yes *sir*."

"And now one of my men will direct you to the quartermaster's, where you'll be supplied with all the things you need."

"Yes *sir*," she said.

Five

Ball, Canister and Shell

"While a battle is raging one can see his enemy mowed down by the thousands, or the ten thousands, with great composure; but after the battle these scenes are distressing, and one is naturally disposed to do as much to alleviate the suffering of an enemy as a friend."

General U. S. Grant, Shiloh, 1862.

i

All through the night, while guns howled and shell explosions tore the earth and air, Paul and the other surgeons labored at their grisly tasks. Most of the surgeons and their assistants had been reassigned to dressing stations in tents hastily erected near other pockets of fighting and only Paul, Saul Simon, Chief Surgeon Britton and several assistants were left in the log house. None had slept.

The pouring rain seemed unending, as did the buildup

of battle victims lying outside in the mud. Although more tents had been thrown up to shelter the more critical cases, Britton estimated that from two to three thousand of the wounded still lay outside unprotected from the thunderstorm.

Untold thousands more littered the battlefield.

"They're so thick out thar," said one patient, "some places yeh kin walk over 'em like on a carpet fer two, three hundert yards in any direction without once steppin' on the ground."

Others told of bands of wild hogs squealing and quarreling over their feasts on the dead during the night, and the shrieks of the living as they were ripped open by razor-sharp tusks.

The loading squads on careening ambulances and munition wagons continuously arriving to pick up the wounded no longer made any effort to differentiate between those already treated by the doctors or those still waiting for treatment. They were simply cargo to be cleared away as rapidly as possible. All showing signs of life were piled in the vehicles and rushed off to the landing; there to be reloaded, close together as bricks, on any vessel available for transport to Savannah, where overcrowding and lack of medical attention were just as bad.

ii

With the first pale streaks of dawn there began a sudden increase in the volume of cannonading across a broad front and a thunderous new fusillade of rifle fire.

Paul looked up wearily from the patient he had just finished bandaging. "So it's starting all over again. . . ."

"You bet it is," said Britton. Except for his bloodshot eyes and unkempt appearance, the gray-haired chief surgeon looked as peppery as ever. "And you can damn well bet it's going to be hotter than it was yesterday."

"How can that be? All the men still alive out there must be close to dead on their feet."

"Abbott, the longer a man fights the ornerier he gets. I've seen soldiers after two or three days of fighting without letup turn into savages worse than any Apache. It's a kind of cornered-rat survival instinct built into the human animal—"

He halted to slap a restraining hand against the shoulder of his patient. "Stop squirming, you miserable yellow-belly! My reference to humans didn't include you. If I'd noticed right off that you'd taken a ball in the back, I'd have thrown you into the dead pile. Any coward who shows his heels to the enemy deserves hanging by the neck."

The cowed patient subsided into inert silence. Britton continued:

"All those new batteries whanging away out there, Abbott, are from General Buell's men. They got here the other evening, and all night Buell's been deploying about eighteen thousand of them into battle lines. Besides that, General Lew Wallace, who never did know his arse from his elbow, finally looked at his compass long enough to find his way down from Crump's Landing—a whole day late—and his men are filling in the gaps. As they say about fools and angels, new troops have a tendency to rush in. As for Grant's green troops of yesterday, there won't be so many of them pouring in today all shot to hell. They're overnight veterans. The ones still alive have learned to keep their arse down."

He laughed harshly. "It's Buell's and Wallace's recruits that will take the worst of it today—and it won't necessarily be their fault. Grant made one big blunder. He was so cocksure that he could walk all over the Confederates any moment he decided, he didn't bother to have his men dig in. Two thirds of our casualties could have been saved if Grant's men had been entrenched. I warrant he'll never make that mistake again. Be that as it may, foxy old Johnston and Beauregard are bound to blast us with everything they've got today. It's their last chance to shove us into the river, and you can be sure they've got plenty of bare-assed reserves to throw at us, so there's a good chance they'll do it. . . ."

Saul Simon, listening with a moody frown, all at once threw his hands up in disgust.

"It's all a bloody farce—the goddamned war, the whole goddamned medical service—everything! All those men out there have gone kill-crazy, and they haven't the foggiest notion of the real reason why—all because the power-mad politicians, money-mad industrialists and glory-mad generals tell them to. And what the hell good are we doing here hacking off arms and legs? We're all part of the insanity—bloody butchers, all of us!"

Paul looked at him worriedly as Simon paused to extract a half-filled bottle of whiskey from his surgical bag and take a long swallow. Until yesterday, Simon had told him, he had never touched liquor. Paul felt strongly that no surgeon should ever drink a drop of alcohol when he had work to do, but he knew that Simon was dangerously close to the breaking point and apparently liquor helped him endure the incredible strain. War had certainly changed him.

The chief surgeon's lips tightened in disapproval. "You people of Hebraic extraction see war differently from the rest of us, because it's not in your nature to face up to a fight."

"Major, are you implying that Jews are afraid to fight?"

"In my long years of service I don't recall seeing many of your brethren in uniform, but you'll find plenty of them among those industrialists you spoke about getting rich from the war."

Simon's pale face slowly tinged with a flush. His slender hands clenched and unclenched.

"I ask you again, Major, are you calling me a coward?"

"Calm down, Simon. You've got nothing to worry about. You don't have to shoulder a gun. Back here you're relatively safe."

The young doctor's grim lips began to tremble. "It would be a thousand times easier to be out there with a gun killing the enemy than it is in here butchering our own men with knives and saws!"

"It's not like shooting at squirrels and stumps out there, Simon. You're forgetting you have to wade through a hail of bullets."

Without another word Simon put down his scalpel and ripped off his bloodied apron. Going over to a corner, he picked up one of the rifles that had been collected from a few of the wounded who had brought them in and strode to the door.

"Where the hell do you think you're going, Simon?" called Britton.

"Out to wade through a hail of bullets."

"You get right back here—!"

Simon rushed out, slamming the door behind him.

Paul started toward the door, unfastening his apron as he went.

"Dammit, Abbott, let him go—" Britton yelled at him. "Your job is to stay with the casualties!"

"That's exactly why I'm going after him—he's one of the casualties."

iii

Paul ran into a tumultuous dawn. Beneath a dripping sky, heavy with dark clouds, the din of battle had swelled into a tremendous chorus. The racket of rifle fire, the heavy thud of artillery, the frenzied beat of drums and thousands of men shouting were continuous. Black smoke billowed over the treetops. From all sides along the fighting lines hundreds of compact little balls of white smoke kept spurting from rifles to float upward and dissolve in the pall of smoke. The air burned with the sulphurous breath of gunpowder.

Against a background of the blurred and agitated forms of troops crossing a field, he spotted Saul Simon running blindly, this way and that, without any apparent sense of direction.

"Saul, Saul—!" he shouted. "Come back here—"

His voice was lost under the banshee shriek of shells, the passionate whine of bullets.

Simon sprinted on—straight in front of a battery changing position at a frantic gallop, scattering troops right and left. One of the horses began to stagger. Terrified, eyes rolling, the animal was carried along by the connecting harness to other horses, dragging its bowels which a cannonball had torn from its stomach. Simon was not in sight.

Paul detoured the melee of plunging horses and men, saw Simon racing ahead toward the thickest billowings of smoke clouds that marked the foremost line of battle. He rushed on.

The fury and storm of gunfire were louder now. Cannons thundered until it seemed the very heavens would burst. Bullets rained through the trees, nipping off leaves and twigs, thunking into trunks. Most of the branches had already been wrenched off by bursting shells, looking as if Titans had been hurling thunderbolts among them.

He passed a young soldier groveling in the dirt from a gaping, blood-gushing hole ripped through his belly. Crimson froth bubbled from his mouth with his final cries: "Mother . . . Mother. . . ."

Nearby a man screamed and began hopping about in a macabre dance. A jagged piece of iron had torn one arm nearly off. It hung by a slender bit of flesh and muscle, flopping back and forth as the man jumped around, crazed with shock and pain; shouting, "Here, boys, here—" before dropping to the ground insensible.

Paul found himself gasping for fresh air in the thick fog of smoke and gunpowder. His ears were ringing, aching from the concussion of cannon. He was aware that soldiers in a ditch were yelling at him, gesticulating. But now he was gaining on Simon, who was only a dozen paces ahead.

"Simon—it's Paul—come back!"

Simon seemed not to hear. As he plunged ahead, Paul suddenly realized why the soldiers had been shouting at them. Simon was headed into a ravine, and from a murky woods on a hill across from them came spurting flashes of red.

An enfilade!

Making a final effort, Paul leaped ahead and caught Simon by the arm, swung him around. "For God's sake, Saul—we're in a trap! Let's get the hell out before—"

Simon knocked Paul's hand aside. "I don't give a damn! Stay away from me, Paul—"

"I'm taking you back." He knew the man was unhinged.

"Like hell you are!" Wild-eyed, Simon raised the rifle. "Don't step a foot closer."

"Don't be a fool, Saul—"

Simon took careful aim. "I swear I'll shoot!"

Oddly, the expected raking of rifle fire from the woods did not come. Apparently the rebels had become interested onlookers to this unusual confrontation between two blue-clad men and were curious to see how it would end.

Paul took a step forward and heard the empty click as Simon pulled the trigger. Either the rifle wasn't loaded or the powder was wet from the rains. Another quick step and Paul's fist caught the crazed man under the chin. Simon's eyes glazed as he collapsed.

Quickly Paul kneeled and loaded the man over a shoulder. Then, bent low under his load, he began running. A spattering of shots followed.

A burning sensation like a red-hot iron stabbed across his left shoulder. He grabbed at it with his free hand, brought it away wet with blood. He kept running.

But now the ground ahead looked queer, as though it were boiling, wavering up and down. He continued to stagger along under a weight that was growing unbearable. *If I can only stick it out another twenty feet . . . to the ditch. . . .*

Something like the kick of a horse smote his hip. There was no pain, just a tremendous shock producing a paralyzing sensation. His legs turned rubbery and he began falling under the whole ominous weight of the dark sky, which kept growing blacker and blacker. . . .

Book Two

VENDETTA

One

The Fox and the Vixen

i

Under a mizzling April rain, a horseman followed by a black man on foot and two pack mules loaded high with bundles wended through a grove of giant cypresses. Rain dripped steadily from Spanish moss bearding the towering trees; it dripped from the wide-brimmed black felt hat and black cape worn by the rider; formed in sparkling droplets in the woolly black hair of the black man who plodded barefoot through the mud, soaked to the skin in his forlorn garments of Osnaburg cotton.

Emerging from the grove, the rider halted his small caravan. Just ahead, the vista had opened suddenly into wide green lawn surrounding a lofty mansion encircled by a gallery and supporting columns of massive Doric design fully forty feet high. Beyond were the long neat rows of slave quarters, sheds, barns and the huge sugar mill with its towering chimney.

For a few moments the rider gazed in admiration at the

classic lines of the splendid whitewashed manor. With the government stockpiling cotton and appropriating crops at prices below the cost of raising them, planters were hard put to keep going. Raw cotton was bringing but five cents a pound and slave labor was of no value at all, yet Osnaburg cotton had risen to thirty-seven and a half cents a yard—too dear to buy for sacking crops, let alone for slave clothes. Planters felt fortunate when they could hire out their slaves for just the cost of feeding and clothing them. As a consequence, many of the big plantations had fallen into sad disrepair.

But this one—the most magnificent plantation he had ever seen—gave evidence everywhere he looked of the finest care and maintenance. Obviously Les Cyprès wasn't suffering from lack of money.

And all of it belonged to the man he hated more than anyone else in the world: Paul Abbott.

Léon Jacquard swore softly. His dark eyes glinted and his swarthy face grew taut, lips stretching back over glistening white teeth.

It had all started before the war at a *grand bal paré* in New Orleans when Jacquard, smitten by the beautiful and aloof Sylphide Beauvais, had sought to dance with her—to be curtly rebuffed in favor of the Yankee Abbott, who was in attendance as her escort. Later, when he challenged Abbott to a duel, he had been further humiliated by the doctor's refusal to accept his cartel—the worst kind of insult.

Or so he had thought at the time.

A far worse, far more humiliating, far more infuriating insult had come later when Jacquard's mistress—the beauteous Micaela Delacroix, for whom he had paid a most handsome settlement to her quadroon mother to guarantee that Micaela would become exclusively his own property—had left him to flee north with Abbott.

Nothing could have wounded his pride and male conceit more deeply. Jacquard had always been vain about his prowess with women. A wealthy and highly virile man, handsome in a savage sort of way, he was accustomed to having his pick of dozens of beautiful women.

But to be rejected by one with black blood for a nobody Yankee was an affront beyond belief. It was unheard of in Creole circles for a colored mistress to leave her *protecteur*. It dishonored him, made him an object of derision.

It had also fired him with undying hate that nothing but full vengeance could ever satisfy—

A painful death for Abbott; punishment worse than death for Micaela.

He would find ways to degrade and humiliate her, as he had been humiliated; he would make her suffer, suffer, suffer, as he had suffered.

Complicating but not contradicting his intensity of hate for Micaela was another emotion he had never been able to quench. His lust for her still burned in his loins. Many a night he went almost crazy remembering her exquisitely shaped warm body, the tender lips, the submissiveness to his most sensual demands.

He had tried numerous times to kill the druglike craving for her by losing himself in orgies of sexuality with other alluring women, but it only served to heighten his seething desire for Micaela; by comparison the others were tasteless.

There was no way to end his obsessive torment except to get her back, and once again possess her body.

That was the reason for his present mission.

ii

Narcisse Duplessis Troyonne was in her dressing room lovingly running a brush through the radiant abundance of her champagne-blond hair when Aimée, her black personal maid, waddled in to announce that Monsieur Léon Jacquard had just arrived to speak to her on a matter of great importance. Aimée extended his card.

Dropping the hairbrush in her momentary flutter of surprise, Narcisse's memory flashed back to the night of that dreadful going-away party for Etienne. Though she had scarcely spoken a word to the man, she remembered most vividly Jacquard's savage face with the horrible scar along one side of his forehead, the unruly shock of coal-black hair, the gleam of animal-white teeth when his lips drew back in a mocking smile. She remembered the tingle of fright that had raced down her spine at the way he had looked at her, felt the same tingle now.

But of course there was nothing to fear. Monsieur Jacquard, a privateer who had done much for the Southern cause by capturing and plundering enemy ships, was of course a gentleman. He had been brought to the party, an uninvited guest, by a most respectable naval commodore of high repute.

"Tell Monsieur Jacquard I shall be down presently," she told Aimée.

Aimée lingered. "Mebby you wan' me ter call in Jobe?" Jobe was the muscular black slave boss.

"For heaven's sakes, why?"

"M'sieu Jacquard—he a bad man."

"Nonsense, Aimée! You do as I tell you."

Nonetheless as she descended the wide staircase, looking poised and regal in a burgundy silk gown that was flattering to her pale skin and hair, she was seized with a nervous tremor at the first sight of her visitor. The tall, swarthy-faced man looked even more powerful, even fiercer than she remembered.

At her approach, he bent into a sweeping bow. It brought into greater prominence the hideous scar of reddish hue extending along his left temple. Rain dripped from his glistening cape.

"Madame. . . ."

"Monsieur, to what do I owe the surprise of your visit?"

Her careful avoidance of the word "pleasure" was not lost on Jacquard. As he straightened, the lines around his smile tautened and in the depths of his dark eyes were tiny flickers, like raw flame.

"I must apologize, madame. I have been remiss in not calling on you sooner. . . ."

Her eyebrows arched. "Indeed, but I had no expectation of a visit from you."

"Perhaps you are unaware that I am one of your closest neighbors. I live but a few miles from here and am presently engaged in the rebuilding of my home. It is the usual custom for older residents of an area to call upon the newest ones, is it not?"

"It is very kind of you, monsieur," Narcisse murmured. She had not seated herself or invited Jacquard to be seated. "But I was of the understanding that you had a matter of great importance to discuss with me."

"Of importance and of great benefit to both of us, madame . . . but that can wait. First, I have brought with me a few trifles and would be most pleased if you would honor me by accepting them as gifts. . . ."

"Gifts?" Her turquoise eyes chilled. "Why should a gentleman who scarcely knows me offer gifts?"

"I am only too aware, madame, of how ladies of your standing have suffered from deprivation of the little luxuries that you are accustomed to." His bold dark eyes swept over her appreciatively before he added:

"Meaning no offense, but I cannot help noting that the exquisite gown you are wearing is of silk moiré, probably woven in Lyons, and has not been obtainable for the last five or six years. . . ."

Astonished, Narcisse felt warmth come to her cheeks. The dress, one of her oldest, was indeed of Lyons weave. She had purchased it in Paris nearly five years ago while on her Grand Tour with her parents when they still had ample money. What sharp eyes he had! But how could any *man* know of such feminine things? And how crass of him to subtly imply that he knew it was a dress of somewhat outdated style!

She shrugged. "It is but an old rag I sometimes wear around the house when I am not expecting uninvited visitors. I would have discarded it long ago except for the scarcity of materials. And now that New Orleans has fallen to the Yankees, I can no longer go there to shop—"

She stopped, suddenly vexed that she had allowed herself to be drawn into conversation with this brash man instead of evicting him with a proper snub.

"*Hélas,* it is sad. With the accursed Yankees now occupying New Orleans, even I have been forced to discontinue running the blockade. The net of Yankee ships is so tight that only the fish can get through. *Quoi qu'il en soit,* I still have a large selection of exceptional items taken from enemy ships, a sampling of which I have brought along for your pleasure."

"You are presumptuous, monsieur. Even from an intimate friend I would consider it shameful to accept goods that came from acts of piracy."

"Madame, your allusion is most unkind. President Jefferson Davis himself signed my *lettre de marque,* authorizing me to seize enemy ships and cargoes. I have also a citation from Congress praising my skills and expressing gratitude for my achievements on behalf of the Confederacy."

"Admirable as that may be," she said in a slightly less cool tone, "it still does not change my attitude. I have no interest in gifts but only in the matter of importance you said you wished to discuss."

"And presently I shall discuss it, but madame—" Jacquard put on a pained smile. "I have ridden far through a miserable rain to bring you these gifts. Pray accord me the favor of at least examining them before rejecting them. I have brought Chantilly lace, Venetian silks and satins, velvets enriched with gold threads from Genoa."

Narcisse felt a warm stirring of interest. Aside from wealth itself, nothing could excite her more than the fine things that only wealth could purchase. Her thirst for riches and precious luxuries was almost sensual, so interwoven with her erotic emotions that she couldn't tell one from the other. Wealth and all its symbols were for her as potent as a mating call.

"It was very kind of you to trouble yourself to such a great extent to bring the gifts, monsieur, and even though I could not possibly accept them, I concede you have excited my curiosity, so—"

At once Jacquard was striding to the door. He pulled it open.

"*Imbécile, fiente*—" he called harshly to his slave. "Remove the bundles and bring them inside!"

Watching him in profile, seeing the hawklike nose, the unruly mass of coal-black hair, the muscular arms and hips, she had a sudden vision of how she imagined he would look aboard his ship, sword buckled at his side and shouting orders at his bloodthirsty crew. It was truly her mental image of a pirate. Her blood quickened.

iii

The bounteous array of elegant fabrics lay spread over a long table. Narcisse, eyes glowing and now seated in a big Empire chair, sighed.

"Never have I seen more luxurious materials—what exquisite gowns they would make!—but as I have already informed you, Monsieur Jacquard, it would be unthinkable for me to accept such costly gifts."

"Would it not change your thinking," he said slyly, "if you considered the articles not as gifts, but as just payment for a very valuable bit of information I need?"

Her eyes widened. "What kind of information could I possibly have that would be of such great value to you?"

Jacquard, seated in a carved walnut chair nearby, took out his gold-inlaid cigar case and withdrew a cigar, smiling. Thrusting the cigar between his hard lips, he took his time about lighting it. He considered himself an excellent judge of women and was convinced that she was now sufficiently baited with both greed and curiosity. He expelled a blue plume of smoke.

"The information I seek may seem trivial to you, madame, but to me it is as important as life itself. I wish to know the present whereabouts of Dr. Paul Abbott and the octoroon woman, Micaela, who ran off with him."

"Ah yes . . . I have heard rumors that he stole your woman. . . ."

Hot blood rushed to his face. "It is an outrage for which I shall never forgive either of them!"

A flicker of a smile touched her lips. "I can well understand the injury to your pride, monsieur, but as the Latins say, *Alis volat propriis*—she flies with her own wings. Better to forget."

Her wit and knowledge of Latin surprised him. Perhaps he had underestimated her. But his anger was unappeased. "Never will I forget! Cost what it may, I shall track them down and wreak my vengeance—"

A pattering of footsteps drew his eyes to the staircase, where a small boy was descending. Jacquard's black eyebrows contracted in a frown and his features grew tense as he stared at the child.

"So that is Abbott's spawn—I see the likeness, the gray eyes—"

Narcisse turned and spoke sharply. "Carson, get back to your room!"

The boy scampered up the stairs.

Jacquard murmured, "The lad, too, is an important part of the matter under discussion. . . ."

"You continue to talk in riddles, monsieur. I must be honest and say that you impress me as a wolf who talks like a fox."

He laughed. "And you, madame, impress me as a vixen."

"Monsieur! You are insulting!"

"*Au contraire*, I am but returning the compliment. A vixen, after all, is a female fox."

She tossed her head, piqued. "Monsieur Jacquard, I do not think there is any way in which I can help you. Take your gifts, *s'il vous plaît*, and depart."

He smiled and took a leisurely puff from his cigar, expelled a cloud of blue smoke.

"Enough of this silly fencing, madame. I have come for a trifling bit of information, for which you will be paid extravagantly. The gifts? They are *rien du tout*—next to nothing. What I am about to offer you is something much more dear to your heart—"

"How would you know what is dear to my heart?"

"Would not ownership of Les Cyprès be dear to your heart?"

She raised a hand to her throat as if to suppress a gasp. "So you even have the audacity to snoop into private affairs of ownership—!"

"Snooping? Everyone up and down the river knows that this plantation belongs to my sworn enemy, Paul Abbott. I have dug out all the details through my legal contacts. Originally this plantation was owned by Pierre Gayarre. Your husband, Etienne Troyonne, who was Gayarre's cousin, owned the plantation known as Terre Rouge and their mutual cousin, Sylphide Beauvais—who later became Abbott's wife—owned Le Paradis. The three plantations were known as 'the Triangle.'

"When Gayarre died, he willed Les Cyprès equally to Sylphide Beauvais and Etienne Troyonne. But out of the goodness of his heart, your husband gave his half of Les Cyprès to Sylphide upon her marriage in exchange for her unproductive Le Paradis so that she could be complete owner of this fine plantation, while he stayed on living here to manage business affairs for her.

"But then came the shocking, premature death of Sylphide during childbirth—which left her husband as the sole owner of Les Cyprès. Only one conclusion can be reached: Paul Abbott, the only doctor in attendance, wanted her to die. . . ."

He paused to puff gently on the cigar, then: "Be that as it may, by Etienne's misplaced generosity you have been cheated out of your proper wife's share of Les Cyprès. Etienne now only owns Terre Rouge and Le Paradis— both of them boarded up and virtually worthless. If the war should end tomorrow, Paul Abbott could come here with his nigger woman and, with the full weight of the law behind him, kick you out to take possession of his property."

He paused again before adding, "And should your husband have the misfortune to be killed during the war, where would you be? I know from the most impeccable, confidential sources that your husband's financial situation is in bad shape. Before the war he had loaned huge sums to Gayarre, on his cousin's word alone. His other monetary transactions have been ruined by the war. You would have nothing. . . ."

Narcisse, who had bowed her head as if beaten into into abject misery by his words, now looked up at him, eyes blazing. "All you have said may be true, as I have already learned from my attorney, but once we have won the war all will be changed! No Yankee will ever be allowed to set foot through my front door, let alone have ownership of one inch of Southern property!"

Jacquard laughed harshly. "Don't be a fool and console yourself with delusions. The war has already been lost but most Southerners are too stubborn to concede it. Remember what happened at Shiloh? When last I was here, during your going-away party for Etienne, you were all quite merry about our successes in pushing the Yankees back into the Tennessee River. Victory was ours, you thought. Your prayers were being answered."

He laughed again. "But Yankees pray, too, and God is always on the side of the army with the most guns. The next morning Grant was reinforced by Buell's army—two to one against us—and all those well-fed Yankee *canailles* sent our starving troops scurrying like a pack of scared mice."

"But that was just one battle—"

"The beginning of the end, madame. The tide has turned against us. The South is already impoverished, whereas the Yankees are still fat with their vast superiority of factories, money, raw materials, food and reserves of men to fight. We are fast being forced to our knees and would do well to surrender before the entire South is burned to the ground and thousands more lives lost."

"That is traitorous talk, monsieur!"

"But true. It is unfortunate that you and so many like you are so blind."

She drew herself up straighter in the chair, regarding

him scornfully. "I do not care to listen to any more such slanderous talk against our gallant fighting men. About the other matter concerning Dr. Abbott, if you continue to talk in riddles instead of explaining yourself simply, I must ask you to leave."

"A wolf with the brain of a fox does not do things simply," he said with a mocking smile. "Such a brute is accustomed to travel in circles, often backtracking on his own trail to confuse enemies, but to preserve your patience as well as your unusual beauty, which is slightly marred when you frown with such annoyance, I shall endeavor to get quickly to the point—"

"Then do so at once, for my patience is at the breaking point."

Jacquard's swarthy face grew tense and he leaned forward, elbows on his knees, dark eyes burning.

"To recapitulate a bit, I would give my entire fortune, everything I own, just for a chance to find Paul Abbott and the octoroon Micaela. Already I have exhausted every other source of information, to no avail. It is known, however, that your husband is a close friend of Abbott's, and that they have been in close communication with each other by the mails. Etienne of course would refuse to divulge such information, but in view of the fact that Abbott is your enemy as well as mine and that you have so much to gain—"

"You mentioned ownership of Les Cyprès. I fail to see what bearing that has on the information you seek."

His lips twisted back into a caricature of a smile. "If Paul Abbott ceases to exist, his entire estate would go to his heir, the child Carson who is presently living here. You and Etienne Troyonne would then be free to adopt the child as your own."

"But what if Abbott has married the octoroon?"

"She too would cease to exist. The child would be the sole heir. Then if you had adopted the child, and should Etienne have the misfortune not to survive the war, you as the legal mother of the child would have complete control of Les Cyprès."

Her eyes narrowed speculatively. "And you can guarantee disposal of your enemy and the woman for just the information I can supply to enable you to locate them?"

He smiled. "Not quite, madame. . . . There is other compensation I would expect. . . ."

She was hesitant, plainly battling with her conscience. "I have not any great amount of money at hand, but I could raise any sum that is reasonable. . . ."

"For such a beautiful woman it would be an insult to mention money. There are many more interesting and pleasurable forms of compensation ready at hand that would cost you nothing. . . ."

Narcisse flushed. "Monsieur!"

Jacquard laughed softly. "Are you forgetting all the riches I shall be helping you to gain? More than that, I have valuable services that will be at your disposal—such as my armed privateer crew to protect you and warehouses full of rich materials. I am a rich man. Additionally, I have acquired influence with the Federal powers now controlling New Orleans, and when the Yankee hordes begin ravaging all of Louisiana, you can be assured that this plantation will be left untouched. . . ."

Her face had blanched.

"My dear, it can be done so easily and pleasantly. I suggest that you ring for a servant to bring champagne to celebrate what I am now confident will become a lasting and pleasurable friendship between us—" His smile broadened. "After that, of course, you may dismiss all your house servants for the evening. . . ."

Narcisse hesitated but a moment. The chill melted away from her beautiful face as she reached for the bell-pull.

Jacquard took a contented puff from his cigar. His evaluation of her had been close to the mark. Quick and clever she was, with the flexibility to adapt to changing circumstances affecting her welfare—but still not quite clever enough to admit to herself her own greed and dishonesty.

With a bit more cleverness and less conceit, he thought with amusement, she would have seen at once that he was offering far too much for too little. She would have been more suspicious and wary and alerted to his long-range goal.

His aim was complete ownership of Les Cyprès for himself.

Two

Micaela

i

Through the gray of dawn a shandrydan, more commonly known as a buggy, jounced slowly over a rutted country road drawn by a plodding plowhorse. A pale mist still hovered over the ground and the air was sweet with the cool odors of woods and meadows. Soon a warm spring sun would dry away the road dampness and a haze of dust would follow any passing vehicle.

On this one, secured by stout cord to the collapsible top of faded black canvas, were piled several portmanteaus and hatboxes. The driver, a black man of such gigantic size that he seemed to dwarf the light, high-hung carriage, sat hunched forward on his elevated board seat striving to coax the horse into greater speed by an unwearied chirruping and an occasional "touch of the string"—a sharp flipping of the reins against the animal's broad rump—to no visible effect.

The lone passenger inside was a young lady of stunning

beauty wearing a leaf-green dress of taffeta with a billowing skirt sprigged with yellow. She had smooth ivory skin, sparkling dark eyes and dark hair arranged in the current Empress Eugénie *fleur de lis* style—a coiffure of bunched curls on the top and sides with a short tail of curls dangling at the nape of her neck. Setting it off was a pert little bonnet, also of pale green and fluted with yellow. Her slim hands, sheathed in white gloves, were nervously fingering the beaded reticule in her lap containing her money and other items. In every way her appearance was the very essence of a proper young white lady. None would have dreamed that Micaela Delacroix Abbott was one-eighth Negro, skilled as any man in the use of a pistol, and had grown up in a sleazy pirate's den.

Leaning forward, she called up to the driver, "Oh Zam, can't you go a bit faster? I don't want to miss the train."

"T'se tryin,' Miz 'caela, 'cept dis hoss pay no 'tenshun ter what *ah* wants. But don' yo' fret . . . li'l furder ahead ah take dat shortcut by de ribber."

Micaela sat back and tried to relax, without success. The night before she had been in a fever of excitement resulting from the letter from Paul that had arrived in the post yesterday.

For two weeks after the battle of Shiloh she had been in torment, awaiting a letter from Paul. The papers were full of reports of the ten thousand men who had fallen on the battlefield, and Paul had not written.

At last the arrival of a long-delayed letter quelled the worst of her fears, but not all of them. Paul had been wounded and had written from a convalescent hospital near Cairo. Although he assured her that his wounds were not of too serious a nature and that he was fast recovering, she feared that he was withholding the full truth so as not to upset her. A subsequent letter gave more details:

". . . *I cannot say it often enough,*" he had written, "*that I owe my life to one of my colleagues, and now a very dear friend, Saul Simon, who though badly wounded himself managed to drag me to safety through a hail of gunfire. I was unconscious at the time, having been wounded in the shoulder by a minié ball and nicked in the hip by a cannonball.*

"Poor Saul fared less well. Among his various wounds was a torn leg with a crushed tibia bone, resulting in the loss of the limb.

"But enough of that for now. The more cheerful news is that I have healed sufficiently so that I can walk with scarcely a limp and have recovered my energy to the extent that I expect to be granted leave within a week. . . ."

But the brief letter arriving yesterday had been a bitter disappointment. He had written:

". . . My hopes for a visit to you and Rill have been dashed. Tomorrow I am to be transferred to Fort Dixon which, ironically, is only about a day's train ride from home, but I shall not be allowed to leave the camp as I have been assigned to a contingent—the identity of which I do not yet know—which is about to embark on a mission of a secret and urgent nature. Why I have been chosen for such an expedition, I can only speculate. . . ."

Micaela had scarcely read the rest of the note, for at that instant she made her decision.

If Paul couldn't come to her, she would go to him!

After that she had gone into a frenzy of preparations. Paul's letter had been dated only a week ago, and if she hurried there was a good chance she could reach the camp before he left. Rill would be safe and well-cared-for in the hands of Bessie Barnwell and Aurora.

That same evening she had sent Zambullah to the nearby village with a handwritten message to be dispatched over the railroad depot telegraph to inform Paul of her arrival the next day, praying he would still be there to receive it.

"Heah de shortcut, Miz 'caela. I turn 'long de ribber now. . . ."

As the buggy began to lurch over the grassy trail that would soon bring them to the village, a fast racketing on the main road ahead drew Micaela's attention. It was a large shiny black barouche-and-four rapidly approaching. Like the one that had come by the farm cottage the day before.

ii

Bessie Barnwell let the curtain of the front parlor window fall back into place and turned away frowning. She was a buxom, motherly-looking woman with graying hair parted in the middle and combed down in severe batwings. Her homemade dress was of brown glazed muslin, reaching almost to the floor, and around her ample waist was tied an apron of white cambric.

"Why law!" she said indignantly to Aurora, who sat in a rocking chair dandling her baby on her knee. "It's the same big carriage out in front again that was snoopin' around yest'day! If they're land buyers like they say, why're they a-hangin' around here after I told 'em plain my farm ain't fer sale? I swear, I never seen the likes of it."

Moving to the door, she opened it a few inches and frowned at the man outside—a different one than the one who had come yesterday but not a bit more prepossessing. He was respectably enough garbed in a suit of current style, albeit somewhat shabby, as was his none-too-white shirt and soup-stained stock. It was something about his face that repelled her most. Crafty, she thought. His dark little eyes had a way of roving back and forth and darting past her shoulder, as if trying to pry their way inside, and the face had a dissipated look. The pores on his red nose were enlarged and his teeth, now showing in an ingratiating smile, were of an unsavory tinge of yellow.

"If it's my farm you're a-hopin' to buy—"

"No, m'um. Ain't nawthin' like that a-tall. We was told in the village that Missus Paul Abbott is residin' here, an' we brung a message for her."

"Well, she ain't here now. You can give me the message an' I'll see that she gets it."

"Can't do that, m'um. It's a personal message, you understand. I will thankee kindly if you tell me where we can find the lady, so I can go there an' deliver the message direct."

"It won't help you any by knowin', sir, because Mrs. Abbott is on a train on the way to an army camp to visit her husband, an' there's no tellin' when she'll get back."

"An' how about the little tyke? We heard it in town that she's got a young-un. Did she take the baby along with her?"

"A mother can't go traipsin' around the country with a baby in her arms. We're takin' care of the little tot right here."

He smiled his yellowish, snaggle-toothed smile. "And is the big nigger here?"

She drew herself up huffily, her expression showing all the scathing contempt she could muster. "I'll have you know, sir, that there are no niggers around here except for the white nigger standin' in front of me right now! Now, if you'll excuse me—"

"One moment, madam—"

A tall, broad-shouldered man suddenly moved into view, elbowing the other man aside. Bessie goggled. Never had she seen a man so elegantly attired. He wore a plum-colored jacket, white silk waistcoat, fawn trousers and shining Congress boots. Diamonds sparkled on his magenta stock and fingers. Sweeping off his silvery gray beaver, he gave her a courtly bow.

"Mrs. Barnwell—" his voice was suave, cultured— "I beg you to forgive my assistant for arousing your displeasure. He is unaccustomed to duties of this nature and it was purely unintentional. I offer my deepest apology for any offense you may have felt."

Bessie was not impervious to gentlemanly charm. In all her life she could not recall any man ever bowing to her, let alone one of such a distinguished appearance— although she was repelled as well as fascinated by his face. The eyes were dark and piercing, and he wore a drooping mustache above gleaming white teeth; he had a terrible red scar along one temple. Luxuriant black hair fell to his shoulders.

"Well, sir, I accept your apology, but I do hope you will teach your man better manners for when he's talkin' about decent colored folks."

"That I shall certainly do, madam, but for the moment please indulge me for a bit longer in the matter of the message I wish conveyed to Mrs. Abbott. Since it is of such importance and will take a few minutes to properly explain, may I come in so we can talk under more relaxed conditions?"

Mrs. Barnwell hesitated briefly, then, "You may come in, sir."

Scarcely had he stepped inside when there came a gasp of astonishment from Aurora. Turning, Bessie saw that the black girl had risen, clutching her child close. Her brown eyes were wide with fright.

"Marse Jacquard!" she exclaimed.

The tall man looked at her with an amused smile. "So you remember me?"

Aurora started backing away. "Miz Barnwell, dat man bad! He from de South. He whip slaves an' do bad things. Yo' tell 'im to git out—"

Jacquard laughed and again directed his charming smile at Bessie. "It is true that I once lived in the South and owned slaves, but my allegiance has always been to preservation of the Union. After the war broke out, I came North and am now engaged in the service of the Federal Government as a privateer with a letter of marque signed by Secretary of War Stanton."

As he spoke, he withdrew an official-looking document from an inner pocket. Unfolding it carefully, he held it up for Bessie's inspection. She peered at it. Sure enough, at the bottom was the beautifully inscribed signature, *Edwin M. Stanton,* and below it, *U.S. Secretary of War.*

"And now, madam, it is urgent that I locate Mrs. Abbott quickly to deliver my message, so if you will tell me the name of the army camp to which she is headed—"

"Don' do dat, Miz Barnwell!" Aurora burst out. "He'll do bad things to Miz Micaela if he find her!"

Jacquard laughed softly. "Your young nigger friend is spouting lies and nonsense."

Mrs. Barnwell bristled. "Sir! I'll have you know that Aurora is a very truthful young lady and is *not* a nigger!"

"Methinks you are making much ado about nothing," he said with a mocking grin. "Words are just words. What difference whether she's called a nigger, a darky or lady of color? She's still a black wench."

"Sir! You will leave my house this instant!"

His voice hardened. "Madam, we are wasting valuable time. Surely Dr. Abbott has writtten to his woman, and his military address should be on such letters. I request you once again to produce that information."

Bessie's face turned pink with outrage. "Well, I *never!* How dare you—"

"I offer you one last chance, madam," he said harshly.

"And I am *ordering* you one last time to git out!" She was quivering with anger.

He shrugged. "I was hoping this could be handled amicably, madam, but since you refuse to cooperate—"

Stepping to the door he opened it. "Jud," he said to the man outside, "call the men in. . . ."

iii

They came piling through the door, one behind the other. Brawny, rough-clad men who had the look of seamen, Bessie thought in growing fright.

"Wot's the word, Mr. Jacquard, sir?"

"One of you tie up the old biddy. The rest—"

Bessie started screaming.

A heavy hand slapped across her mouth, silencing her. Muscular arms from behind locked her in a viselike grip. Her heart was fluttering crazily in her ears and she was afraid she was going to faint.

"The rest of you," Jacquard continued as if there had been no interruption, "shake down the house and find

111

every scrap of letters or telegraphic messages sent by Abbott. Also tie up the nigger—gag her if she starts squawking—and wrap up the two brats in blankets and get them all out to the coach. Lively now!"

"Aye, aye, sir."

By this time Bessie had recovered her breath but not her wits. "You'll pay dearly for your dastardly deeds!" she shrilled at Jacquard. "I've got your looks fixed good in my head, scar and all, so I can describe you down to the last inch when I report this to the police—"

Her brave words faltered, ceased—stopped by the sudden change in Jacquard's face. Under heavy scowling eyebrows his eyes seemed to turn coal-black except for pinpoint glints of fire in their depths. The terrible scar on his temple turned flaming red and his white teeth gleamed under tautly drawn-back lips in an expression as vicious as that of any snarling animal she had ever seen.

But an instant later the face softened and he spoke in a gentle, almost sorrowful tone:

"Madam, I regret exceedingly your foolish words, which allow me no alternative—" Turning toward one of the men, he made a swift hand signal.

"Aye, aye, sir. . . ."

The man drew a long knife from his belt as he approached.

Again Bessie started screaming. A moment later the screaming ended.

Three

The Kidnapping

i

Zambullah was dejected and angry. About twenty minutes before, he had delivered Micaela to the station, unloaded her luggage, then waited to make sure that she got aboard the train safely. As usual, even that early in the day, a small crowd of villagers had gathered to watch the arrival and departure of the train. It was always the big event of the day.

As usual, too, Zambullah was an object of curiosity. Even back at the farm when out in the fields plowing or hoeing, farmers often stopped in wagons to gawk at him, awed by the physique, the sheer bulk of him. It had quickly passed around the township that the big black man was a sight to behold. One hot afternoon, sweating profusely, he had removed his shirt and as he worked down a row near the road had overheard a lady in a buggy exclaim indignantly, "Well, I never! Showing hisself nakkid like that—shameless as any animal!"

At the station he had heard some of the muttering comments from bystanders as they gaped at him. Said one man, without attempting to lower his voice, "A mean looker, that one. Iffen it was me, I'd never trust 'im in the same house with two white wimmin."

It irked him, filled him with boiling anger at the injustice of it, but he carefully masked any show of his feelings.

Now, as he drove slowly along the narrow country road, he brooded about the strangeness of white people. At first he had hated all white skin with a deadly passion—until discovering goodness in Massadoc Abbott and Miz Micaela. Then after they had helped him escape to the North he had found, to his surprise, that most of the Yankees were kind enough and quick to accept him as a free man—though not as an equal. One of the confusing things about the "free" North was the fact that quite a few Yankees still believed in slavery and had slaves of their own. Then why were they in a war against the slaveholders of the South? Was it not to free the blacks?

And he did not understand why the Yankees did not allow him or any blacks to join them in the war against their common enemy: the Southern slaveholders. Did they think that he—a great warrior and killer of leopards—was too puny? Too cowardly? It was an insult to him, to all blacks! And foolish as well. Were there any whites who had more reason to be fierce fighters against those who wished to keep the black people enslaved?

He was happy enough about having Aurora and their infant son, but how could he be truly happy doing farm work that could be done by old men and women while others were out fighting his enemies?

Just the thought of his enemies started a rage growing in him until his whole body tensed and seethed with the desire to kill.

His enemies, symbolized by all slave masters, were those who had trapped him in the jungle with nets, clubs and maces; had degraded and killed his first woman,

114

Tembah; had tried countless times to beat him into a whimpering, abject state of subjugation.

That they failed was because of help that came from the leopard, his brother—all leopards were his brothers. For Zambullah, known among the Ebos as the mightiest of leopard killers, slew them not out of hate, but only in fair battle as proof of his bravery and skills; proof that there was no greater warrior than he.

The leopard—the largest of all that he had slain—came to him one night in a dream and lay down beside Zambullah to lick his wounds. And the spirit of the leopard entered into his body to teach him cunning. Thereafter there was nothing the white men could do to break his spirit for it was joined as one with the spirit of the leopard.

But now the leopard within, lean and savage from feeding on hate and frustrations, was pacing about ever more restlessly. Impatient with waiting. Turning, twisting, seeking a chance to spring.

And kill.

ii

The warning came when he was within sight of the house.

It came, Zambullah knew not from where or why, in the form of a familiar, prickling sensation crawling up his neck. The same feeling he had sometimes experienced in the jungle foretelling danger he could neither see nor know about.

Moments or minutes later he would see the slinking shadow of a leopard in the bushes, the weaving reared head of the deadly black mamba with its needle-thin darting red tongue poised to strike or one of the other jungle perils.

Now, Zambullah saw a big coach standing in front of the farmhouse. The warning sensation was still prickling up his neckbone.

Lifting the slender buggy whip, he brought it swirling through the air to crack sharply against the broad haunches of the startled plowhorse. Never before had he used the whip except to snap it harmlessly in the air; Zambullah's own back was too ridged with crisscrossed scar tissues—grim mementos of more beatings than he could ever remember—to bring himself to touch a whip to any beast unless in the direst emergency.

His usual gentleness with the horse was in sharp contrast now to the savagery of the cracking whip. The horse bestirred himself into a clumsy gallop.

iii

When the buggy came lurching down the road, Jacquard, carrying Micaela's baby wrapped in a blanket, was just emerging from the house with four of his men. His assistant Jud was already in the barouche keeping a watchful eye on Aurora and her baby.

Seeing Zambullah leaning forward on the buggy's front seat wielding the whip, Jacquard bellowed at his men:

"Stop that big nigger! Dispose of him, but don't use a gun! And be careful—he's a mean one—" Even as he shouted he was hustling toward the coach with the baby.

The buggy creaked to a halt and Zambullah vaulted out, started running toward the barouche.

At once he found his way blocked by four men. One carried a short club which Zambullah recognized as a belaying pin used on sailing vessels to secure ropes; another had raised a fist on which was fastened a strange contraption of knobbed metal over the knuckles that could tear flesh; the other two had drawn knives. Grinning, the four began separating, circling slowly to surround Zambullah.

The barouche was suddenly careering away, its four magnificent black horses plunging their full weight against the harness.

At that moment, in an abrupt movement that few would have thought possible in a man of such huge size, Zambullah spun around and in one leap caught the belaying pin in a powerful grip, wrenched it from the surprised man's grasp. In the next instant the stout little club smashed against its owner's skull, felling him to the ground.

Again he whirled—just in time to dodge a blow from the man with the iron knuckles. The belaying pin swung in another blur of movement. Iron Knuckles howled and stared aghast at his broken wrist for a split second before the huge black shape was upon him. Great hands gripped his head as if it were a mere pumpkin and raised him aloft. His suspended limbs began jerking in the air.

"Lon—" screeched one of the men, his voice keening with hysteria, "git yer knife in the bastid from in front an' I'll stick 'im from behind!"

But now Iron Knuckles' heels were flying through the air as Zambullah swung him around like a horizontal windmill. Crackling, snapping sounds came from the flying man's neck as spinal bones separated. Only stretched skin and muscle tissues still held the head to the body.

After a swing and a half around, the black man released the body, well-aimed. It soared several feet, whumped heavily in collision with Lon, sent him floundering backward to the ground with the wind knocked out of him. His knife went slithering over the grass.

Zambullah pounced for the knife, plunged it into the recumbent man, then twisted up from the ground with the crimsoned blade in hand and lips stretched back over gleaming teeth to face the last man and his knife.

"Look heah, mistuh," squalled the other man with the knife. "Ah ain't got no quarrel with you! Now you jus' cool down an'—"

His gaze swerved, as did Zambullah's, toward the sound of the buggy creaking into movement. In the driver's seat whipping the plowhorse mercilessly was the first man Zambullah had felled. Apparently he had been knocked out only briefly by the belaying pin.

"Hey, Reuben!" bawled Zambullah's last opponent. "Wait up for me—" He began running.

He ran less than a dozen feet before the black shape caught up with him. His last protests gurgled into silence as he slumped to the ground, blood spurting from his throat first vigorously, then more and more weakly as his life ebbed away.

iv

Zambullah stared down at the grisly spectacle of Bessie Barnwell crumpled on the floor in a pool of her own blood. Guttural sounds of rage came choking out of his throat. With them was a screaming alarm in his head. Where were Aurora, their baby, Micaela's baby?

He raced through the house searching, his rage driving him as on wings through every room, peering into every closet, nook and cranny even though the strong sense of emptiness in the house told him it was hopeless.

The closets were in disorder; dresser drawers were open, the contents strewn on the floor. What had they been looking for? Money? Micaela's jewels? It didn't matter.

All that mattered was that his woman and the babies were gone.

Slowly, reason began to calm the turmoil of his emotions, bring order to his thinking. Grasping at the uppermost straw of hope, his intelligence told him that his loved ones were still alive. Had they intended to kill them, the bodies would be in the house along with Mrs. Barnwell's. Perhaps they had been stolen away for ransom. Zambullah knew much about ransom, for in tribal wars during his youth, hostages were often taken and held alive to exchange for cattle, young women or other prisoners held by the enemy.

The enemy, clearly, was Marse Jacquard, whom he had seen running toward the big coach carrying a bundle.

One of the babies? Jacquard was the Southern slaveowner from whom Zambullah had escaped.

From whom Miz Micaela also had escaped.

All at once Zambullah understood. He knew of Marse Jacquard's cruelty toward Miz Micaela when she had been his woman—but he also knew how Marse had prized her, lavished money and finery on her. He well understood the driving forces of a proud man's passion for a woman. He knew of nothing stronger.

As he reasoned it, Marse Jacquard had come North to get his woman back. And not finding her, had taken hostages—

Suddenly intruding into his thoughts came the sound of approaching wagon wheels.

He hastened back into the parlor, drew aside a front curtain to peer out. A farmer with his wife beside him on the seat of an open buckboard had just reined his team of horses to a halt and was gaping at the three bodies sprawled around in the grass. A muffled scream burst from the woman. Terror distorting his face, the farmer seized his whip and began flaying his team with vigor. The buckboard went rumbling away toward the village.

Soon there would be many wagons, many whites, some on horseback with hounds and guns, seeking the killer.

Zambullah looked down at the bloodied knife still gripped in one hand; his gaze shifted away to where the still figure of Bessie Barnwell was lying on the floor in a pool of her blood. The harsh truth smote him.

Never could he prove to the white people that he had not murdered Bessie Barnwell. Never could he prove that the three men lying dead outside were his enemies who had stolen his wife and child and tried to murder him. Zambullah knew from much experience the cruelty of whites and had little faith in white man's justice. Those who had never felt the whip on their back felt no sympathy for those who had. Those who had never fought for their own lives could not understand when one had to kill to survive. He had heard them talk; to most of the whites he was little more than an animal.

A crazed animal to be shot or hanged by the neck.

Even as these thoughts were flashing through his head, he was moving toward the back door, slipped out. He started in a long, easy lope toward the distant woods.

Headed South.

For without having to go through the full thinking process required by most people before reaching a decision, Zambullah's jungle-sharpened brain had already unerringly reached a conclusion. The only possible conclusion.

First, he had to escape at once to avoid being killed.

Second, and most important, he had to find his worst enemy, Jacquard. Kill him. Get his woman and child back.

His instincts and intelligence told him that Jacquard would be taking them back to his plantation in the South.

As he ran, Zambullah cast an experienced eye up at the sun. He had always lived close to nature, had now learned the white man's directions. By daylight he could tell the points of the compass almost to the degree by the sun's shadows; without sun, by subtle signs such as the way the trees had bent through the years to the north wind, where the moss grew most heavily on bark. By night he had the eternal stars to guide him.

He had no choice. He knew nothing of geography and had only a vague idea of the distance, only that it would be many days, or weeks, perhaps months of travel. He knew that wherever he went would be white men, most of them enemies. He knew he would have to travel through battlefields where soldiers from the North and South were fighting to their death. If and when he ever reached the South, every white man would be his enemy.

Without food or money he would have to do this. With only his knife.

But he would do it.

Four

The Fox Calls the Tune

i

Paul was fuming with frustrations. . . .

Micaela, after twenty-six hours of exhausting train travel, had arrived yesterday morning. By frequently badgering the telegraph operator at the station, Paul had been able to get an estimated arrival time of the long-delayed train. Armed with that knowledge he had only a three-hour wait.

Joyous as was their reunion—the first time they had been together in nearly a year—various discomforts and obstacles to happiness were quick to accrue.

First of all was the conveyance by which Micaela was brought to the camp. It was a two-wheeler ambulance, commonly referred to as a "dead cart," which was the best the camp had to offer for the transport of wives and other visitors since the four-wheeler ambulances were preempted by high-ranking officers for their own personal quarters.

The cart was equipped with two kegs of water, beef stock and bandages, two mules and a soldier driver, who made privacy of talk or behavior impossible—hardly feasible in any case because of the violent jarring of bones produced as the springless vehicle jolted over uneven ground.

Adding to the discomfiture were the sleeping accommodations. The camp, being but a temporary base hastily thrown up as a staging area for military units soon to leave for the battlefront, could provide only wall tents for the visiting wives of officers. Ordinarily the commandant would have allowed an officer to share a tent with his wife for a night or two, but it so happened that a visit from General Henry Wager Halleck, general-in-chief of all the nation's armies, was expected on the following day. There was a shortage of tents because of a sudden influx of visiting wives hoping to meet the exalted general, so Micaela was obliged to share a tent with the elderly wife of a senior officer.

Thus Paul had slept alone with his loins aching for his beloved, who slept only a hundred yards away.

And now on the second evening, his frustrations were becoming excruciating. He had just picked her up at her tent to escort her via ambulance to the ball that was being held in honor of the general-in-chief, and the vision of her radiant loveliness was almost too much to bear. For the occasion she wore a close-fitting gown of rich gold satin, elegantly simple down to the in-curve of her slim waist before frothing outward over a series of hoops in its sweep to the floor. The décolletage was low—too low for Paul's puritan sense of propriety, so low as to arouse his passion to the level of pain.

In the back of his thoughts was the vagrant notion that after the ball was over he would dismiss his ambulance driver and take over the driving himself. And since it was a warm, balmy evening . . .

Light from hundreds of flickering candles and whale oil lanterns along the walls cast its lambent glow over the colorful assemblage of dancers. It was a strange contrast of the wild and primitive blended with the courtly splendor of a dress ball. The "ballroom," a rude boxy structure about seventy feet long, had kept scores of enlisted men busy for two days cutting and erecting long posts to support a roof of poles thatched with pine boughs. The walls were of canvas and the floor of rough sawn boards from a nearby sawmill. A pleasant mingling of tangy pine, new-cut wood and French perfumes scented the air.

The men, all staff or line officers, were resplendent in dress uniforms, many with sabers hung smartly from their belts, some even wearing spurs. But the liveliest sense of color and movement came from the ladies as their rainbow-hued, voluminous hooped skirts swirled to the music of a small military band while they laughed or smiled gaily at the officers who held them as closely as the conventional embrace of the dance permitted. Some were visiting sweethearts but most were wives. All were determined to be gay, to block out reality for the evening, drive away all thoughts of war and the grim certainty that many of the men present would die before the war ended.

"*Chéri*—" Micaela smiled up at Paul. "You look so *triste!* Are your wounds hurting? Does it bother you to dance?"

"Hardly at all except for a little stiffness. But I would gladly endure the worst torment just to hold you like this —though it's not as close as I'd like."

"*Ah, mon pauvre chéri!* I too long for the moments to hold you much, *much* closer to show you how starved my love is for you. Your *officier commandant* must be a miserable man without an ounce of the understanding of

123

love in his heart, not to permit a good soldier such as you, who have been wounded, and his loving wife to be private together—"

"Be careful of your words—" Paul cautioned. They were near the entrance and over Micaela's shoulder he saw two high-ranking officers appear in the doorway. "The camp commandant and General Halleck are just entering."

"I say poof to them! If your great *généralissime* does not like my honest words and dares to criticize, I shall snap my fingers in his face and tell him he is no gentleman." She twisted her neck to look.

"Ah, then he must be the tall one with a beak like a hawk, *trés héroique*, and medals of great bravery all over his chest!"

"No, the tall one is only Brigadier General Staughton Frazer, our camp commandant. Halleck is the shorter one."

"Non! He with the bulging eyes like a bullfrog and little pursed lips like a priest? Even with a toothpick in his mouth? How *gros!* Such a man could have no soul! It is no wonder he cares not for those who love."

Her intuition was close to the mark, he thought. Many an army man would have agreed with her appraisal of General Halleck. Paul remembered the sick and wounded at Shiloh, dying from lack of medical supplies after Grant's requisitions had been returned as incorrect by the nit-picking Halleck.

Following the Union victory at Shiloh, Halleck had taken over full field command of the joint armies of Grant, Buell and Pope. His hate and distrust of Grant unabated, Halleck had further humiliated Grant by elbowing him aside, going over Grant's head to select lesser generals to begin the march on Corinth. Whereas Grant had intended to advance rapidly and within a matter of days engage the enemy, Halleck with an overwhelming force three times as large was presently pressing the march on Corinth at a timid few hundred yards a day, entrenching deeply every night. Already weeks had passed. The main lesson of Shiloh, *speed*—in battle never to lose a moment's time but to press on with every available man

124

giving a defeated foe no time to rally—had been utterly lost on Halleck. Meanwhile General Grant and his military genius languished idly on a shelf. It was rumored that he was about to resign his commission and was drinking heavily.

"To show you I care not a fig for what your *officiers* think—" She slid arms around him to pull him close and gave him a lingering kiss on the lips.

Among nearby dancers eyebrows were raised. Morality was shocked. Some of the ladies regarded Micaela with open disgust and hostility; a few of the men grinned. Men could be more tolerant of social indiscretions committed by a young lady of such dazzling beauty of face and figure, especially one dressed so richly in a high style that plainly marked her as a lady of quality.

Indeed, it was this costly look of Micaela's golden gown that was beginning to bother Paul most. He could not afford to buy her such a dress. His modest military pay, as in the case of most soldiers, was several months overdue because of insufficient funds released by a penny-pinching Congress.

The money had come from the goodly sum of gold coins sewn into her garments and a small hoard of valuable jewels Micaela had brought with her when fleeing from the South.

All of it but a part of the riches that had been lavished on her by her former protector, Léon Jacquard.

Often Paul was plagued with doubts. Had it really been love—or just impulsive infatuation—that had prompted her to leave Jacquard and run off to marry him? How could a young woman so accustomed to opulence and excitement find happiness in her present humble circumstances? Perhaps by this time she missed the many luxuries that Jacquard had provided for her and was restless.

Adding to his uncertainty was the feeling that he didn't really know her—that he was dancing with a beautiful stranger who had reappeared from a brief past chapter of his life. It was hard for him to keep in mind that they

125

were actually married, that she had borne his child, the child that he had not yet seen.

"What is it, my darling?" she said with concern. "Your face has suddenly grown even longer, and you are so quiet."

He forced a laugh. "It is only that I am trying to concentrate on my dancing. You float around light as a shadow and I am so clumsy at it."

"*Mais non!* It is not that—you dance no more badly than other Yankees. You are hiding something from me. Is it worry about where the army will send you next? I am your wife and you must tell me what troubles you. I insist."

"I have nothing to tell. I have been told nothing. I have only heard rumors that a secret expedition is being formed and that I may be a part of it. Beyond that I am still in the dark."

Again she stopped dancing and her eyes grew fluid. "War is so terrible, and so stupid!"

He saw that tears had sprung to her eyes, brightened them as if they were dark jewels. Her feelings were always close to the surface but ran deep.

Twining her arms around him, she drew his face down to hers. He felt the wetness of her tears against his cheek. The pressure of her body started his blood rushing, seething through his veins in a kind of urgent arousal that he had almost forgotten. For nearly a year blood and death had all but suspended such erotic urges. Now they awakened with a tumultuous urgency.

"Are you losing your faith in me, *bébé?*" she murmured close to his ear. "Can you not believe that in your absence my love for you is just as strong, even stronger than ever before, and that I am your woman—your woman only—for eternity?"

How accurately she had read his doubts!

Overcome with shame and a new outpouring of feeling, and for the first time in his life without the impediment of self-consciousness or concern for a breach of etiquette, he held her with a jealous, almost frightening greed of possession while kissing her long and lovingly on the lips.

iii

A sharp tap on his shoulder ended the moment of bliss.

"Sorry, Captain. . . . I regret having to interrupt you during your, uh, dance with such a lovely lady. . . ."

The speaker was a young lieutenant with exquisite, almost feminine features. He had silky blond hair that fell in ringlets below his ears, languid blue eyes, a fine straight nose and a wisp of cute mustache above very red Cupid's-bow lips. His complexion was like milk and pink roses. Never had Paul seen a young man so pretty.

"I have been instructed by General Frazer," said the pretty one, "to inform you that you are to report to Colonel Keyes of the cavalry in the command tent immediately."

"As you can see, Lieutenant—"

"Lieutenant Sheldon Verlandigham, sir. I am the colonel's aide-de-camp."

"Lieutenant Verlandigham, isn't this a most inappropriate time to intrude with matters of a military nature?"

"I entirely agree, sir, but after Colonel Keyes has explained the urgency of the situation, I believe you will understand the necessity of your reporting for duty at once."

"For duty? Good grief, man! My wife has traveled far to visit me, and knows no one else here. The colonel can scarcely expect me to abandon her on the dance floor alone and unescorted while I report for duty."

The lieutenant directed a charming smile and brief bow toward Micaela. "If you will allow me, sir—with the concurrence of Mrs. Abbott—I would be delighted to finish out this dance for you while you report to Colonel Keyes. I am confident that he will take all proper steps to assure the safety and care of your wife during your absence."

Colonel Rodney Keyes could have stepped out of a
maiden's dream. Still in his mid-twenties, he was tall,
slim and graceful with a golden beard and dimpled
smile. His father was a rich industrialist with powerful
connections in Washington, which had its due effect in
enabling his son to enter service with an army captaincy
granted by Secretary Stanton himself. Soon after he was
elevated to colonel. Despite the favoritism, Keyes turned
out to be an excellent soldier, quickly adding to his
glamour by leading several daring though relatively minor
cavalry raids in which he distinguished himself for
bravery in action. His present ambition was to plan and
win a brilliant victory that would surely propel him to the
rank of brigadier general.

". . . the particulars of my plan," the colonel was
saying to the small assemblage of officers crowded around
him in the command tent, "are secret, known only to
some of my staff officers. In due time you'll all be
informed, but for the present I will sketch out only
our broad objective.

"As you all know, General Halleck's forces are
presently advancing toward Corinth, which is held by
sizable Confederate forces under Beauregard. Under the
circumstances, General Halleck's presence here this
evening may seem odd to you, but there is a military
reason for it. You are all aware that we are in a state
that abounds in copperheads who report every move we
make to the rebels. Halleck's presence here, therefore,
is intended to lull the Confederates in Corinth with a
degree of complacency. The enemy will be bound to
conclude that Corinth is under no immediate threat
while the general is not with his forces."

The colonel paused to briefly display his dimpled grin.
"Frankly, the general-in-chief was not much in favor

of my plan at first, but after I was able to win the enthusiastic support of Secretary Stanton, with an endorsement from Lincoln, he is giving full cooperation and has ordered Sherman to provide two thousand of his best troopers for our expedition.

"Getting back to our main objective . . . Corinth is greatly dependent on the Memphis and Charleston Railroad and the Western and Atlantic line that ties in with it at Chattanooga for the bulk of their food and ammunition supplies, as well as for reinforcements. The obvious strategy is to cripple this rail network so seriously that Beauregard's forces will be trapped in Corinth—cut off from supplies as well as escape—"

Again he paused, this time looking very solemn.

"The key element of the plan involves you officers who have been selected for an advance contingent of five hundred well-appointed troopers on a deep stab behind Confederate lines below Corinth. Your duties will include the burning of bridges, destruction of rail and telegraph lines and in all ways possible the prevention of Beauregard's forces from escaping when General Halleck attacks Corinth. This phase of the plan is so all-important—and so dangerous—that I have decided to lead the advance group myself. Major Stewart Younger has been assigned to lead the other fifteen hundred, who will leave tomorrow in full visibility to divert Confederate attention in quite another direction.

"Prior to that—this very night while the ball is still in progress—our small group will slip out under cover of darkness. You are all ordered to now return to your tents and make preparations to leave within the hour. Horses and the necessary field equipment have been readied for all of you. Leave all personal articles behind. You are to bring only your field uniforms and sidearms. Are there any questions?"

Paul, who had been listening in growing dismay, spoke up: "Colonel, I have a problem. . . . My wife, whom I had not seen in nearly a year, is presently visiting me—"

"I am aware of that, Captain Abbott." The colonel rippled into another smile. "In fact, all of the officers have been buzzing with talk about what a great beauty you have as your wife, and I was in hopes of meeting her myself—but unfortunately duty comes first. I would have considered assigning another surgeon in your place, but the only other available doctors are either too old or city-bred and could hardly stay in the saddle over the rough country we'll be traveling through. You are young, strong, and your record indicates you grew up on the prairie and are an accomplished horseman. As for Mrs. Abbott, have no worries. The commandant will see that she is properly escorted back to the station and safely put on a train home."

"May I have your permission, sir, to at least return to the ball to explain matters to my wife?"

"You have my permission only to bid her goodbye. You are not to breathe a word about the nature of our mission." Turning away, he spoke to the group as a whole:

"You are all dismissed to return to your tents and change into field uniforms. Make haste, gentlemen. . . ."

V

Micaela was annoyed and worried. How inconsiderate of the army to take her husband away in the middle of a dance! What did it mean?

At least young Lieutenant Verlandigham who had brought the general's orders had been courteous enough about it. A perfect gentleman. And very attractive as well. Some ladies would be all aflutter just to be dancing with him, but for Micaela it was no more exciting than if she were dancing with a brother. She early had learned, with help from a worldly mother, how to sort out the many different types of men. She had known instantly that the lieutenant lacked amorous interest in women. It had nothing to do with his beautiful face or delicate grace.

for there were many of his kind who were plain of face, clumsy and strong as oxen. This strange difference in men was something she could always sense unerringly, but it was nothing she condemned or pitied. Her dearest friend on Balize, Jean-Baptiste, had been like that, although a man in all other ways, a strong and brave fighter with a charming gallantry toward women, even though in lovemaking he preferred boys.

But regardless of whatever type he might be, she was grateful to Lieutenant Verlandigham for easing the embarrassment of having been robbed of her husband's company. She smiled up at him.

"You dance so smoothly, Lieutenant—almost like a Southerner."

His eyebrows arched in surprise. "An acute observation, Mrs. Abbott. The fact is I was born and reared in the South. Then my parents moved North, at which time I got an appointment to West Point. After that, by slow degrees, I became a Yankee."

"But of course in your heart you must still have a great love for the South."

He frowned. "You must remember, Mrs. Abbott, that I am an officer in the Union army. I am as much of a Yankee as you are, who are married to a Union officer—and yet you also come from the South. . . ."

"*Vrai!* But how could you know that?"

His smile was knowing. "Perhaps you, too, dance so much more smoothly than any Yankee."

She began to laugh, stopped suddenly in cold shock.

A tall, powerful-looking man had stridden up behind the lieutenant to tap him on the shoulder.

"M'sieu," came a familiar, deep, suave voice, "if you don't mind, madame is an old friend of mine and I wish to dance with her."

During her momentary discomposure she was only half attentive to the lieutenant's courteous reaction, his little bow and murmured thanks for the pleasure of the dance before withdrawing. She was staring almost unbelieving at the swarthy face and mass of dark hair tumbling to his

131

shoulders, at the great hawk nose, sensuous lips, the burning dark eyes and a terrible purplish red scar—something new she had never seen before—running along one side of his temple like some brand of the devil.

"Jac!" she gasped. "What are you doing here?"

Already Jacquard had lightly swung her into a whirling dance, graceful as a panther. He looked down at her with a thin, mocking smile. "You should be flattered, Micaela. I am here only because of you."

"I don't understand—how could you know I was here?"

He laughed. "I have many ways of getting information and many influential friends in the North to help me. When I visited the drab little cottage you live in a couple of days ago, unfortunately you had just left to visit your husband at this camp. Of course I could have waited for your return, but I am a busy man with much business to conduct in the North. I am also a very impatient man. I had but to telegraph a most important congressman in Washington, a friend, to get his telegraphed order authorizing an army pass for me to travel by troop train. I arrived only a day after you did."

"But why, Jac, why? You know I'm married to Paul—"

"Cela suffit!" His face darkened with sudden rage. "I had the prior right to you, Micaela. You still belong to me, and always will. I intend to take you back to my plantation!"

"You dare to threaten me? All I would need to do is inform General Halleck and the other officers who you really are—a Southern slaveholder and secessionist, an enemy who has infiltrated into the North and come here to molest me, and perhaps for other nefarious purposes. You would be put under immediate arrest."

Jacquard's anger left as quickly as it had come. He laughed heartily.

"You are so naïve, my sweet. Nothing you could say would harm me. How do you think I am able to pass so freely anywhere in the North? Even when I arrived here today in a private coach I rented in town, th camp sentries saluted me when they saw my credentials and did not so much as question me. I have become a personal friend of your Yankee General Butler, who now rules New Orleans with an iron hand. I have done him many favors, for which he is very grateful. I am even making him rich by handling the cotton and sugar he confiscates from planters and delivering it to a secret cartel of Yankee commodity brokers who thank me for their swelling fortunes. Do you think for one moment that such rich, influential men, with the power to force Lincoln to yield to their bidding, would not rush to protect me—and their fortunes—from any aspersions cast against my character and the business dealings that bring them great profits?"

Micaela thought desperately. "Even if all you say is true, you know you can't steal me away from my husband, a Union officer."

Jacquard threw back his head and again laughed, at the same time whirling her into a faster dance tempo. It occurred to her that anyone watching would see them only as a merry couple immensely enjoying themselves—which may have been Jac's intention.

Then his smiling face bent close, but the smile had an evil twist. "My sweet, suppose I revealed the truth about you—that you are a woman who sold her flesh to me? How humiliating would that be to your Paul Abbott, if all of his officer friends were to discover that you are an octoroon, deserving no more respect than a woman who walks the streets?"

In fury she started to whip up a hand to slap him, but cat-swift, he caught it by the wrist. Still smiling, he leaned close to her ear, as if saying tender words, and hissed:

"Hear me out, little fool! I am determined that you shall leave with me. Tonight, this very minute. . . . We will now stop dancing and you are going to walk out of this building with me. We will be smiling and gay as if only going out to gaze at the moon—"

"You must be out of your mind, *dément*, to think I would ever do that!"

Still smiling, he reached into an inner pocket and withdrew a delicate golden chain to which was attached a tiny golden locket. He dangled it close to her face.

"Does this look familiar?"

A terrible sense of dread chilled her. It was the baby locket her mother had given her and which in turn she had placed around Rill's neck as a talisman.

"Where did you get that, Jac!"

"There's no time to waste words. Your child is now in my custody. If you wish to hold her in your arms, come outside with me to my carriage in the manner I have already directed you to do—otherwise you will never see her again."

Numbly, feeling faint, she moved toward the entrance with his strong arm hooked through hers, giving support. Her heart was beating in her ears like great black wings of hopelessness. But Jacquard, acting the part of a gallant, was smiling, laughing in his rich sonorous voice, now and then leaning toward her to chat with gay words that in her numbed state were only a blur of sound.

Outside, through a balmy, starry night she allowed herself to be escorted toward the vague, ominous silhouette of a carriage. He opened a door.

"Into the back seat, my sweet. . . ."

In the deeper darkness inside she could see nothing at first; then a man seated in a rear corner.

"But—but where's my baby?"

"The brat is safely on my ship, anchored on the Potomac."

Her brain sprang to life and she made a sudden move to back away. Jacquard caught her and gave her a powerful shove that sent her tumbling inside.

"Grab her, Jud!"

As rough arms caught her, she cried out, "You lied to me, Jac—you told me my child was out here!"

"Patience, my sweet. I only told you that your only chance of ever seeing her again was to accompany me outside. In due time I'll return your brat—after we set sail for New Orleans."

With a wail of anguish she tried to twist free, but the rough arms held her as in an iron trap.

"Keep holding her, Jud, and I'll drive. If she makes an outcry, gag her and tie her tight as a drum."

Moments later she heard the crack of a whip and the carriage began moving.

vi

Paul hastened back fuming with bitter frustration. After weeks of inactivity while recuperating from his wounds, weeks of boredom and futility, to be finally rewarded by a visit from Micaela—only to have the army snatch him away even before he'd had a chance to be alone with her!

His hatred for war and the heartless monsters called armies was growing with each passing day.

Reaching the ballroom, he saluted his way past the two armed honor guards outside, entered into a blare of light and thumping band music. The floor was quite crowded with dancing couples now. The younger officers, faces shining from the ardor of their exertions, zigzagged sinuously among the older couples, whirling their partners frequently, which allowed them to grasp slender waists more firmly and sometimes even brush daringly against the corseted torsos. Since there was a preponderance of men, many without their women were congregated around a makeshift bar of planks set on barrels.

Paul's glance skimmed the room. Micaela was nowhere to be seen. He began another visual check, spotted Lieutenant Sheldon Verlandigham, who at the same instant saw him. The lieutenant came toward him, smiling.

"Ah, Captain Abbott . . . you're looking for your wife, I presume?"

"Yes, Lieutenant. I left her in your care. Where is she?"

Verlandigham rolled his blue eyeballs in an expression of helplessness. "As a matter of fact we were enjoying a dance together when an old friend of hers suddenly appeared and robbed me of the pleasure. I had no choice but to relinquish her to her friend and they continued to dance."

"A friend? But she's an utter stranger here!"

The lieutenant's smile held a touch of malicious mischief. "Ah, but this one, Captain, was obviously a *very* dear friend of long standing. . . ."

"Explain your implication, Lieutenant!"

The smile vanished. "I'm implying nothing out of order, sir," Verlandigham said hastily. "It is only from the way that they laughed and joked together and apparently much enjoyed each other's company that I inferred that naturally Mrs. Abbott was a very dear friend of Mr. Jacquard's."

"Jacquard!"

"Why yes sir. Certainly you must be acquainted with Léon Jacquard?"

Paul felt suddenly as if kicked in the stomach. How could Jacquard suddenly crop up here? Dancing with Micaela!

It could hardly be a coincidence.

Yet how else explain it? If Micaela had planned to see her old protector, certainly she wouldn't have picked such an unlikely time and place. A tryst with a Confederate enemy at a Yankee officers' ball—

His voice shaking, he spoke again to the lieutenant: "Where are they now?"

"I much fear I cannot answer that, sir. The last I saw of them they were strolling arm in arm out of the ballroom, chatting quite cozily. They went out into the night. I haven't seen them since."

"How long ago was that?"

"About fifteen minutes ago, sir."

Turning, Paul strode out. The whole thing was building into a bad dream. A nightmare!

It was all too confusing. And with it Paul's rage was beginning to rise. She had gone out with Jacquard willingly, according to the lieutenant.

All of Paul's misgivings were flooding back. His

thoughts in a sick swirl in his head, Paul strode out into the dark.

vii

Strong arms held her immobile, but her brain raced. The carriage was rolling along faster now. Soon they would reach the sentry post, and beyond that—all hope of Paul's help sliced off. Forever.

A desperate plan was forming in her frantic brain. To allay suspicions, she allowed herself to relax, felt a similar relaxing of the strong arms that imprisoned her. She cuddled against him in a contented way, as if to sleep.

Jac's voice hooked back from the front seat: "She still struggling, Jud?"

"Naw sir. She's settled down comfy as a kitten." His hand inched out slyly to stroke her breast.

In that instant Micaela turned into a whirlwind of movement, using all the force and agility of her supple young body to twist free of her captor's lax arms and propel herself toward the carriage door.

"Damned bitch—!" Jud's arms snaked after her, clutched at her shoulders.

In another twisting movement she turned and raked clawed fingers across the man's eyes. He yelped hoarsely, brought his hands scrabbling to his face.

A moment later she had the carriage door open, jumped out and began running. The hoop skirt, all the pantalets, impeded her. The heel of one shoe caught against a rock. She fell sprawling.

Jacquard's voice bellowed: "After her, Jud! Catch the slut and get her hog-tied!"

Up and running again; now at a frantic, hobbling gait because one dancing pump was gone.

Through the darkness she could see rows of pale white army tents stretching in endless lines, here and there dottings of campfires like winking red eyes. Wood smoke and wafting odors of cooking food mingled in the piney night air. Her fall had cost precious moments. The pounding steps of Jac and his assistant were close behind, gaining on her.

On impulse she headed for the nearest campfire, around which lounged several soldiers. Their eyes goggled as she raced up.

"Those men—" she gasped, pointing back, "—are attacking me. Please help—"

One of the men, a burly sergeant, put down his tin cup of coffee and jumped up with a hand upraised to stop her pursuers. Another rose, reaching for his rifle.

"Jest a minute, misteh!" barked the sergeant. "Hold it right where yeh is! Wat'r yeh doin' ter this pore girl?"

"Uh, you see, Sergeant, she's my wife and we've just had a little quarrel—"

"A wife, hunh? An' she runnin' from yeh like a scairt rabbit?"

"Dammit, Sergeant! Have you never heard of lovers' quarrels?" Jacquard had produced a sheaf of bills, thrust some of them at the sergeant. "She gets over it quickly but it's a delicate matter. It would be embarrassing if my friend the general—your commandant General Frazer— were to know that my dear wife and I had quarreled, so I request of you as a personal favor—"

Even as she saw the sergeant hastily stuffing the bills in a pocket, Micaela slipped around the tent and started running. She knew human nature only too well—especially when money was involved.

She heard male cursing from behind as she raced on. With her head bent low, darting this way and that among the tents in the darkness, there was no way they could know which way she had gone.

After several minutes she began to slow down, breathing raggedly, sighing with relief.

Relief that changed to dismay a second later when she collided with a bulky, shadowy object that had lurched out of the darkness.

"*Hey* now! Wot th' thunderin' hell yez mean runnin'

spang inta me—?" Brawny arms grabbed her; heavy alcoholic breath wheezed in her face.

"B'gad, if it h'ain't a leddy! Purty 'un too. . . ."

"Let me go—!" She struggled against the brawny arms. "I've got to get to the general at once!"

There was a burst of raucous laughter and she was aware of other blurred figures rising up around her in the darkness. A stray beam of moonlight glistened on a bottle held by one of them. Apparently the men had been seated in the darkest shadows between two tents drinking—probably against camp rules. Several were staggering.

"The gen'ral, she sez? Mmmnnnnn . . . git a smell a thet purfoom. Bet she's one a them fancy doxies thet gits a hull dollar a jump."

"Wal, ef she's good a-nough fer the gen'ral, she's shore good 'nough fer me."

"Release me at once!" Micaela said furiously, straining and kicking against the beefy one holding her.

"Don' yez worry none, purty leddy. We'll pay a hull dollar fer the hull of us."

"I on'y got me a nickel fer my share, but I bin without it so long I figger I kin make it quick as a wink."

One man wobbled toward her with his bottle extended. "This'll loosen yeh up down thar. Take a good long swig—"

She snatched the bottle. With catlike speed she swung it against the skull of the brawny one. His arms slithered away from her as he slumped to the ground like a loose bag of grain, making not a sound.

Holding her voluminous skirt high, she began running.

viii

Rushing through the night. Frantic, disheveled, distraught. . . .

Paul . . . I must reach Paul . . . only Paul can help me. . . .

Limping, lame from a wrenched ankle suffered in the the fall she had taken, she finally reached the rude structure that was the ballroom. A few idling soldiers stared at her in astonishment. The two honor guards standing under the flare of lanterns hung above the entrance raised their rifles nervously, momentarily flabbergasted by the sight of her stumbling out of the night.

She suddenly realized what a sight she must be—hair disarrayed, dress torn, one shoe missing.

At that moment the door opened. Music and light flooded out behind two emerging figures. One was the lumpish figure of the man she had been told was the general-in-chief of all the Union armies, General Halleck. The other was Lieutenant Sheldon Verlandigham.

With the courage of desperation she rushed up. "General Halleck—!"

At the sight of a strange, bedraggled female rushing toward him, Halleck scurried a few steps backward, an arm raised in self-defense.

"I need your help, General," she continued, her words tumbling out faster than she could control them. "I have been attacked by a man who has also kidnapped my daughter. He was trying to steal me away from my husband—"

Halleck, his courage somewhat recovered, stared at her with his large bulging eyes. He had a bulbous brow, a short dimpled chin, heavy cheeks sagging into gray sideburns. Between his pursed lips was a toothpick. He turned to Verlandigham with an annoyed expression.

"Lieutenant, who is this woman?"

"Captain Abbott's wife, sir."

"Who is Captain Abbott?"

"A surgeon, sir. From Grant's medical service."

"Oh. . . ." Halleck shrugged. "That's hardly a recommendation."

Anger added bite to Micaela's voice. "Did you not hear what I said, General?" Remembering then that she was talking to one of the most powerful men in the country, she softened her tone. It was imperative that she try to talk and act like a lady.

"Monsieur Jacquard, who kidnapped my daughter and has just now tried to force me to run off with him, is still in this camp. He is a secessionist and slaveowner, and a dealer in stolen goods from the South. I demand that he be put under arrest at once."

The schoolmasterish face stared at her long and intently. He scratched one elbow in deep thought. He had, Micaela noticed, soup stains down the front of his uniform, which had a most shabby look.

"Lieutenant," he said at length, "is there an ounce of truth to this female's ravings?"

The handsome young lieutenant's face showed consternation. "None that I know of, sir. Mr. Jacquard has the highest credentials from General Butler, Secretary Stanton and members of Congress."

"Hmmph! I confess that I have never been able to understand hysterical females. My time is too valuable to trifle with such matters. I'll leave it to you, Lieutenant, to dispose of this matter as quietly as possible. And keep in mind that the honor of the Federal army must in no way be impugned or slandered by whatever this wild-looking woman has to say." Frowning, he turned a stern face toward Micaela.

"As for you, madam—" the toothpick wobbled between his pursed lips "—it appears that you have been rolling in the dirt. Very unladylike. I should hope that your husband will reprimand you most severely."

Turning, he waddled away with great dignity.

Lieutenant Verlandigham's expression was most commiserating. "Mrs. Abbott, I am truly sorry for your discomfiture, and I wish there was some way I could relieve your distress."

"But my story is *true*, Lieutenant, and my husband can verify it. Please help me locate him."

"I regret to say, Mrs. Abbott, that your husband has been ordered into immediate active service and has already left."

A great cold weight seemed to settle over Micaela. It was as if all walls were closing in around her. All she had left was anger.

"And no effort will be made to apprehend this criminal before he escapes?"

Verlandigham shook his head sadly. "You must realize, Mrs. Abbott, we have no evidence whatsoever that what you say is true. You see, it's all a political matter. When such important men vouch for Jacquard, what can we do? I would be stripped of my commission and doubtless General Halleck would also suffer if we gave credence to your story without solid evidence. I hope you understand."

Micaela bent her head and tried to hold back her hot tears. She understood only too well. It was the same the world over when women raised their voices in protest against men; as meaningless as a breeze down the Mississippi.

"I suggest," the lieutenant said soothingly, "that you return to your tent, Mrs. Abbott, and get a good rest. In the morning you will be escorted to the station and put safely on the train for your return home."

Book Three

THE RAIDERS

One

Boots, Saddles and Sabers

i

As the bugle, stridently off-key, wailed out "Boots and Saddles," Private Jory Jones leaped up from her morning campfire and began buckling on her saber and revolver. In a few moments she was running toward the horse line. The bugler paused briefly for breath and then began to blow "To Horse."

Within minutes she had her horse, Thunder, saddled and was among the milling horses falling into line. The bugle sounded again.

"Right, forward!" bellowed a sergeant. "Fours right!"

The weeks of hard drill, day after day, had paid off for Joreen. With tired skill she guided Thunder to the right as the long line of horses wheeled with precision into segments of four abreast and began walking through the morning mist that had settled over the woods and fields. It had rained during the night and soon the muddy, puddled road was thickly noisome with the clop-splash of the hoofs of fifteen hundred horses in extended formation for nearly a mile.

Joreen shivered and hunched forward a bit, scrunching her neck down as low as she could into the collar of her heavy blue uniform. It was less from the chill than from a habit she had acquired of curling her torso forward to prevent her young breasts from pushing noticeably against the cloth. Fortunately her uniform was a couple of sizes too large and the stiff fabric did not mold to subtle contours.

The biggest worry involved more delicate matters. A prime fear had been the preliminary examination by an army doctor—which turned out to be little more than the taking of her pulse and a perfunctory glance at her tongue. Another concern had been her need for privacy when performing her morning functions following reveille—the signal for soldiers to "arrange their toilet." This was not a very difficult procedure as the men slept in their clothes, rolled up in a blanket on the ground. Quickly she had discovered that most of the troopers didn't bother to hike to the latrine—a long pole propped up horizontally to sit on over a slit trench—but preferred to urinate or hunker down amid the nearest trees. For washing, the best she could do was scrub her hands and face with a cloth dipped in a tin cup of cold water; more thorough bathing she did with a bucket of water and bar of soap at the horse line during the night, screened by her own mount.

As for her ability to successfully act out her masquerade as a male, she had no worries. It had become almost second nature to her, having its roots in the love-hate relationship toward her father and the formless resentment that for most of her young life she had felt toward the male world in general.

Old Isaac McNally had never tried to be tactful about it. Kindness, or even the semblance of it, was alien to his nature. From the day of Joreen's birth he had been unhappy about her being a girl. It had set him off into a temper. "Why couldn't both twins have been boys?" he raged at his hardworking wife, as if somehow it had been

146

all her fault. His wife was already "enough woman" to have around the house to do the cooking, washing, canning, sewing, mending and other female chores. What he wanted most were more sons for the plowing, planting, harvesting and other hard chores that brought in the money. Joreen would be just another mouth to feed.

Joreen had striven with might and main to please her father, to prove that she was equal to a boy in every respect. In due time she became a better shot, a better hunter, a better rider and a harder worker than her brother. She became also something of a daredevil, always the first to ride the wildest colt on the farm, the first to climb to the highest point on buildings or trees where Jody feared to follow, or undertake some other mischief. It greatly worried her mother.

She had grown up lithe and hard-muscled with a fiery determination. Conversely, brother Jody grew up as the weaker one, more given to books and quieter pastimes. Joreen sometimes even protected him from bullies at school—usually guilt-stricken about it afterward because she feared it damaged his self-respect. But she could not help herself because she adored her brother, as he adored her.

Yet nothing she did could ever change her father's opinion of the wide gap between males and females. Even after her mother died of overwork and pleurisy when Joreen was about fourteen and Joreen took over not only the numerous female chores but continued to keep up with the field work, Isaac's only concession to her worth was the grumbling comment, "Why couldn't *you* have been born the boy and *he* a girl!"

The twins had just turned seventeen when the War Between the States broke out, and Isaac at once ordered Jody to enlist. Fighting the accursed Confederates, he was sure, would bring out Jody's manhood.

Whenever she thought about it her heart grew heavy. Jody had never been cut out to be a soldier. He was too dreamy, too soft-hearted; it had always bothered him even to shoot game for food. Why couldn't it have been her instead of Jody who was sent to Shiloh? She wasn't afraid of fighting—and killing too, if she had to. The dirty rebs had killed her father, and maybe Jody. Oh, she'd do her share and more of killing every dirty rotten one of 'em she saw, soon's she got the chance!

The horses were now clopping along through a heavy mist that obscured the landscape, enclosed them like a giant phosphorescent tent. They could see less than a hundred yards in any direction and had no idea where they were or where they were headed. Three days of riding, lame muscles and boredom had reduced the minds of the men to a condition of limp indifference and most of them no longer cared.

Still, it made for one of the limited topics of conversation now and then to break the monotony.

Said Private Mike Yancey, grumpily, at Joreen's left, "I can't figger why they don't tell us nothin'. I ast purty-face Lieutenant Verlandigham where we's headed and he jist said with a kinda smirk, 'Prob'ly straight to hell, soldier.' That ain't right. Us men as does all the fightin' oughter be told fair an' square what we're goin' into."

Another voice, preluded with a gust of sarcastic laughter, put in:

"You jist don't understand the army. I was a regular for five years afore you volunteers come along, an' one thing I learned is they go out of their fuckin' way to pick the dumbes' they kin find to make into off'cers. Now take any enlisted man you can point a finger at who's been through fightin' an' put him in charge an' the war'd be ended overnight. Only the fat-arsed rich don't want it that way 'cause the longer the war lasts, the richer they git."

"Bull m'nure!" hooted another. "If yer so all-fired agin' the army, why were yeh five years in the regulars drawin' pay for jist settin' on yer ass most of the time? Iffen yer warn't smart 'nough ter become a dumb off'cer, t'ain't nobody's fault but yer own."

Still another: "Y'all sound like a flocka wet hens cacklin' in the barnyard fer the kitchen scraps."

148

"All I was sayin'," said Mike Yancey, aggrieved, "is I shore wish t'hell I knew where we're headed."

A scathing retort followed:

"All of you is too dumb even to be off'cers! If yer'd used yer God-given eyes, yer'd all know that up to yestiday mornin' all the farm folks along the way jist smiled and waved an' the wimmin blew kisses at us but by afternoon all we got was dirty looks. It means we're gettin' deeper an' deeper into secesh territory. I wager at this very minute there's rebs all around us jist waitin' fer the fog to lift afore they start shootin'—"

A sharp voice barked out: "No loud talking in the ranks!"

Lieutenant Sheldon Verlandigham came riding up along the column on a fine bay stallion. He continued:

"Men, we're on a special assignment of great importance. I expect you to maintain proper military deportment at all times. Loud talking and laughter will not be tolerated. Anyone failing to heed my orders will be subject to the harshest discipline."

A stony, sullen silence fell over the troopers within earshot.

The lieutenant's horse was keeping pace close to where Joreen was riding. He was eyeing her critically.

"Private Jones!" he snapped. "Sit up straight! Erect. . . . I said *erect!*"

She stiffened into the straightest posture she could manage. Too much, she suddenly realized. How could the lieutenant possibly miss the way her small breasts were now pushing out against her uniform?

"That's better," he said after a few moments. "Much better. . . ." He spurred the bay and rode ahead along the column.

Beside her, Mike Yancey turned to grin and gave her a heavy wink. "I see purty boy still has the eye for ya. . . ."

"Keep your mouth shut, Mike!" she hissed and Mike turned his face away, shrugging.

149

That had been part of her first few weeks among the soldiers—the joshing and ridicule from some of the men, due to her slight figure and obvious youth. On the whole it had been good-natured bantering, except from Mike, whose gibes had been crude and cruel—and sometimes too close to the mark. . . .

"What'n hell's a baby-faced kid like you doin' in a man's outfit?" he had said once, innocently enough. Then adding, " 'Less it's ter play lovey-dovey with our purty lieutenant."

Other soldiers had guffawed. They would endorse anything he said. Mike, once a sergeant, had been broken back to a private and fined six months' pay because of drinking, brawling and "accidentally" tossing an officer overboard from a river troop transport when the officer had tried to intervene in a fight. This had made Mike a hero among the enlisted men.

But Joreen had flushed with the realization of how obvious it must be to the other men—the undue attention that Lieutenant Verlandigham was showering on her. Frequently he rode his fine horse up beside her, ostensibly to criticize but usually ending up with the virtually unheard-of accolade of an approving nod and a pat on the back. "You're smartening up, soldier. Keep up the good work. . . ."

At first that was one of the things that had puzzled her, the approving pats on the back or shoulders. The lieutenant just couldn't seem to keep his hands off her. But soon enough, she was sure she knew why.

The lieutenant had guessed her secret. He knew she was a female.

Yet he hadn't reported her. Why? It seemed plain enough, the way he was always offering her small favors, now and then giving her smiles that he never bestowed on the other men. It was his way of letting her know that he knew her secret, had a warm feeling for her, was protecting her. She was enormously grateful.

Then Mike had taunted, "The lieutenant's got the eye for ya, kid. Afore long he'll be offerin' to share his tent with ya. . . ."

In a spate of fury she had leaped up and shouted, "Close that ugly mouth of your'n or I'll—"

"Or you'll *what?*"

With a metallic swish she hauled out her saber, which always looked hugely oversized for her slight figure. She waved it in the air and said furiously, "Or we'll duel it out here and now!"

Mike first looked astonished; then he guffawed.

"Well, by thunder! If this ain't the damnedes' thing! I never thought the little cuss had thet kinda blood in 'im." He stood there, a hulking muscular man, grinning at her.

"Fight! Fight!" she shrieked at him, dancing around as she flourished the sword.

"Look, kid, everybody here knows how many men I've sliced with my sword. I don't hafta prove nothin'. I could lop off yer ears an' scramble yer guts afore ya got one good whack at me. But why should I? Yer just a raw kid with no experience an' ever'thin' yet ter learn. But ya got the right kind of guts. Now put back that big sword afore ya cut yerself. Wait till ya've been through a couple *real* fights with the secesh—then if ya still wanta make a try at slicin' me, I'll give ya a chance. But fer now, let's jist be friends." With a broad grin he thrust out his hand and reluctantly Joreen put out her slim hand, which was soon overwhelmed by the brawny muscularity of his grip.

After that the gibes ceased, for Mike was her unspoken friend and protector. Besides, she was winning respect because she rode so well and at target practice proved she could shoot better than most of the other men.

That helped her situation but did nothing to relieve the constant dread she lived with—the fear of what might happen if they ever found out she was a female.

The sky grew murkier; the mist thickened, beginning to form into fat drops of rain. A drizzle started, soon turning into a steady rainfall that drenched the riders and their mounts and turned the road to mire. Except for occasional curses, the men rode on in silence broken only by the clopping footfalls of the sad-faced horses muffled by the sound of rain.

Joreen shivered. Despite her poncho, there was no way

to keep the rain from trickling down her neck, dripping from the rim of her cap. It soaked her trousers, ran down into her boots. The rain turned chill, penetrating her to the very marrow. The whole world seemed suspended in a sliding gray sheet of monotony.

In late afternoon the welcome order came that the column was to go into bivouac. Horses and riders swung out of line and became a scene of disorganized, milling activity as the men sought out elevated spots in as sheltered a location as possible. Blanket rolls were tossed down, establishing individual spots for sleeping. Numerous fires were started, over which pots of coffee would soon start bubbling and salt pork frying to fill out the rations of hardtack.

But first the horses had to be cared for. The mounts were always fed first, rubbed down affectionately, slipped extra rations of stolen hay or tidbits of corn whenever possible. After that the exhausted men could look forward to the luxury of eating their own Spartan fare, a pipeful of tobacco, then seeking wet pine boughs and bunches of grass for a mattress on which to spread a poncho before rolling into a blanket, feet to the fire.

Joreen was still rubbing down Thunder when a voice called from behind.

"Private Jones!"

Turning, she saw Lieutenant Verlandigham, still mounted, staring down at her.

"You will report to my tent at once," he ordered, and swung the horse away.

ii

Lieutenant Sheldon Verlandigham was in high feather. But nervously so. . . .

The nervousness was an outgrowth of the visit from the Southern spy Léon Jacquard several days ago, and the act that he, Verlandigham, had committed.

The lieutenant had imparted to Jacquard all the secret details of the cavalry expedition presently headed into secessionist territory.

For Verlandigham, born and raised in the South, still loved his homeland with a fervency that only a true Southerner could understand. His years at West Point had not changed that. After the war broke out, most of the Southerners among his classmates had returned to their home states to accept commissions in the Confederate army. Verlandigham would have done likewise, except for his father, who, to escape financial troubles in the South, had moved to the North to become a highly successful cotton broker. The old man's orders had been blunt:

"You will stay in the North, Sheldon, and take a commission in the Union army at once."

Verlandigham, who feared and hated his father but always knuckled to his demands, protested weakly. "But Father, you know my loyalties are with the South."

"And so are mine. But we are in the fortunate position of being well-situated in the North, where we can be of considerable value to the Confederacy."

"You mean as, uh, spies?"

His father's heavy, authoritarian face grimaced in distaste. "Copperheads, I think, is the term the Yankees use for such as you and me. The fact is, due to my numerous contacts with Yankee industrialists, I have already been approached by an emissary from Jeff Davis in connection with this matter, and I further intend to place you in a sensitive position where for once in your frivolous life you can do something worthwhile."

"And where might that be?" Verlandigham had asked stiffly.

"Through my friend, General McClellan, I shall see that you are commissioned and assigned to headquarter duties under the Army of the Potomac. If you weren't such a worthless little shit with, ah . . . certain tendencies which I deplore deeply, I could probably get you commissioned immediately as a major, or at least a captain, but that might involve responsibilities too far beyond your capabilities. Your only talents seem confined to riding, so you will probably be assigned to a cavalry unit, where your job will be to ingratiate yourself—another of your talents, I must admit—with your superior officers, and of course gather any information of military value."

"But even if I should be able to get such information, how could I get it to the Confederacy?"

"The South is presently creating an intelligence network extending to all parts of the North. Sooner or later you will be contacted by an intelligence agent from the South."

And thus it came to pass. The lieutenant found it quite exhilarating to think of himself as an important part of the spy network. The practice of secrecy and deceit came quite naturally to him. Gave him a thrill, in fact. He felt no guilt, considering it an honorable thing to do all possible for such a noble cause as the Confederacy.

That, at least, is the way he had felt prior to the arrival of Léon Jacquard.

The unexpected visit from that big, savage-looking, magnificent specimen of maleness had thrown him into a dither of excitement after Jacquard had established contact with his credentials.

"However," Jacquard had explained, "my primary reason for coming here is to settle another matter of a personal nature. It was only when checking over my list of contacts in the area that I noted your name as one situated in this camp. I am one who believes in exploiting every opportunity, and trust that we can be of great mutual benefit."

"I shall certainly strive to prove worthy of that trust, sir."

Even during those first words, Jacquard's glance had slashed across the lieutenant's face, up and down his neat uniform, then around the smallish wall tent. One corner of his lips had curled in contemptuous amusement.

"So you're *that* kind. . . ." had been his comment.

Verlandigham flushed. He well knew the innuendo "*that* kind." It was something he had prided himself on hiding so carefully that even at West Point it had never been discovered—officially, that is. True, he had skirted close to disaster when once he had allowed his hand to stray too intimately with a fellow cadet with whom he had struck up a warm friendship. To buy the cadet's silence had cost him a hundred dollars. But how could Jacquard possibly know?

"I beg your pardon, sir!" he had responded with a touch of anger.

Jacquard shrugged. "It means nothing, Lieutenant. Each to our own. . . . Now as to the information you have for me . . ."

It was the first time in his role as a spy that Verlandigham had ever been called upon to produce secret military information, but not until it was a *fait accompli*, irreversible, did the full realization of what he had done, the enormity of his crime, really hit him. All his fond and romantic notions of being but an idealistic, clever Southerner performing a dangerous and admirable mission out of loyalty to his beloved Southland were submerged under the flood of new fears and apprehensions that seized him.

The stark reality was that he was worse than a mere copperhead, worse than a professional spy. A spy could expect, if caught, a quick hanging or execution before a firing squad. Still he could hold his head high, carry his pride unto death.

His case was different. He was a traitor to the uniform he wore, a betrayer of his comrades. The highest kind of treason. Punishment would be far worse than quick death.

Contempt, loathing and a lingering stigma attached to his name.

Thinking these thoughts now as he paced a few feet back and forth within the limiting confines of his tent, a trembling as chill as the rain beating against the canvas roof slithered down his spine.

The new burden of fears made that other burden seem trivial by comparison, that "other burden" being the "tendencies" so abhorred by his father, the affliction that had dwelled in him as long as he could remember. It was a quirk of character—he refused to think of it as an abnormality—that was condemned by most as something shameful, reprehensible. Among the military, especially,

155

if he were ever found out, he would be treated with as much loathing as if they had found a snake in their midst.

It was most unfair. It was a part of his nature impossible to change.

Nor would he have wished to change it even if he could. Denied the relatively easy means of sexual gratification available to most men, it had become the obsession of his life.

Fears, stress and tensions only heightened his hunger for the kind of fulfillment he so ardently and continuously desired.

A heady fulfillment he expected soon to enjoy.

With that lovely lad, private Jory Jones.

He had delayed making a move for several reasons. One was that it was too dangerous in any of the rear, well-organized camps. One slip and he could be stripped of his commission in disgrace. On a field expedition, as they were now, the discipline was much more lax, opportunities easier to create.

Another reason was the need to go slowly. Especially with such a prize.

From the beginning he had detected it in the boy—the incredibly smooth young face without yet a trace of the fuzz of a beginning beard, the graceful ways he moved now and then, other little subtle signs. . . .

Without doubt, Jory was potentially one of his own kind, but too naïve, too unsophisticated to know it, still unaware of his own delicious potential.

Slowly and patiently the lieutenant had worked at opening Jory's eyes. By meaningful looks, occasional touching, words with double meanings—along with constant stress on the necessity of obeying *any* orders given—he had induced an increased receptivity in the boy. He sensed growing responsiveness, warmth, even admiration in Jory. Until now in his innocence, Jory doubtless thought of it as ordinary friendliness. Soon he would begin to realize it was something much deeper. . . .

Soon, very soon, the dear lad would be introduced to such ecstasies as he had never dreamed were possible.

The lieutenant almost swooned at the thought of the delightful possibilities that were almost in his grasp.

iii

Joreen paused uneasily in front of the closed flaps of Lieutenant Verlandigham's wall tent. The cold drizzle fell steadily, pittering against the tent walls, dribbling from her cap and poncho. Droplets trickled down her neck. Hesitantly she called out:

"Lieutenant Verlandigham, sir—?"

The response was instant. "Who is it?"

"Private Jones, sir."

"Come in, Jones."

Bending, she drew a tent flap aside and stepped into the humid warmth of the semi-dark interior. Pale light glowed from a small brass oil stove hanging from a tent pole. Along one low tent wall was a folding cot boasting a field mattress and several blankets. The air was faintly unpleasant with the odors of oil, tobacco smoke and whiskey. The lieutenant was seated on the cot. The collar of his uniform was undone and in one hand was a glass half full of a dark liquid.

"Quite cozy in here, don't you think?" he said. "I regret, of course, that such comforts can't be extended to the entire group of enlisted men, but this is one of the privileges only allowed to officers during active field service. Too many tents would be a hindrance to the swift movements that may be required in an expedition of this kind. You understand that, don't you, Jones?"

"Yes sir."

Slowly, languorously, the lieutenant lifted his glass and took a delicate sip.

"But still, Jones, some of the comforts I enjoy during field service could be available to an enlisted man who has the wit and intelligence to know how to avail himself of them. Do you follow me? Wouldn't you like to be enjoying the snug comfort of this tent during such a rain as this?"

"No sir. I couldn't enjoy being in a tent while the other men are sleeping out in the rain."

Verlandigham gave her a tolerant smile. "You're still a young fool, Jones. With time you'll learn that any smart person takes everything he can get, whenever he can get it in this most unfair world—and to hell with the hindermost."

"Begging your pardon, sir, but isn't there something you wished to see me about?"

The lieutenant took another slow sip from his glass, at the same time watching Joreen steadily through blue eyes that seemed to her uncommonly bright.

"You realize that I am empowered to assign any sort of duties to you that I wish. I could put you to work digging latrines, send you out on guard duty or picket duty, anything at all—I could make your life so difficult and miserable in so many ways that you'd almost wish you were dead. But I haven't done that, have I?"

"No sir, you've been very kind to me."

"The truth is, as a general rule I'm not a very kind person, Jones. But I find you to be a very special individual. Why do you think that is?"

"I-I don't know, sir."

"You *do* like me, don't you, Jones?"

"Why, yes sir," she said almost gratefully.

"Ah! And I like you, too. *Very* much. I'm sure you understand that for cautionary reasons I considered it more circumspect not to show it. I've been bearing down hard on you at times, trying to shape you up into a good soldier. Other times I've ignored you completely. But that's all for the sake of appearances. . . ."

He paused to take another sip from his glass while keeping her under the gaze of his bright-glazed blue eyes. Then he continued:

"But now that we're on field duty, I think the time has come to have you assigned to my personal service, as of now. . . . That implies a willingness on your part, of

158

course. You would like to serve as my orderly, would you not?"

"Yes sir. Whatever your orders are, I'm glad to obey."

"That's an intelligent response. Now come over and stand closer to me so I can get a better look at you. . . ."

She moved forward, oddly disturbed. A delicate trembling seized her. He was so handsome—the smooth rosy cheeks, bright blue eyes, golden hair. . . . He was everything that her innocent young girlish imagination had ever fantasized as the type of man she could fall in love with. Indeed, on some nights he appeared in her dreams, and then she would wake up warm with excitement.

The lieutenant's tongue flicked lightly over his very red lips. His eyes roved over her in a bold way. From her face down the torso to the crotch area, lingering there. She felt heat rise to her face.

"You're dripping wet, Jones. Don't you think you'd be more comfortable if you unbuckled that heavy saber and revolver belt—and then removed your wet uniform?"

"I-I'm more comfortable the way I am, sir."

His eyebrows arched in mock surprise and his lips compressed into a thin, mean smile. He shifted his position on the cot as if preparing to stand. Some of the liquor spilled from his glass. She realized he was a little drunk.

"That wasn't a request, soldier. It was a direct order. I'm sure you must be aware that I have only to call in the guard and have you arrested for disobeying a direct order from your superior officer."

"But that's not a proper order, sir!"

Instead of the anger she expected, he only smiled tolerantly.

"You have so, *so* much to learn, Jones. Naturally the order you refused would go down in the guard book as something quite different—and very proper. And of course the word of an officer against a private would not be questioned. . . ."

He took another sip of his drink, continued: "But I don't want to see you suffer the consequences of your

159

rash insubordination, which can be very severe. In a theater of war, as we happen to be in now, it can even mean the death penalty. In view of your age—perhaps even younger than the eighteen you claim to be—I shall be lenient and give you another chance. Now relax and start taking off those wet clothes. . . ."

Her heart was thudding fast. Her face burned. This wasn't the handsome, princely lieutenant of her dreams, but someone horribly different. There was something about his eyes . . . shining and cold as a lizard's . . . something calculating and even corrupt in his expression, the parting of his lips, the way he kept his eyes roving over her body.

"But I c-can't do that, sir . . . *please.* . . ."

Again the anger didn't come. Instead his expression grew crafty, his grin knowing.

"Jones, let's stop pretending. I know much, much more about you than you realize. I've been watching you for weeks—your movements. . . . They are, should I say, a bit . . . delicate? Not like those of most of my swaggering young bloods. I would even go so far as to say at times you seem almost . . . feminine." His grin became a smirk.

Her heart began thundering in her ears. So he had known her secret all along! He had only been playing a game of waiting, like a cat with a mouse, waiting for the right moment to pounce, to expose her. . . . Her face was hot with embarrassment, her voice pleading:

"Oh please, sir—don't tell on me—!"

Momentarily he looked puzzled, then laughed. "Tell on you? I wouldn't dream of revealing what I know about you. That would only bring about your dishonorable discharge from the army and spoil the little pleasures we can have together. . . ."

Panic seized her. Plainly he intended to use his knowledge of her masquerade as a club over her head to force her to do his bidding . . . what Steen Saxton had done to her . . . as if she were no more than a common whore. And to think that once she had thought she could fall in love with him! It was all so callous, so hideously unromantic, sickening. . . .

"You misjudge me, sir! I-I'm not the kind who could ever do anything like that."

He laughed softly. "So you really are a virgin? I suspected as much. But have no fear. I'll teach you everything you need to know—"

He lurched to his feet, tossed his empty glass aside. His face turned hard. "But I expect cooperation. We're wasting valuable time. For the last time, soldier, I am ordering you—*get your clothes off!*"

As he spoke, one hand had reached down to unbuckle his trousers. The fly parted. She could see the swelling of his stiffening organ.

With the panic of despair beating in her ears despair was also an upsurge of anger. "I can't—I won't—!" she gasped, backing away. "You can't make me—"

With a sudden pounce he grasped her by the arms. "We'll see about that!"

A moment later his arms had encircled her tightly and his burning lips were crushing against hers.

It shocked her into passivity. Unlike the savage, painful biting at her lips when Steen Saxton had raped her, the lieutenant's kiss, though passionate and greedy, was softer, more sensitive. The fiery pressure of his lips sliding over hers, parting slightly, was the first real kiss she had ever known. Against her will she relaxed, began to respond. . . .

"I'll get you hot, lad," he said huskily.

A hand reached down roughly to get her belt unbuckled, tore at the fly of her trousers. Fingers snaked inside and down toward that most private part of her—

Suddenly a hoarse yowl of astonishment, horror, outrage.

"Oh my God! Oh, my *God!*—"

Joreen had broken away, was backing up, at the same time rearranging her trousers and rebuckling her weapons belt. The lieutenant was wiping the back of a hand across his mouth as if scrubbing away taint. Revulsion was ugly on his face.

"You and your pretense of innocence—!" he ranted on. "You lied your way into the army just to get close to our fine young lads—" His voice had taken on a righteous tone of fury. "No doubt to seduce them, corrupt them—"

"But sir—I don't understand. I've done nothing—"

"Nothing! Why you've even tried to seduce me! After I've been so nice to you. I'll fix you—!" He started toward her with clenched fists.

Joreen was flabbergasted. The lieutenant was unhinged! Out of his head! From the look of fury on his darkened face as he advanced, he intended to inflict great bodily harm, perhaps kill her.

She whipped out her saber. "Don't you dare touch me, sir, or I'll—"

"You *dare* to threaten me? To attack an officer—?" He lurched toward his sword, which hung suspended in its scabbard from a tent pole, and unsheathed it. When he faced her again, swaying a bit from tipsiness and his blade gleaming evilly in the pale light, his grin was exultant.

"Now you've given me the perfect excuse to silence you forever. . . . A deranged private attacking me with a sword! Fortunately at West Point I had excellent training in fencing."

He advanced in a rush.

Trapped in a corner of the tent, frenzied with fright, Joreen jabbed out defensively, blindly, with all the force of her hard young muscles. The lieutenant's saber slashed down to knock her blade aside. The clang of steel against steel merged suddenly into a high-pitched scream.

His defense tactic, slowed by alcohol, had been a moment too late, or perhaps he had underestimated the vigor and speed of her thrust. Her blade had only been deflected downward below his belt before it pierced flesh.

She watched in horror as he fell away backward to the grassy floor of the tent, began rolling around with both hands cupped over his crotch, screaming in agony. The first several inches of her saber were crimson.

"Christ almighty," he moaned, "you've *ruined* me—right through the most precious thing I've got—my manhood. . . . I'll kill you for this—I'll have you hanged—!"

Hastily, Joreen sheathed her saber. Her heart was *lunka-lunka-lunking* in her ears, madly, thunderously. She had to run. The lieutenant would surely accuse her of attacking him—also reveal that she was a female.

Where could she go? Where could she hide? Her heart was thundering louder than ever, galloping—

Suddenly she realized that it wasn't her heart.

The thunderous, galloping sounds were coming from somewhere outside. Men were shouting. And above the tumult, another, more piercing level of sound:

"Eee-yi-yay . . . eee-yi-yay—!" The chilling rebel yell.

Thinking only of escape, she rushed out into the drizzle.

Into a scene far more frightful than the one she had just left.

iv

'Fall out! Fall out, everyone!" a voice was bellowing. 'We're under attack!"

It was Major Younger on his fine white horse riding through the camp. Troopers were leaping up from around campfires or tumbling out of their blanket rolls under the trees. From somewhere a bugle began the faltering, soggy first few notes of "To Arms"—suddenly sliced off as the bugler received a bullet in the chest.

Major Younger galloped past again, bellowing orders, raging at the men. "Hurry, hurry—it's an all-out attack!" His words were soon muffled out by a crashing volley of rifle fire from a copse of woods only a few hundred yards away.

One of the captains came riding up without a jacket, without a hat. The major reined in close to him, cursing utterly. Joreen overheard him telling the captain, "We're

163

greatly outnumbered! They couldn't have been so prepared if there wasn't a leak!"

"Some accursed copperhead in our midst, I warrant!"

The major swung his horse away, barking over his shoulder, "Get the men formed in line along the edge of the field. Quick, quick!"

Amid the melee of action and sounds, Joreen raced on toward the horse line. She passed Mike Yancey, hat askew, running awkwardly with his Sharps rifle in one hand while buckling on his saber with the other.

"This sure beats hell," he said sourly. "I was jist gettin' snugged inta my blanket."

At the horse line Thunder, still saddled, was pawing the ground and weaving around nervously amid the rising battle commotion. Swiftly Joreen mounted. A few of the other troopers had managed to saddle their horses, were plunging around, disorganized. Some had drawn their revolvers and were shooting blindly at the spattering of Confederate fire that seemed to be coming at them from all directions.

Major Stewart Younger was galloping past again, shouting, "There's no time to saddle! All dismounted men fall into battle line on foot—*double quick!*"

By this time about half of the troopers had already rushed to the edge of the field and fallen forward in a prone position on the grass to begin firing at the charging rebels. A Confederate colonel mounted on a large bay came boldly dashing past the Union troopers, miraculously unscathed, right into the midst of the campsite.

"Who's in charge here?" he shouted. "I demand your surrender—"

The jacketless captain rode toward him cursing, raising his revolver. The rebel officer approached at a furious gallop, saber aloft. It came slashing down with a sickening thud across the captain's neck just as the revolver fired—but not soon enough. The bullet was deflected harmlessly into the sky. The captain swayed sideways in the saddle, his half-severed neck spouting blood.

Joreen witnessed the gory spectacle as she rode from the

horse line. Shocked into reaction, she took quick aim with her revolver and fired. The colonel slumped in the saddle, began falling. His hat fell off. He was elderly with silvering hair. He kept falling until he was hanging from his horse only by one foot caught in a stirrup. His head went bumping along the ground as the horse plunged away.

Somebody shouted, "There's a hull new column of 'em headed for us from behind. They got us under crossfire—!"

His words were followed by an increased rattling of musketry coming from an opposite direction. Hastily a new battle line started forming to ward off the attack from the rear. By this time, Joreen had unsheathed her Sharps rifle from its scabbard beside her saddle. The revolver was good only at short range. She began looking for targets, but in the growing dusk it was difficult to distinguish blue uniforms from the butternut and gray of the rebels. At random she selected a moving figure in butternut and shot. She saw the man pitch forward. She shot again and again at other targets. The bodies dropped.

Killing was so easy! A kind of exhilaration seized her. It was like killing poisonous snakes. They were all of the same rotten breed who'd killed her father, robbed them, perhaps had killed her brother. She felt the blued steel of her Sharps grow ever hotter until it was scorching to her touch as she kept firing as fast as she could reload, oblivious of the enemy bullets zipping around her like angry hornets.

About a hundred yards away, she noted, the cavalrymen's big three-inch Rodman gun was finally swinging into action. Its crew of eighteen men along with the gun had been loaned to them by the 22nd Ohio Battery. That would soon stop the teeming Confederates, she thought with relief!

A trooper came rushing past. There was terror on his face.

"Our Rodman's got took—!" he shouted wildly. "They kilt our gun crew an' are turnin' it around at us—"

165

Before he had finished, the big gun went off, recoiling with an ear-splitting crash. Its shell tore like a thunderbolt through the thickly packed pass of troopers milling around in the midst of the camp. Joreen watched in horror. Their Rodman was shooting down their own men! The rebels were yelling with jubilance. Another shell slammed through the camp; then another and another. . . .

But already that first solid shot of the Rodman had ended the cavalrymen's desire to fight. They knew they were overwhelmed on all sides, sitting ducks to be slaughtered at ease. Some of the men, realizing what had happened, were already stripping their Sharps carbines and revolvers of their slides and cylinders, throwing them away in the murky twilight to make the guns useless. The spattering of Confederate rifles quickly died away.

Joreen saw why. A Confederate officer was fearlessly riding into the camp toward Major Younger, who had raised a piece of shelter tent upon a pole as a signal of surrender. The advancing rebel line had halted.

"Who is in command of this force?"

"I am," replied Major Younger.

"Then sir," said the rebel officer, "I demand your sword."

Groans rose from the cavalrymen. Overcome with rage and humiliation, many more of them began hurriedly stripping down their guns to make them worthless. Their curses mingled with the moans and shrieks of the wounded, the slurred downpour of rain and the triumphant yells of the rebels as they began invading the camp bent on plunder.

A hot flash of fury and shame overcame Joreen.

Their commander had surrendered—but she would not!

She wheeled Thunder around and spurred him into a furious gallop.

She had fought as well as she could. She had killed and killed and killed. But it was all so useless.

Even if they had won, she would have been arrested and perhaps hanged for attacking the lieutenant. Nothing she could say would have an ounce of credibility against

166

the word of the lieutenant. It was all so unfair and useless.

From behind she could hear new yells and the hoof-beats of horses setting out to catch her.

But she wasn't worried. Thunder was the fleetest horse in her company. Leaning forward in the saddle, she gave him the spurs and raced off into the dismal gloom of evening.

She had not the slightest idea of where she was headed.

Two

Ambush

i

For most of the dark and dreary day under an overcast sky, the cavalcade of five hundred cavalrymen had been riding over narrow, muddy roads winding through hills overgrown with tangles of scrubby brush, vines and stunted trees. Having no command or military obligations other than medical duties, Paul was free to ride anywhere he wished alongside the procession and Colonel Rodney Keyes had invited him to join him at the head of the column.

But Paul had proved to be a poor conversationalist, as had the colonel. After a bit of desultory talk of a polite and perfunctory nature, both men, weary and saddle-sore, had relapsed into their own separate worlds of introspective silence.

For Paul that meant the usual haunting, sensuously goading, enraging memories of Micaela, who dominated his thoughts during most of his waking hours, inflamed his dreams.

And left him heartsick, leaden with despondency.

How could she have betrayed him? He had given her his fullest trust. She had been so loving, ready to give up everything for him. Yet try as he would, he could find no explanation of Micaela's defection with Jacquard except that it was what she wanted. She had danced with Jacquard, gone off with him laughingly, willingly.

Yet his love for her still burned in him unabated—burned with the added sickish pain of frustration and unrequited passion.

Reason told him that for the sake of his very sanity he must do all possible to extinguish all feeling for her, end the searing agony. But he could not. Micaela was eternally in his blood.

ii

Forcing himself out of his morose brooding, Paul scanned the rough countryside and wondered at the lack of any sign of human or animal life. They had passed a number of ramshackle farm buildings, but all appeared to be abandoned. Why? Even the scrubby woods seemed empty of the usual sights and sounds of wildlife. Having grown up on the frontier and having done a considerable amount of hunting and trapping in the wildest sectors of Iowa during a period when Indian raids were not uncommon, Paul had almost unconsciously absorbed a "feel" for things subtly out of balance in woods country, something he could not put a finger on but filling him with unease, a sense of things wrong. He knew they were in secessionist territory, but where were the civilians, the farmers, the livestock? Certainly by this time they should have seen at least one of the natives gaping or glowering at them.

To the colonel he commented, "There seems to be a conspicuous lack of people along our route."

Keyes laughed. "That's to be expected, Doctor. Naturally a body of troopers of this size can't expect to sneak through enemy country without being well heralded in advance by the locals. Most of them are probably hiding out in cellars, or have taken to the woods with all their movable possessions."

"Then certainly the enemy soldiers must know of our presence."

"Of course, but they're stretched too thin to pose any threat other than minor skirmishing action."

"How can you be sure of that?"

"My little plan has been carefully worked out, Doctor. Be assured that no detail has been overlooked. We know for a fact that all available Confederate forces in this sector have been assembling at Corinth under Beauregard in anticipation of an attack by our much larger forces commanded by Halleck. Part of our strategy is the diversionary tactic I have assigned to Major Younger, who has been instructed to proceed flamboyantly enough to mislead the enemy into thinking he may be making a thrust at Chattanooga—a natural enough conclusion since Chattanooga is the virtual linchpin of the Memphis and Charleston Railroad where it connects with the Western and Atlantic. With the bulk of the Confederate forces tied up to defend Corinth, the enemy will be so hard put to scrape up a handful of men to defend Chattanooga that our rather small detachment will be largely unobstructed in the performance of our mission.

"You see, Doctor, our plan is not simply to destroy the railroad network—all that can come later—but to grasp a great opportunity to capture Beauregard's entire army. Our mission is to rush in and totally destroy vital segments of all rail lines and roads below Corinth so that the enemy will be, in effect, bottled up, not only cut off from badly needed supplies and reinforcements—but from escape."

The colonel laughed again, a bit smugly. "Beauregard and his army will be trapped. It will take weeks to repair the sabotage we intend to inflict. Before they can begin to do that, Halleck will move into Corinth with his overwhelming forces and capture the whole kit and caboodle of them. It will so seriously cripple the Confederacy, the war could be over in another few weeks."

"How soon do your sabotage operations begin?"

"Very early tomorrow morning. Hours before dawn."

"You must have an excellent espionage system to have pinpointed all your objectives so clearly."

Colonel Keyes gave him a mysterious smile. "The best in the world! Did you perchance meet Major E. J. Allen, the short, stocky, bearded man who visited our head-quarters recently?"

"I had not that opportunity."

"The name is only a pseudonym. He is in reality Allan Pinkerton, head of the famous detective agency in Chicago. General McClellan has put him in complete charge of our military intelligence, espionage and counterespionage alike. Pinkerton has most thoroughly collaborated in the preparation of plans for this mission, so we can be virtually certain it will run like clockwork. . . ."

Paul, remembering the endless tales of Indian cunning from his boyhood days on the frontier, was not reassured by the colonel's air of confidence.

"Trickery is a two-edged weapon available to both sides," he said mildly, "and I suspect the weaker side grows more skilled at it since they're more constrained to make up in cunning what they lack in strength."

The colonel smiled tolerantly. "Meaning no offense, Doctor, but I suggest you confine your doubts to your bone saws and medical nostrums, and in regard to this mission put your faith in our seasoned military judgment."

Paul shrugged and looked ahead at the narrow valley into which they were now entering. The sides were sheer, rain-slashed cliffs of red clay; everywhere else the terrain was thickly strewn with boulders and overgrown with dense underbrush. An eerie prickling started up his spine.

If it were hostile Indians they were facing, what a perfect setup it would be for an ambush!

Yet highly improbable. Army pickets were continuously riding well in advance of the cavalry column, scouting the terrain for just such dangers. Even so, Indians had often been known to waylay advance scouts, killing them before they had a chance to make an outcry.

He tried to relax. These were all battle-hardened, experienced cavalrymen. His imagination was working overtime.

But still the prickling feeling remained.

iii

They were well into the valley when the first shot came.

In the next moment gunfire exploded from all sides. The startled cavalrymen seized their weapons, glancing around. On both sides, high on the ridges, was a bristling of bayonets and rifles, each one sending up little white puffs of smoke as their gunfire swelled into a heavy fusillade. Shouts and screams erupted. An appalling number of men started falling from saddles.

Almost simultaneously men and horses appeared in a plunging line from ahead, cutting off their advance. A cul-de-sac!

"Retreat—!" bellowed the colonel. "Retreat at full gallop!"

Snorting horses swerved and reared. The advance section of the column became a blurred and turbulent mass of men and horseflesh as they attempted to swing around and escape the trap. Sabers and revolvers were out, but there was no chance to use them. There was no letup in the raking fire from hidden rebels above. Men kept toppling. Wounded horses reeled, buckled to the knees, tumbled forward, throwing their riders. Hundreds of voices were shouting as the survivors of the advance company—less than half—managed to get turned around in the melee and begin their galloping retreat.

Paul, riding near Colonel Keyes, saw that his face registered fury and disbelief.

"Hell and damnation!" he spat out. "They couldn't possibly have prepared such a trap without advance information! There had to be a leak in our headquarters security—!"

Hoofs thundered over the rock-strewn ground. Fire and smoke kept spurting from hidden Confederate rifles. Men were falling on all sides.

From ahead came a swelling surf of sound, a sudden uproar from hundreds of maddened voices raised in a fury of frustration. The reason was soon apparent.

A large body of rebel cavalrymen confronted them at the mouth of the valley, completely blocking their escape.

The colonel's voice bawled out, "Charge, men, *charge* —our only hope is to break through!"

Too disorganized to deploy into proper battle formation for the charge, the Federal troopers nonetheless advanced at a furious gallop, all of them braced for the onslaught of the rebel horsemen. It came in a fury of agitated movement. Rearing, snorting horses, steel clanging against steel, a flare-up of explosive gunfire.

In the frenzy of the assault, Paul, caught amid the plunging horses, could scarcely see what was happening beyond a few feet away. His ears were ringing from the concussion of continuous firing. A trooper riding close to him took a bullet in the chest, the missile hitting him with such impact that it almost lifted him from the saddle. He fell to the ground and his panic-stricken horse dashed away.

Men and horses were falling on all sides. The ground was sprinkled with men in butternut as well as blue. Paul, who carried no sidearms, having sworn never to kill, tried to guide his horse out of the swirling melee but was blocked on all sides. Not far ahead he saw that Colonel Keyes's horse had been shot beneath him, tumbling the colonel to the ground. Unscathed, Keyes leaped up and raced toward a riderless horse, which he quickly caught and mounted. But unfortunately his officer's insignia made him a sudden target for a hail of bullets that once again brought the doomed officer tumbling to the ground, riddled with shot.

At that moment Paul's horse lurched violently. Paul tried to twist from the saddle, but not soon enough. The horse had fallen to its knees, nickering in terror and pain, then rolled over sideways, hoofs flailing. Paul was trapped.

Book Four

THE SEARCHERS

One

Washington

i

Seated in the back of a barouche, Micaela gazed out at
the fine homes lining a tree-shaded street in an affluent
neighborhood of Washington and tried to find comfort
in the thought that soon she would be meeting the one
person who could, if so disposed, give her the help she
needed. . . .

Since that terrible night at Camp Dixon when Jacquard
had unexpectedly appeared, she had been disconsolate.
Already in near shock from the kidnapping of her child,
she had returned home to the horror of an empty cottage
and to gruesome tales of Bessie Barnwell's murder. Neighbors and the police were convinced that Zambullah was
the culprit; that he had absconded with his wife Aurora
and the two children. Searching parties with hounds were
striving in vain to pick up their trail.

Nothing Micaela could say was able to convince them
that Zambullah was innocent, that a man they had never

179

heard of, Léon Jacquard, was the guilty one behind it all. They thought she was addled from grief.

Then had come notification from the War Department that Paul was missing in action. Newspaper stories soon followed telling of the annihilation of the cavalry group to which Paul had been attached. Names of the dead were not yet available. Some of the cavalrymen were believed to have been taken prisoner; some may have escaped; a few severely wounded men had been found by a Federal foraging party and taken to a field hospital, but their identities were unknown.

For Micaela it had been blow after blow.

Emotionally devastated by the loss of both child and husband, she had cried until she was too numbed for more tears. Yet for all her heartbreak, she could not believe that Paul was really dead. *Le bon Dieu* was surely protecting him. If Paul's time to die had come, she would *know*. In her heart of hearts burned the mystic conviction that somewhere Paul was still alive and in need of her help.

Believing that, she at once decided that she *must* find Paul. According to news reports, Paul's cavalry group had been attacked in the vicinity of Corinth and Memphis— both of which towns had since been captured by Federal troops. Her plan was to get to Memphis, and from there begin her search. Naïve as her plan may have seemed to others, to Micaela's ingenuous but determined spirit it was the only logical course open. Once she had found Paul, together they could decide on plans for recovering their daughter, Rill, who by now must be somewhere deep in the Southland, held hostage by Jacquard.

But obstacles blocked her. Steamship offices informed her that all river traffic was now under government control. No civilian passengers other than very important men with special military approval were allowed to travel south of Cairo. One sympathetic clerk added, "If you're so set on gettin' to Memphis, madam, the only chance for a female is to join the Sanitary Commission. They're shipping big batches of nurses down there these days to take care of the wounded."

Further inquiries soon disclosed that to join the Sanitary Commission was not easy. Whereas the large organization had numerous branches in the North, none of the heads of local chapters had the authority, let alone the audacity, to accept women to aid in their noble work without the express permission of their national leader, who insisted on personally examining the qualifications of every applicant.

The name of this autocratic woman was Miss Dorothea Lynde Dix, a lady of wealth with a passion for justice. Her life and fortune had been dedicated to improving the condition of paupers, lunatics and prisoners. She accomplished many reforms, correcting abuses and securing favorable legislation for their relief. When the war broke out she offered her services to the government to organize hospitals and a nursing corps. In 1861 Secretary Cameron vested her with the sole power to appoint women nurses, a power later ratified by Secretary Stanton, who succeeded him. As superintendent of war nurses she became the scourge of slack hospitals and incompetent doctors, who were jealous of her power, fearful of her authority. They called her arbitrary, opinionated, severe and capricious. Nonetheless, she and her hundreds of devoted nurses were said to have saved more lives and done more good for wounded soldiers than the entire U.S. Army Medical Service.

This was the woman whom Micaela was about to see.

ii

The barouche rolled to a stop in front of a stately house. It was of red brick, its powerfully plain facade dramatically accented by brownstone Palladian windows and crowned by a projecting cornice. The rounded, elaborately detailed portico was graced with four Corinthian columns that also supported a second-floor balcony. It gave the impression of a costly but not gaudy home of a woman of culture and good taste.

"Are you sure this is the right place?"

"Oh yes, ma'am. This 'ere's the residence of the famous Miz Dix, an' a finer leddy niver lived."

Paying the driver, Micaela stepped out into the sun-dappled street. It was a Sunday afternoon in June and the warm air was rich with the scent of fresh green leaves and fragrance of blossoms from well-tended flowerbeds. It was hard to believe that only two or three hundred miles away battles were raging, men were killing, suffering and dying amid rivers of blood.

The woman who admitted her was large and mannish in appearance. Her forbidding face was framed with black hair combed down tightly on each side in batwing style. She wore a long dark gown reaching to her heels and on which the only touch of femininity was the little white lace-frilled collar around her heavy neck. She looked at Micaela with disapproval.

Micaela announced her name, adding that Miss Dix was expecting her. She had arrived in Washington yesterday, checking in at the Willard Hotel, from which she had dispatched a note to Miss Dix by messenger requesting an interview. Miss Dix had responded at once, by the same messenger, giving this day and hour as the earliest time she would be free to receive her.

"You will follow me, please," said the large lady.

She passed through rich and somber rooms paneled in cherry with curled maple beams, hung with bronze gas-oliers, adorned with brocaded furniture and works of art. Window drapery embellished with heavily fringed and tasseled lambrequins cut out the sun. On upstairs to an elegant, if lugubrious, reception room completely up-holstered and curtained in black silk satin. Her guide knocked discreetly on a door at the end of the room, and after a few words with the one inside turned to Micaela.

"Miss Dix will see you now."

Entering, Micaela was at once confronted by two bright little China blue eyes appraising her from head to foot. The eyes belonged to a slight and delicate-looking lady of sixty, seated behind a mahogany writing desk piled neatly with sheaves of foolscap, opened correspondence and a miscellany of other papers. She wore a high-necked gown of dark blue silk well suited to set off her gray hair, some of which hung in cute little curls around a comely face. She indicated a plain, stiff-backed wooden chair near the desk.

"Please be seated, Mrs. Abbott."

Micaela felt a sudden, sinking sensation in her stomach as she sat down. The bright blue eyes and prim mouth registered disapproval. Perhaps, Micaela thought in dismay, Miss Dix was discerning enough to detect her Negro blood. Or perhaps she was not garbed conservatively enough for these older ladies. For the occasion she had chosen a summery dress of pale green organdy with a dark green velvet sash at the waist and a thin band of matching material around her neck. But the neckline was low, almost down to the upper slopes of her breasts. And for this decorous background, her hat—which was of dark green with a moderately wide brim tilted forward at a slanting angle and from which rose a saucy cluster of pink-colored feathers—doubtless seemed impudent.

"You are a very beautiful young lady, Mrs. Abbott."

Micaela was a bit flustered. "Why . . . thank you, Miss Dix. You are very kind."

"No personal compliment was intended," the older woman said dryly. "It was only a comment pertaining to your qualifications. Your note to me made no reference to your appearance or age. I had expected a much older woman. How old are you?"

"Twenty-four."

Miss Dix frowned. "And what are your motivations for wishing to serve in the Sanitary Commission?"

"You see, my husband, who is an army surgeon, is missing in action, and—"

"A surgeon! I do hope he is more competent than the average. The majority of them seem to have a mania for sawing off arms and legs, whether necessary or not. They don't know how, or care enough, to cleanse wounds and dress them properly. You have no idea how many hundreds of our poor, heroic soldiers I find in the hospitals in agony or dying from shoddy treatment from our inept, callous army doctors!"

"I assure you my husband is most competent. But as I was about to explain—"

Miss Dix silenced her with a graceful wave of a frail hand. "Further explanation is unnecessary. It is already apparent that your motivations are quite personal—not at all based on the broad, unselfish love for all humanity that I require in my nurses. By the way, what is your religion?"

"I was baptized as a Catholic but cling to no particular creed other than a love for God."

"All of my nurses are Protestants, as are most of our soldiers. It could be unduly disturbing to many of our wounded, thus hindering their recovery, to find they are receiving ministrations from one of another religious persuasion."

Micaela felt her face growing warm. "But Miss Dix— not once have you asked me about my medical and nursing experience! Being married to a doctor, I have absorbed and been taught a great deal—"

"Laudable as that may be, you fail to meet my primary requirements on all counts. These are: my nurses must be Protestant; they must be over thirty years of age—"

"But why so *old?* Cannot a younger woman work harder, longer?"

"Women over thirty are less likely to be shocked by male nudity when such exposure is necessitated by dressing wounds or bathing, nor are they as apt to adopt flirtatious mannerisms."

"I am not shocked by the human body, Miss Dix. I am also a happily married woman and do not flirt!"

"I can make no exception to my rules, regardless of your personal merits. Even if you were fully qualified in other ways, I could not possibly accept your application because you fail to meet my most important requirement, which is that all nurses I appoint must dress plainly, be plain of face and figure and devoid of all personal attractions." She hesitated a moment and then with a sad little shake of her head added:

"I regret that I am compelled to say that you are simply

too beautiful—far, far too beautiful—to serve in the Sanitary Commission."

Micaela stared at her, flabbergasted. Miss Dix herself had a comely face, a soft and musical voice, a graceful figure.

"What is it you have against attractiveness in a woman, Miss Dix? You yourself are very attractive. I dare say when you were my age you must have been considered to be a great beauty. Men must have flocked around you. . . ."

The great lady's eyes momentarily grew dreamy, then hardened.

"Mrs. Abbott, as much admired as female attractiveness may be—mostly by men—it is but a misleading veneer of a woman's true worth. How far more admirable are the golden virtues in a plain woman's heart! Physical attractiveness is too often a tool of the devil's. It incites the blood of men, stirs them with unholy lust. In a hospital full of helpless but virile wounded men, the proximity of a young woman such as you could be devastating to the health of their minds and bodies."

Micaela stood up abruptly, now thoroughly angered. "Obviously I have been wasting your time."

"I regret the inconvenience it has caused you, my dear."

Micaela strode to the door, turned. "May I ask you one last question?"

"Of course."

"Miss Dix, have you ever experienced the glorious thrill of feeling a man's throbbing passion for your naked body?"

The older woman's face flushed a hot pink.

"Young lady, you will please leave—*at once!*"

iii

Scorning a carriage, Micaela walked and walked. Thinking, brooding. . . .

In this great free Yankeeland her child had been kidnapped. An attempt had been made to kidnap her. Bessie Barnwell had been murdered. Zambullah and his wife and child had vanished.

She knew who was behind it all, but neither the police nor the military had believed her.

And now, for biased and unfair reasons the superintendent of nurses—her best hope for gaining passage to Memphis to begin a search for Paul—had rejected her.

Was there nobody in the country who could or would help her?

Several heavily laden army wagons rumbled slowly past. Soldiers were everywhere. On the streets, marching and drilling on lawns; some encamped in stretches of woods. A number of them accosted her with flirtatious invitations; a few of them were lewd.

Ignoring them, she kept walking, feeling safe enough since the streets were also populated with Sunday afternoon strollers. Fine coaches and carriages clattered past. There was a strange holiday atmosphere mingled with a sense of the urgencies of war.

Just ahead of her the sidewalk was blocked by a congregation of about two dozen women, all bonneted and dressed in a varied collection of gowns. They were clustered in front of an iron gate, which was open but blocked by a blue-uniformed man wearing a badge and an odd high-crowned derby with a comical tiny brim. "Your passes, ladies," he was saying, "I must see your passes. . . ."

One of the ladies waved a paper at him. "We don't have passes, officer, but here is a letter from Secretary Stanton inviting us to visit the Executive Mansion. We are all members of the Mothers of Heroes Brigade from Chicago and have been promised an audience with President Lincoln."

The police guard briefly scanned the missive and motioned them in.

On sudden impulse Micaela fell in behind the excited throng of women as they eagerly flocked onward. Past their bobbing heads in the distance she could see the stark severe lines of a two-storied structure topped by a fortress-like balustrade. The squarish portico in the center was crowned by a projecting, triangular cornice in the Federal style, supported by four columns. A few scrubby trees obscured the lower portion of the building but left visible a row of eleven second-story windows. Close to the entry a cow and two sheep were munching at the unkempt grass around the base of a statue of Jefferson.

. So this was the President's residence! Impressive as it might be, Micaela had seen grander-looking houses.

Inside there was more to admire. A guide had appeared to lead the ladies on a tour. They were led through spacious banqueting halls, sumptuous drawing rooms, dazzling saloons embellished with gold, silver, crimson, orange, blue and violet decorations, with marble mantels, Italian black and gold fireplaces, gilt eagle cornices, rich cut glass and gilt chandeliers suspended by Grecian chains. They passed through the East Room, garnished with huge gold-framed mirrors as big as barn doors. On to the Blue Elliptical Saloon, said by the guide to be the choicest room in the Mansion. It appeared to be a grand apartment, rich in French furniture, showy drapery, costly gilded ornaments and in general furnished, according to the guide, after the style of the most brilliant drawing rooms at the Tuileries.

Tagging along, Micaela was bored, but grateful to have her thoughts temporarily removed from her immediate problems. Until finally—

"Ladies . . . *the President of the United States!*"

A polite rippling of handclapping rose from the assemblage of females as a tall man, surrounded by a cluster of important-looking men, appeared in a doorway.

Micaela stared at the tall, ungainly man whose half-staggering gait and strangely introverted look made him appear as one walking in his sleep as he emerged from the doorway. A deeper gloom filled his expression than that of any person she had ever seen. Indeed the homely, melancholy face could not have looked more ghastly or rigid, she thought, if he had been lying in his coffin.

Mechanically, in an absent way, he began taking the hands of the ladies in the forefront until their leader piped up:

"Mr. President, we are all members of the Mothers of Heroes Brigade from Chicago."

"So you are from Chicago?" said Lincoln in a deep, warm voice. A broad smile seemed to awaken him from his sleeplike state. "I hear you've been through a bad and muddy winter, but I'm sure our Washington mud could have beat you all to pieces in that respect. And what is it that you ladies wish to know?"

"All of us have sons in the Federal army, Mr. President, and we have come to hear what you can tell us in the way of encouragement, something to cheer and stimulate us."

The homely face dissolved back into its usual melancholy. "I fear I have no words of encouragement to give. The military situation is far from bright. . . ."

The ladies waited in deep and painful silence for his next words:

"The fact is, the people haven't yet made up their minds we are at *war* with the South. They haven't buckled down to the determination to *fight* this war through. They've got it into their heads that we're going to get out of this fix somehow by strategy—that's the word, *strategy!* General McClellan thinks he can whip the rebels by strategy, and the army has got the same foolish notion. They have no idea that wars are carried on and put through by hard, tough fighting that hurts somebody. And no headway is going to be made while this delusion lasts."

Some of the ladies appeared shocked. "But Mr. President, aren't you overlooking how many thousands of our loyal sons have rushed to arms at the call of the country, how bravely they fought at Forts Henry and Donelson, Shiloh and New Orleans, and how gloriously they triumphed?"

"True enough," Lincoln said soberly, "but many thousands of lives were unnecessarily lost because such a large proportion of our men committed to battle shirked their duty and were not at their battle stations. I return to my original statement. The people *haven't* made up their minds that we are at war. They think there is a royal road to peace, and that General McClellan is to find it. As an example, ladies, when you came to Washington, I'm sure you found the trains and every conveyance crowded with soldiers. You won't find a city on the route, a town or a village, where soldiers on furlough are not plenty as blackberries. There are whole regiments that continuously have two-thirds of their men absent—a great many by desertion and a great many on leave granted by company officers, which is almost as bad. General McClellan is continually calling for more troops, and they are sent to him—but the deserters and furloughed men outnumber the recruits. To fill up the army is like undertaking to shovel fleas. You take up a shovelful—" Suiting his words, the President made a comical gesture of shoveling. ". . . but before you can dump them anywhere they are gone. It is like trying to ride a balky horse. You coax and cheer and spur, and lay on the whip; but you don't get an inch ahead. There you stick."

"Do you mean that our men *desert?*" one lady asked incredulously, for plainly in her glorification of soldiers she could not conceive of any Yankees becoming deserters.

"That is *just* what I mean! Desertion of the army is just now the most serious evil we have to encounter. At last count, General McClellan had the names of about one hundred and eighty thousand men under his command. Of these, seventy thousand were absent on leave granted by company officers, which as I said before is almost as bad as desertion, for the men ought not to ask for furloughs with the enemy drawn up before them, nor ought the officers to grant them. About twenty thousand more were in hospitals, leaving only some ninety thousand. McClellan recently went into a fight with this number, but in two hours after the battle commenced, *thirty thousand had straggled or deserted,* leaving only sixty thousand—or only one-third of the total of men who should have been available for fighting."

One lady held up her hand, and at the President's nod, asked anxiously, "Is not death the penalty for desertion?"

"Certainly it is."

"And does it not lie with the President to enforce this penalty?"

"Yes."

"Do you intend to enforce it, then?"

"Oh no, no!" Lincoln said, shaking his head ruefully. "That would be unmerciful, barbarous. If I should go to shooting men by scores for desertion, I should soon have such a hullabaloo about my ears as I haven't had yet, and I should deserve it. You can't order men shot by dozens or twenties. People won't stand it, and they ought not to stand it. No, we must change the condition of things in some other way. The army must be officered by *fighting* men."

The ladies fidgeted uneasily in the glum silence that followed. One of them spoke up timidly, "I find myself greatly depressed by your words, Mr. President. Do you consider our national affairs hopeless?"

"Oh, not at all!" he said earnestly. "For we have the right on our side. We did not *want* this war, and tried to avoid it. We were forced into it; our cause is a just one. And let us also hope it is the cause of God, and then we may be sure it must ultimately triumph. But between that time and now there is a great amount of agony, suffering and trial for the people that they do not look for, and are not prepared for."

The talk ended a few minutes later, and to the last moment Micaela listened as if hypnotized—not so much by the words or even the deep, soothing voice, but by the inner beauty that shone through that haggard face, so ravaged by care, anxiety and overwork, so permeated with sadness, compassion and understanding.

Certainly *he* would understand.

Finally the ladies were dismissed, all shaking hands with the President one by one. The important-looking men began crowding round the President again, waiting impatiently for the last lady to leave. Micaela stayed in the background.

"Mr. President, we've got to do something soon," said

one of the men. "The idea of Grant getting back in the thick of it is intolerable!"

"Well, whom do you prefer, Senator?" Lincoln said mildly.

"Why, Halleck should stay where he is, of course, but—"

"Senator, are you forgetting the weeks that were wasted while Halleck was edging inch by inch toward Corinth, hoping by his 'strategy' to capture Beauregard's whole army—and by the time he at long last got there, Beauregard had long since slipped away and Halleck was able to 'capture' a town without a single enemy soldier to resist him? Now if Grant had been commanding that campaign, he would have been in Corinth within two days, have taken thousands of prisoners if not the whole army. And you still think that Grant should not be back in command?"

"But Mr. President, a man of his sort, who drinks—such a grave responsibility . . . how can we in good conscience put the lives of thousands of loyal soldiers in the hands of a man who cannot be depended on—who might be drunk at a time of great emergency?"

Some of the other men around Lincoln added their assent, shaking their heads ominously.

A gentle smile touched Lincoln's lips. "So you think General Grant is a drinker, do you? Well, he's also a fighter. We've had many generals—McClellan, Halleck and others—who seem to be geniuses—on paper—but when it comes to fight, where are they? I'll tell you, gentlemen, if you want to further the interests of the country, please find out for me what brand of whiskey General Grant drinks. I would like to buy a case of it to give to all my generals." With that he turned and in his ungainly, awkward way, started back toward his office.

At that moment Micaela rushed up. "Oh, Mr. President—"

The tall man turned tiredly and looked at her just as a guard rushed up and caught her by the arm.

Lincoln motioned the guard away. "The young lady in-

191

tends me no harm. There is no need to restrain her." And to Micaela, "What is it, young lady?"

"Could I—could you spare me a few minutes, Mr. President?"

The smile now lighted up Lincoln's face with a radiance that made him seem years younger.

"As busy as I am, I can always spare a few minutes for a lady—especially one so enchanting as you."

He turned and opened the door. "Please enter my office, young lady, where we can talk with a bit more privacy. . . ."

iv

After Micaela had finished her story, the President scrunched his brow in thought for a few moments.

"So Miss Dix has turned you down, has she? She's a wonderful lady whom I admire greatly, but I concede she has her blind spots, as we all do. However, I have done many favors for her—in fact there is now a request before Congress for additional funding for the Sanitary Commission, which I must either approve or veto. And she is much in debt to me for various favors, so I think it only fair that she return a small one for me."

His smile broadened. "I might even let her know that if I were sick or wounded languishing in a hospital, my recovery would be greatly hastened if my nurse was a young lady with as cheerful and beautiful a visage as you have, my dear."

Micaela flushed.

"And so, my dear girl, if the President has any authority at all in this country, you have your wish. I shall contact Dorothea Dix at once and have whatever arrangements made that are convenient to you both."

As the President stood up, indicating their little talk was over, Micaela's eyes blurred from her deep feeling and on impulse she went forward and with a quick embrace kissed him on the cheek. "Oh thank you, thank you, Mr. President!"

Lincoln's face glowed with a broad smile. "Don't thank *me*, young lady—on the contrary, I thank *you* for having brought to me one of the brightest moments I have had for many days. . . ."

Two

Ladies at War

i

Micaela peered, as best she could, through the streetcar window, which was trickling on the outside from a steady drizzle and fogged on the inside from the hot, humid breathing of the crowded passengers. The view was dull. Chicago's rain-slicked cobblestoned Madison Street on this early Monday morning presented nothing more interesting than a dreary congestion of drays, carriages and coaches of all kinds; the wet board sidewalks thronged with the bobbing parasols of pedestrians trudging to work. Within the car, seemingly indifferent to a nauseous mingling of the odors of cigar smoke, cheap perfumes, garlic and body sweat, the passengers endured the ride in a resigned silence broken only by the clickety-clacking of the iron-rimmed wheels of the horse-drawn streetcar over steel rails.

Micaela's mood was just as dismal. After two weeks as

a volunteer worker at the headquarters of the northwestern division of the Sanitary Commission, she felt no closer to her objective than when she had started. On arrival she had immediately told the Commission head of the Chicago branch, Mrs. Sarah McCogg, of her desire to be included among the first contingent of nurses shipped downriver to Memphis. The rule, Mrs. McCogg had informed her, was that she must put her application in writing and at the proper time the Commission would make their selection of ladies to be sent and the list would be posted.

Thus far, no such list had appeared.

Getting out at the next stop, Micaela arranged the hood of her cape over her dark hair and hastened toward the Commission building.

The main entrance was located beneath the McVickers Theater fronting on Madison Street. It was hardly an auspicious location for a para-official organization that someday would become the great American Red Cross. All day long it was subjected to the multitudinous footsteps of bustling pedestrians just outside the windows, a continual racket of carriages, omnibuses, horse carts and heavily laden wagons rolling past, the coarse shouting of draymen unloading and loading huge boxes. Once inside the din was further increased by the incessant hammering and pounding of big crates being opened, sorted, stamped, repacked and nailed shut again.

Worse than the noise were the smells that to Micaela were a perpetual torment: sauerkraut and codfish, pickle and ale, onions and potatoes, smoked salmon and halibut, whiskey and ginger, salt mackerel, kerosene, tobacco, benzine, marking paint—all their pungent exhalations collected into one villainous assault on the olfactories at one's entry, clinging tenaciously to clothing for hours after departure.

Rooms on the lower level were set aside as the "Receiving Area" into which poured each day endless barrels and firkins, baskets, bundles and multiform packages of all sizes—food, hospital stores and all sorts of contribu

196

tions for soldiers from aid societies in several surrounding states. One floor above were the sewing rooms, where between thirty to forty Singer sewing machines were in constant operation all day.

Having no sewing experience, Micaela had been assigned to one of a row of several tables set up as desks on the first floor to read and answer mail and help attend to a steady stream of callers on every imaginable errand.

Her co-worker at the next table, Lottie Claghorn, was already on duty sorting through mail and packages. She was a large-framed woman of middle age garbed in a long dark gown caught at the neck with a brooch, and above that the usual narrow white frilled collar. Her plain but sweet face, usually placid, this morning registered excitement as she greeted Micaela.

"Reckon you h'ain't yet heard the news. . . ." she said.

Micaela admitted she hadn't.

"Mrs. U. S. Grant herself is visiting us today! If I'd knowed, I would have wore my Sunday dress."

"How nice," Micaela said mechanically, but thinking it was hardly anything to get in a dither about. She began looking through the bundles and mail on her table.

The letters were typical. One came from several patients in a hospital bitterly complaining that the doctors and nurses gobbled up all the delicacies and none was saved for them. Another was from an agonized mother begging piteously that the Commission search out and send tidings of her only son, who had not been heard from since the battle of Shiloh. Several were versions of a common type received from young ladies passionately pleading that they be sent as nurses to any of the sad, cheerless, faraway hospitals where they could raise the spirits of the poor, sick soldiers.

The packages and bundles—usually containing dainty foodstuffs or knitted items of clothing—often included notes clearly conveying the senders' romantic motivations. Young ladies described themselves in detail, requesting that recipients of their gifts write to them and similarly tell all about themselves. One lass appended a P.S. *"If the*

197

recipient of these socks has a wife, will he please exchang
socks with some poor fellow not so fortunate!"

Meanwhile the stream of callers had begun and Micae
was soon busy taking notes on all manner of requests fro
mothers and wives of soldiers seeking information (
wishing messages delivered because many of them couldn
write.

Always surprising to Micaela was the vehemence wit
which these loving mothers urged their sons to kee
fighting.

"You tell my boy he got no call ter worry about us
home at all," one sweet woman told Micaela. "I g
enough work an' the county allowance of three dollars
week, so tell 'im jest ter keep his mind on the fightin' a
never think of deserting. Tell 'im *stand it like a man!"* Th
whole family was praying to the Virgin for him.

Equally important to mothers was that their sons re
main morally pure and innocent while killing rebels. On
asked Micaela to make particular inquiries about he
Fred's habits. Did he drink? Swear? Smoke? She wante
to be sure that Fred was told that his mother would rathe
that he be sent home *dead* than return alive and dissipatec

Another woman, who had grayed hair and the seame
features of premature age from drudgery and worry, ha
brought along a bushel-sized wicker basket full of hickor
nuts and ginger snaps—her boy Willy's "fav'rit treat"—
that she wanted sent to him.

Toward noon, Micaela broke off to go upstairs for
cup of tea. Starting up, she encountered one of her co
workers, Jane Quincey, a tall and angular woman of abou
thirty-five, hurrying down with great excitement on he
beaming face.

"I'm so thrilled!" she told Micaela. "I've been appointe
as one of the nurses to leave on the next boat to Memphis
Mrs. McCogg told me to rush right home and get packed
as we're leaving tomorrow!"

Micaela felt a sinking sensation in her stomach. Wh
hadn't *she* been notified? "How did you find out about it
Jane?"

198

"Well, Mrs. McCogg told me, but a list of all the names is posted on the bulletin board outside her office."

Micaela raced upstairs to the bulletin board.

Her name was not on the list.

ii

Mrs. Sarah McCogg, a portly, prim-mouthed lady wearing tiny oval spectacles with golden wire rims perched on her chubby nose, peered up at Micaela from behind her cluttered desk. An embarrassed frown flawed the calm symmetry of her round face.

"I am quite aware of your desire to be sent out as a nurse, Mrs. Abbott, but I do not recall *promising* you that your wish would materialize. In her communication directing me to accept you into the Chicago Commission office, Miss Dix left it to my discretion as to the type of duties you were to be assigned. Qualifications for nursing responsibilities are very rigorous and all applicants must be approved by our board members. Your name was submitted, but the board felt that in good conscience it could not endorse you for service that, uh . . . entailed any personal contact with our soldiers."

Micaela's temper flared. "But *why*? Is it a sin to be young and attractive to men? Are our soldiers such lusting beasts that even though wounded, and perhaps dying, a young woman such as I would not be safe from them—or they from me? I think it is an insult and a terrible injustice both to me and our soldiers to think so badly of us!"

"I can only say that I am extremely sorry, Mrs. Abbott, but the matter is out of my hands. Perhaps if you wish to appeal to the board—"

"Never, never! I can no longer waste another moment battling with opinionated, biased minds!"

"Nor do I have any more time to waste," said the Commission head, her face pink, "as I have several more applicants to interview this forenoon. . . ."

Micaela rushed out, heartsick.

Her tears began streaming before she had gone a dozen steps, forcing her to bow her head and seek refuge in the nearest corner until she could get her emotions under control. Her shoulders quivered and unwelcome hot tears gushed down her face for several long minutes, it seemed, before she felt ready to continue on her way, dabbing with her handkerchief.

"Oh my goodness, young lady! What's wrong?"

Through blurred vision she saw a rather plainly dressed, squint-eyed but pleasant-faced woman of middle age staring at her. Her slightly crossed eyes were expressive of deep sympathy as she put a hand on Micaela's arm. "Is there anything I can do?"

"Thank you—there's really nothing anybody can do. I've got to help myself. . . ."

She hurried on. The plain-faced woman would doubtless be accepted at once for nursing duty. She was certainly a kind person—and it was unlikely that any wounded hero would lust after her.

iii

Back in her cheap rented room, Micaela studied herself in the mirror. She had done everything possible to look as drab as she could; cheap neck-high dresses, hair drawn down tight on both sides of her face and knotted severely at the nape of her neck. No jewelry but her wedding band. What more could she do?

In a rush of anger and sudden determination she ripped off the ugly dress, and going to the small closet began rummaging through it for her most elegant traveling dress of rich topaz silk.

She had tried it their way, tried to play by the rules and got nowhere.

Now she would do it *her* way, in accordance with her natural instincts.

One way or another, however and whatever she had to do to manage it, she was going to be a passenger tomorrow on that boat to Memphis!

Three

Stowaway

i

Carrying a large box tied with pretty ribbons, Micaela wended her way through the crowd collected around the quay at Cairo. It was a warm, sunny afternoon and the bustle of passengers, noisy vendors of food and trinkets, loading crews and the usual assemblage of idlers with nothing better to do than gape lent a holiday air to the scene. The paddle wheeler *City of Memphis*, lying long and majestic at the dock, was scheduled to sail in ten minutes.

Micaela, having arrived much earlier on the Illinois Central Railroad, had waited as long as she dared before the boat's departure time in hopes that she could slip aboard unnoticed in the last-minute rush. She had found out by this time that the paddle wheeler was primarily a hospital boat that would be carrying mostly military officers, medical supplies, nurses and a handful of high-ranking civilians such as representatives of the Chicago

Chamber of Commerce, members of the Legislature, influential cotton brokers and a few of their wives.

Falling in close behind a group of civilians she started up the gangplank saucily, lugging her big box. It contained the absolute minimum of clothes and toiletry articles, by her standards.

"May I see your pass, miss?" The voice of the boat officer at the head of the gangplank was courteous enough, but the sharp eyes held a glint of suspicion.

She flashed a smile. "But—I didn't think a pass was necessary just to deliver a package."

"I'm sorry, miss, but this boat is under War Department regulations. No visitors are allowed aboard without special military passes."

"Oh dear, I've got this package to deliver—"

"Give me the name of the party and I'll see that it gets delivered."

"But—I simply must deliver this package *personally* —" Her eyes darted around frantically, trying to find some way of getting past this obdurate man. She simply *had* to get on the boat! Her glance momentarily lingered on a slim young army officer who seemed to be eyeing her appreciatively. His intent eyes and tentative smile were of the kind she'd seen countless times, and on instant impulse she blurted, "Oh, there he is—!" And as if carried away by overpowering emotions she rushed past the man blocking her toward the young military officer.

"Oh, darling—" she cried, "I was so afraid I'd miss you—" And throwing herself against him, she gave him passionate kiss on the lips.

Before the astonished, flustered man could speak, she thrust the box at him. "I brought this for you—please hold it so I can catch my breath. Then perhaps we can go where it's more private so I can explain—"

Recovering his aplomb as if accustomed to strange young ladies falling into his arms—which could perhaps be true, for she saw now that he was very handsome and wore the insignia of a full army colonel—the young officer called to the dubious official at the gangplank:

204

"It's all right, mister. I'll be responsible for the lady. . . ."

Then grasping the box with one hand and taking her arm with the other, he guided her away from the immediate danger zone.

ii

Seated at a small table in the crowded ship's saloon, Micaela finished telling her story.

". . . so you see, sir, that is why I have been so bold. I was desperate. I saw no other way of getting aboard, and I simply must get to Memphis!"

He had listened intently, a look alternating between concern and disbelief on his aristocratic features. He was of a tall, slender build with eyes of deepest blue and dark wavy hair, and had a way of occasionally lifting one eyebrow in an arrogant manner belied by a humorous quirk of the lips.

"A deeply moving tale, my girl. Either you have a most fanciful imagination or are captive of one of the rarest of human emotions—a grand passion. Having neither witnessed nor experienced such an emotion, I have no way of evaluating your credibility."

"You doubt my story?"

He smiled. "It is easy enough to see how many a hapless male could become hopelessly enamored of your charms, but not so easy to imagine a heavenly creature like you losing her heart to a mere mortal man—and a sawbones at that."

"Sir, you insult my husband by demeaning his profession!" she flared. "And you insult me by implying that I am not capable of deep feelings!"

He inclined his head in a mock little bow of apology. "I withdraw my words. Such a fiery temperament could certainly rise to great emotional heights, and I have every

205

respect for conscientious doctors of the kind I assume your husband to be. I can only say that he must be a very determined and heroic type indeed to have won you away from what, I am sure, must have been a virtual horde of other admirers."

"It is I who was the determined one who sought to win him."

His laughter was interrupted by the deep-throated blooting of the boat whistle. He grinned at her.

"The gangplank has been lifted and the boat will presently be moving. You are now an official stowaway. Do you know what that means?"

"I suppose I shall soon be arrested."

"That's the least of it. There's nothing a boat captain hates more than stowaways. They upset a nautical man's sense of order and tidiness, all his precise calculations of space, weight, displacement, food supplies and so forth. On the high seas a stowaway is lucky to be put in irons. Usually they're tossed overboard to the sharks. On the Mississippi, a stowaway is more likely to be put overboard in a small boat to drift where the current may decide. The shorelines are mostly swampy as well as teeming with crawling and deadly reptiles, and the few villages along the river—if you were so unlucky as to reach one—are generally populated with ignorant, brutish sorts of men who would rape you in two shakes of a nannygoat's tail, and—"

"But I have sufficient money. I am hoping that a small room can be found for me, for which I am willing to pay liberally."

"A room?" He laughed. "Do you realize this boat is so crowded that most rooms are filled with double or triple their usual number? Fortunately, in my case, my rank as a colonel entitles me to a room of my own—small and not overly fancy, of course—but I am always willing to help a damsel in distress. . . ." He looked at her with a speculative grin.

She returned his look with a suspicious frown. "You would sell me your room perhaps?"

"Now you insult *me* with the implication that I would take advantage of your pitiful situation to turn a profit! No, no, I had no such dastardly thought in my mind. Instead, out of the generosity of my heart I am offering to *share* my room with you, free of charge."

She looked at him scornfully. "Share a room with you, sir? Please don't misjudge me. As I told you, I am a married woman—"

"Well now, I don't hold that against a lady as beautiful as you are. It makes the situation even more intriguing. A married woman, naturally, is not accustomed to sleeping alone, so—"

"Sir! If such is your intention, I shall go directly to the captain and declare myself a stowaway!" She stood up.

"Please sit down, young lady, and don't do anything rash. Certainly you don't want to be set adrift in wild country. Perhaps we can work out some sort of arrangement. . . ."

"I will have no part of any 'arrangement'!"

"But you haven't yet heard my proposal, which is that I will promise to respect your wishes in every way and do nothing to bother you. You may have my bunk and I will make do with blankets on the floor. Whenever you require complete privacy, I shall leave the room."

"And why would you do all that for me?"

"Out of the goodness of my heart."

"Then I accept. But be warned, I am not as completely innocent and defenseless as I may appear. If any facets of your nature other than 'goodness' obtrude, I am fully capable of handling myself."

"You grow more fascinating by the minute," he said with a smile. "And now that you have agreed to share my room—if not certain less than good facets of my nature—let me introduce myself. My name is Pace Schuyler, of the New York Schuylers, and I have a notorious reputation as a worthless scoundrel and wastrel. I have no talents of a useful nature, particularly as a military man, since I abhor killing. I was given a colonelcy only because of my father's high connections in Washington and as yet have no idea as to what good or bad use I shall be assigned. And what, may I ask, is your name and background?"

She gave her name, at first intending to invent a simple background as a small-town housewife, then decided to tell the truth. Why not? What did she have to lose?

"I too abhor violence and killing, but I early became accustomed to it because I was raised on a tiny island of mud off the Louisiana coast called Balize—a refuge for pirates, murderers, thieves and all sorts of criminal riffraff hiding from the law. My *maman* taught me as a child to use a pistol and I grew expert enough to shoot out all the spots in a playing card at ten feet. I would not hesitate, if necessary, to shoot to maim or kill, which a few silly men have already learned, to their misfortune. At seventeen I became the mistress of a *très riche* planter, who refused to marry me because I am an octoroon—one-eighth Negro—and then—"

Schuyler laughed uproariously. "No need to scare me any more, my girl! You have given me a perfect picture of yourself. What a fanciful imagination! I see you clearly as a dreamy lass trapped in the role of a small-town housewife, left alone for months at a time while your husband is off to war, and thus forced to amuse yourself with wildly romantic fantasies—a charming and most harmless pastime. In all truth, such a female as you describe I would dread to share a room with out of fear she would shoot me should I grow too bold."

Remembering the little pearl-handled pistol hidden away among her effects, Micaela smiled demurely. "Then let us hope, sir, that you will remember not to grow too bold, and you shall have nothing to worry about."

"And would a proper little housewife like you consider it unpardonably bold of me to address you simply as 'Micaela'? Of course I would expect you to call me 'Pace.'"

"It matters not, Pace, as long as you keep in mind the limits of our temporary relationship."

"Splendid. Then I suggest a brief visit to our mutual cramped quarters so I can divest myself of this heavy box you have inflicted on me, and after that a promenade on the deck to look over our floating abode and at the same time work up an appetite for dinner. . . ."

iii

The tiny room, floored with a dull brown carpet, contained a single berth covered with a flowered cotton spread and mosquito bar; above it the room's only window, adorned with a red bombazette curtain. Against the opposite wall was a short sofa, one chair and a gilt-framed looking glass.

After depositing Micaela's large box on the berth, Pace flopped on the sofa to gauge its length. It was much too short.

"The floor it'll have to be for my slumbers," he lamented.

"*Mais non!*" she said quickly. "I will sleep on the sofa."

"Absolutely not! If you were to sleep on this board-hard sofa, you would awaken in such a vile temper I couldn't stand you. The berth, I am told, is stuffed with the finest Spanish moss, which will enable you to sleep in enough comfort to indulge in more of your wild romantic dreams. Mayhap it will soften your attitude toward your humble cabin mate."

"And mayhap," she said coldly, "*you* are getting overly preoccupied with romantic fantasies. To get back to unromantic realities, where is the washroom?"

"Unfortunately, as a mere colonel I do not rate a private bath. The ladies' and gentlemen's washrooms are about twenty feet down the corridor. . . ."

About fifteen minutes later they were promenading on the upper deck. Many others thronged the walkways and were lined along the railings, for the breeze was balmy and the view of great interest to city dwellers. A forest crowded the shoreline, the intense green of its massed foliage crowned with gold from the sun and hazed with purple in the deepest shadows. Now and then a deer appeared among the trees to watch them glide by, unafraid, its large luminous eyes as eloquent as the silence. In the unending panorama of wilderness was a haunting sense of isolation and remoteness that seemed to reach in and stir Micaela's own ever-present sense of loneliness. Poignant memories of Paul, who might be dead, and of her child, Rill, for whom her arms yearned, tugged at her. To hide the tears that suddenly swam in her eyes, she looked down at the swirling, fast-sliding brown water. She shivered.

"You see what I have saved you from?" said Pace, also glancing at the sullen water.

Unanswering, for she did not trust her voice at the moment, she turned away from the rail and they continued their stroll. Pace appropriated her arm.

"Lost in your dreams again?" he said. "Or do you find my conversation too dull?"

Again she didn't answer—but this time for a different reason.

Strolling toward them, less than a dozen feet away, were Mrs. Sarah McCogg and her bevy of Sanitary Commission nurses. All of them were staring at her and Pace, eyes goggling in astonishment. Jane Quincey blurted out:

"Micaela—is it really *you!*" Her eyes raced up and down Micaela's low-cut, richly tailored gown, then to her handsome companion and back again. "H-how did you get *here?* Why . . . I thought—"

"By good fortune," Micaela said coolly, "I encountered a friend, who is escorting me to Memphis."

"Well! I never—!" said Mrs. McCogg. "It would seem that my judgment has been fully confirmed. Come along, girls. . . ." Her face was pink and her lips compressed into a tight little line.

After they had passed beyond earshot, Pace turned to Micaela with a wry little smile. "So that's the group of nurses you tried to join? A more unattractive flock of hens I've never seen. And they're going to be inflicted on our poor defenseless soldiers? I shall take great care never to be wounded!"

"Pace, please don't be unfair! Truly, most of them have hearts of gold and are of great service to our country. I was rejected only because of a few stupid rules."

iv

She knew not how long she'd slept, nor what had awakened her, only that the room was pitch dark and that a chill of apprehension was racing down her spine. . . .

The dinner had not been the finest, due to the Spartan nature of supplies on a military vessel, but satisfying enough. Afterward Pace escorted her back and, seeming to sense the tensing of her body as they neared the room, had said reassuringly:

"Have no fear, my dear. I shall leave you now to retire whenever you wish. As for myself, I beg your leave to go and enjoy the evening with some of my comrades. If I return late, you may be sure that I shall not bother you or disturb your pleasant dreams." With a bow he had left.

Now she knew what had awakened her—the metallic scraping of a key in the lock.

A moment later the door was flung open and a man stood outlined against the corridor lighting outside. The door closed behind him and again the room was intensely dark.

Involuntarily she let out a gasp of fright.

"You still awake, m'dear?" came Pace's voice, lazy and slurred with alcohol. "Thash a shame . . . didn't want to disturb you. . . ." Stumbling footsteps followed. A chair crashed over. A match flared, briefly highlighting his face like that of the devil himself as he leaned toward the wall and lit the whale oil lamp.

The glare of the lamp did little to restore Micaela's peace of mind. Its yellow rays slanted across the rumpled berth where she was half sitting up, making her feel almost nakedly exposed in her thin, filmy nightdress. His eyes were fixed on her intently as he got his jacket off and tossed it aside.

"How lovely you look, lyin' there in bed. . . ." He lumbered toward her. "Don'sh you thinks you owe me a li'l kiss for making thingsh so comfor'ble for you?"

"Sir! We had an agreement!"

He towered beside the bed. Alcohol was strong on his breath. "Agreements not satisfact'ry to both parties ought to be changed. Now I've been thinkin' thingsh over—"

"Drinking things over, don't you mean? You're not at all sober, Colonel Schuyler!"

"Just a dram or two. . . ." He shrugged amiably. "But whatever, the gist of my thinkin' ish that you're not a virgin, of course, and any fool knows that a woman accustomed to the supreme pleasure of a man's embrace in bed gets mighty lonesome sleepin' without it. . . . Oh, I'm not shayin' you don't love your husband, but human nature being sush as it is, an' hot blood not havin' a brain of its own, you cannot make me believe thash you wouldn't welcome the arms of a man 'round you at thish very moment—"

"Pace! You will cease this type of talk at once or I'll—"

"Or you'll what?"

"Or I shall leave at once!"

He leered deliberately as his glance slid over her nightdress, lingering at the breasts. "In thash flimsy piece of gossamer? And where would you go? To our woman-starved troops on the lower decks? To the crew? The captain? Or jump overboard 'mongst the crocodiles? Don't forget, my lovely, I hold all the winning cards in this li'l game you're playing."

"I am not playing games, sir!"

He guffawed drunkenly. "All thish balderdash 'bout being born in a pirate's den 'n' other buncombe! What you really want is some man to take you by force so you can still feel pure and innocent—while enjoying it to the limit. Well, ma'am—" He gave a short, drunken bow. "Being the gentl'man that I am, I am prepared to grant your wishes—"

He lunged forward and caught her in a clumsy but hard embrace. His mouth sought her mouth while she kept battling and twisting her head to avoid his kisses, and at the same time she was struck with a terrible realization.

It is true, she thought. *I am hungry for a man's arms, and Pace is a very attractive man. . . .* It shocked her that such thoughts could pass through her mind.

With a renewed surge of fury she clawed a hand across his face, bringing a yelp of pain, and in the next instant twisted out of his grasp and scrambled off the bed. She remembered the little pistol packed away in the box, which was on a rack above the berth, but knew that she couldn't use it against Pace even if she had it within reach. She darted toward the door, but in one long leap he caught her in an angry grasp.

"You little hellcat—" Before she could twist away again, his lips crushed down on hers. For a moment her struggles ceased as the warm pressure against her long-starved lips began to have its effect on her and the pulse and beat of her blood stirred long dormant amatory reactions throughout her body. A warm flush pervaded her loins, her breasts, and up into her head. With a desperate movement she broke away from him breathing hard.

"Sir! You have maligned me and broken your word, and are certainly no gentleman!" She had reached back as she spoke and grasped the doorknob.

"And your hot kiss, my dear, jus' proved to me that you're no lady." He reached for her.

Yanking the door open, she slipped out.

"Damn li'l fool—come back—!" He lunged after her.

She had raced scarcely a dozen feet down the corridor before his long legs outpaced her. Catching her roughly by the shoulders, he swung her around. At that moment a door opened and an elderly female face, ludicrous in a floppy nightcap, thrust out.

"What in the world is all this commotion?"

The woman's face was strangely familiar . . . something about the oddly unfocused eyes. Then with a sinking sense of dismay, Micaela recognized her as the squint-eyed lady who had been so solicitous near Mrs. McCogg's office.

"Come 'long quietly now—" Pace hissed close to her ear, "before we wake the whole ship." He took her arm and tried to lead her back.

"*Non, non*—I will not!" She struggled to free her arm.

Footsteps approached rapidly from behind her. An authoritative voice demanded: "What's going on here?"

Pace released her, grinned at the speaker, a uniformed boat officer accompanied by two burly fellows dressed as ordinary seamen. He laughed with an easy air of male bonhomie. "It's nothing but a li'l lovers' quarrel, mates . . . you know how it is. Nothin' to fuss about. Soon's we get back to the cabin and make up, she'll be sweet as pie again. . . ."

The officer smiled knowingly, and turned to Micaela. "Miss, we don't like to interfere in personal matters. Now why don't you relax and do like the colonel says?"

"I won't! I—I'm a stowaway and demand to be taken to the captain!"

"The captain wouldn't like being roused out of bed, miss, and if the colonel here vouches for you—"

"You heard her, officer!" said the older woman in the doorway. "You do just as the young lady says! I happen to know she's telling the truth."

"Why, yes ma'am," said the boat officer with remarkable alacrity and courtesy. "Anything you say, ma'am." And to Micaela, "Come with me, miss. . . ."

V

The captain's office was abovedeck just forward of the roundhouse. It was elegantly fitted out with rosewood paneling, a fine desk on which reposed a globe of the world, red flowered Brussels carpeting that harmonized tastefully with several polished brass spittoons, a few

214

carved walnut chairs and along one wall a leather-covered bench.

Micaela was huddled on the bench wrapped in the white, gold-buttoned jacket of the boat officer who, showing a sensitivity that surprised her, had offered it as a more decorous, if not complete, covering than her filmy nightgown as they awaited the captain's arrival.

"The cap'n's a real whinger for high-fangled style," the officer said pridefully as he glanced around the office. "But when it comes to duty, he's a hard man. Gets mad enough, he'll throw a fellow overboard quicker'n a wink without so much as a how-do, and leave him to sink or swim."

"How does he feel about stowaways?"

"Hates 'em like poison, but seeing as you're a lady—"

The door burst open and a scowling captain entered, hastily dressed, flaming red hair tousled, and still rubbing sleep from his eyes. He was a big man, over six feet, with a sturdy physique somewhat going to fat. The chin was blurring into his throat and there was too much belly, but he was well-featured and clean-shaven except for sidewhiskers. He appeared to be in his mid-thirties and had a firm mouth and chin and a big nose with a slightly flattened bridge as though from a blow long ago. All in all it was a handsome enough face.

"Bedad, an' 'tis the divil's own toime t'be wakin' a man from his slumbers!" he was grumbling. "Damn, what kind of officers have I got on this floatin' volcano that can't handle a wee stowaway problem?"

At the sound of his voice, Micaela stared, then leaped to her feet.

"Mike!"

The red-haired captain stared back. His jaw sagged. "Well, strike me! Micaela, me little beauty—!"

The boat officer watched in astonishment as the two rushed toward each other and embraced. Micaela's spirits soared. She hadn't seen the former Mississippi gambler since just before the war. Mike had been one of Paul's best friends. He had helped them escape from the South— and prison for Paul—by taking them as sole passengers on his steamer—won in a poker game—to New Orleans, where others had feared to venture during the height of the yellow jack epidemic.

Mike drew back, grinning. "And now, me little dove, f'what's all this fuss about?"

As briefly as possible she told about Paul's being missing in action in the Memphis area, her frustrated efforts to get passage there herself, up until her final desperate act of becoming a stowaway.

"Stowed away, say you?" Mike slapped the heel of one hand against his head as if he couldn't believe his ears. "Ah, me lass, you had only to ask and the whole boat would be at your disposal! If it's hard up for the coin you be—"

"Captain—" Pace Schuyler stood in the open doorway, obviously embarrassed. His appearance had been tidied up and he looked considerably sobered. "I am afraid that I am responsible for this unfortunate turn of events. There's been a terrible misunderstanding. In all sincerity and with the best of intentions I offered Mrs. Abbott refuge in my cabin, never dreaming that—"

With a sudden, lionlike roar of rage, Mike leaped at the young colonel and catching the front of his uniform jacket with both hands literally lifted him off the floor for a moment or two as he shook him. "Hah! So now 'tis clear enough. You lured this innocent, heavenly creature into your cabin with lecherous intent! Bejabbers, if you've so much as harmed a hair of her head, I vow I'll throw you in irons!"

"Captain—have you forgotten that I'm a colonel in the Union army, and that this vessel is presently under the command of the military?"

With an expression of disgust, Mike released the colonel and shoved him away. " 'Tis not only a scoundrel you are, but an ignorant one. Jist so there's no misunderstanding, Colonel, I am not only the captain of this ship but also the sole master and owner. I have let out to the government the service of this ship only—not my authority. On all matters of the comfort and safety of my passengers not even your highest general can gainsay me. Now then—"

"Gentlemen," cut in a gentle voice, "may I speak a word or two?"

Micaela's eyes swerved toward the voice. It was the squint-eyed lady, still wearing a flowery nightcap on her uncombed dark hair but now robed in a loose, light pelisse that reached all the way to her ankles.

Mike, surprisingly, had at once straightened to his full stature, then smiling broadly, gave a low sweeping bow.

"Ah, Mrs. Grant, what an honor! My apologies if the perturbation has disturbed your slumber, but let me assure you that all is now under control and there will be no more vellications or ebullitions on deck this night." Micaela thought "vellications" and "ebullitions" were rather extreme, even for Mike.

"Oh, don't be concerned about me, Captain. It's only this young lady I am so worried about. You see, I happened to hear all about her story from Mrs. Sarah McCogg, who as you may know is in charge of the nurses who are presently your passengers. Now I want to be sure she is properly treated on this boat. She seems to have placed her trust unwisely."

Schuyler's face reddened. "But it was all a misunderstanding, Mrs. Grant, and I would like a chance to explain—"

"No need to explain, young man, but you certainly should be ashamed of yourself! As for the young lady, I would like her to have a berth in my suite."

Micaela had been staring at the older woman as in a trance. Mrs. Grant!

At last she found her tongue. "I thank you deeply for your concern, Mrs. Grant, but I really couldn't presume—"

"Then don't presume, young lady," Julia Grant said tartly. "I am a very good judge of people, I believe, and also have an excellent memory. I read my husband's letters over and over, and in one of them I distinctly remember his writing how impressed he was by Dr. Paul Abbott, who treated his leg when he hurt it before the Shiloh battle, and therefore I feel the least I can do is become your chaperone for the rest of this trip." She glanced at Pace, who avoided her eyes in embarrassment.

"In fact," she went on, "I *insist* upon it! With the kind of men we apparently have aboard this ship, you certainly need a chaperone. Come along, Mrs. Abbott, and we will make preparations to move your effects into my suite."

Four

Memphis

i

The army ambulance, mule-drawn with a black driver, jolted and racketed over the uneven corduroy road. Micaela, its sole passenger, sat on a hard board seat inside, battling to keep her balance while enduring the jarring punishment to her spine.

So this was what wounded soldiers must suffer. It was a wonder that any of them were delivered to the hospital still alive.

Still, it was nothing compared to the horrors that awaited them in the hospitals. . . .

During the two days she had been in Memphis, Micaela had gone to all the city's eleven military hospitals in her search for Paul. Each visit seemed more sickening than the last. The hospitals, most of them "regimental hospitals"—always the most comfortless—were usually located in rotting old buildings or warehouses overrun with rats and vermin, and stifling with a stench of blood, gangrene and slops that filled the air outside for hundreds of yards in all directions. All were overcrowded and constantly seeking space for the boatloads of new patients arriving daily from points below. Not all were battle casualties; the majority came from the waterlogged encampments in pestilential swamps and bottomlands above Vicksburg, from camps flooded by rains and almost sunk in unfathomable mud. The toll of sickness was far greater than that caused by rebel bullets.

Never had she seen sadder sights. In some wards, hundreds of aching, unwashed bodies lay side by side on board floors with their knapsacks for pillows, with no food except the usual army fare of hardtack and half-spoiled salt pork, with no nursing but the little help they could get from other soldiers less sick than themselves. Lice infested their hair and clothing. They were tormented by lazy fat flies during the day, devoured by mosquitoes at night. On all sides they were dying. Dying of typhoid, pneumonia, blood poisoning, gangrene or unknown swamp diseases. Dying swiftly, silently, having exhausted their last reserves of energy. It was the younger men who went first. They were less inured to hardship than the older men.

Horrified and outraged by her first visit to such a hospital she went seeking a doctor to complain—only to find that the sole doctor for the entire hospital was dead drunk in bed, where he spent most of his time.

At the larger and better-staffed hospitals it was no more reassuring, for there she could hear the screams of the amputees, see the tense white faces of mangled men waiting for their turn, stomachs already curdled with fright and the surgeon's dreadful words still filling their ears: "I'm sorry, lad, but there's no help for this arm. See that bluish inflammation? It'll have to come off. . . ."

Much as it sickened her, she had forced herself to go through most of the hospitals, for having failed to find Paul's name in the patient registry, she had insisted on a personal inspection of any as yet unidentified patients, and there were usually a few.

Her first surge of optimism had come when one registry clerk told her they had an unidentified patient who might be her husband since he was a captain of about the same age, but was unable to speak. She had gone back to see the man with a strangely contradictory mingling of dread and hope—hope that at last she had found Paul but at the same time hoping it *wasn't* Paul, with wounds so serious as to make him voiceless.

He had been a young man whose entire lower jaw had been shot away, and his tongue cut off. His physique was so much like Paul's that she felt dizzy for a few moments, unable to know for sure because plasters and bandages concealed the face. A surgeon came to remove the dressings. The process of healing had begun, drawing down and so terribly distorting that part of the face adjacent to the ghastly wound that she still would not have known —except for the eyes. They were blue, not at all like the smoky gray of Paul's. A deathly faintness had come over her as she hurried to the outer air for recovery.

Now her nightmarish search of hospitals was ended, and she was almost relieved—relieved to know that at least Paul was not among all those pathetic, suffering men so negligently treated by the country they had served.

ii

The ambulance was now close to the river, and swerved off on another corduroy road that ran parallel with the levee. The vehicle was a military courtesy obtained through the good office of Julia Grant, with whom she had become very friendly on the boat. Otherwise the remainder of Micaela's trip had been uneventful. Several times Pace Schuyler had approached her to beg forgiveness and each time she had coldly rebuffed him. The only other incident from which she derived some small satisfaction was having dinner at the captain's table one night with Mike Quinn and his honored guest, Julia Grant— and becoming the object of astonished, envious stares from

Mrs. McCogg and her Commission nurses at a nearby table.

On arrival in Memphis there had been a military escort awaiting Julia. Micaela had been transported to the Gayoso House where high-ranking officers and the Commission nurses were quartered, and Mrs. Grant had gone on to rejoin her husband, promising to enlist the general's help in gathering information about Paul. Later that same day, General Grant's chief of staff had visited her with a message from the general requesting that she visit him in about two days, which would give him time to first have all possible information gathered about Paul, and in the meantime his staff would furnish her with anything she might require in the way of escorts, passes or transportation.

The two days had ended, as had her fruitless hospital search. The only and last possible hope left was that the general might have good tidings for her. `

Soon she would know. . . .

As the ambulance proceeded over the bumpy road, her gaze drifted off to the swollen, rushing river, which in places seemed to have seeped through or run over its banks. In some places were stretches of dull turbid backwater as far as the eye could reach, a vista enhanced in its dreariness by the skeleton cottonwood trees hung with funereal moss, quite appropriate to her melancholy mood.

The ambulance stopped and the driver called back. "Missy, yo' g'wine have t'walk de rest de way. Dis am'lance won't go no farder in dis mud."

"But where's General Grant's boat?"

"Yo' jest walk over ter de levee, but watch fer dem water holes—dey deep—an' climb up de levee an' it bring yo' smack dere."

She began walking, still unsure of how she was going to get there, for terra firma seemed to be nowhere. Mostly she was wading through puddles, and where it was not water it was mud, and the mud was so liquefied she sank into it above her ankles as if she were slogging through porridge. Here and there lay the rotting carcasses of horses and mules that apparently had become helplessly mired and left to die.

Awkwardly, feeling most unladylike, she clambered up to the top of the levee, where to her relief she found a board walkway. General Grant's headquarters boat, the *Magnolia,* was only a short distance ahead.

Reaching the gangway of the vessel she was confronted by a guard.

"I wish to see General Grant," she said. "I have an appointment."

"Jist go right up the stairs to the saloon, ma'am."

At the head of the stairway to the saloon she was halted by another guard, to whom she repeated the same words.

"Pass around behind the screen, ma'am."

The saloon of the *Magnolia* had been partitioned into three compartments by movable green baize screens. She passed around the first screen as directed and came upon a group of staff officers lounging and chatting. One of them was a frail-looking man with a pallid face and bushy black hair and beard—the same officer who had brought the message from Grant two days ago. Recognizing her, he rose swiftly. "Ah, Mrs. Abbott . . . I presume you've come to see General Grant. This way, please. . . ."

They passed around the second screen, behind which was another group of officers, who appeared to be busy poring over reports and documents. They evinced great interest in Micaela, but her guide ignored them and led her around the last screen and into a blue haze of cigar smoke. Micaela was suddenly nervous. She had heard so many stories about the famous general. It was widely rumored that he was a drunken, irresponsible officer, that the slaughter at Shiloh was due to his bad generalship, that he was a bloodthirsty monster with no regard for human life and had already vowed that he would move in and take Vicksburg in so many days even if it cost him three-fourths of his army.

Grant was sitting at a table wearing his hat, a cigar in his mouth, one foot on a chair, and buried to his chin in maps, letters, reports and other military documents.

"Mrs. Paul Abbott to see you, General. . . ."

At once Grant rose to his feet, clumsily knocking over his own chair in the process. Whatever *mauvais honte* Micaela may have felt in thus obtruding herself on the general was speedily banished by his discomposure. For a few moments he seemed the most bashful man she had ever encountered as he hastened around placing a half-dozen chairs at her service, begging her to be seated, removing his hat and taking the cigar from his mouth, then quickly and unconsciously replacing both.

"Do please be seated, Mrs. Abbott," he said again after she had already selected a chair and was seating herself.

"Thank you, sir."

He was not at all as she had visualized him. He was dressed quite carelessly, the jacket of his uniform unbuttoned, one hand jammed in a pocket. Nor was he as tall as she had imagined, certainly not over five feet eight, a slight-figured man with a meek face more like that of a schoolteacher than a great general. His dark brown hair was a bit mussed, his beard scraggly. The eyes were sensitive and lonely, giving his expression a look of softness—until one noticed the thin mouth, as hard as a slit of steel.

At the same time she was sharply aware that Grant was not intemperate. Having been raised on Balize among roistering men, she was practiced in diagnosing all the short- and long-range effects of alcohol and could tell instantly that he was not a drunkard. His eyes were clear, his skin clear and firm and the hand holding the cigar had not the slightest tremor. *The rumors are all lies,* she decided, at least as they concerned the way he was now.

His face had warmed with an engaging smile. "Julia has told me all about you, Mrs. Abbott, and how much she enjoyed your companionship. I want to thank you for helping to make her trip more bearable."

"But *non!* It is your wonderful wife who deserves all the thanks for making the trip bearable for me, and I am very grateful."

She waited for Grant to continue talking, for surely he knew why she was here, but instead he had begun pacing back and forth, puffing thoughtfully on his cigar. Either he was an extremely shy and reticent man, she thought— *or he has only bad news that he is loath to tell.*

"Sir," she ventured, "have you gathered any new information about my husband?"

His eyes clouded. He looked at his cigar held in one hand and spoke in a bemused way, as if to himself, "The whole thing was an ill-conceived operation. Had I been in command at the time, I never would have given my approval."

"But about my husband—?"

"There is but one known survivor, Mrs. Abbott, and he has been interrogated most carefully. . . ."

At that moment as if by some sort of spiritual telegraphy, she knew the worst. Fighting off an overwhelming sense of faintness, she bowed her head to hide the wetness suddenly swimming in her eyes. "Then—?"

"We have no knowledge of any prisoners being taken, Mrs. Abbott. Your husband has been officially listed as missing in action."

She lifted her head. "Please don't try to spare my feelings, General. Uncertainty and false hope are worse, far worse, than facing the most dreadful truth. As an experienced military man, do you believe there is any slightest chance that my husband might be alive?"

General Grant examined his cigar thoughtfully, cleared his throat. "In all honesty, Mrs. Abbott, since you are of that admirable type who will have it no other way, I must say that my best judgment is in favor of one of our common maxims: 'In this army, missing in action means dead.' "

iii

Heavyhearted and forlorn, Micaela crossed the pillared portico of the Gayoso House and entered the lobby. *So now the trail is ended,* she thought dismally. Paul was

225

no more. Yet life must go on for her and Rill. Without Paul to help it was up to her alone to find a way to locate her child and rescue her from Jacquard. But how?

In her benumbed state as she threaded her way through the vestibule, she was scarcely aware of the bustle around her. The Gayoso House had a well-earned reputation for high style and low living. Its marbled floors and tapestried walls announced that it was expensive. Once it had been the hotel of choice for rich travelers and prosperous salesmen, and no questions were ever asked concerning private entertainment with their *femmes de joie* as long as discretion was observed. Since the Yankees had captured the city it had not changed overmuch except that its clientele now consisted mostly of Union officers, and their female entertainment came almost entirely from *femmes publiques*—town whores of black, brown, yellow and a few white complexions slipped in during the night by obliging hotel servants in exchange for coveted Northern greenbacks. The nature of idle military men being such, there were nightly drunken rows and fights, the crash of glasses, ribald songs, drunken mirth and profanity.

It was in this boisterous atmosphere that Micaela, as well as all the Sanitary Commission nurses, had been quartered. Thus she studiously avoided meeting any male glances invitingly directed her way as she proceeded through the smoke-hazed, crowded lobby.

"Mrs. Abbott, may I have a word with you—?" A tall figure loomed in front of her. Pace Schuyler.

"Colonel Schuyler, I have repeatedly told you that there is nothing I care to discuss with you."

"But Mrs. Abbott—since I may soon be shipping out for points south, this may be the very last opportunity in my life that I'll ever have to convince you that I'm not really the beast you take me to be. It is true that my behavior was utterly disgusting and it weighs heavily on my conscience. I only beg of you that you grant me one small word of forgiveness so that I shall not be burdened for eternity with the feeling that I have insulted a lady for whom I have come to feel the greatest admiration and respect."

So he's leaving for the South! Perhaps . . .

"Colonel Schuyler, I'm willing to consider all past unpleasantness as water under the bridge. The only thing that concerns me at the moment is to find passage to New Orleans. Perhaps if you could find some way to help me—"

He groaned. "Oh my God—it's an impossibility! See all of these men—?" He gestured at the surrounding lobby. "All of these officers and *attachés* are waiting—they may wait for weeks—for passage south. Do you realize that the river below here is like running a gauntlet? Guerrillas, Confederate soldiers, and even rebel farmers hide in the bushes to shoot at every passing Yankee vessel. Our pilots have to be protected by steel plates around the pilot house. Should I be lucky enough to get passage soon—" He laughed humorously. "I couldn't even sneak you aboard to share my cabin again. Neither man nor beast will be allowed to leave Memphis for points south without a pass from the commander of the Department. Until Vicksburg falls to our forces, there is no slightest chance that any female will be allowed on board."

"Thank you anyway, Pace." She gave a wan smile. "And in saying goodbye, be assured that I shall harbor no ill feelings toward you."

"Thank you, Micaela. I pray that we may meet again under more favorable circumstances."

She allowed him to grip her hand heartily in a final gesture of parting, and continued on her way.

Just ahead she saw several well-groomed women who by their dress and manner could easily be recognized as Southern gentlewomen. They were part of a group of about a dozen Memphis ladies who had been rounded up and put under arrest by the Union army as they were known to have been acting as spies and sending information to their husbands, fathers and brothers in the Confederate army. Although they were being treated with the utmost consideration until such time as they could be passed under a flag of truce to the enemy lines, they were doing all possible to make themselves obnoxious. In every petty way they manifested their aversion to Yankees, including Micaela and the Commission nurses. They had bumped into her furiously in the halls and on the stairways, would make a general stampede from the parlors whenever a Northern woman entered, and were not above uttering such sneers as "Northern white trash" and far more vulgar epithets.

To avoid them Micaela veered in another direction, but not so quickly as to prevent them from bringing their lacy handkerchiefs to their noses, as if to mask the smell, and quickly drawing their skirts away to prevent any taint of contact.

Micaela hurried on, only to be stopped by a soft hand on her arm.

"Mrs. Abbott—are you feeling quite all right? Your eyes are red and the expression on your face—" Sarah McCogg was peering at her worriedly.

"I shall be all right soon, Mrs. McCogg, thank you."

Mrs. McCogg had not removed her restraining hand. "My dear, I am so sorry things did not work out differently. . . . Had I known—but this is no place to talk. Come, let us have a cup of tea and a chat. . . ."

iv

As they were seating themselves in the salon, Micaela noted that four of the Southern ladies were at an adjoining table. Instead of their usual insult of hastily rising and leaving the room, they continued to sit there staring at them boldly. Finally one of them condescended to speak:

"We have been told that you Yankee women have come here to look after your sick Yankee soldiers."

"That is quite true," said Sarah McCogg.

The Southern lady gave a short sarcastic laugh. "It's high time *somebody* came down to look after them. They're all dying like sheep and get no care at all."

"You're quite mistaken. They're getting the best of care possible under the circumstances."

228

The Southerner shrugged. "Well, anyhow, you're the first women who've come down here to look after them. So far all we've seen are the wives of Yankee officers—all cold-blooded, white-faced, lank lean women, decked out in cotton lace, cheap silks and bogus jewelry. Women who are their own servants at home. What do they care whether Yankee soldiers live or die?"

"I dare say," said Mrs. McCogg, "that Yankee women are fully as concerned about their soldiers as any Southern women."

"Hah!" snorted the Southern lady. "I myself happen to be the wife of a member of the Confederate Congress and am accustomed to wearing silks and jewels, but we Southern women are now done with wearing such luxuries until the war is over. I sold my jewels and gave the money to our hospitals, and I'd come down to wearing 'nigger cloth' and eating corn bread mixed with water, prepared with my own hands, before I would allow any of *our* men in *our* hospitals to want for anything!"

"Madam, I respect your devotion to your soldiers and only regret the wrongness of your cause. In the North we are equally concerned for the welfare of our men but you are mistaken in supposing that we are as poor as you are in the South. The war is not impoverishing us as it is you. Our women can afford to wear silks and jewels and *still* provide everything needful for our soldiers. Should it become necessary, we are as ready to make as great sacrifices as you."

"Hah! But your soldiers aren't *worth* the sacrifice, as ours are! *Our* men are the flower of our youth! The best blood in the world flows in their veins—*gentlemen,* every one of them. But your Yankees—ugh! The dregs of your cities—guttersnipes, drunken, ignorant—"

"You will please stop such calumny!" interrupted Mrs. McCogg, pink-faced. "I well know just the sort of 'gentlemen' your soldiers are, as we have seven thousand of them at Camp Douglas in Chicago, taken prisoners at Fort Donelson. If *they* are the 'flower of your youth' you are worse off for men in the South than we had supposed."

"And I have seen much of *your* soldiers too, to my sorrow and horror. They are barbarians. They came to my husband's villa after he had gone to Congress, leaving me alone with my servants, and they destroyed everything—*everything!* My plates, china, pictures, carpets—even my imported furniture. The wretches burned up everything!"

"If your manners were as unbearable to them as they have been to us for the past several days, you are fortunate to have escaped cremation with your villa and furniture. The whole world knows of your bad manners and your cruelties—particularly to the colored people."

"You dare to call us cruel to the niggers!" she retorted hotly. "That's just more of your wicked Yankee slander. Why, no one could be kinder to such people than we are. We feed them and clothe them, and try to educate them, despite their low intelligence and slothful ways. Why else are they *all* so devoted to us? They *love* us!"

"Perhaps they act that way only out of fear of getting whipped."

"Whipped you say!" the Southern lady fairly screamed, almost purple with rage. "Why, they're never whipped unless they *deserve* it!"

Listening to all this, Micaela suddenly perceived a way out of her dilemma. Turning to Mrs. McCogg, she said firmly, "I regret that I must disagree with you. It happens that I have lived most of my life in Louisiana, and nigger blood runs in my veins—"

"I thought so!" said one of the women at the next table. "She has that certain look that I am quite familiar with, having myself come from Thibodauxville in Louisiana, where we have many mulattoes, quadroons and octoroons and that sort."

Sarah McCogg looked at Micaela in surprise. "Well, it matters not to me, of course, whether one is black, white or whatever. The point is—"

"But it *does* matter!" said the first Southern lady, with her bright eyes now fastening on Micaela. "Here we have clear enough proof. Tell us, young lady, have you ever experienced mistreatment in the South because of your nigger blood? Or known others of your race to be punished without just cause?"

Avoiding the shocked eyes of Sarah McCogg, Micaela said with false sincerity, "Speaking for myself, I can only say that I experienced nothing but the kindest treatment from all the white people I knew in the South."

"It would appear so," said the Southern lady, "from the costly look of your dress and your general deportment. I am only wondering why you ever left the South to join the Yankees?"

"In my heart I never left the South. I only went North because I fell in love with a Yankee, who is now dead." She bowed her head as unfaked tears shone in her eyes. "My dearest wish is to be able to return to the homeland I love."

"Hah! You have proven our point, young lady. If given the opportunity, would you care to join our group to return to your homeland in the South?"

"Ah! To return to Louisiana is my greatest desire!"

Even as she was speaking, Mrs. McCogg rose abruptly to her feet and after giving Micaela a scathing look of contempt, walked stiffly off.

"I think we can grant your wish, young lady. Come with us to our rooms and we can arrange matters with the Yankee officers." With a haughty smile she added, "You must understand, however, that you cannot expect to be one of *us*. You will travel as my personal maid."

Five

Zambullah

i

He was guided by the sun during the days and by the stars at night, and slept only when his body refused to take another step. Usually he walked, and sometimes he ran at a long-legged, easy lope that consumed distance with the speed of a trotting horse. How many days, weeks or even months he had been traveling, he had not bothered to count. He could only estimate the distance he had covered by the soles of his shoes, which had worn through in places, and by the calluses that grew on his feet. His trousers and shirt were in shreds from plunging throught thickets and brambles when farmers set after him with guns and dogs, for no reason except that he was unwittingly trespassing across their fields. And because he was black. And of fearsome size.

Because of the fear and hostility he inspired among the whites, he bypassed all towns and stayed as close as possible to streambeds and swamps to elude dogs. He could easily outdistance farmers on foot, but dogs were another matter. Several times he had been forced to use his knife to kill hounds that had caught up with him—but not without cost. He had quite a few slow-healing, deep tooth gashes on his arms and legs. Fortunately he had not been followed by men on horseback. Yankee farmers apparently used their horses only for plowing, not riding.

Food had been his main problem, for his huge bulk required a lot of it. He tried to satisfy himself by eating acorns and cracking wild hickory nuts between rocks, and by stuffing down blackberries, which were plentiful at this time of year. Craving more solid food, he looked for the silvery flash of fish when he was following streams. He used his knife to cut a long willow sapling, sharpening it to a point on one end, and gashing into the wood to raise jagged little spurs which would prevent a fish, once impaled, from slipping off. He would remain poised for hours at a time over a deep wood with endless patience until he had speared a fish or two. He ate them raw.

He had with him a few matches that he had always carried wrapped in a bit of oiled paper. He saved these for the rare occasions when he was able to snare a rabbit or catch a bird sleeping during the night. On a couple of occasions he raided a farmer's hen coop and raced off with a couple of chickens after breaking their necks. He discontinued that after being chased one night by an irate farmer with a shotgun blasting at him in the dark.

Still, it was never enough to provide all the nourishment his great bulk required. He had lost many pounds. His ribs were beginning to show and his face was gaunt.

ii

A light rain started at dusk, increased its volume steadily until by dark it was pelting down like hard little pellets of ice against the skin of his back where his shirt was torn.

Zambullah forced himself into a slow run, scanning the

murky landscape for trees that might afford some shelter, but saw none. He staggered continually. For much of the previous night and all day long he had tramped on mechanically except for a few brief rests when he could find secluded spots. His only food that day had been green apples shaken from a tree in an orchard. They had brought on cramps and diarrhea, so weakening him that he had been able to continue only by a great force of will.

Coming upon a well-worn path leading across a broad meadow, and emboldened by the extremity of his physical condition—for now he was starting to shake and his teeth chattered—he began to follow it. Rain as well as darkness had the double advantage of driving farmers indoors, so there was less need for concealment, and paths could lead to sheds or barns where he might find shelter.

Coming over a knoll, he saw looming ahead a dark, silent shadow that brought him to a standstill. For a moment he hesitated, his primal instincts alert for possible dangers. He could see now that the structure was a barn, and in the background were the vague outlines of a farmhouse. But no dog had barked, and his dire need for rest and shelter were so great that heedlessly he strode ahead toward the gaping black cavity of opened barn door.

Inside, he could just barely discern a row of several stalls along one wall. In one corner was what appeared to be a pile of straw.

He stumbled toward it, half falling into the softness, and within a matter of minutes was in deep sleep. . . .

iii

A scream jolted him awake.

Rolling his head and eyes only toward the sound, he kept his body motionless like a startled animal.

Silhouetted in the rectangular barn opening and back-lighted by the blaze of morning sun was a white girl. One hand held a bowl against her trim waist, the other hung beside her unintentionally dribbling bright yellow kernels of corn. Chickens gathered around her, clucking and pecking at the ground.

Slowly, Zambullah rose to a sitting position, propped on one arm. He must not startle her. Where there were females, there were men. Men had guns. He saw the girl's eyes widen as her gaze took in the full size of him. He stumbled to find reassuring words.

"Missy—"

At the sound of his deep voice she let out another scream. Dropping her bowl, she ran off to one side.

Zambullah's catlike reflexes brought him quickly to his feet. He had intended to awaken before dawn and slip away, but his exhaustion had been too great. Now was his last chance to start running and hope to gain enough distance before the man of the house came out and started shooting.

But the problem was the girl.

She hadn't fled, as he had supposed; instead she had darted only a few feet to grasp a pitchfork against a wall just inside the door. She now raised it with its shiny tines pointed at him.

"Don' you try t' touch me, you big black nigra, or I'll poke 'is fo'k right through your eyes, hear?"

He stared at her in surprise and consternation. A white girl who would fight! She stood crouched like a tigress ready to leap, lithe and nimble, the fork poised. Her lips were drawn back, baring her teeth, and a hank of her rope-colored hair had fallen forward to obscure one eye; the other one blazed at him like pale blue fire. Her cotton dress was so old that she had outgrown its cheap shapelessness in every direction, particularly where it stretched taut across her hips and breasts.

"Why, missy, I ain't gwine hurt you. I jes' want t' git 'way from here an' go my way."

"Don' you try t' git away either, hear? I know whatcher are! You're a runaway, an' I ain't a-lettin' you go! Hear?" She gave an angry little toss of her head to get the hank of hair away from her eye.

Zambullah could have in an instant leaped and wrested

the fork from her with ease, but like most big men he felt a great depth of gentleness toward women and children. He was powerless to hurt a woman in anger, even if it meant his life.

"Please, missy—"

A masculine voice cut in: "Hold it right thar, nigra—!"

An elderly man approached holding a double-barreled shotgun aimed full at Zambullah. He was a thin man, his body bent from a lifetime of plowing, and his long-nosed face with its dull eyes was marred with deep wrinkles that were dirty in the furrows. Close behind him came a younger man limping on a twisted leg and holding a musket.

"Now what in tarnation be you doin' in my barn, nigra?" demanded the oldster, brandishing the shotgun close to Zambullah's face. "What's yer name?"

"My name's Zam, massa. I ain' done no harm. I jes' slept here to git outta the rain."

"I bet he's a runaway, I do!" said the girl, keeping her pitchfork poised fiercely. "I found 'im first an' iffen any bounty hunters comes 'round t' claim him, I git the reward."

The oldster glared at her. "You kin put that fo'k down, Loah. Me an' Lud kin handle 'im."

The younger man, Lud, was staring openmouthed. "Lookit the size of 'im! I bet 'e's got more muscle'n all three of us-uns."

The oldster was squinting at Zambullah shrewdly. "A runaway, hunh? From the looks of the rags he's wearin' an 'is ribs stickin' out, he's come a might far way from whar he started out. Ain't likely no bounty hunters'd ever find 'im 'less we advertise."

"Iffen you turn 'im in, Paw," the girl said sullenly, "remember I gits the reward money."

"Don't be hasty, Paw," said Lud. "We still got a lot more plowin' to do an more crops t'git in. Big buck nigra like 'at could be a lot of help. We kin allus c'lect the reward later. Or mebby claim 'im fer ourselfs iffen nobady comes around he belongs to."

"I ain't studyin' to turn 'im in jest yet. I figger he's a

237

runaway all right. He jes' give 'is name as 'Zam' an' he called me 'massa.' But 'e's far 'nough north so's I don't look fer any bounty hunters t' come pokin' around. Iffen any secesh come around, we kin allus say we was jes' a-holdin' 'im prisoner 'til we l'arned who he belongs to. Any Federals come, we say we're jes' pertectin' 'im from the rebels. Federals don't give a hill of beans if nigras is free or slaves anyhow."

He turned to Zambullah. "All right, Zam—how'd you like to work fer a spell? We'll feed you good an' let you sleep in the barn."

Zambullah grinned broadly. It would be a chance to rest. To recover his strength. To think. "I sho' be glad to work fo' you, massa. An' you don' have to worry 'bout me, massa. I'se a peaceful man. You don' need dem guns."

His quick readiness stirred the oldster's suspicions. "Iffen yer such a peaceful nigra, watcher runnin' away from?"

"I show you, massa. . . ."

Zambullah turned halfway around and pulled down his ragged shirt so they could see the crisscrossings of long scars on his back.

The girl breathed, "My Gawd—!"

"I been runnin' from my old massa, who whupped me alla time. I'se lookin' fo' a new massa who be kind an' nebber whup me."

The older man now lowered his gun. "Waal, you won't have to worry none with me, Zam. Long's you work hard an' don't try nothin' funny, you won't git whupped 'round here."

The girl plunged her pitchfork into the ground and leaned against it, pouting. "Jes' remember he's my nigra, Paw. I found 'im first."

Six

Loah

i

Loah Strake rocked back and forth in fast tempo on the old rocker on the back porch. The angry rhythm was accompanied by an angry creaking from the half-broken rocker, which had been flung around often enough by the old man when he was having a temper fit. As she rocked her fingers moved nimbly with needle and thread, sewing. She hated sewing!

Especially, she hated sewing when it was for a nigra, but the old man had ordered it.

"Them rags is fallin' apart," he said one night. "Ain't even fittin' to be seen by anyone when there's a woman in the house. Neighbors come by an' see 'im in rags fallin' apart, his pants hardly coverin' what he's got below the belt, they'd think of us wuss'n animals. They'd think we ain't treatin' our nigra right. Loah, git yourself busy an' start sewin' him a shirt an' pants to cover him up decent, y'hear?"

Loah didn't argue. Some things she could argue the old man about, some she couldn't. She always knew when to keep her mouth shut. Besides, she had other ways to handle him.

So Lud had been sent to town to get a few yards of Osnaburg cotton. Even that cost dear, because of the war, but the old man didn't begrudge it because Zam had been with them for over three weeks now and doing more work than both the old man and Lud put together. He'd done most of the work of clearing another forty acres, had them plowed, set out with corn. The old man was going to profit right smart by the luck of that nigra coming along when he did.

But Loah didn't like it. She didn't like having a big nigra around and having to cook for him, though thank God the old man didn't let him come in the kitchen to eat. He was fed on the back porch and at night went to his mattress of old straw in the barn, and got locked in so he couldn't run away again.

Zam was a good enough nigra, polite all the time, but awful dumb. He didn't understand half of what she told him to do. She knew he couldn't help being so dumb, but it riled her all the same. It riled her even more having to make a shirt for an ordinary nigra! Well, not an *ordinary* one, that's true. She'd never seen anyone bigger. Three weeks had put back a lot of weight on him. You couldn't see his ribs now and his waist was as flat and hard as a board. She wasn't sure there was quite enough material to cover those broad shoulders, though. It would mean piecing together little bits here and there to make it big enough to fit him. Doing it for a nigra! Sometimes when she thought of those rippling elastic muscles under that broad torso that she had to fit out with this shirt it made her get so hot with anger she wanted to spit!

At least she'd gotten back at the old man with a trick she'd used many times. Loah was a big girl—at eighteen she'd grown up almost to five feet eight and filled out amply in all those certain places that made dresses hard to fit her—but big or not, she disliked physical exertion. Sewing wasn't so bad—except doing it for a nigra—because it allowed her to sit down. But all other chores like chopping firewood, hoeing the garden, feeding the chickens and doing housework she hated with a passion. What she'd done was ask the old man to let Zam do some of the chores that she wanted done around the house but hadn't got around to.

"Whatcha mean, gal? Talkin' 'bout female chores? That big nigra kin do the work of two, three men outten the fields whar he belongs."

"But Paw—" Loah had begun in a practiced way, putting her hand up to her forehead, eyes half closed, and letting herself drift back into one of the kitchen chairs. "Paw, it's that female time a the month agin an' it's gittin' worse alla time." She made her face wince with conjured pain. Men, she had discovered, had a reluctant acceptance of that mysterious female weakness against which they were so utterly powerless.

"What be it you need 'im fer?"

"I need a little garden spaded up by the kitchen, Paw. I ain't yet got the dill planted for the picklin' or the citron for the jam. There's a messa little things t' plant yet. An' the stove wood's gittin' low. An' mebbe he kin shore up thet corner of the porch thet's saggin' almost to the ground. There's lots he kin do, Paw."

The old man eyed her sharply. "Waal, iffen I hafta, I hafta, on account of that derned female sickness. You kin have him fer today an' tomorra." And turning to Lud he added:

"I guess tomorra's as good as any time to take in a load of eggs an' chickens. We kin leave early in the mornin'."

"An' leave Loah here all alone with thet big buck nigra around?"

"I ain't figgerin' on any trouble from thet nigra. I ain't never in my life seen a more scared, dumb nigra. You couldn't ask fer a better-behaved one either. Knows his place. P'lite as all git-out. He knows he's found hisself a good home an' ain' about to mess it up. Besides—" he winked slyly with a sideways glance at Loah "—you know how a woman gits at her time a the month. That nigra ever fergits his place he gits 'is eyes scratched out, you bet!"

"Still, Paw, I don't like the idea of it. Hit don' look right."

Silas added his clincher. "Ain' you fergittin' somethin', Lud? It's been nigh a fortnight since you was last in town. I bet thet little lady friend of yourn's gittin' mighty lonesome to see you agin. . . ."

Lud had grinned and forgotten his worries about Loah.

Loah, pretending not to listen, knew well enough what was meant. For Lud had gotten drunk one hot afternoon from drinking too much hard cider while reaping the hay. He'd fallen under the reaper and got a leg mangled. There'd been no doc to look at it until the next day. She didn't know whether any bones were broken but it did something to the muscles and nerves of the leg and never healed right. Wasn't no good any more for anything but walking like he had a wooden leg. Was kinda shriveled up and ugly. Turned away the women. So he'd started goin' to the sporting houses in the nearest towns. She knew because when she got to town now and then some of the older girls she was friends with told her where he went and that her old man went there too.

That had been yesterday. This morning the old man and Lud had gone to town to sell the eggs and chickens and wouldn't be back until evening. And now it was getting close to noon. She had the shirt nearly finished.

ii

Against her will, her eyes kept moving to watch that huge body. He had finished the spading and was using the ax now, chopping firewood. Now and then when the ax bit into a section of log, pieces of stove wood would fly into the air and with one hand he'd catch them and stack the wood on a pile while continuing to chop. Watching that elastic, muscular, glistening body was almost hypnotic.

Whether at work or at rest, his body was real graceful. *Oh God,* she thought with a soft moan, *if only his skin was white!*

He had quite a pile now, and straightening up he sank the ax with one hand into the chopping block, then swept up an armful of wood and moved toward the house. Loah's lips opened as she watched him approach. The lips felt dry and she closed them again tightly, ran her tongue between to moisten them. She shivered as Zam's footsteps pounded across the rickety porch. He could break her in two with one hand. He entered the kitchen and she heard the wood as it was tumbled into the box beside the cooking stove. She called over her shoulder, "While you're in there, git the water pail and fill it."

"Yes, missy."

She heard the dipper rattle in the water pail as he lifted it and carried it to the well.

She watched him at the well lowering the heavy bucket with its rope into the cool depths, then with short jerking strokes pull it up again. He filled the kitchen pail without spilling a drop and started toward the house again.

Again Loah watched him approach. She didn't know why she was watching him that way wherever he was, whenever he moved. She couldn't seem to help it. He wasn't a white man and he was always on her nerves, but she just couldn't help watching him.

After he had gone into the kitchen with a bucket of water she laid aside the shirt and stood up. She was a big girl, so well figured that she was literally bursting out of the dress she wore. She brushed some of the cotton lint from her apron, tightened it and raised a hand to brush back strands of tarnished blond hair from her forehead. Her pale blue eyes glistened brightly as she went into the kitchen.

He had just put the water bucket down and straightened, pausing a moment, awaiting any further orders. She looked at him for a few moments with eyes as intent as a bird's, full lips parted. Her lips clenched shut again.

"Well, what you waitin' for, Zam?" she said crossly. "Git outta here!"

With a shrug and smile he turned to go.

"Zam—!"

He stopped and turned.

"You like working here, Zam?"

"Yes, missy."

"Well, you better git out thar an' work extry hard for the resta the day, 'cause the old man an' Lud'll be right mad if they come back an' you ain't made a good showin'. They gonna be gone all afternoon, maybe till after dark, so's they'll 'spect a lot of work done."

"You tell me whut work you want done, missy, I do it." He edged toward the door in a hesitant way, awaiting further orders.

Loah was not looking directly at him, but at the wall behind him at a level near his waist.

"Well, what you waitin' for?" she said. "Git outta here!"

As he was going through the door she called, "The shirt on the rockin' chair thet I was sewin' for you—take it to the barn an' try it on. If it don' fit right, I'll try an' fix it."

"That sho' nice of you, missy," he said and went out to pick up the shirt.

"It's 'bout noon," she called after him. "Wait in the barn an' I'll fix you some eatin's an' bring 'em out."

She watched him walking away. He moved smooth and easy for such a big man. She remained standing in the same position until after he'd gone into the barn and vanished in its murky interior. She turned away from the door, angry, feeling waves of heat pass through her body. She was angry because not once in the slightest way had the big nigra looked at her as a man should look at a woman. He looked at her as if she was just another piece of wood—a part of the house. And him just a nigra! During visits to town, all men looked at her with appreciation. She knew what she had. But this nigra was so dumb he wouldn't know the difference if she was a hag a hundred years old.

And a good thing too, 'cause if he ever did look at her in that dirty way, she'd kill him! She would swear to God

244

she would! The idea of a black nigra like that having bad thoughts about her! Anger pulsed in her blood, making tickling, itching sensations race through her body. What right did he have to have all those muscles and a body like that inside a black skin?

Going to a wall cupboard, after getting a box to stand on, she opened the top door and got out the old man's bottle of whiskey. Standing there she uncorked the bottle and took a long drink. It slid down like a little ball of fire into the seething turmoil of her stomach. She had another long drink for good measure, corked the bottle and put it back. The old man would be in such a good mood when he got back from town in the evening, he wouldn't notice any gone.

iii

Zambullah waited patiently in the barn for the girl to come out with his "eatin's."

She finally came, but with no food that he could see.

"How's 'at shirt fit?"

"Ain' tried it on yet."

"Whatcher waitin' for? Take off them rags yer wearin' n' put the shirt on."

He felt uneasy. It didn't seem right, changing his shirt in front of this white girl alone in the murky dimness of the windowless barn.

"Go ahead an' git it off, you dumb black ape! You skeered of girls or somethin'?"

Out of modesty, he walked away a few feet and carefully took off the tattered remnants of his old shirt. She followed with a bright glint in her eyes and watched as he tried on the new shirt. It was a little tight across the shoulders and in the arms, and too loose in other places, but a big improvement over the old shirt.

"How's it feel, Zam?"

"It feel fine, missy."

"Now I gotta measure you for the pants. They're harder t'make, 'cause iffen you don't measure right, what a man's got down thar—" She giggled. "Hit shows too much."

She took a frayed old cloth tape measure from a dress pocket and kneeled down. He stood stiff with embarrassment as she ineptly began stretching the tape across his waist and hips. He could smell that she'd been drinking whiskey and knew it had gone to her head.

His embarrassment mushroomed into fear as he felt her fingers fluttering lightly around his groin. This was the highest kind of danger! A white woman's fingers touching him could be deadlier than a rattlesnake. Worse, far worse, as her hands continued to brush across that most private part of him, was the involuntary arousal—a stiffening of his organ that was utterly beyond his control. She was a comely young female and his virile body had been too long without a woman.

She rose up now, giggling again. "I'd hafta be blind not to know what's goin' on in thet black head of your'n." Her eyes were bright as if she were in a fever and she let out a short laugh that was half a sneer. "I kin see right through nigras like you. . . . You're jus' achin' to git your big black paws on me, ain't you?"

"No, missy, no!"

"I kin see it in your eyes. I kin see the way you let 'em lid over—you're tryin' to hide it, but it's plain to me. You can't keep your eyes off my breasts, can you? You'd jus' like to git those big hands right on my breasts, an squeeze 'em, wouldn't you?" She threw out her breast only inches from him and pulled down her dress to expose them. "See? That's what you're dreamin' 'bout, ain it?"

"No, missy, I got no dreams lak dat in ma haid." He backed away from here as he would from a rattlesnake. In the Ebo tribe where he had been reared, the women were noted for their chastity and a man who sexually violated a tribal woman not his own was put to death. And ingrained in him even more strongly was the untouchability of a white woman.

Yet he was a man of strong needs and the flaunting

this white girl's charms was a torment, had started a slow fire in his loins.

With a knowing smile she followed as he backed away. She glanced at the pile of straw in the corner. Over it had been spread an old blanket. "Is thet whar you sleep, Zam? I bet you is jes' leadin' me back here to show whar you sleep."

"I ain' leadin' yo' noplace, missy."

With a little laugh she ran over to the pile of straw, and drawing her skirt above her knees, sat down.

Zambullah looked down at her in something akin to terror. She stretched back on the straw bed with her hands behind her head and knees bent. The skirt had slipped far above the knees. He knew it was all wrong for him to look, but he had never seen a white woman's legs before and they held his gaze with a raptness as if he was being compelled by the devil himself.

She smiled at him broadly, lewdly. "You'd like to see more, I bet. Come closer, Zam. Come sit here." She patted the blanket beside her.

"No, missy, I don' aim t'git near no white lady."

"Then why'd ya bring me over to your bed like this iffen it ain't what's in yer haid . . . an' in yer pants?" She giggled.

He started backing away. "Missy, I got wo'k ter do—I gotta git back. I—"

"No, you stay right here! Yer my nigra! You b'long t'me an' gotta do jes' what I say. You come here right 'is minute an' get down beside me!"

He hesitated, torn by a terrible conflict of emotions, knowing that he should turn and run, but held there in the grip of a raging desire aroused by this big ripe girl with the tantalizing white body and her dress pulled way up, waiting. She now began boldly, brazenly undulating her hips and moaning softly in a way more inflammatory to the senses than any words could be.

"What you skeered of, Zam? Git down here, hear? Pa 'n' Lud'll never hafta know. I ain' never gonna tell, I promise."

Knowing this was the wrongest thing he could do, but

driven by a devilish lust that was fast overpowering his will to resist, he moved over to the bed and sank to his knees. Stayed frozen there. The blood was pounding in his ears.

"I'm a-waitin' on you, Zam—" Her voice was thick, honeyed. "I'm a-needin' a man bad, an' I'm gonna close my eyes so's I won't even know you're black."

The pounding in his ears had subtly changed. His whole body stiffened as his jungle-trained ears picked up another sound . . . the rumble of a wagon in the driveway.

"C'mon, Zam . . . do it . . . *do it*—!" Her eyes eyes were closed, head sideways, and she appeared half in a swoon. Her legs were opened wide.

He began to rise. "Missy, they's a wagon comin'—!"

"My Gawd, Zam, don' keep me waitin' no longer!"

His voice grew harsh. "Git up thar, girl! Yank yo' dress down quick—dey's comin'! Hear dat wagon?"

His changed tone shocked her out of her sensually drugged state. Half-risen, resting on one elbow, she listened.

"Oh damn, damn, damn!" she spat out. "It's the ol' man's wagon—I'd know that ol' squeakin' wreck a mile away!" And then before his astonished eyes, with a hard, determined look on her face, she gripped the neckline of her dress and pulled. There was a long ripping sound. She began screaming.

"You git away from me!" she screamed. "Stop—*stop!* Lemme go, you big black nigra!"

Zam raced to the barn door, her screams following. Peering out, he saw the wagon had reached the barnyard and Lud was hollering:

"I tol' ya, Paw! We shouldn'ta never left thet nigra alone with Loah! I tol' ya we better git back early—!"

"Git yer rifle an' I'll take the shotgun!" shouted the old man.

With one leap Zambullah was outside and racing toward the corner of the barn.

The old man's voice rose in querulous fury: "Git 'im, git the black bastid afore he gits away!"

Zambullah took a long low dive toward the ground a bare second before the rifle cracked, heard the ball splinter through the barn siding. Already he was rolling around the corner of the barn. The shotgun boomed, followed by the rattle of pellets into the wood.

Moments later he was on his feet sprinting across the field.

Book Five

MONTHAVEN

One

Capture

i

Paul's whole left side ached, burningly. Somehow he must have torn a few muscles from the fall, or cracked a rib. But his left leg, trapped under his horse, had no feeling. It might be crushed, or simply numbed from blocked circulation.

More tormenting were the tickling, itching sensations on his face that came from the huge bluebottle flies. Blood spouting from his horse, dead from a hole ripped through his chest by a cannonball, had soaked his shoulder, an arm, and stained much of his face. Buzzing, swirling hordes of flies were constantly alighting on the sticky, coagulating areas to drag their hairy feet through the blood as they fed on it greedily. He was going crazy from wanting to scratch, but dared not. A few of the rebels had ridden among the fallen men to take last shots at any Federal showing signs of life.

But nearly a half hour had passed since the last shot

was fired, and the only sounds were the moans and feeble cries of the wounded who had been overlooked amid the blood and dead bodies strewn everywhere.

Carefully, Paul began working his leg loose from beneath the horse. It took several minutes to extricate it, and then another several minutes of massaging the leg before circulating blood began to clear away the numbness. Slowly he drew himself to a sitting position, wincing from pain, and looked around at the ghastly aftermath of the massacre: dead horses, upturned wagons, pools of blood, numerous corpses. A fair number of gray and butternut uniforms were sprinkled among the blue. The Federal cavalrymen had given a good account of themselves, considering the overwhelming odds against them.

About a dozen feet away he saw a man trying to crawl. One arm was dragging, shattered near the shoulder, bleeding profusely. Automatically Paul began unstrapping his medical saddlebags. A quick inspection revealed that their contents were relatively undamaged.

Limping over, he at once began stripping the shirt away from the wounded soldier's arm. The man twisted his head and looked up. His eyes were scrinched in pain and bright with terror. It was a middle-aged face, prematurely graven with wrinkles, gaunt from undernourishment "Whut'n tarnation—!"

"Hold still," said Paul. "I've got to get a tourniquet on your arm before you bleed to death."

"You be a doc?"

"That's right." Paul was quickly arranging the tourniquet.

"This beats all! Cain't you see the color a mah unifo'm?"

"I don't treat uniforms, soldier."

"Gawd A'mighty! Yer the fust Yankee bastid I ever see who'd turn a li'l finger t' he'p one 'v us-uns. But don' g wastin' yer time on me, doc. Right over thar's one 'v o off'cers who's bleedin' in the hip. You go fix 'im up fust

"I'll take a look at him after I've done what I can f you."

"Shucks, I ain't 'v much account, suh, but over thar, he a colon'l. Ain't right t'do me fust."

254

"You're talking like a damn fool! Who the hell cares about rank in the graveyard? Which is where you'll end up very soon if we don't get this blood stopped. Now relax and count your blessings, because if I'm able to keep you alive, I doubt you'll ever be able to use this arm again to salute any officers."

Finished with the cleansing, dressing and bandaging of the man's wounds, Paul slung his medical saddlebags over a shoulder and started limping toward the Confederate colonel, but stopped short at the thunderous sound of approaching hoofbeats.

Moments later a band of about thirty mounted rebels came racing up.

"Chris' A'mighty—!" bellowed one of the riders at the sight of Paul. "How'd we ever miss 'at bastid? Waal, ah'll sho's hell take care 'v thet in a hurry—!"

He lifted his Sharps rifle—only to have it roughly knocked aside by the saber of a young lieutenant who rode up beside him.

"Put your gun down, Semple! We don't shoot down defenseless men like the damn Yankees do! This man is a prisoner of war and under the protection of the Confederacy."

ii

Three days later Paul and a miserable collection of fellow prisoners, mostly enlisted men, arrived in Bristol, where they were reloaded into ancient, dilapidated box and stock cars, closely packed as pigs. The cars were putrid with cattle and hog dung. The journal boxes above the car wheels were dry and the axles unlubricated, causing the cars to screech and groan in a continuous nerve-jangling clamor on the long trip to Richmond. The engine puffed along barely faster than a man could walk, frequently running off the track, to be pried back on the rails again by prisoners under rifle guard.

After skirting the base of the Blue Ridge Mountains, past Lynchburg and the Peaks of Otter, through the valleys of the James and Appomattox rivers, the train finally crossed the long bridge over the Appomattox into Richmond in the dead of night and came to a grinding halt.

From there the men were herded from the cars and marched down the main street past the capitol, and finally to a long dark street lined on both sides by brick warehouses and former tobacco factories which were now being used as military storehouses and prisons.

It was all Paul could do to last out the enforced march. The damage to the leg that had been trapped under his horse made walking torture. His shrunken stomach rumbled and ached from the prisoners' fare of three hard slices of mildewed bread daily, with sometimes a fragment of spoiled fat pork and brackish river water.

Worse, his saddlebags and entire supply of medications had been taken from him, so there was no way he could treat his own ailments or those of his fellow prisoners, many of whom were staggering along in far more serious shape than he was.

The column was now halted in front of the largest warehouse on the block. A large sign above the door read:

THOMAS LIBBY & SONS
Ship Chandlers and Grocers

The notorious "Libby Prison"!

iii

A queasiness turned his stomach as Paul looked down the numerous bugs floating on the surface of his tin cup of thin potato soup. Arresting an involuntary impulse retch, he clumsily began trying to skim off the bugs with finger. A few hours in Libby Prison had taught him th nausea was to be his chronic condition, for everythi about the prison was foul and disgusting, but he couldn't afford to let squeamishness overcome his need for nourishment if he expected to survive. The cup of soup and a handful of coarse-ground, uncooked cornmeal was typical of a full day's ration.

"Here, use my spoon—it makes it a lot easier to skim off the little buggers. . . ." Lieutenant Wilbur McAvoy, a slight, wiry young man with bright blue eyes and rust-colored hair, extended his spoon. "Paid a dollar for it when I first got here a couple months ago," he added with a touch of bitterness, "and used up the rest of my money on 'extras' like six apples for fifty cents, a watermelon for five dollars, the same for a pound of coffee, and potatoes at twenty-five cents apiece. Now I'm down to the standard prison fare." He made a grimace of distaste.

Paul reached for the spoon, halted just short of it. McAvoy's wrist was gray, crawling with lice.

Noting Paul's hesitation, the lieutenant laughed. "Bothered by the vermin? You'll get used to it, Captain. That is, you'll learn to endure it. Within a week you'll have thousands of them feeding on your blood. It's the custom here to spend most of the day skirmishing for lice in our clothing. You sort of crunch them between thumb and forefinger. Get good enough at it, you can keep the number feeding on you down to a tolerable limit, say a few teaspoons of the buggers. If you don't work at it, or get so sick as to be unable to help yourself, they'll increase into millions, or so to speak, into pints and quarts."

Paul took the spoon. Fastidiousness was another habit he would have to forgo.

"Don't they ever fumigate?"

McAvoy laughed bitterly. "What good would it do? Even if they gave a damn! We're on the basement level—the only dirt floor in the whole prison—and you've seen the toilet facilities—two pits dug in the far corners, with a trench to drain off the urine. That stink alone is bad enough, but it doesn't end there. The slimy ooze around those pits is just crawling with billions of white maggots . . . and spreading, contaminating more floor space all the time. You see, coarse cornmeal raises hell on the stomach. Half the men in here are suffering from diarrhea, dysentery or other stomach ailments. Nobody blames them when they have to go right where they are, on the instant, or mess up their pants. There's hardly a place left to lie down and sleep without some kind of indescribable filth for a pillow."

Paul upended his cup of soup, spilling it into the dirt, and handed the spoon back to McAvoy. With his professional knowledge of strange, teeming and often deadly bacteria that accompanied filth—knowledge that the majority of doctors still scoffed at—McAvoy's graphic description was simply too much for the present queasy condition of his stomach.

"You'll regret that, Captain," said McAvoy. "A husky man like you never gets enough to keep him going as it is. I'm lucky in being down to less than a hundred pounds. It's the big strapping ones—they get no more rations than I get—who always go first. Hardly a day passes that two or three of them aren't carried away to the so-called hospital and that's the last anybody ever sees of them."

"I'm already ashamed that I didn't first offer it to you or somebody else," Paul said with a sorrowful shake of his head. "Next time I'll endeavor to swallow my qualms—and the bugs. After all, bugs can be considered as nourishment. Birds thrive on them. But if this is the kind of treatment and slop they give officers, what do the enlisted men get?"

"It's no different as far as I know. Fact is, Captain, over half of the men you see here *are* enlisted men. Of course you couldn't be expected to know that, with so many of them without jackets, half-naked or wrapped in filthy blankets."

"I thought officers were kept segregated from the enlisted men."

"I can't speak for the rest of the prison, but down here they aren't. Down here we're not treated like regular officers."

"For God's sake, why not?"

"Because you must have served under a fighting general—I'd swear to that. Probably Grant or Sherman, or maybe 'Old Rosy.' I myself was under Pope. The Confederates have a bitter hatred you can hardly believe toward Pope and Grant and all their commands down to the last humble lieutenant. Because we licked them a few times and killed plenty of them, they think of us as bloodthirsty butchers—their own rebel hands being lily-white clean, in that respect, of course." He paused, then with a wry grin continued:

"On the other hand, if you'd been one of McClellan's officers, or under one of the other pussyfooting generals, you'd stand a chance of being incarcerated on the main floor just above. We call it the 'Showcase Room.' They get fresh-baked bread, clean soup and sometimes, I hear, even mattresses. But they're never allowed to see any of the rest of the prison. They're the first ones to get paroled in exchange for Confederate prisoners—the idea being that they'll return North and tell everybody what decent treatment they got at Libby."

A stark naked man tottered toward them. He was thin and frail, his ribs standing out sharply against his shrunken torso. His mouth hung half open slobbering spit and his vacant eyes looked at Paul as if not seeing him. His voice quavered as he held out a hand:

"An apple . . . please sir . . . may I have just one bite out of that nice big red juicy apple you're eating?"

Gently Lieutenant McAvoy steered the man away. "Sorry, Major, but we've got no apples today. Maybe tomorrow. . . ." And to Paul, "That was Major Franklin—he was okay until a couple weeks ago, when I guess he couldn't take it anymore. You can get to forget for a while the stench, the heat, the lice, the maggots, the dead and dying around you, but it's impossible to forget the craving for food. You'll find a number of madmen in here, all of them babbling and maundering about something to eat."

Later, wandering among the men, Paul saw even more appalling cases. In many, diarrhea and scurvy had set in, wasting them away until their muscles and tissues almost disappeared, leaving the skin lying flat upon the bone. In some of them the gums had swollen so grievously that they protruded livid and disgusting beyond the lips and their breath was so unbearably fetid that even in that malodorous place it took an effort to go near them.

"I've seen some of them where their teeth start falling out and the gums break off in chunks which they either swallow or spit out," volunteered McAvoy. "They've also got ulcers in all parts of their body just crawling with maggots."

Paul was shaken. He'd seen frightful enough cases in the workhouses and insane asylums of Scotland, and enough horrifying sights among the war casualties, but nothing as ghastly as these walking dead, rotting away even before they reached the grave.

"Good God!" Paul said angrily. "What kind of inhuman people are running this prison? Don't they know how easy scurvy is to control? In a southern climate like this, fruit should be plentiful, and just a handful of almost any kind of fruit fed to the men now and then could have prevented all this!"

"General Winder and Captain Turner run this place. Any man who dares complain too loud, the general has him taken out and shot as a troublemaker."

"Well, troublemaker or not, somebody has to do something about this!"

Striding over to the iron-barred door, Paul banged on the metal with his tin cup. "Guard! Guard!"

In a few moments a booze-reddened face with mud-colored eyes thrust close to the bars. "Who'n hell's raisin' the fuss aroun' here?"

"My name is Abbott—*Doctor* Paul Abbott—and I demand to talk with General Winder about the despicable rations that are killing off these men!"

"Dr. Abbott, you say? An' ya craves t'see Gen'ral Winder, hunh?" The face grinned. "Waal, I sho'll see thet the gen'ral gits t'heer ya got complaints 'bout our hospitality. . . ." He swaggered off.

McAvoy and a group of other prisoners were standing around gaping as if Paul had gone crazy.

"You shouldn't have done that, Captain," said McAvoy.

"It won't do us a bit of good, but will surely bring hell down on your head. . . ."

Within five minutes a uniformed Confederate captain appeared. He had a hard slit of a mouth and hard blue eyes that searched past the bars.

"Which one of you is Abbott?"

"I am Captain Abbott."

"You're a surgeon, and your full name is Paul Abbott?"

"That is correct, sir."

The officer turned to the jailer. "Open the door and let the captain out."

Lieutenant McAvoy gave Paul a commiserating glance as he left.

iv

The man with the two stars on the epaulets of his gray uniform, a handsome man with silvering hair, rose from behind his desk when Paul was escorted into his office by Captain Turner. It was mystifying enough to Paul that a major general would rise at the entrance of a mere captain—and a prisoner at that—but more mystifying when he walked around the desk with an outstretched hand.

"Captain Abbott, I can only say that I am sorry for what has transpired since your arrival here," he said as Paul numbly shook the proffered hand. "But perhaps we can make amends. . . ."

"I am afraid I don't understand, sir." Indeed, Paul's mystification had begun earlier when he had been taken before General Winder and the latter—a chunky man whose stolid face with its sharp rodent eyes and florid complexion had been wearing an uncomfortable smile—informed him that an unfortunate mistake had been made. Without explaining, he had ordered Captain Turner to escort Paul to General Cooper, the adjutant general of the Confederate army. It was just a short walk from the prison, and Turner, after leaving Paul in General Cooper's office, had departed.

"I can well understand your surprise, Abbott," said the general. He indicated a chair near the desk. "Be seated and I shall explain. . . ."

When both were seated, Cooper continued:

"General Winder, by the way, expressed profound regret concerning your incarceration. Apparently it was due to carelessness and the misspelling of your name on the part of the recording clerk. The fact is, I had left explicit instructions that as soon as you arrived among the prisoners, you were to be brought to me at once. Had you not registered a complaint, correctly giving your name, the mistake might not have been discovered for a long while."

Noting Paul's puzzled expression, the general laughed. "You see, Captain, word of your medical talents and—perhaps more important—your medical impartiality preceded your arrival. If you recall the day of your capture, I'm sure you will know what I mean. . . ."

An inkling of why the general was showing such courtesy began to dawn on Paul. He had treated the wounded Confederate private to the best of his medical ability. A wounded Confederate colonel had witnessed this, and after the group of rebel cavalrymen had returned and were about to take him prisoner, the colonel had ordered them to find all wounded soldiers in the area, regardless of whether they were rebels or Yankees, and to give Paul full cooperation in doing all possible for them.

There had been no Union men found still alive, but he had done the best he could for all the wounded rebels, including the colonel.

"Colonel Robertson, whose hip wound you dressed, was most impressed by your medical competence—also by your generous spirit and willingness to help our men." The general favored him with a smile of appreciation.

"I am quite aware that your own medical service suffers from an inadequate number of doctors," he continued, "and we have worsened the situation by filling all your hospitals back in Washington, Chicago and all along the

Mississippi with more casualties than your generals had ever dreamed of." He shrugged, somewhat cynically.

"But as bad off as your medical service is, ours is in far worse shape. The cavalry unit that attacked yours, for example, was not accompanied by a doctor. We simply have too few of them. Sad as it is, a majority of our wounded men who might have been saved are lost on the battlefield from lack of medical care."

The general sighed. "Even more discouraging, the biggest toll of our men, by far, is not from bullets but from sickness. It seems that sickness is more redoubtable in our army than Yankee guns. We have so many thousands *hors de combat* from typhoid fever and all manner of ailments that, were they well, they could more than double the size of our army. More than guns, our need is for good doctors."

"I think that the same assessment could be made on our side too, though perhaps not to that extent," Paul ventured.

The general smiled thinly. "And unfortunately your side has lost a good doctor, whereas the Confederacy has gained one."

"Sir, I hope you are not suggesting that I change the color of my uniform."

"If I recall correctly, Colonel Robertson overheard you telling one of our casualties that the color of his uniform didn't matter, that you treated the man, not the uniform. I take that as an indication that you are a true doctor whose humanitarian convictions toward the human race in general take precedence over the ideological differences of war."

"That is largely true, sir, but I am still a Yankee whose first obligations are toward my own comrades."

"Let me correct you, Captain, by pointing out that you are also a prisoner of war who no longer has any choice in the matter. Which brings us to the point at hand. . . ." He leaned forward over the desk and his voice took on an edge of urgency.

"It so happens that one of my best officers and a dear friend, Brigadier General Adrian Ashley, was killed in

263

battle about a year ago. His wife Christina has since devoted all her money and energies to the care of wounded Confederate soldiers. To take some of the load off our already badly overcrowded hospitals, she has opened up her rather large plantation and several tobacco warehouses for this purpose, and put all her slaves to working solely for the care of the patients, who number into the hundreds and are steadily increasing. She has only one aging, infirm doctor to handle all the medical aspects—an impossible task, of course. Mrs. Ashley has been begging us for more medical help, but we simply have none to spare. I am officially unable to transfer one of our scarce doctors to a quasi-official hospital such as hers when our fighting units are constantly crying out for more doctors. But in the case of a Yankee doctor, who is also a prisoner of war—" He leaned back with a smile. "That's where I am sending you, Captain Abbott."

Paul's whole reason for wishing to see General Winder, which he had not yet been given a chance to discuss, came tumbling back into his thoughts.

"But sir, I could not in good conscience give all my medical aid to your casualties and sick when my own comrades in Libby Prison are so desperately in need of help." Quickly he went on to give a graphic picture of the frightful conditions he had found.

The general nodded sympathetically. "It is all too true, Captain, and no one regrets it more than I do. But I wish to point out that the conditions among our own men are hardly much better. Unlike you Yankees, who have so much more money and vast stores of supplies, we are hard put in trying to meet our most basic needs. The uniforms of many of our soldiers are in tatters. Some are actually without shoes. Nearly all of them are cruelly undernourished. Scorbutic cases have begun to crop up even among our fighting units."

"I don't understand," said Paul. "Certainly you should have a plentiful supply of fruit which could prevent such a disease."

The general grinned wryly. "Apparently you are unaware of the success of your units in disrupting much of our rail network. In some areas we have an oversupply of various fruits and vegetables. Other places are barren of all farm goods, either because the orchards have been neglected while the farmers are fighting or they have been ravaged by warfare, and our crippled transportation system is simply unable to achieve proper distribution."

General Cooper shrugged. "However, I shall instruct the commissary general to do all possible to improve the diet and general conditions of all prisoners. It is the best I can do, Captain."

He stood up, adding, "As of now you will no longer be considered as a prisoner of war, but are paroled on your word as a gentleman to proceed on the morrow, accompanied by a military escort, to Monthaven Plantation to begin work unstintingly for the benefit of wounded or sick Confederate soldiers. While there you will be accorded full freedom of movement and all the courtesies appropriate to your situation."

"But General, about my prison comrades—"

Affecting not to hear him, General Cooper frowned at Paul's uniform.

"Your clothing is a mess, Captain. But I'm sure that one of my aides can arrange to have it properly cleaned, or find another uniform more suitable—a Yankee one, of course." Then walking to the door, he opened it and spoke to the orderly outside:

"Notify Lieutenants Yardley and Tibbs to make arrangements for the escort of Captain Abbott to Monthaven at the break of day tomorrow."

Two

Christina

i

That night Paul enjoyed the luxury of a good bed at Richmond's Exchange Hotel and his first real bath in weeks. After shaving, brushing his hair and getting into the uniform they had provided—not a new one but clean and tolerably well-fitting, probably once owned by an officer now dead—he began to feel more like his old self. A substantial dinner of broiled chicken added considerably to his feeling of well-being—at the same time giving him deep twinges of guilt in remembrance of the underfed prisoners. He could only hope that General Cooper would keep his word about doing all possible to improve their diet.

The following day was pervaded by a dreamy sense of unreality. Clean, refreshed, amply fed and provided with good horse, the ride through forested hills and rolling plains seemed more like a pleasure jaunt than the lot of a prisoner of war. The blue-hazed vista of distant mountains and valleys was breathtaking. Magnificent oaks, hickory, ash and maple mantled the hillsides; the valleys were green with orchards and crops; meadows were colorful with profusions of wild flowers that filled the air with honeyed perfume and lulled the senses with the murmur of innumerable bees. And his escorts, Lieutenants Yardley and Tibbs, turned out to be friendly lads who laughed and joked and tactfully desisted from any reference to the war. Yardley was the sprightlier of the two, a slender chap with curly dark hair and a cheery disposition. Tibbs, stocky and towheaded with shrewd blue eyes, was quieter in deportment and at all times maintained toward Paul the rule-book courtesy due a captain's rank. Neither of the young officers had as yet experienced any action in battle and it was hard for Paul to think of them as the "enemy."

By evening they reached Lynchburg, where they took rooms at the Piedmont House. The hotel was full of Confederate officers, and contrary to his expectations, Paul was more an object of curiosity than one of animosity. The attitudes of the rebel officers, who of course knew he was a prisoner of war, were uniformly civil and courteous.

They don't hate me because I'm a Yankee, he thought in surprise. *Under normal circumstances many of them could well be my friends. What a crazy thing war is!*

By contrast, during the next day's ride, when several times they passed through small villages or near humble farms, the lowborn citizens, including women and children, shook fists at him, made ugly faces and shouted obscenities. Tibbs and Yardley, he realized, were escorting him as much to protect him from the ire of the populace as to prevent an effort to escape.

The long ride brought them, in late afternoon, to Mont haven.

The first view of the huge plantation was from th crest of a hill, which afforded a panorama of broad field of tobacco and grain, sprawling apple and peach orchard scattered herds of cattle and hogs and meadows spotte with wild flowers. A pastoral dreamland! And in the fa

268

distance the manor house, impressive as a castle, gleaming white under the slanting rays of the sun.

Not until they were riding closer to the outlying tobacco-curing houses and other farm buildings did something less pleasant obtrude. In the warm breeze, sweet with the wholesome scents of greenery, fresh-tilled earth and clover blossoms, was carried a whiff of something evil. The rot in Eden. The faint but sickening exhalations of gangrene from dead, decaying flesh.

Tibbs said, "I guess we'll have to ask one of the niggers to direct us to Cade Ganty. That is, *Sergeant* Cade Ganty—" He let out a snort of amused disgust. "First time I've ever been ordered to report to an enlisted man!"

Yardley laughed. "As I've heard, the sergeant was General Ashley's orderly, and the general thought so highly of him that on his deathbed he added a codicil to his will directing that Ganty was to be put in full charge of the management of Monthaven, subject only to the desires of Mrs. Ashley."

ii

Cade Ganty, seated behind a pine board desk in the plantation office building, looked up with a frown at the entry of Paul and Lieutenants Yardley and Tibbs. Ganty had black, stringy hair and beetling black eyebrows over dark, piercing eyes that seemed to be emitting sparks. The whole muscular but stocky build of him seemed to exude a hostility as prickly as a porcupine. The corrugation of scowl lines in his forehead and the set grimness of his wide mouth gave him the look of an angry bulldog. For all of that, he was not an unattractive man. He was neatly dressed in a Confederate soldier's uniform, the sleeve of his right arm tight from bulging muscles and prominently displaying sergeant's stripes, the left sleeve hanging limp and empty.

"You are Sergeant Ganty?" Tibbs asked politely.

Ganty considered that for a moment before allowing that he was.

Tibbs's face pinked. "Sergeant, isn't it the custom to rise and salute when you are approached by an officer?"

Ganty considered that for a longer moment before apparently deciding it wasn't worth answering. "Something you wanted to see me about, Lieutenant?"

Tibbs's flush deepened. "I am Lieutenant Tibbs. Lieutenant Yardley and I were instructed by General Cooper to escort Captain Paul Abbott, a surgeon of the Union army, into your custody—"

"What th' hell—! A goddamn Yankee?"

"Captain Abbott has been sent here on parole in response to Mrs. Ashley's request for medical and surgical help." Tibbs dropped a thick, official-looking envelope on the desk. "The general's letter to Mrs. Ashley will explain. . . ."

Ganty skimmed a glance of fury at Paul, transferred it to Tibbs. "You can turn right around an' take this fuckin' bastard right back where you found 'im! Mrs. Ashley don't want no goddamn Yankee sawbones going around killin' our patients. The general must be out of his mind!"

Yardley stepped forward with a languid smile. "Sergeant, Mrs. Ashley gave General Cooper the understanding that she was most seriously in need of a competent doctor. Captain Abbott's competence has been fully established. Colonel Robertson and dozens of his men had their wounds treated on the battlefield by the captain and the colonel has nothing but the highest praise for his skills and compassion toward our casualties."

"Robertson, hunh? He's one of the best damn colonels we got. . . . Well, I'll leave it to Mrs. Ashley to decide, but you two hang around in case you have to take him back." With an air of dismissing the officers, he turned to Paul. "Abbott, you come with me. . . ."

It was too much for Tibbs, who was still rankling from the insulting lack of respect from an inferior.

"Sergeant! You may be sure that your rude manner

270

and lack of military courtesy will be reported to General Cooper, and Mrs. Ashley shall be informed as well."

Ganty started rising with a growling sound in his throat. "Look here, you little shit—I don't need any of your pissy, birdshit regulations spouted at me!" He had risen to his full height behind the desk and now they saw that he had one peg leg. "I've given an arm and a leg in this war, but you two errand boys are still nothing but a coupla fancy stuffed uniforms to me. Now get the hell outta my sight until I send for you!"

iii

Christina Ashley had been gently bred. For generations her people had been gentlefolks, the *crème de la crème* of Virginia society. Exquisitely figured, favored with dreamlike beauty, she was a creature of peach-blossoms and snow, reared most properly to exhibit all of the lady-like attributes: a manner languid and quiescent, sometimes saucy; now imperious, now melting, frequently aggravating but always bewitching. Her speech had been trained to be soft and sweet, low-toned, musical. She had been accustomed since childhood to be waited on by servants quick to do her every bidding; unaccustomed even to putting on her dainty slippers or combing her Titian-red hair.

But that had been yesteryear. The brutal shocks of war and the loss of her aristocratic husband—his handsome visage shattered by the mushrooming impact of a leaden Yankee minié ball—had brought out an unexpected core of steel, exposed her velvet-sheathed claws, filled her with an undying hatred of everything Yankee.

It was a far different Christina Ashley that Paul saw now in the manor library as she sat at her Chippendale mahogany writing table with its gentle *s*-curved legs reading the missive from General Cooper. The auburn hair, flecked with highlights of gold, had been too hastily brushed; a few disarrayed strands of it hung down the sides of her pale face. Now and then her glance lifted up from the letter to flick over him in appraisal—unfavorably it was plain, for the greenish eyes sparked with hostility. The beautiful face looked a bit haggard, tired. She wore a simple lime-green calico dress, somewhat soiled and spattered in a few places with what Paul was sure was blood.

He surmised the reason. Previously he had been led through a once elegant living room but now so crowded with hospital cots that it was difficult to maneuver past them without brushing against the sheets. All the fine furniture—giltwood and marquetry consoles, marble-topped tables, Directoire mahogany armchairs, low sofas with claw feet—had been shoved back against rosewood and silk-lined walls to make room for them. Every cot was occupied. On all sides lay the sick, wounded and dying. Some lay stiff and still; some writhed, moaning, groaning, sobbing. Everywhere was pain; everywhere were bloodied bandages, the stench of sickness, sweat, blood, excrement. A few black people, both male and female, were moving among them changing sheets, bathing faces, changing dressings. From the looks of Christina Ashley's dress, it was obvious that she had been doing her share of the nursing.

She let the letter drop from her hand as her eyes swept over him with an expression of virulent hatred and scorn.

"If it were not for my great respect for General Cooper I would drive you off my property, although I would prefer to have you shot down like a dog."

Paul was more amused than angry. "And why, may I ask, would you wish to do that?"

"You dare to ask? As you entered my home, did you not get a glimpse of what your Yankee bullets have done?"

"I assure you it's no worse than what rebel bullets have done."

She stood up, head held high and haughty, and Paul saw that she was almost as tall as he was. The green eyes were frozen ice. "You overlook one great difference, Dr Abbott. In the South we did not seek war. We wanted—and still want—only separation. It is your loathsome arm of criminals—murderers!—who are shooting us down. You are the invaders and attackers. We are only fighting to defend our rights of self-determination."

"Madam, I have no desire to argue the rightness or wrongness of the war. I myself did not carry a weapon and do not believe in killing. I am interested only in helping the poor fools who have been caught up in this holocaust of misunderstanding. My medical abilities are at your disposal if you so wish. If not—"

"Enough!" she said in a cold, tight voice. "In his letter General Cooper assured me that you are a most competent surgeon. Even though it strains my credulity to trust a Yankee, our need for medical help is desperate. You will be allowed to remain here, but you must understand that even though you have been given your parole, you'll still be considered a prisoner of war, with limited privileges."

Paul gave a curt little bow. "And from whom shall I take my orders—aside from you?"

"Dr. Langdon Stanberry, who is in charge of the hospital, will supervise your medical duties. Cade Ganty is the plantation manager and will issue all other necessary instructions. As for your sleeping quarters . . . In view of our severe shortage of space, and since you Yankees are so ostentatiously democratic about Negroes, I'm sure you won't mind being assigned to one of the slave cabins—" With a tight little smile she turned toward Cade Ganty, who had been standing in the background.

"Cade, take him to Mammy's house."

iv

"Mammy's house," which was at the head of a long row of whitewashed slave cabins, was a bit larger than the others. Its most distinguishing difference, however, was not size, but the dead-white horse's skull that had been nailed to the front door. The empty, shadowed eye sockets regarded Paul balefully, revealing much.

Neither Cade Ganty nor Christina Ashely had any way of knowing that Paul, a Yankee, had for several years lived in Louisiana in close contact with hundreds of black slaves among whom voodooism was a most awesome and important part of their lives. He knew, for example, that the skull of a horse was the prime symbol usually marking the abode of a voodoo priestess or "conjure woman."

"Why is this cabin vacant?" he asked Ganty.

Ganty suppressed a grin. "Nigra woman who occupied it died a while back. Ain't been any need for it since."

Because no blacks would dare live in the former home of a voodoo priestess.

Nor would any Southern white lower himself to live in black quarters. It was Mrs. Ashley's way of insulting a Yankee.

Inside, the stale air had the musty smell of long-dead rodents. The only ventilation came from a broken pane in one of the two small windows. A floorboard was missing and the adjoining boards around the gaping hole were littered with hard little mouse turds. Here and there on the walls, which were papered with yellowed newsprint, were exotic symbols, some scrawled on with blue chalk, some smeared on with what Paul surmised was blood. A few withered plants and roots hung from the ceiling, and scattered about on the floor were several boxes of strange objects: one appeared to be full of dead mice, shriveled bats, a few dried-up snakes; another contained a collection of colored broken bottle glass, pebbles, rusted nails and bolts. Still another held balls of bright-hued yarns, chalk and misshapen crayons probably handmade from wood dyes mixed with melted bayberry wax, tallow or beeswax. A rusted iron cot with moldering blankets was the only furniture.

"This place will have to be cleaned out and repaired before it's habitable," Paul told Ganty.

Ganty could scarcely conceal his amusement. "I'll send Hunch down to talk it over with you. Hunch is our nigra overseer, you see. Nigras is like mules. Hunch is the only one who can make them move right smart." Turning, he stumped off on his peg leg, chuckling.

Hanging his jacket on a nail in the wall, Paul dragged out the filthy old cot. One by one he carried out all the boxes of voodoo esoterica and piled them on the bunk. In the midst of his endeavors, Lieutenants Yardley and Tibbs appeared. Both seemed embarrassed.

"We're leaving, Captain," said Yardley. "We just wanted to bid you goodbye and wish you luck."

"But isn't it rather late in the day for leaving? Hasn't Mrs. Ashley offered you beds for the night?"

Tibbs made a grimace of distaste. "She did—on cots right next to all those poor devils who are moaning, sobbing and dying all around here."

"And the stink. . . ." Yardley added. "Have you been in the warehouses where the worst cases are kept? Such filth and misery! I swear to heaven, hell can't be any worse. It's one part of war I'd rather not know anything about. No, we can hardly wait to get away from here. We'll take our chances on finding an inn before dark, or we'll sleep on the ground. Sorry we had to bring you into a situation like this, Captain."

Paul glanced around the miserable shack, grinned. "Well, I must say that even this is an enormous improvement over where I just came from."

After a final handshake, the Confederate officers departed.

A minute or two later a muscular black man strode up. His wide shoulders were grievously lopsided, one side rising inches above the other and the whole upper back bulged into what was commonly known as a "hunchback." Automatically Paul made his silent diagnosis: the man's malformation of the enarthrodial or ball-and-socket joint of the shoulder and the distortion of the large globular head of the humerus as it was received into the glenoid cavity of the scapula were probably due to the tuberculous inflammatory affection known as Pott's disease, either congenital or acquired early in childhood. Or it could have resulted from accidental injury or numerous other causes. In any diagnosis Paul was acutely conscious of his medical ignorance, of how little he, or any doctor, really knew about the endless, baffling assortment of human ailments.

Even more pronounced than the man's deformity was his manner. Beneath lowering eyebrows his dark eyes glared with hostility and the lips were drawn back in a tight line. The woolly hair matted close to his skull, his way of leaning forward, due to the humped back, and the long arms with their bunched muscles dangling a bit in front of him added to the impression of a very powerful gorilla seething with anger—but an impersonal anger directed permanently at the whole world and the cruel fate that had doomed him to that unsightly, hateful abnormality that kept his head bowed. But not his spirit.

"Mistah Ganty tol' me t'come down heah," he said sullenly, showing none of the Southern black man's usual subservience toward a white. "What yo' want, Yankee-doc?"

"I want this place cleaned thoroughly." He pointed to the floor. "Have that floorboard repaired and the place scrubbed down. Everything thrown out. Then I'll want a clean cot, clean blanket and sheets, a table, washbasin and a chair. There'll be other things, but that will be all for now."

"Yo'll git no nigra t'come in heah an' do any of dat. I send down de stuff an' leave it outside. Yo' have t'do de rest yerself."

Paul smiled. "Your people are afraid because your conjure woman died here, isn't that right?"

Hunch looked startled. "How yo' know 'bout conjure woman?"

"It's plain enough—" Paul walked over to the open door, took a firm grasp of the horse's skull and yanked it loose, tossed it rolling over the ground a dozen feet away. Hunch and a scattering of Negroes outside who had been watching stood petrified with horror.

His audience grew as he took several of the chalks and crayons from the voodoo box and began a sketch on the front door. Paul was not without skill at drawing, having done innumerable anatomical delineations during his training at the Edinburgh College of Surgery. Quickly he drew a vertical staff, and on top of it two wings. Around

276

the staff he made looping lines which soon became recognizable as two intertwined snakes. The blacks watched with wide-eyed wonderment and obvious fright as he started embellishing the drawings with colors. Yellow crayon gave a golden cast to the staff and wings; a crisscrossing of scales on the snakes in bright green drew gasps—green snakes being sacred in the voodoo cult. For good measure he added long forked tongues of crimson to the snake heads. His rendering was a rough replica of the ancient caduceus—the staff reputed in mythology to have been carried by Hermes, and which since the sixteenth century had been the symbol of medicine.

Above the sketch he printed in bold letters:

DR. PAUL ABBOTT
Surgeon and Doctor of Medicine

Turning, he smiled at Hunch. "I'm sure your conjure woman's medicine was strong, but you can tell your people that the Yankeedoc's medicine is much stronger."

Hunch glared back at him, his animosity seemingly undiminished.

"Now I'll thank you to get someone in here to clean and repair my cabin right away," Paul added amiably.

Hunch waited a few moments before responding, reluctantly, "Yassuh, Marse Yankeedoc, I do dat right away."

V

Within a half hour a procession of black workers began the renovation of Paul's cabin. A skilled carpenter came to rip up defective floorboards, replacing them with new-sawn white pine boards. Another replaced all cracked or broken windowpanes. Several women busily swept and scrubbed. A new cot with a fresh moss-stuffed pallet, clean

277

blankets, sheets and pillow arrived. Then a table, chair, washbasin and water pitcher. A cracked mirror. More than he had asked for.

Before they had finished, a slender young man of perhaps twenty-six appeared in the doorway. He had pale blond wispy hair, prematurely receding from his forehead, almost colorless blue eyes and a manner that was at once supercilious and diffident, as if unsure of his welcome. He glanced around with obvious distaste before his eyes sought out Paul.

"My name is Haywood Cheeves," he said by way of introduction, thrusting out a hand. "Mrs. Ashley sent me down to show you around a bit and apprise you of the medical situation." His tone was a strange blend of arrogance and meekness. His handclasp was soft, limp, effeminate.

"Then you are an assistant to Dr. Stanberry?"

Cheeves made another grimace of distaste. "Hardly that. I am the ultimate catchall of all the odious chores that nobody else has the time or inclination to perform. I do assist at operations but primarily I am the chief of bedpan nursing—a pure euphemism, since I lack all proclivities for such noble work and I lack any staff to speak of. You'd be astonished at how quickly all my Negro helpers are suddenly overburdened with other, more urgent tasks when I try to round up an excremental cleanup squad. I also serve, when she so desires, as Mrs. Ashley's secretary, and as her bookkeeper."

Paul smiled. "I'm sure that such chores are far more valuable to your cause—and to mankind—than shouldering a rifle and adding to the violence."

Cheeves flushed. "Are you implying, sir," he said huffily, "that I fear to shoulder a rifle?"

"Not at all. It goes against my personal belief to take the lives of good men to prove a point that ought to be settled by calm reasoning."

Cheeves's eyebrows arched. "You have no idea how surprising it is to me to hear a Yankee express some of the same thoughts that have troubled me since the beginning of the war. In any case, my lack of enthusiasm for carrying a gun was interpreted as the attitude of one with, uh, deviant tendencies, and I made no effort to disabuse the recruiting officers of such a belief. I happen to be a distant cousin of Mrs. Ashley's—from the poor side of the family—and it is due to her influence that I am now in this exalted position. Safe from bullets but not from the blood and gore. But I talk too much. . . . Would you care to have me show you around Monthaven?"

"I'd be most appreciative."

As they left the rows of whitewashed cabins that housed the field slaves, Cheeves pointed out and explained the uses of the various other types of buildings they passed. There were smokehouses for curing hams and bacon, a carpenter shop, wash houses and the quarters for the house servants, who were more privileged than the field hands. Their cabins were more substantial, with a chicken house and yard closed in by split palings for each family. Almost every inch of their small plots was crowded with vegetable and flower gardens and a fruit tree or two. Pyracanthas hedged the boundaries; honeysuckle ran riot over the palings; yellow cowslips splashed their brightness against cabin walls while sweet peas, pinks, dahlias and hollyhocks encroached everywhere they could gain root-hold. All trees were heavily leaden with ripening fruit.

Cheeves laughed. "Even when the plantation orchards fail, you can be sure that the black people's fruit trees will somehow bear cherries, peaches, apples or pears in mysterious profusion."

The fecundity of crops, the panoply of rich colors and fragrance of blossoms bespoke of happy days past—the splendid life that the Southerners were striving to preserve.

But so hopelessly, Paul thought with a touch of sadness. The tides of harsh change could not be held back. The grand old way of life for rich Southerners was fast crumbling, decaying—rotten at the core as symbolized by the stench of sickness that everywhere filled the perfumed air.

As they proceeded toward the long low tobacco warehouses, the stench grew stronger. One whiff of the putrid exhalations of rotting flesh, sour sweat, excrement and the other odious smells would have turned back most laymen, but Paul had long since trained himself to ignore it, and apparently Cheeves was also inured to fetid odors.

"These are the two main warehouses," said Cheeves. "Both filled almost to overflowing with patients."

"Where do they come from? How are they brought here?"

"General Ashley was rich and influential enough to get the railroad to build a spur of private line—a little over two miles of rail—for the purpose of transporting his tobacco crop. As you can see the rail sidings run right up alongside the loading dock—actually an ideal situation for unloading patients."

"How long were the casualties in transit before arriving here?"

Cheeves shrugged. "It could be a day or a matter of several days, depending on where they were sent from. Normally all casualties are sent to official military hospitals and we get the overflow. We get a new carload or more of them every few days."

"Where are you going to put them when all the buildings are filled?"

Again Cheeves shrugged. "The fact is," he said soberly, "they leave almost as fast as they come in—to the grave-yard, that is. Many are dead when they arrive and a large percentage die shortly after. About a half mile back behind the orchards, Mrs. Ashley has established quite an extensive cemetery for the poor devils who don't make it."

Inside, the noxious smells were so overwhelming that even Paul had to steel himself to continue. There were no cots, only rough pallets on the floor stretching out in end-less rows with bare walking space between each row. Lying there in the stifling heat pooled by sun beating on the roof of the windowless warehouse, patients lay almost shoulder to shoulder, head to feet, many of them adding to a cacophony of groans and moans, and some cursing as they tried to wave aside the swarms of buzzing flies that crawled over their faces, drawn by the blood and stink. A few lay stiff and still, dead or close to it. From all sides came the usual appeals for water. Several slaves walked among them with pails of water and dippers.

My God, Paul thought, *how can one doctor, or two—or even dozens—be expected to do much for these hundreds of desperately sick and wounded men!* It was more like a charnel house—a place where the wounded came to die.

As they walked along slowly between the pallets, rows of agonized eyes followed, begging for mercy. Some showed delayed surprise, then scowling hatred when they recognized the Yankee uniform. Paul ignored the hostility. In his eyes they were no different than the Yankee casualties, all pathetic, all victims of the same war machine. Again, as had happened so often during the war, he felt a depressive sense of utter futility. And hopeless rage. Men were dying on both sides by the thousands, but less from bullets and sickness than from sheer lack of the most elementary kind of medical help. On almost every other man were bloodied bandages made from torn sheets, strips of uniform, any old rag. Clumsily applied. Caked, stiff with pus and blood. Everything filthy. Gangrene, "hospital fever," pyemia, suppuration, erysipelas, mysterious intestinal inflammations, vomiting, general peritonitis, every type of infection ran riot in such conditions. Basic cleanliness was an impossibility. Each of these men was in desperate need of the skilled medical attention that he could never get, and as a consequence an appalling percentage of them would die. It was one of the bitterest lessons of war: the needs of the few had to give way to the needs of the many.

"Over here," said Cheeves, pointing to a corner of the warehouse, "are the most critical cases."

Paul's trained glance ran over the unfortunate men. They were all too familiar: victims of every manner of bodily destruction from smoothbore balls, the bursting charge of canister slugs or the newer soft-lead minié bullets that splintered bones so horribly that no medical magic could save a limb. Any abdominal or chest wound from such a bullet, tearing intestines and blood vessels as it did, was invariably fatal.

He noted one young fellow twisting about and groaning

from the intensity of his pain. Bandages swathing his right upper thigh were bright crimson from fresh seeping blood.

"That man's injury looks recent."

"He just came in today."

Going over to the man, Paul kneeled down and carefully drew aside the bandages. He frowned.

"This wound obviously hasn't been cleansed since the patient arrived, and it has already started gangrening."

"Dr. Stanberry said it wasn't necessary to fuss with it, since he intends to amputate tomorrow. At the hip, I believe."

"Amputate! Tomorrow? And where is Dr. Stanberry now?"

"He had an engagement in town to deliver a baby."

"To deliver a baby! Good God, any midwife can manage that! This man needs immediate surgery!"

Cheeves appeared embarrassed. "I am not in a position to question Dr. Stanberry's judgment, Doctor."

Paul made an instant decision. His medical saddlebags, which had been returned to him after parole from Libby Prison, were back in his cabin. They contained his surgical instruments as well as his bottles of carbolic acid, which were always with him since he learned of the theories of sepsis and antisepsis from Lister in Edinburgh.

"Mr. Cheeves, will you please return to my cabin and fetch my saddlebags. Also have someone bring a couple of basins of water, preferably hot, clean dressings, alcohol and if possible, a charcoal brazier."

"Surely, Doctor, you don't intend to operate on the patient now!"

"Why not now?"

"Dr. Stanberry would want to give his approval first. For another thing, it's rather late, almost mealtime—"

"Tell me, Mr. Cheeves, could you in good conscience enjoy your meal knowing that every passing moment was bringing this man closer to certain death? At this point think there's still time to excise the gangrene and save the leg, as well as his life. By tomorrow the gangren might have invaded the hip-joint, and then nothing could save him."

Flushing, Cheeves turned away. "I'll do my best to get everything you need, Doctor."

Three

Flowers of Evil

i

Paul moved wearily from pallet to pallet, making his first round of examinations of all patients. It was late forenoon, and due to the sweltering summer heat already above 100 degrees in the warehouse, he had removed his jacket, a habit common to battlefront surgeons, who often worked stripped to the waist.

It didn't help much. His exhaustion was greater than the heat. On the previous evening he'd worked until long after midnight. First had been the young fellow with the gangrening upper thigh wound. Cheeves and his assistants —two recuperating patients who could hobble about— had removed the patient to a table in the operating area and brought lanterns to illuminate the table. Cheeves, fortunately experienced in the use of chloroform, had produced the required amount from the medical cabinet. The torn tissues and splintered bone had been in the iliac portion of the thigh, a ghastly mess of inflamed flesh turning purplish with the whitish edges of necrotic tissue. Luckily, the great saphenous vein had not been severed. Paul had worked on far worse cases, but in this instance the need was to quickly halt the gangrene before it reached the hip joint. A hip joint amputation such as Stanberry had planned was a most formidable amputation at best. Few of the world's greatest surgeons had succeeded in doing one successfully. But if the gangrene had progressed too far, no surgery could help.

Lister and even the great Syme had praised Paul for his skill and great speed with a knife. It took Paul less than eighteen minutes of the most intense but at the same time delicate effort to extract splintered bones, trim away abraded tissues, tie off blood vessels, excise all diseased flesh and complete his applications of dressings soaked in his carbolic solution and covered with foil held with bandages. Cheeves had watched raptly, but with mystification.

"Are you using a new procedure, Doctor? I've never seen that done before."

"Yes. I'll explain it to you later, but for now I want to do what I can for some of the others."

For several more hours Paul had worked with a fury that seemed to infect Cheeves and the others. Willingly they raced around, doing his every bidding, fetching more water, keeping it hot on the brazier, bringing dressings. Paul insisted that each of them wash his hands in the stinging carbolic solution before going to other patients. Under the lash of such concentrated surgical and medical efforts, Paul always lost awareness of tiredness, aching bones, hunger—everything but the problem at hand. It lifted him into that state of grace that can only be induced by the total submergence of self.

This is what I was put on earth for. . . .

Later, they had been served coffee and food by Negro servants.

Then he had slept. . . .

But now as he bent over patients, exhaustion pulled his movements, rasped at his nerves. He had slept on four hours before being awakened by the clangoring of the slave bell.

From close behind, a low icy voice intruded.

"I see you're hard at work already, Dr. Abbott."

Turning, he saw Christina Ashley regarding him haughtily. Today she wore a bright yellow cotton frock, and tied about her waist an unbleached muslin apron. Her red-bronze hair was severely drawn back and tied at the neck with a yellow ribbon. Had there been a touch of sarcasm in her voice, he wondered?

"It's hardly early, Mrs. Ashley. It's getting close to noon."

"Still, one hardly expects a Yankee doctor to be in any hurry to treat Confederate soldiers—even before he's received any instructions."

Paul glanced around. "Well, thus far I've seen no Confederate doctor doing anything to help them."

A tinge of pink suffused her pale face. "Dr. Stanberry has been delayed in town. As soon as he returns I'm sure he'll give you all the proper instructions."

Noting her eyes running over his naked torso, he felt sudden embarrassment.

"I hope you'll excuse me for the informality of my attire. I had forgotten that there might be a lady present."

"I have been working among soldier patients for some time now, Doctor. If I'm not accustomed to male nudity by now, I never shall be." She paused; then her voice softened a trifle:

"By the way, Haywood has told me that you worked very hard and late last night, and I wish you to know that our efforts are appreciated—though of course I have no way of knowing whether the results will justify the efforts. I understand that you're using a new medical technique. I would prefer that you abstain from using it any further until I hear Dr. Stanberry's opinion."

He choked back his anger. He had seen enough and heard enough already to conclude that Stanberry was indifferent and callous as well as medically incompetent.

"I too am anxious to hear Dr. Stanberry's opinion. There is much I would like to discuss with him."

"I'm sure he'll be just as anxious to talk to you when he returns." With a parting nod, she hurried away.

ii

Lunch was served at a rough wooden table set up under an apple tree near one of the warehouses for Paul, Haywood Cheeves and the several ex-patients who were helping with the nursing. Henceforth, Cheeves had advised him, Paul would be taking all his meals with the white nursing staff.

It was a simple meal of soup, fresh white bread and butter, hot tea and peaches—just reaching maturity in the plantation orchards—for dessert. They ate in unnatural silence, which Paul attributed to his being a Yankee. He attempted to break the constraint with a question:

"Is Mrs. Ashley always so hardworking and attentive to the patients?" Since his talk with her, he had seen Christina Ashley, followed by a black female slave lugging a huge basket of peaches and cookies, going from patient to patient distributing the tasty items. Usually she paused a few moments to chat with each one, sometimes called for a basin of water to bathe a fevered face.

His question apparently touched upon a wellspring of warm opinion:

"You ask is she hardworkin'?" said one of the assistants. "Why, I seen Mrs. Ashley day after day working from the crack a dawn till dark. Sometimes after dark. Don't hardly take any time out to eat, either. Can't figger how she keeps goin' like that. Always cheery as a sunbeam, too. She's shore as close to bein' an angel as any female you'll ever find in this world."

"She's more'n that, Jeb," said another in a slightly reproving tone because the praise had been too scant. "There h'ain't no finer angel in heaven than Mrs. Ashley. Why, I wouldn't hardly be here today, 'cept for her. The was nights when I was so a-painin' and blue and so dam' fed up with ever'thing, I just *wanted* to die. Sooner the better. Then one night she comes around with a lantern and catches me bawlin' like a baby. Ain't shamed to admit that anymore. Man gits weak enough, he can't help it. Anyway, she kneeled down beside me an' held my hand for quite a spell. Even sang to me in the softest, prettiest voice ever heard on God's earth, or in heaven either. Right after that I knew I *had* to live. Just to please her. It's her I credit, not ol' Stanberry, for pullin' me through."

"Lucky you're such a homely bastid, Pike," said the man beside him. "Cade would've seen you to perdition, else—once she'd held your hand an' sung to you." There was a ripple of laughter, followed by:

"Yeah, it shore don't pay to be too good-lookin' when you're around Mrs. Ashley. I recall one young lieutenant, handsome as all git-out, came in here not hurt too bad— would have been fixed up an' out of here in a week, 'cept he mistook her kindness for the glad-eye an' kept flirtin' like a fool. Cade was fit to be hog-tied. One night the lieutenant's bandages got pulled off, kind of, while he was sleepin', which started him a-bleedin', an' he was dead before anyone found out. Now I ain't accusin' anybody, but—"

"But nothing, you fool! You gabble too much."

A moment's silence, then, defensively, "Why hell, I ain't sayin' nothing everybody don't already know. After Doc Abbott's been here for a while, he'll see for his-self. . . ."

"Ain't just Cade," added another. "Hunch is just as pertective. Hates everybody in the hull world—his own nigger tribe included—except for Mrs. Ashley. That nigger kisses the ground she walks on. Anybody hurts one little hair of her haid, Hunch, he'd rip 'is guts out."

Cheeves grinned at Paul. "As you can see, Dr. Abbott, Mrs. Ashley is our resident angel, and there's not a sinning devil around here who wouldn't protect her to his dying breath."

One of the black servants approached the table. "Doctah Abbott, suh, Doctah Stanberry asked fo' yo' to come right 'way to de numbah-two warehouse."

iii

Dr. Langdon Stanberry, hands clasped behind his fawn frock coat, stood peering down at the patient Paul had operated on the evening before. He looked to be in his sixties, with a beautiful mane of silvered hair, bushy eyebrows and claret-red cheeks in an otherwise pale face in which two small eyes blazed in anger as he turned and saw Paul.

"You are Dr. Abbott?"

Paul struggled to maintain affability through the fog of his tiredness and the air of hostility that greeted him.

"Yes sir. I'm pleased to meet you, Dr. Stanberry." He extended a hand.

Stanberry ignored the hand. "*Major* Stanberry, if you please. I hold a reserve commission." There seemed to be loathing in his face. Paul could now see the shriveled look of his neck, the parchmentlike texture of his skin around eyes and cheeks; age was creeping up on him rapidly. He wore a bright stock of lavender on a pristine white shirt. A diamond flashed from one finger.

"Yes, Major," Paul said stiffly. "What can I do for you?"

"Tell me, Dr. Abbott—what have you been doing to *my* patients?" He jabbed a finger at the patient Paul had treated on the previous evening. "Specifically, this one."

The patient, whose name was John, a sturdy young man, watched the confrontation between the doctors with worried eyes.

"My intention, sir, was to save his life."

"Which was precisely *my* intention, Abbott. Again I ask, by what authority, by what outrageous presumption, have you dared to interfere with the treatment of one of my patients?"

"Were you aware, sir, that the patient's wound had gangrened?"

"Of course. What else would you expect? Any open, lacerated wound will develop pyemia or gangrene within one to three days. That is why I planned to amputate—as you were informed by Mr. Cheeves. It is on record. That is why I still intend to amputate on the man today."

A look of stark fright passed over the patient's face. He cast a beseeching look at Paul.

"But there's no longer any need to amputate, Doctor. The gangrene is gone."

"Impossible. Gangrene doesn't just disappear by itself."

"I excised all the diseased tissues, Doctor—as you can see for yourself, if you care to examine the trauma with the dressings removed."

"I don't have to look to know what I'll see. Of course it's possible that you have cut away the superficial signs of gangrene, but that would only be temporary. As you well know—or should know—they will reappear soon enough. The poison is in the limb and there's no way to stop it—no way at all except to amputate."

"Even if there's no sepsis?" He had used the word "sepsis" although he knew it would ring strangely in Stanberry's ears. He was doubtless one of the majority of doctors who still attributed infectious ailments to miasmas that rose from swamps, basements, almost any dark corner, or even from the patient's unhealthy state of mind.

"My prognosis is already on record, Abbott. I shall advise Cheeves to have this man brought into the operating room at once."

"And that I shall not permit," said Paul.

Stanberry's mouth dropped open.

"You dare to countermand me—!"

Ignoring the man, Paul went forward and kneeled down beside the patient. With gentle hands he removed the bandages and then the strip of tinfoil. Under the foil was a piece of cotton bandage, hardened by blood and seepage from the wound. Carefully he pulled it away.

There was no pus, no stink, no scarlet inflammation—none of the dirty gray coating of gangrenous flesh. Instead,

291

the wound, albeit bloody, was clean, rosy and showing the beginnings of granulating flesh.

"As you can see," said Paul, "gangrene has not returned. This is a healthy, healing wound, and therefore there is no need to amputate."

Paul, expecting that he had proven his point, and would win some sign of grudging acknowledgment, was surprised at quite the reverse:

"No pus!" exclaimed Stanberry. "No laudable pus! Why, you have removed the most healing substance known to medicine!"

Paul fought back his fury. He should have known better than to think that he could bring enlightenment into the obdurate brain of a man basically stupid with probably no more than a country horse doctor's training who treated humans because it was more profitable. Stanberry's ignorance, however, was not totally his fault. The so-called "laudable pus" that seeped from all suppurating wounds had for thousands of years been considered by the medical profession as a sign of healing. Only in the past few years had the better-educated doctors in Europe, and a sprinkling of them in America, begun to recognize that this was not true.

"Right or wrong, Dr. Stanberry, a hip amputation such as you propose has rarely been successful. Even if you were a surgeon as great as Syme himself, the chances of this man surviving would be very slim. And since there's no gangrene now, why not wait a few days and see if it reoccurs before you subject this man to almost certain death, when, at the present state of healing, he stands an excellent chance of remaining alive."

Stanberry's voice rose to a thin, indignant bantam squeak. "Because I say so! For any Yankee dunce to question my procedures is an outrage beyond belief! I won't permit it. On the contrary, I intend to expose you for the ignorant surgeon you really are. I direct *you* to amputate this man at the hip."

He's just making noise now, Paul thought. *He siruts*

about like a turkey gobbler until his bluff is called. Then he resorts to barking like a scared dog. He doesn't really mean it.

"I realize you are only speaking in anger, sir—"

"Did you not hear me? I'm your superior, Abbott! I say, amputate that man's leg at once. That's an order!"

The patient's agonized eyes were riveted on Paul's face. Not speaking, Paul carefully replaced the dressings. As he was doing so, he noted that Christina Ashley was standing in the background. Frowning. How long had she been there, he wondered? Had she heard all the stupid words spoken? He stood up.

"That's an order I refuse to obey, Doctor—if you really are a doctor. You may arrest me, shoot me, send me back to Libby Prison—anything you want. I shall neither carry out such an improper order, nor stay here and continue to treat patients in any way but in accordance with my medical knowledge."

Christina Ashley walked up. Anger sparked from her brilliant green eyes. "Under the circumstances, Dr. Abbott, don't you think you're being out of order?"

Paul hazarded one of the few gambles he had ever attempted, since he was not a gambling man. "Have you heard our disagreeing words, Mrs. Ashley? Both sides of the argument?"

"I have."

"Then you be the judge. I'll submit to whatever your decision may be—whether Dr. Stanberry will doom this man to an amputation that almost certainly will lead to his death—or whether you will allow me to continue treating him and give him a chance to live."

"Your words are weighted in your own favor, Dr. Abbott. Let us see what Dr. Stanberry has to say—" She turned to the older doctor with a questioning expression.

"I say amputate!—*amputate*—!"

She looked down at the patient. Tears were streaming down his face.

"I'll leave it up to you, John," she said softly. "It's your body, your leg, your life. You decide."

"Please God—" he cried out, "let the Yankee doctor take care of me. . . ."

iv

In his cabin Paul lay back on the narrow little cot and tried to sleep. The night was still early, but he was drugged with exhaustion, a keyed-up exhaustion that crowded his head with racing thoughts and images and made relaxation difficult. It came from an undercurrent of elation due to winning a first round against the pompous Dr. Stanberry. Christina Ashley's support of the new aseptic procedure he was using to heal the patient John had sent Stanberry off in a huff. He had not reappeared throughout the day as Paul continued working at a feverish pitch, aided by the willing Cheeves and his assistants, in a drive to seek out and treat as quickly as possible every patient at Monthaven with suppurating wounds and/or gangrene. By some mysterious fashion, favorable words about the Yankee doctor had spread swiftly among the patients and all signs of hostility had vanished. Still, it was a Herculean if not impossible task to treat all of them. In any case, Christina Ashley's tacit approval of his method was a victory—his major medical victory since his entry into the war. . . .

In truth, Paul's experience as a surgeon for the Union forces had been continual frustration, disenchantments. With men being slaughtered by the thousands, the first dictum of war—*the good of the whole is more important than any of its parts*—was always uppermost. There was no time to treat a wound properly, even if the average undertrained army doctor knew how. It was always quicker, simpler, to lop off hands, arms, legs, cauterize or tie off the gouting blood, then bandage the butchery job. Give each a parting kick on the ass and get on to the next one. Paul's efforts to save limbs and lives by the use of carbolic had been foiled on every side, if not by the pres-

294

sures of time then by the inflexibility of the army establishment. Time and again his superiors ordered him to discontinue his carbolic treatment of wounds. Military surgery, except for recent acceptance of chloroform and opium for anesthesia, had barely advanced beyond the entrenched methods that had been used for hundreds of years.

It was ironic that having been forbidden by his own Union army to follow his new procedure, he was now in a position to prove its virtues for the benefit of the enemy. It was a procedure he believed in fervently. Once accepted by all doctors, he was convinced, it would revolutionize surgery, save untold thousands of future lives.

All thanks to Joe Lister. Paul would never forget that fateful day in Edinburgh when young Lister—then a supernumerary clerk to Professor Syme—had invited him to the Boar's Head for a glass of ale and the talk that was to change Paul's entire outlook on the profession he had chosen.

Inspired by the studies of Louis Pasteur in the new field of bacteriology, particularly those concerning putrefaction and fermentation, Lister was determined to find ways to apply the same theories to surgical procedures. Pasteur destroyed deadly bacteria by heat, or "pasteurization," which could not be used on humans without cooking them. Lister was striving to do it with chemicals, but until then had found none strong enough. Out of their talk had come the suggestion that carbolic acid—then being used in Edinburgh to good effect to disinfect and kill the stench of the sewage drains—might be equally effective in killing any kind of sepsis germs.

Lister had been jubilant at the thought, and both men had parted to carry on their separate experiments. Paul, first diluting the powerful acid with alcohol and water, had been astounded by the incredible successes of his own experiments achieved with the solution, and had made it a part of his doctor's armamentarium ever since.

As for the brilliant Joe Lister—whom Paul fully credited with the whole concept—he had not seen or heard from him since. Often he wondered where Lister was now, and how his experiments had turned out. . . .

Yes, today had been a success, of a sort. Even Cheeves and the assistant nurses had been much impressed by the new techniques. Already they were learning how to dress wounds in accordance with his teachings. His supply of carbolic was nearly gone, but Cade Ganty was departing on the morrow to obtain a new supply from commercial sources.

He rolled over on the cot, seeking a more relaxing position, but knew that sleep would be long in coming. It wasn't just because of his keyed-up state.

It was more because of that other thing—the loneliness that closed in like a dark, gloomy sky whenever he was alone, had a chance to think, to remember—

Micaela.

Never a night passed when he was not tormented before falling asleep, and even in his dreams, by the visions of her face. By sensory memories of her soft warm firm body in his embrace. At such moments he would turn and twist in the intensity of his desire and frustration.

Whatever she had done, whether she had betrayed him or not, his love for her remained as much a part of him as the pulse and beat of his heart. He could forgive her anything, but forget—never. *Never* would he be able to scrub from his memory that knowledge of her departure from the ballroom, happily laughing, with her former lover, Léon Jacquard. . . .

A knock on the door intruded into his dismal thoughts.

It was the black servant who had followed Christina Ashley carrying the basket of peaches.

"Massa Yankeedoc, Miz Ashley said fo' yo' to come to de liberry."

V

The door opened at once to his discreet knock and h found himself staring into her bright green eyes.

"Come in, Doctor. . . ." Christina Ashley's voice was low, melodious, with no trace of the animosity that usually iced her voice when she spoke to him.

As he entered, quietly closing the door behind him, his gaze was again drawn to her eyes, which seemed unduly bright. Or was it a trick of the lighting? A wall girandole cast its soft radiance over her face, highlighted her hair, which was now brushed out loosely, like burnished copper. She was wearing a simple gown of emerald green.

"Would you care for a drink, Doctor? A glass of brandy, perhaps?"

The unexpected cordiality and offer of a drink surprised him. It had been weeks since he had tasted liquor and he would have welcomed a few swallows, but something—some intangible sense of wrongness—made him hesitate. "Thank you, Mrs. Ashley, but—"

"Don't you dare refuse! It is by way of apology that I have asked you here for a little drink and a chat. Haywood Cheeves has told me so many admiring things about you that I feel shamed by my ungracious behavior toward you when you first arrived. You've been working so hard that I'm sure your nerves must be under strain, as mine are. I shouldn't have to tell a doctor that there are times when strong spirits are the best medication. So—" She looked at him expectantly with her bright emerald eyes and a tiny smile on her lips.

"The truth is," he said gladly enough, "I would much appreciate a bit of brandy, Mrs. Ashley."

"Ah, that's better. Do sit down and I'll get it." She indicated a chair, and going over to a sideboard, poured a crystal goblet half full from a cut glass decanter. Returning, she extended the glass.

"You must understand that I cannot join you with a drink. Southern ladies do not drink brandy—at least not when alone in the evening with a strange gentleman—although to be frank, I am uncertain as to whether I can still consider myself a lady. . . ."

"I would say," said Paul gallantly, "that never have I known one more deserving of the term. Your unselfish devotion to your cause, your hard work for the benefit of

297

others, the love and respect you have won from every-body certainly qualifies—"

"Nonsense! A prostitute devoted to our cause, or al-most any black female servant, might well perform the same duties, but by no stretch of imagination could they be considered as ladies." Her smile was mocking and her brilliant eyes gazed straight into his as if daring him to disagree.

Paul took a sip of the excellent brandy and kept his silence.

"In the South," she went on, "the definition of a lady embraces a far broader spectrum. To begin with, it is based on a proper background—something that no amount of money can purchase. You must inherit it just as roy-alty inherits the throne. It involves proper manners, yes, but all the proper, ladylike behavior in the world will not make a true Southern lady if she lacks the right ances-tors. However, I don't expect a Yankee to understand."

Was she trying to provoke him, he wondered? She wouldn't know, of course, that he didn't need to be told what was expected of a Southern lady. His first wife, Sylphide Beauvais, had been the essence of an aristocratic lady from a distinguished Creole family. He couldn't imagine Sylphide ever inviting a man of any class, high or low, into any kind of room without servants or others present to have a drink. Or talking as Christina Ashley was now. She was certainly acting strangely. And the ab-normal shine in her eyes. . . .

As if reading his mind, she laughed. "I do gabble on compulsively, in such a silly way, don't I? Not ladylike at all. It's my nerves. At the end of every day I feel so—so frazzled, so squeezed dry of all emotions. I've poured it all out. By day's end I could scream. But thank God I have my medication. It helps. . . ."

As she spoke, she walked toward a console against the wall. Her movements were languid, graceful. So unlike the energetic but tense way she propelled herself about during the day. From a silver tray on the console she picked up a small brown bottle and a spoon. Removing the bottle stopper, she poured out a spoonful of the contents and quickly swallowed it; then took another spoonful, after which she licked the spoon in a most unladylike way before replacing it on the tray. Turning, her smile washed over Paul in a bemused way.

"If it weren't for my medication," she said softly, "I would go crazy."

"And what is the medication you are taking, Mrs. Ashley?"

"It's just a sedative that dear old Dr. Stanberry mixes for me. I take it only in the evening when I want to escape from the horrors of the day. It does wonders for me. . . ." She shrugged jerkily, as if with a sudden chill. "But I don't want to discuss medicine or other morbid matters tonight. I am too conscious of seeing nothing but poor, maimed creatures who are already half dead, who will never again be the strong, vital men they once were. I cry for hours at night for the youth and beauty they have given to their country and will never, *never* regain. It is such a horrible price to pay—and for what? I no longer believe we have a chance to win the war, but we're still paying the price. All of our glorious youth are going down the drain, many of them dying before they've had a chance to live . . . the rest of them so crippled that if they do survive, they can never fully enjoy life again."

She had begun pacing restlessly, with the limpid fluidity of a puma, as she talked. "I can't seem to escape the subject, can I? It is the main reason I asked you to come here tonight, to help me forget war. I want so badly to talk of other matters, pleasanter matters, with a man. A *whole* man. . . ."

Paul was feeling increasingly uneasy. "Can you not talk of pleasanter matters with Cheeves or Dr. Stanberry?"

"Poor Cheeves is not quite a man in the sense that I mean it, and as for Langdon Stanberry—he's just the dry husk of a man. . . ." She stopped in front of him, weaving slightly as she looked down at him. Her lips parted in a smile.

"But you, Doctor, have escaped with your body undamaged. Please rise so I can see you standing, straight and proud."

Wishing to humor her and uncertain how best to handle the situation, Paul set his drink down and stood up. "As you can see, Mrs. Ashley," he said with a grin, "there's nothing remarkable about me."

She gazed at him as if pleasurably hypnotized. "But you're so wrong! I saw you unclothed to the waist today. . . . It has been many months since I have seen a *whole* man, still young and vigorous. Please unclothe to the waist again so that once more I can admire your hard-muscled, beautiful young torso."

"That would be improper," he said gently. "After all, I am not a slave on the auction block."

Her eyes narrowed. "You, a *Yankee,* are telling *me* what would be improper!"

"I have no slightest doubt that your late husband would say the same thing even more forcefully."

Her lips pressed together tight and thin. "Let me enlighten you on that matter, Dr. Abbott. My departed husband always held his head high and was a model of all human virtues. He was sweet, kind and loving to me always. I loved him throughout our marriage, was always a most dutiful wife, and now I cherish his memory. No greater love for me could any man have shown. But from the height of his awful majesty—quick to scold and scorn any woman who did wrong—he too had another side— such a different side as you are seeing in me tonight.

"Sooner or later you will notice at Monthaven—as you can see on almost any Southern plantation—a scattering of mulattoes who carry in their veins the same blood as their masters. It is one of the duties of a Southern lady never to see these things, but sometimes during the cold, pitiless hells of sleepless nights, we cannot avoid seeing most starkly the things we do not wish to see. Often I have wondered if that is the way God intended such marriages to be. If the strongest and most loving of husbands cannot always control his primal urges, is it not possible that loving wives too are sometimes tormented by physical forces which their brains seem to have lost the power to direct? Is moral perfection to be expected from women only, and never from men?"

Paul's embarrassment increased. "I don't think, Mrs. Ashley, that I am quite fitted to be the recipient of confessions of such intimate matters."

"Of such matters I shall say no more—I have already said more than enough to relieve any perceptive man of a sense of guilt. . . . Tonight I am not the same Christina Ashley you have seen during daylight hours—and shall see again tomorrow. Tonight I am just a woman full of vital juices who found herself excitingly stirred today by the sight of your naked torso—"

As if in a dream she floated against him and her arms encircled his fervently. "Hold me, Doctor . . . hold me tight. I am so starved for strong arms around me. . . ." Her head was tilted up, her lips parted. He saw now that the pupils of her glazed eyes were dilated. "And kiss me, please, please . . . for over a year I have not known the touch of a man's lips."

With ardent strength she drew his head down and her lips, fever-hot, crushed against his.

All too easily, Paul gave in to the intoxicating sweetness of soft female lips, the delicious, clinging pressure of her body. He too was starved. His arms tightened around her fiercely and the kiss was long-drawn-out, but in the background of the swirling turmoil of his aroused emotions, a faint alarm bell seemed to be ringing.

The glazed eyes, dilated pupils, her compulsive behavior. A woman possessed. . . .

With difficulty and almost as painfully as if losing a vital part of his body, he gently started disengaging her arms.

"No, no . . ." she whispered thickly. "Don't draw away. Unfasten my gown at the neck and help me disrobe. . . ."

This was not Christina Ashley talking. It was something else—

Freeing himself, he strode over to the silver tray on the console and snatched up the bottle of medication, un-stoppered it, sniffed. To make sure, he poured a bit into the spoon and touched it to his tongue. The characteristic odor and bitter taste beneath the sweetness of the men-strum were unmistakable.

Opium!

Yes, it would relax her, allow her to sleep and tempo-rarily forget the nightmares of the day—but all too soon create far worse nightmares with its subtle poison finally taking over full control of her body and brain.

She stood standing as in an uncomprehending daze. Her arms reached out for him again. "Doctor—don't you desire me?"

Holding the bottle, he walked over and grasped her firmly by the shoulders. "How long have you been taking this medication?"

"What difference does it make? Dr. Stanberry started giving it to me a month or two ago when I couldn't sleep. It's been the most blessed thing. Without it I couldn't—"

"There's nothing blessed about being addicted to opium. If you aren't already hopelessly addicted, you soon will be." He thrust the bottle in a pocket. "I'm taking it away from you tonight, and tomorrow I want to talk it over with you. You don't need this stuff."

"H-how dare you!" she began angrily, then immediately her smile grew soft. "But why should you care, Doctor? It makes me so happy, so loving. . . ." Her arms snaked around his neck again. "And your kiss told me that you're just as starved as I am. . . ." Again her hot lips sought his.

Again he disentangled himself from her arms, more roughly this time.

"I'm sorry, but you're not at all yourself, Mrs. Ashley. You're under the influence of a drug and tomorrow you'd regret everything—and so would I. I'll have to bid you goodnight for now."

Her eyes flared wide in disbelief and anger. A moment

later she swung. The flat of her hand smacked against his face smartly enough to jar his head back.

He retreated a step and bowed slightly. "Until to-morrow, Mrs. Ashley. Have pleasant dreams."

He strode out. He felt eyes of hate following him.

Four

Lady in Hell

i

Paul began his medical rounds early the next morning.
His sleep had been bad. He felt snappish, his nerves strung
out. By contrast, Christina had without doubt slept like a
log.

He knew because her behavior last night had indicated
the first phase of the effects of opium: pleasurable stimulation and excitation, often accompanied by hallucinations.
During such a phase the pupils of the eyes usually narrowed to pinpoints, but prior to the secondary phase—the
induction of sleep—the pupils tended to dilate, as hers
had been dilated.

Which was also a serious danger signal. Dilated pupils
resulted from the slower breathing induced by the drug,
and in the case of an overdose heralded the lack of oxygen
known as asphyxia. Death by suffocation.

None in the medical world knew how much opium it
took to constitute such a lethal dose—it varied widely

with individuals. It was known, however, that deaths from an overdose were a common occurrence in the East, especially in India, where some of the ayahs had the reputation for starting the craving for opium in infants by administering poppy juice to stop their crying.

No doctor in the world knew of any cure or counteracting drug for asphyxia from opiates.

Paul's knowledge about Eastern drugs had been gained from experiences in the asylums and workhouses of Edinburgh, where students from the Colleges of Medicine and Surgery were often sent to practice on the insane, indigents and malefactors in exchange for corpses needed for pathological studies. A surprising number of them were the emaciated victims of the Oriental poppy *Papaver somniferum,* which along with Indian hemp, or hashish, was easily available almost anywhere due to the continuous supply brought in by sailors and spice merchants. Some had begun their addiction innocently enough by getting intoxicated from eating the Oriental candy known as *manzouls*—a mixture of hashish and chocolate, honey or sweetened oils—commonly sold in confectionery shops, and then as their craving for stronger stimulation increased, moving on to opium. By then it was too late to break the habit, and they had no desire to do so. They lived only to reach those transient moments of drug-induced euphoria, and soon became incapable of honest toil, by necessity turned to prostitution and crime for the pence, shillings or pounds needed to gratify their increasingly insatiable cravings.

He had seen all of the deleterious effects—the scrawny, emaciated bodies, the deathlike coma, the moanings of those rolling around in their own excrement from intense pains in their gastrointestinal tracts or urinary systems, the demented, screaming ones in the "monkeys" from withdrawal. A more pitiful type of humanity he had never seen, for they had none of the nobility of the mangled victims of war.

They were considered as the scum of the world, and some of the luckier ones were hanged by the neck for thievery or other petty crimes created by their addiction. It made Paul's blood boil.

The ones growing fat from the profits of selling such drugs—well knowing the destruction they were wreaking on human lives—were the ones who should be hanged by the neck. Without compunction! It was just another example of weak laws and the lopsided forces of a money-crazed world that favored the knaves and punished their victims.

And Christina Ashley, a most generous, unselfish, cultured lady, was one of the victims. . . .

He continued moving among the patients, giving whatever aid and comfort he could, until Haywood Cheeves arrived.

"You're up early, Doctor." The blond young chief nurse was still rubbing sleep from his eyes.

Paul smiled. "My sleep was not as compelling as yours appears to have been. Tell me, Mr. Cheeves, how much opium do we have on hand?"

Cheeves was instantly alert. "As I think I told you yesterday when you inquired about our stock of anesthetics, there's been great difficulty in obtaining opium. Its scarcity is due to the Yankee blockade, I understand."

"But certainly you have *some* in stock."

"A very limited amount that Dr. Stanberry reserves for only the most painful, dying cases, and there's never enough even for that."

"You have the key to the medicine cabinet. I would like to see for myself the amount of opium on hand."

With apparent reluctance, Cheeves led the way to a wall cabinet in the smallish supply room at one end of the warehouse and unlocked it, revealing row upon row of glass-stoppered bottles and apothecary jars. He picked out a bottle clearly labeled *Opium* and handed it to Paul.

"This is all we have. As you can see, there's not much left, but Dr. Stanberry is hoping to receive more soon from the military."

The bottle was about one quarter full—nearly 1,000 ng., Paul estimated. It had the brownish-red look of unrefined opium that resulted after the milky latex juice of the poppy was fully dried, became brittle and fell into the raw powder form. Diluted in a tincture as laudanum, it would be sufficient to alleviate the agony of many patients.

Or sufficient to keep Christina sliding down the euphoric road to hell for weeks to come. . . .

If an overdose didn't kill her first.

"You may lock the cabinet if you wish, Mr. Cheeves, but I will retain the opium."

Cheeves's eyes widened in alarm. "You can't do that! Dr. Stanberry gave me strict orders that he alone is to dispense it."

"You may tell Dr. Stanberry that I will take full responsibility."

"You seem to forget that you are a prisoner on parole, Doctor. Granted that you are doing much for our patients, Dr. Stanberry is still in charge, and a very opinionated man. The least you can expect is that he will send Cade Ganty down and put you under arrest the moment he finds out. And of course, I shall be obliged to report all of this."

"I will take care of that when the time comes. I regret putting you in an awkward situation, Mr. Cheeves, but in this instance there is no alternative. By the way, did not Sergeant Ganty go to town today to get more carbolic?"

"He left early this morning with Hunch. They went by wagon since there were many other supplies needed."

Leaving the warehouse, Paul started back toward his cabin, passing Christina Ashley on the way. She nodded at him with a perfunctory greeting and the trace of a smile, making him wonder if she even remembered about last night.

In his cabin he took a hammer and pried up one of the old floorboards. In the ground below he dug a shallow hole with the claws of the hammer and put in the opium bottle wrapped in a cloth, covered it with earth, then hammered the board back in place.

308

ii

Repercussions came swiftly. . . .

Scarcely had he returned to the warehouse when Langdon Stanberry came storming at him. The elderly doctor's silvery hair was uncharacteristically askew, his pale blue eyes seeming to emit sparks, his cheeks flaming.

"In God's name—" he raged at Paul in his high bantam squeak, "what ever possessed you to confiscate our opium supply?"

"It was not confiscation. I felt obliged to take over the responsibility for dispensing it properly to prevent abuse."

"Sir! You are presumptuous and insulting beyond belief! You will return that opium at once!"

"That I must refuse to do."

A feminine voice intruded:

"Gentlemen, what is this altercation all about?" Christina Ashley approached.

"This man, this insufferable Yankee ass, has stolen— *stolen* I say—our scanty supply of opium and I want him arrested immediately!"

Christina looked at him with a flush of anger. "Is that true, Dr. Abbott?"

"I appropriated the opium for medical purposes, yes."

"Then you shall return it promptly to Dr. Stanberry."

"With all due respect to you, madam, I cannot do that."

"You refuse to obey an order? Do you realize I can have you imprisoned—or even shot?"

"I doubt that you would do that, Mrs. Ashley, since you must be aware that it would cost the lives of many of your wounded that otherwise I could save."

"Don't listen to the fool, Christina!" exploded Stanberry. "Call Cade and have him put under arrest!"

"But it's true, Langdon. We do need all the help we can get. Besides, isn't Cade to pick up the shipment of

309

opium that you're expecting? And then it won't really matter, will it?"

She turned to Paul with the shadow of a smile. "Your arrogance is insufferable, Dr. Abbott, but I will yield to it for the present in the interest of the patients. I shall expect you, of course, to continue treating them as you have been. As for your prescribing the medication I need—or forcing you to return my medication—I shall do without, thank you. When Cade returns, I'm sure that Dr. Stanberry can replenish all of the medication that I require." She turned and walked away.

Still glaring, but silent, Stanberry also departed.

At the end of the day when Paul returned to his cabin, another surprise awaited. The cot was upturned, the sheets, mattress and mosquito netting scattered on the floor. Some of the floorboards were pulled up or loose. His few garments and the contents of the medical saddlebags were also strewn about.

He was staring at the mess in dismay when Haywood Cheeves appeared in the doorway.

"I'm really sorry about this, Dr. Abbott. Cade returned late this afternoon without the opium shipment that was expected. Military supplies have run out and there was none to spare. Dr. Stanberry was fit to be tied and ordered your cabin searched."

"Was Sergeant Ganty able to obtain the carbolic?"

"Oh yes, there's plenty of that available. But Doctor, I don't think you know what a serious plight you're in. I'm sure Cade will be calling on you sooner or later—and he's a very dangerous man. . . ."

"I'll face Cade when the time comes."

"Meanwhile," Cheeves continued, "Mrs. Ashley is fast losing patience. She sent me down to get the medication you took from her and said that if you refuse, she'll take strong measures."

Paul took a small stoppered bottle from a pocket that he had already prepared with a teaspoon and a half of the opium menstrum. He handed it to Cheeves.

"You may tell her that I am putting her on decreasin

310

medication. Here is her dosage for tonight. Tomorrow I shall have another—a smaller one—ready. If she wishes to lock me up, there will be no more at all."

"We'll hope for the best, Doctor. Meanwhile I'll send somebody down to put your cabin back in order."

iii

Throughout the next day Paul wondered why Cade hadn't come to bully him into returning the opium. Had Christina decided to go along with his terms? Last night's dose had been his estimate of one-half of the usual amount she had been taking, and tonight it would be one-half less again. It was a brutal treatment that had been effective with some opium addicts. But it only alleviated and in no way saved them from the hellish pains of withdrawal.

Several times during the day he passed Christina in the warehouses and she would acknowledge his presence with the barest nod, her features again tensed tight, hostile. Soon the restlessness and beginning pains would grow worse and the craving become excruciating.

He only hoped that the reduced dosage he would send her tonight via Cheeves would enable her to get some sleep.

iv

With darkness a soft rain began. Its gentle whisper against the tarpapered roof made a pleasant, relaxing sound— the first pleasant sound he'd heard since he'd been at Monthaven.

Now again the loneliness was closing in around him like the mist that was rising from the drizzle against hot earth. Again the poignance, the pain of memories of Micaela. . . .

There was a timid rapping on the door. Not at all the way Cade Ganty would knock. He went to the door and flung it open.

She was wearing a hooded pelisse that muffled her to the chin, giving her a look that was almost nunlike in the evening murk. Before he could speak, she quickly slipped into the cabin and the hood fell back, revealing the copper aureole of her hair. Her face was sheened with the dampness of the mist.

"Close the door quickly, Doctor. I wouldn't want anyone to see that I've come here."

Paul closed the door. "You seem distraught, Mrs. Ashley."

"I am—*very*. Exhausted as I am, I can't sleep. I need the medicine that Dr. Stanberry mixed for me."

"I sent a dosage to you via Cheeves. Didn't he give it to you?"

Her eyes flicked down. "I-I'm sorry, but I was so nervous . . . I spilled it."

He knew she was lying. "That's a shame, Mrs. Ashley." He stepped closer. "Now look up at me so I can examine your eyes."

"Is all this necessary?" she said, frowning up at him. "All I'm asking for is my medication that you stole from me."

The pupils of her eyes had shrunk almost to pinpoints again. The harsh, unmistakable odor of opium was on her breath. Her face, too, was pallid. As she looked up at him she seemed to draw inward as if in a sudden chill. She began to quiver. He took one of her hands. It was ice-cold. She yanked it from his grasp.

"My God, Doctor—can't you see I'm *suffering?* I've been suffering all day—I'm in pain—I need sleep *badly* If I can get a good night's sleep, I'll be all right. Please stop torturing me like this and give me the medication need!"

"I can mix you a sedative of twenty grains of sodiu

312

bromide—it's very effective for sleeplessness and far less harmful—"

"But I don't *want* any other sedative—!" she half-screamed at him. "Why are you torturing me, Dr. Abbott?"

"It's the opium that's torturing you, Mrs. Ashley. Please try to understand what I'm saying. You're worse off than I feared. To give you opium to induce sleep now, I'd have to increase the dosage so much it would put you into a stupor. And tomorrow you'd need even more—and every day still more—with less results. Can't you see it's sucking you in deeper and deeper toward hell? There's nothing left for you to do but go along with my withdrawal program."

"Please, Dr. Abbott—can't you see the pain I'm going through? My whole body's on fire! Every bone aches . . . my stomach. . . . Please, *please,* give me some of my medication—quick!"

He looked at her sadly. He knew that communication with her was next to impossible. Opium had a way of destroying reason as well as the sense of morality along with the deterioration of mind and body. A true opium addict lied glibly, would promise anything, *do* anything for more opium.

If he could only break through to that fine intelligence he knew her to have—

"Forget your own pain for the moment, Mrs. Ashley, and think of the multiplied pains of the hundreds of men out there in the warehouses. Do you realize how many of them could have used a bit of opium to alleviate their pain? *They* must suffer without it. Did you ever stop to think that perhaps the medication you've been taking could have saved some dying soldier from agonies beyond belief? Agonies of which you have not yet the barest idea. But tomorrow you'll get a greater taste of it. For the next two or three days I'll give you decreasing dosages. There's no way I can save you from so much misery you'll wish you were dead. But you'll have to stick it out. There's absolutely *nothing else* that can save you—except death itself."

Her arms shot forward and caught his jacket with

frantic hands. "I don't *care* what happens tomorrow—I don't care if I die. Understand that, Dr. Abbott—I have no *desire* to break the habit!" Her voice rose to a shrill scream. "All I want is my *medication!* I want it *now!*"

Paul stood unmoving. The easiest way would be to put her in a stupor now with enough opium, but it would be only temporary and make tomorrow even worse. Each day that went by the more difficult if not impossible the act of breaking it off would be. Before he could decide on an answer, her trembling hands released her grasp on his jacket. Her eyes grew sly; filled with tears. Her hands slid up and suddenly pulled aside the pelisse, then darted to the front of her low-cut gown. Ripped. A thin tearing sound. Her breasts gleamed palely in the lamplight.

"Now, Doctor," she whispered huskily, "I will pay the ultimate price . . . anything. You may have me now. My body, everything. . . . Just don't make me wait any longer. . . ."

Her hands tore at his jacket and trousers, ripped at his belt. Wild sounds, half laughter, half shrieks, keened from her throat.

It took all his strength to subdue her, get her locked in his arms until her struggles ceased.

"You can let her go now, Doc—"

The speaker was Cade Ganty, who stood just inside the door with a pistol in one hand.

"You don't understand, Sergeant—"

"I understand plenty. I was right outside listening to every word." Stuffing the pistol under a belt, he stumped forward on his peg leg. "For your information, I was also outside the library door the night she asked you to come there. I was ready then, an' just as ready tonight, to blast you to hell if you'd took advantage of her condition."

"Then you know why Mrs. Ashley is not herself tonight?"

"I didn't know before but I do now. I seen enough poppy-heads when I was out prospectin' for gold in California to know what it does to people."

Christina, meanwhile, had bowed her head and was weeping silently. She submitted meekly as the two men drew the pelisse back around her to hide the torn dress and began escorting her back to the manor.

"By the way, Doc," Cade added, "any kind of help you'll be needin', just ask me. I'll back you all the way. Stanberry's no favorite of mine."

Book Six

NEW ORLEANS

One

The Beast

". . . hereafter, when any female shall, by word, gesture or movement insult or show contempt for any officer or soldier of the United States, she shall be regarded and shall be held liable to be treated as a woman of the town plying her vocation."

Order from General Benjamin Butler during occupation of New Orleans, 1862.

". . . in an address published to his troops, General Beauregard has referred to the infamous and beastly proclamation of Major-General Butler, of New Orleans, with respect to the women of that city. The terms of the order are of the most outrageous description. It is proposed that the Yankee soldiers shall revenge themselves for any insult or scorn, by word, gesture, or movement, which the women of New Orleans dare offer to the invaders of their homes, by being free to treat them in such circumstances as common harlots. The proposition is hideous, but characteristic of the Northern mind. If any appeal was wanting to steel the nerves of our soldiers, and to make them dedicate all they have of labor, of blood and of life, to the destruction of their enemy, it may

be found in this vile and brutal proclamation of the notorious libertine and coward who insults the unhappy fortunes of New Orleans by a proposition to license in its streets crimes that would shame a Comanche."

From an editorial in a Southern newspaper, 1862.

i

The forenoon sun was bright and cheery, but did nothing to lighten the heaviness in Micaela's heart as the barouche rolled down Royal Street. The last time she had seen New Orleans, the city had been pervaded with gaiety, an ebullience of spirit that no previous deprivations of war, holocausts of fire, epidemics of yellow jack or other fearsome pestilence had been able to quench. Normally the streets had been thronged with hawkers, peddlers, bright blanketed Indian women, red-turbaned mulatto women, check-suited gamblers with diamond rings on their finger and gaudy *femmes de plaisir* clinging to their arms; and mingling among them, quite democratically, a sprinkling of the gentry garbed more richly but only a bit less flamboyantly in the latest Parisian fashions.

Today, the streets were all but empty; cloaked in the silence of fear. Within view were only a few creaking wagons, a stray dog, a cat slinking up an alley, several civilian pedestrians and a group of swaggering Union soldiers. On April 25 in this year of 1862, New Orleans had fallen to Union troops under the command of General Benjamin ("Beast") Butler. The Beast now ruled the city with a cruel, iron hand.

On arriving back in New Orleans two nights ago, Micaela had gone directly to the home of her close friend Danielle D'Indy, in whose elegant coach she was now riding. Danielle, a sparkling-eyed beauty who dimpled whenever she smiled, was, like Micaela, an octoroon. Danielle's mother, a quadroon, had been the lover of a very wealthy Creole bachelor, now deceased, who had left his entire fortune to the mother and daughter, so Danielle had need to seek a rich *protecteur* of her own. She had met Micaela's friend Mike Quinn the gambler, and had fallen in love. They would have married except that Louisiana law forbade marriage between whites and those with even a drop of black blood in their veins, and Danielle would not change her residence to where such laws did not prevail because she wished to stay near her mother, who was gravely ill. When the war broke out, Mike's steamer had been in a Northern port and was commandeered by the Yankees. Danielle had not seen him since, though letters from him still got through and their love remained strong.

The two friends had spent half of the first night exchanging news, but concerning Jacquard and the information Micaela most fervently sought—news about her child, Rill—Danielle could offer little:

"I know that Jacquard is back in New Orleans—profiting greatly from shady schemes he works out in collaboration with unscrupulous Yankee politicians and army officers, they say—but I know nothing about his household. However, my servants can easily find out from other servants everything that goes on behind closed doors. Tomorrow I shall send them out to inquire."

The next day the joyful information was brought back. Yes, there was a white baby at Jacquard's town house; also Micaela's former maid Aurora and her baby!

Micaela could scarcely wait to rush off to a high-ranking Union officer—perhaps to General Butler himself—and make her complaint, confident that with the proof at hand—her baby in Jacquard's custody, and Aurora to testify to the kidnapping—any reasonable official would surely help to redress the wrong.

But Danielle cautioned her: "You've not been here long enough to know that the Yankees, by order of their highest general, treat all Southern women as scum." She then told of General Butler's infamous order that authorized any soldier or officer of the Union army who felt insulted or displeased by a Southern lady's attitude to treat her as if she were a common harlot.

"It is why today you rarely see a lady on the streets—

and why I only venture out in a coach with the curtains drawn."

"*Mon Dieu!* Have they no respect for womanhood?"

"None! Nor for the church. Our clergymen have been ordered to include, in every morning prayer in all churches, the words 'for the President of the United States and all in civil authority.' Those devout clergymen who believed that in their prayers to His Holiness to give equal importance to secular individuals would be sacrilege, and therefore refused to comply, had their churches locked up by General Butler."

"*Mais, c'est terrible!*"

"*Hélas*, that's not the worst. One of our most patriotic citizens—a Monsieur Mumford by name—could not tolerate the sight of the Union flag flying in Jackson Square. He climbed the flagpole and tore it down—a most rash thing to do, of course, but he was impelled by his own loyalties to the Southern government. General Butler ordered him hanged by the neck like a common criminal."

"*Mais non!*" Micaela gasped.

"So now you see that you cannot expect much help from the Yankees."

"But since I am the widow of a Yankee officer—surely they will show me consideration, *n'est-ce pas?*"

"*Peut-être.* Perhaps that will make a difference. . . ."

ii

The man behind the desk had a lumpy, oversized body. He was double-chinned and pot-bellied. His major general's uniform, however, was immaculate and impressive. One of his eyes, which were focused in two separate directions, appraised Micaela. A touch of scorn curled his heavy lips.

"I am a very busy man, madam, and I'm so sick and tired of the imperious sluts of this town demanding my time to complain about my troops carrying out their lawful orders that I wouldn't have allowed another female in my office, except that I was informed by my orderly that you are the wife of a Union officer."

"The widow, sir. My husband, Captain Paul Abbott, who was lost in action, was a surgeon in the Army of the Tennessee."

"Grant's army, hmmph? My only comment to that, madam, is it's a shame he wasn't assigned to the service of a more competent general. Your complaint, whatever it is, should more properly be taken to Grant's headquarters, or to Washington. But since you're here, please state your business, and make it as brief as possible."

"My reason for seeking your help, sir, is because my child—our child—has been kidnapped by a citizen of New Orleans who is holding her for ransom."

General Butler's eyebrows arched. "Ransom for money? How much?"

Micaela flushed. "Not for money, sir. This man has demanded that I leave my husband—he does not yet know that he is dead—and join him."

Butler essayed a smile. "Madam, I don't see the problem. If your husband is dead and this man is that enamored of you, why not grant his desires and go live with him?"

Her flush deepened. "But I do not love this man, sir. I detest him. I beseech you to go to this man, whose address I now have, and force him to return my child."

"I have only your words to go on, madam. How do I know you're telling the truth? All women have fanciful imaginations. What evidence do you have to support your allegations?"

"My former maid, a Negro girl named Aurora, was kidnapped at the same time and is now living at the home of the kidnapper as a captive. She can testify to the truth of my statements."

Butler gave an impatient shake of his head. "Black people are notoriously unreliable as witnesses. Since it is just your word against this alleged kidnapper, I would like to know his side of the story. What is his name?"

"Léon Jacquard."

The general looked startled. "Jacquard, you say?" Frowning, he rose from his chair and began pacing back and forth behind the desk, brows scrunched in deep thought. Then:

"I'll tell you what I'll do, madam. I'll have the provost marshall's office check into the matter at once. Meanwhile I have urgent duties awaiting my attention. You can wait outside in the anteroom until I've had a chance to think this over further, and I'll call you back after I've decided on the action to be taken." He gave a nod of dismissal and Micaela went out feeling less hopeful than when she had gone in.

As she left the office, heading toward a chair in the anteroom, an astonished voice accosted her from behind:

"Micaela! Is it really you?"

She turned and saw a most attractive young woman with a pale cocoa complexion emerging from another office. An officer wearing a colonel's insignia stood just behind her, self-consciously adjusting his clothing.

"Solange! What are you doing here?" Solange, who had been one of the Madame Silkwood girls that Micaela had known years ago, rushed up and embraced her with a cry of delight.

"I'm surviving, so to speak," Solange answered with a laugh. "The situation in New Orleans for such as you and I is not what it used to be."

"What of your *protecteur*? Does he not take care of you?"

"*Hélas*, I have no *protecteur*. All rich young Creole gentlemen have gone off to war, so I must do what I can to maintain my style of life. Fortunately, Madame Silkwood is of great help to me."

"Then you are still living with her?"

"Ah, *non*, her home is no longer the same. The elegance is gone. It is only a place of business to supply Union soldiers with the pleasures they seek. I myself have my own apartment, and Madame Silkwood arranges for me to meet only gentlemen of the officer class."

Micaela was suddenly aware of the colonel, still in the doorway of his office, leering at her with an appreciative smile. She felt embarrassment both by the officer's stare and by Solange's implicit admission that she was but a prostitute.

"What a shame," she murmured.

Solange shrugged philosophically. "One must do what one has to do. The only important thing these days is just to survive. But I must go now—perhaps we shall see each other again soon. . . ." She hurried off.

Finding a plain wooden chair against the wall in the anteroom, she sat down to wait.

Officers came and went, most of them walking stiff and erect, on errands to see General Butler. A few of the callers were civilians from the North—she could tell because they always seemed more brashly dressed than Southern gentlemen, and their voices were often loud and coarse, carrying plainly through the office door. One of them spoke angrily:

". . . makes me sore as hell, Ben, all these goddamn Jews that Grant's been letting through his lines to buy cotton."

"Why are you worried? Don't you already have all the cotton contracts you can handle?"

"Sure, but it's the principle of the thing gets me. Here you are, my own brother, setting right here on the whole pile of shit and letting the Hebrews in to take advantage of the war situation. They're gonna make ungodly millions."

"Business is business. They're paying double the percentage you're paying."

"I ain't complaining of that, Ben. You've been fair, like a man should be to his own brother, but Jesus to hell—*Hebrews!*"

There was the clink of glasses. Oaths. Laughter. Another snatch of the general's words:

". . . can promise you one thing. If anybody is going to make ungodly millions down here, it won't be the goddamn Jews!"

More laughter, clinking of glasses. . . .

After another interminable wait, an orderly appeared.

"General Butler requests that you come to his office, ma'am."

Reaching the open doorway of the general's office, she stopped in sudden shock. A tall, swarthy man stood there watching with a sarcastic grin.

"Jac! H-how did you get here?"

Jacquard bowed slightly in mock courtesy. "I entered the general's office by a side door to add to the pleasant surprise I see on your face. You see, my dear, I have been expecting you to arrive sooner or later, and the moment I received the general's message I hastened here at once."

Micaela was stunned. "You-you're a friend of General Butler's?"

"More than that, my dear. We are business associates. But that doesn't concern you. . . ." Jacquard swung toward the general, who sat behind his desk with a formidable scowl on his face. "General, will you please explain to madame the things we have discussed."

The general cleared his throat. "Madam, facts brought to my attention by Mr. Jacquard have completely altered the picture. Mr. Jacquard claims that the infant in question is his own."

"*Mais non! Impossible!* It is my child, fathered by Paul Abbott!"

"You can prove that?"

Instantly she realized that was impossible. She had been living with Jacquard up until the day she escaped via boat to flee North with Paul Abbott. They had married almost immediately. She *knew* the child wasn't Jac's, *couldn't* be Jac's, but how could she prove it? Even the birth records in the North would not be conclusive.

"I would swear on a thousand Bibles that Paul Abbott is the father."

Butler let out a snort of laughter. "I was trained as an attorney, madam. There are as many lies sworn on th

Bible as there are criminals. To get on, do you admit to cohabiting with Mr. Jacquard?"

"Yes."

"Do you admit that you signed an agreement to cohabit with Mr. Jacquard, in accordance with accepted Creole custom, in exchange for a substantial amount of money paid to you, your mother and a certain Madame Silkwood who was the intermediary?"

"I signed such an agreement, yes, which specified that Monsieur Jacquard was to become my *protecteur*."

"And did you not default on your written agreement by absconding with another man?"

Micaela flushed. "Monsieur General, it is the obligation of a *protecteur* to treat the woman he has selected with the same kindness and consideration that is accorded any wife. It is a matter of the highest morality among Creoles and according to custom, a woman is also free to leave a *protecteur* if he defaults in his obligations. I left Monsieur Jacquard because of his brutality toward me."

"The law is never concerned with the moralities of a situation, madam, only the legalities."

"But in any New Orleans court where Creole customs are honored—"

"At present I am the law in New Orleans by authority invested in me by the United States Government, and as such, I have heard all I need to know."

"What about my baby—?"

"Madam, you seem to be unaware that you have broken the law in several serious respects. When you signed that agreement with Mr. Jacquard, you indentured yourself under a firm contract, and since you broke that contract, Mr. Jacquard is entitled to redress."

"But—"

"I'm not finished, madam! You have also made charges—very serious charges which, if unsubstantiated by strong evidence, could send you to prison for uttering such infamous slander. However—"

He leaned forward on the desk and focused one eye on her sternly. "Since I am a very fair man, I am willing to have all charges against you dropped—with Mr.

327

Jacquard's consent—if you are prepared to fulfill your signed agreement by returning to him and your child."

Micaela's heart sank. She knew she was outmaneuvered. Her position was hopeless.

"Come, my dear . . ." Jacquard said gently. "I forgive you freely. Come home with me and you shall have your child again—and I promise to treat you with the kindness and consideration that you so richly deserve."

Numbly she stood up and without another word walked out, utterly desolate, with Jacquard close behind her like her own inescapable shadow.

Two

In the Lair of the Fox

i

Clasping her child in her arms finally, feeling the beat of the small heart against her own, a great weight seemed to fall away from Micaela. All the obstacles she'd had to overcome, everything she had suffered, had not been in vain after all, if only for this moment. Rill had grown and changed, even in so short a time—and so plump! Obviously she was healthy and well cared for, and now was cooing with pleasure to be cuddled in her mother's arms again.

Jac, out of some unsuspected sensitivity, or for less noble reasons unknown, had left her alone with Aurora and the two children after their first joyful, tearful reunion. Aurora had sobbed and Micaela had sobbed as the two women embraced, and even Aurora's child, Samuel Paul Lincoln, gurgled with joy. They had been treated well, Aurora assured her. Jacquard's lavish house in a fashionable area of the city had a beautiful walled garden in the rear where Aurora was allowed to take the children each day. Otherwise she was not permitted to leave the house with Rill and there were always one or two rough-looking white guards to assure that Jacquard's orders were obeyed.

Micaela's happiness was all too short-lived. It ended with the sudden appearance of Jacquard in the doorway.

"Follow me, Micaela . . ." he ordered.

Nervous tremors raced through her as she followed the tall, powerfully built figure. There was a certain angry tightness in his stride that filled her with forebodings. Now that he had her so completely in his power, what did he intend to do with her? He continued up a winding staircase and into a pleasant sitting room. Swinging around, he faced her with a thin smile.

"Are you quite satisfied that your child is in the best of health, my dear?"

"I am so relieved! I must be honest and say that one of my worst fears was that you might have mistreated her. You are an evil man, but you also have goodness in your heart, and for keeping Rill healthy and happy I am immensely grateful."

One corner of his mouth pulled down in the sardonic mannerism he had when about to say something hurtful. "You give me too much credit, my dear. It was not out of the goodness of my heart that I have seen to the well-being of your brat. It was only because of her value to me in getting you back under my control again."

"What is it you want of me, Jac? Did you go to such extreme, dastardly steps just to get me back to be your mistress again?"

He broke into a harsh laugh. "What a presumptuous question! After all the shame and humiliation you've made me suffer, do you think we could ever just pick up where we left off? You fool! Have you forgotten that you had your opportunity—but instead chose to spit in my face and then to rub salt in my wounds, run off with that despicable Yankee, my worst enemy?"

330

"If you can't forgive me for loving him, you should at least be able to forget, now that Paul is dead."

His voice swelled with rage. "Forget? Never in a million years! You have dishonored me, stabbed me to the heart, made me a laughingstock among my friends. For years the pain has been like a thousand devils eating me away inside. I can find no rest, no peace until the score has been settled—"

"Settle the score—?" she cried. "You have already more than settled the score by your cruelties and foul deeds! If it's my life you want—"

Again his harsh laughter. "Your life? That would be too easy. Even if you had a thousand lives and I could crush each one of them as slowly and painfully as possible, it would not be enough. No, I have plans for you that will make you wish you were dead, but you won't take that way out because it is only while you are alive that no harm will come to Rill."

A cold sinking feeling chilled her. Jac did not make idle threats. There was something insane in the way his jet eyes shone as if from deep fires within. What could he do to her beyond his normal sexual brutality? Whip her? Disfigure her? She shrank back from him. "You must be insane, Jac, to have so much hate in you!"

He bared his white teeth in a smile. "Call it what you wish. But it is all I have been living for the past year, to get you completely in my power and—"

"And what, Jac?"

"And turn you into the lowest, rottenest whore in town. The whore that you really are at heart. All the *canailles,* the scum and dregs of the Union army, will have their fill of you. You will live in the basest, foulest whorehouses with vermin and lice crawling over your face while the most scrofulous riffraff from the gutter crawl over your belly until you have lost all your freshness and youth and beauty, until even the basest whoremasters kick you out into the street with the other discarded, pimply strumpets; until even the drunken niggers will scorn you and turn away in disgust."

"There's no way you can make me what I am not! Never have I allowed any man to touch me without love! Had you not professed to love me in the beginning, I would not have agreed to live with you. I intended my affection for you to grow into love and it could have if you had shown me a little of the love I craved—"

"Come now, your sentimentality is out of place. As for what you *choose* to do, you'll do exactly as I tell you because you have no choice. If you do not, accidents could befall your beloved brat—a fall from her carriage, perhaps under the wheels of a coach; a crushed leg, a lost eye—who knows? She could grow up crippled and ugly."

She shrank away from him. "You could find it in your heart to harm an innocent child as a way of hurting me?"

He almost spat it out: "There's *nothing* I wouldn't do to hurt you in the most painful way possible!"

"Jac—your hate has destroyed your mind—you talk like a mad beast!"

"You should be grateful that I am. I would put my plans for you in operation immediately—except for that crazy side of me I cannot control. . . ."

"And what is it besides your temper that you cannot control?"

He bared his teeth. "The one thing I still cannot control is the animal in me. My brain is for naught when I am a captive of physical desire. I've lain awake more nights than I care to remember thinking of your accursed body in my arms. I *hate* you, yes—such a deathly hate I can never for a moment forget, and yet—even yet—my body burns and yearns for your body with a greed that nothing but the fullest satisfaction can ever assuage. So enjoy it my dear, while I get my fill of you before I throw you aside to your wretched fate."

Again she shrank back in horror. "Surely you can't want my body when you feel such inhuman hate for me!"

"How little you understand male nature, my dear. . . ." Striding over, he caught her hand brutally in an iron grip and yanked her toward the doorway at the end of the sitting room. "I shall now give you a taste of wha

332

you spurned when you gave me up for that miserable doctor!"

He pulled her through the doorway into what was plainly the master bedroom and threw her sprawling on the silken-sheeted bed.

ii

Scarcely waiting for her to recover from her sprawled position, he half fell across the bed and hooked furious fingers under the low bodice of her expensive gown. Ripped. Kept ripping, tearing—petticoats and all—like a starving dog after a choice piece of meat, until the nakedness of her body was exposed all the way down the front.

Rigid, sick with revulsion and dazed with shock, she gazed up at him in disbelief that even he could be so savagely insensitive. He was standing now, eyes shining in a frenzy of passion as he began pulling off his own garments.

"You no longer have the need for respectable gowns." His cheeks were taut with the anticipatory grin that always preceded further cruelties. "Henceforth you will only wear dresses appropriate to your status as a whore."

She forced herself to lie still as the bed sagged under his weight. Hurting hands gripped her knees, bringing pain, parted them with a fierce disregard for anything but the frenzy that now possessed him. He was on his knees, towering over her like a dark, avenging devil. The jet black eyes—those terrible burning eyes—stabbed down at her with such a fury of hate that she wanted to avert her head, but could not because they were so hypnotic. Long black hair tumbled down both sides of his face—a face of drawn tight lines that transformed the evil in it into something almost ascetic from the very intensity of his passion. Everything about him seemed flexed to an overwound, tight readiness, like an animal poised to spring: the wide, muscle-bunched shoulders, the broad furred chest tapering to the hard flat belly, flanks—and the thing jutting from between—

When bruising fingers moved over her body, grasping cruelly at her breasts, the nipples, she had to fight back an impulse to struggle, knowing it would be worse than futile; it would only incite him the more. She turned her head and stared stonily at a wall while his hands continued greedily exploring the vulnerability of her cringing flesh. In spite of the heat she was cold—so cold! How could she stand it? How could she endure the violation of her body by this cruel lusting beast who was now so much worse than she'd ever remembered, a beast who knew nothing of love?

She closed her eyes, her memory fleeing back to Paul. To love. Love was the seething pulse of blood in her veins when Paul embraced her. It was like the seethe of flames roaring through dry grass. Flames that lifted her soaring to the clouds in arms that were as gentle as they were strong and urgent. It was Paul needing her as she needed him.

Not like this—

He could wait no longer. His hips jerked, thrusting downward, and he penetrated her with one fierce plunge. Inwardly she screamed wildly, but kept her body lax. Lax with despair, pain, hopelessness.

Without withdrawing he lay over her for a moment as if wounded, exhaled a demented moan: "*Mon Dieu,* have waited an eternity for this . . . !"

But a moment later he drew back and began thrusting anew, as if in a frantic need to devour her. . . .

Slowly, with a sense of horror, she became aware of a beginning response in herself. Small pulsating tremor started in her vitals. An expanding heat. Mentally she struggled against it—oh, treacherous body! Despite her long-pent-up hunger for love, how could her body betray her to a beast she despised? She moaned deep in her throat and began to meet his thrusts with a deepening urgency of her own.

Instantly he was aware of her arousal. "Hah!" he exulted. "You have proven you are a born whore! You pretended to be cold on the surface toward me, but your body is like a furnace at highest heat now that I've set you aflame." The vigor of his thrustings increased in their insatiable fury.

She sobbed in outrage and anger as the unwanted sensations in her body mounted.

A triumphant laugh burst from him. "Now, foolish slut, maybe you'll see what you lost! After knowing me, how *could* you—how could *any* woman—ever prefer him to me!"

iii

She awoke in the grayness of morning; into a gray fog of sickness so nauseating, so loathsome that she wanted only to fall back into the blackness of slumber and never wake up. Inside she felt all sore, emptied, dirtied; a used, discarded receptacle. She couldn't remember how the evening had ended; only that Jac had forced his groaning, thrusting pleasures on her again and again, maddened with insatiable sexuality. Untiring. Brutal. Not just sex; certainly not love. Rape. She had escaped into unconsciousness before he was finished. All through the night she had lain in a half-sleep, half-conscious state of numbness, dully aware of only two emotions: self-disgust—and hate.

Never before in her life had she known what it was to truly hate. Anger, yes, but never to the extent of the icy fury that roiled through her now. Given the opportunity, she knew she could kill Jac without the slightest compunction.

But an impossibility, because she also knew that punishment would swiftly follow. Jac was an important man among the Yankees, whose iron ring encircled the town. Then what would happen to Rill?

335

Because of Rill, another alternative she longed for—suicide—was out of the question.

The only alternative left was to endure his heartless bestiality.

She glanced around at the disarranged bed, at the forlorn remnants of her torn garments on the bed and floor. None of Jac's clothing was in sight; there was no evidence of his having slept in the room. Where was he now, she wondered?

The bedroom had a private bath, in which she bathed and scrubbed until her skin shone pink. She searched in closets for apparel, but found nothing she could wear except one of Jac's robes. Shuddering with revulsion she put it on. There was no choice.

She found Aurora downstairs in the nursery with the two children. The black girl's eyes were sad. She knew.

Micaela forced her voice to sound normal: "Where is Monsieur Jacquard?"

"He go out," Aurora said sullenly. "Don' know when he come back."

Micaela glanced at the door leading into the garden. "Aurora, do you think there's any chance I could slip out with Rill and find a place to hide?"

Aurora shook her head vigorously. "Nebber! Dey a guard in de garden an' one in de front. Dey bad. I hear 'im say to guards watch sharp yo' don' try to run away."

"Where are the babies?"

"Dey takin' de naps."

Micaela went in and looked down at her sleeping child, yearning to pick her up and hug her, and at the same time thinking, *Someday she'll grow up and know what her mother will have become. Could I ever expect her to understand—and forgive me?*

Feeling chilled, she went back to where Aurora was preparing a *petit déjeuner* for her. She ate listlessly, without appetite. Before she had finished, she heard someone entering from the *porte cochère*; then heavy, purposeful footsteps approaching. Moments later Jacquard loomed in the doorway.

"Upstairs with you," he said brusquely.

Heavy with resignation but burning with that new undercurrent of hate, she followed him. What did he plan for her now? Surely not more of the same!

On the stairway she noticed he was not alone. A black servant accompanied him, arms laden with large cartons.

Jac was in the master bedroom, the boxes piled on the crumpled bed and the black man leaving, eyes averted, when she got there.

"Open them," he commanded.

The first box open made her gasp with surprise. It was a ball dress of deep gold silk overlaid with magnificent ivory lace.

"Jac—! I don't understand. . . ."

He scowled. "It is the finest gown I could purchase, but not from generosity, I assure you. I would prefer to dress you in the flaming red of a whore so the world would know the kind you are. But not yet. By a stroke of fate—whether for good or bad I do not yet know—you were seen by a most important gentleman when you were in the anteroom of General Butler's office. His name is Lord Crittendon, a personal envoy from Queen Victoria to evaluate the situation in New Orleans. He was very much intrigued by the sight of you and beseeched Butler to arrange a meeting. He is a notorious libertine and assured the general that he was willing to pay most handsomely for favors from one such as you. You will wear that gown and the accessories tonight at the *grand bal paré* at the St. Charles, where you will meet him."

"Then you even have General Butler to help you pimp out women for your filthy profits?" she said acidly.

"Shut your slut's mouth! You understand nothing of how things are done in politics. Britain is now divided between whether to throw their support behind the South, because of their need for cotton, or to the North because the British frown on slavery. Butler considers it imperative to win Britain on the side of the Yankees and Crittendon has great influence with the Queen. Your job is to charm him and do all that he desires before he falls into the hands of some Southern seductress."

"How can you know I would not tell him my entire story and seek his support?"

Jac flashed his wolfish grin and spat out one word: "Rill."

Three

Alliance de Convenance

i

Under the faceted brilliance falling from ornate chandeliers and soft candle backlighting from heavy silver girandoles on the ballroom walls, Micaela was uncomfortably aware that she had become a cynosure of attention: male eyes showing admiration; female eyes reflecting envy. True, she had worked hard to look her best for this evening. Her heavy dark hair, with Aurora's help, had been artfully teased and piled above her lovely face, with a few stray ringlets falling over her back and shoulders against the creamy paleness of her skin. The golden gown with its rich ivory overlay and daringly low décolletage was a perfect fit. Jac was very familiar with her sizes from past experience in purchasing dresses for her, and had excellent taste.

They had arrived only moments ago. Jacquard as usual was resplendently garbed in costly high fashion, his very haughty arrogance in itself a part of his striking appearance. The ballroom was crowded, and as the orchestra struck up a new tune, the floor became a swirl of dancing couples. It was a scene of opulence and gaiety. Most of the men were officers in dress uniform. The women were quadroons and octoroons with just a sprinkling of whites —the wives of officers or businessmen from the North —no respectable Southern white lady cared to be seen socializing with the Yankees. All were richly dressed. The air was filled with the scents of expensive perfumes, rustlings of silk, the sparkle of gems. And with the swaggering pride of the Yankee conquerors mellowed only slightly by the submissiveness of their purchased partners.

As they entered, she saw a familiar face along the sidelines, a most handsome woman with grayed hair, elaborately coiffured, and splendidly gowned in violet taffeta. She was Madame Silkwood, who had once been Micaela's tutor in the arts of being a lady and charming men. New Orleans' most prominent procuress. She was at the moment chatting with two attractive young quadroons, doubtless under her tutelage.

"Jac, I have just seen an old friend, Madame Silkwood. Will you permit me to go and speak to her for a moment?"

His eyebrows arched. "Why certainly, my dear. I have implicit faith in your good sense. Meanwhile, I shall find Lord Crittendon and bring him to meet you."

Madame Silkwood came forward to meet her with outstretched arms. Diamonds glittered in her fingers, ears, and around her heavy neck.

"Ah, *chérie,* it has been so long!" she gushed before embracing Micaela. Then standing back she examined her with a critical eye. "And more beautiful than ever! But I am surprised to see you back in New Orleans. There were incredible rumors that you had absconded with that impecunious doctor to marry him in the North. Tell me it was not true. You must tell me *everything. . . .*"

Micaela had difficulty in fighting back anger, keeping in mind that Madame Silkwood had great influence and could perhaps find a way of helping her, or at least offering advice.

"It is true, I married Paul Abbott and am now his widow, as he was killed in the war."

"Ah, it is sad. . . ." She shrugged her heavy, powdered shoulders. "But *tout est bien qui finit bien*—all's well that ends well. You were a silly goose to leave such a rich man as Monsieur Jacquard, but thank God that's all water under the bridge, and I see you back with him. I hope you realize how fortunate you are now to have won back his attention and forgiveness."

"Madame, there is little time to talk, because monsieur will soon return, but I must tell you all is not as it seems. I am now in the hands of a monster! Monsieur Jacquard is keeping me and my child prisoners against my will. He is so cruel, so full of hate, and is forcing me to do things I do not wish to do. I beg of you, madame, for the sake of our old friendship and the affection we have for one another, please—"

"Quiet, quiet—say not another word!" Madame Silkwood's eyes were wide with astonishment, scorn and anger. "What a crazy little fool you are! Have you not yet learned that men of course expect to have their way, and women should be quite happy to charm and gratify them in all ways possible? Especially when they have such wealth and power as Monsieur Jacquard." She paused to catch her breath, eyes narrowed at Micaela haughtily, then continued:

"I myself am presently employed by Monsieur Jacquard, who now owns or controls most of the bordellos in town, but mine remains the finest. I and all my girls are completely at his disposal. No, my silly little fool, I can only recommend—" She broke off as her eyes slid past Micaela and a smile of great sweetness rearranged itself on her heavily powdered face.

"Ah . . ." she murmured. "Monsieur is returning, with a fine gentleman. . . ."

A moment later, Jacquard's deep voice intruded: "Ladies, I wish to present Lord Crittendon. . . ."

His companion was an older man of slender build, slightly stooped, with thinning gray hair, an almost colorless mustache and pale watering blue eyes. His thin lips were stretched in a smile over somewhat yellowed teeth, except for two that were of glaring white, obviously false, and his florid complexion was webbed with the tiny, purplish broken veins of an aging alcoholic. Otherwise he was most impressive in a perfectly tailored white linen frock coat, a burgundy watered silk waistcoat, ruffled shirt and formal black stock set with a diamond stickpin. He was all gentility and suave manners, bowing low to kiss the hands of both women as Jacquard made the introductions.

"I have heard so much about the beauties of New Orleans," he said in a hoarse, gravelly voice, "but the reality far exceeds my expectations."

Madame Silkwood simpered; Micaela smiled. Lord Crittendon directed his stretched lips at Micaela.

"And to make the reality even more entrancing, I would be most grateful for the opportunity of dancing with this lovely young lady."

On the dance floor, Micaela was surprised to find that Lord Crittendon was an accomplished dancer, but she found his way of pressing her close quite distasteful, and his quick hot breath smelled bad. He also had an annoying mannerism of frequently clamping his jaw shut with a clicking sound to set his false teeth back in place when they loosened while he was trying to dance and talk at the same time.

During a brief intermission between dances, she happened to glance toward the sidelines and at once saw a familiar face staring at her as if transfixed.

Pace Schuyler!

The music started and again Lord Crittendon swept her into a dance, but this time he seemed more intent on talking than dancing.

"I believe, my dear young lady, that Mr. Jacquard has made my desires known to you, has he not?"

"I have been told nothing, sir, except that you desired companionship."

"Ah yes, that has been settled. I have already arranged the monetary matters with Monsieur Jacquard, and you will be returning with me after the ball to my quarters at the Pontalba Arms."

"Tonight!" She was suddenly horrified at such an immediate prospect and sought an excuse. "But I have no articles of clothing or *toilette* with me and—"

"Nonsense, my sweet. Such items are easily obtained and I do not wish to delay my first taste of the delightful intimacies you have to offer." Not too subtly an arm tightened around her drawing her close and his fetid breath was in her face as his wet lips sought to kiss an ear.

She shuddered with loathing and bent her head away.

"What is it, my dear? Are you feeling ill?" he said with concern.

"A faintness has seized me. I need a breath of fresh air."

"Of course, my pet. I shall escort you outside."

"No, please—I prefer to be alone for a few moments. . . ." Turning she hurried away.

ii

Feeling sick with revulsion, she leaned against the balcony railing outside of the ballroom trying to still her pounding heart. A fresh breeze from Lake Pontchartrain fanned against her flushed face, fragrant with the perfumes of flowering trees and blossoms. In the courtyard below couples strolled hand in hand amid the flamboyants; some sat at small tables under the shadowy branches of magnolias holding hands or sipping from iced cordials. All was light talk, laughter, youth—romance—just the reverse of the situation from which she had just fled. But only briefly: soon she would have to return. The thought of lying in the odious embrace of an aging body fired not with love, but only with jaded lust, started her shuddering again. Her position was so hopeless! How could she possibly endure it? All of her feelings of frustration were boiling up in her, a pressure that suddenly vented itself in an outpouring of hot tears.

A quiet voice spoke from close behind:

"You seem unhappy, Micaela—"

She turned, chagrined by the tears that ran down her face, and through blurred eyes saw Pace Schuyler standing tall and erect in his splendid colonel's dress uniform. "I'm sorry to have you see me this way, Pace, but it is just a temporary indisposition."

His eyebrows arched. "You seemed quite content when you were dancing with Lord Crittendon—and because of the disparity in your ages I assumed that it was only because you were aware you would be paid quite liberally for your assignation with him tonight." His voice was cold.

She gave a soft, hurt cry. "But how could you know?"

"Seeing you arrive in the company of the notorious Jacquard should have told me, but I didn't dream it was you that had been selected for his lordship until I saw you with him. You see, I have been assigned as his personal aide while he is in New Orleans and was quite aware of the entertainment he was seeking through the sordid offices of Jacquard. Still, it astonished me to find that the scoundrel would pimp his own ex-mistress—and even more so that you would acquiesce."

"You believe that I would do such a thing of my own free will!"

The hard set on his face softened. "If you have a good explanation, I would certainly like to hear it."

She bowed her head. "I cannot tell you. You would not believe me anyway—nor could you help me if you did."

"That remains to be seen. Remember, I already know much about you from your revelations on the boat. At first, I ridiculed your stories as wild fabrications. I learned, to my shame, that you told only the truth. Now I am most anxious to hear—and believe—what has happened to you since. . . ."

As calmly as she could, she related all of the misadventures she had suffered since she had last seen him in Memphis, up to the present moment with Jac still keeping her child hostage as a means of punishing her by forcing her into a life of prostitution. When she had finished her tears began welling again. She turned her head away in embarrassment. Arms slipped around her and gently Pace drew her against his chest.

"Cry all you wish, my heroic little lady. I believe every word of your story and will do everything in my power to help." Leaning down, he tenderly touched his lips to each of her tear-sodden eyes while his embrace tightened protectively.

A hoarse gravelly voice barked at them: "Colonel, what is the meaning of this!"

Micaela tried to draw away as she saw Lord Crittendon in the doorway glaring at them, but Pace kept a possessive arm around her firmly.

"Sir, you are intruding upon a reunion with the girl that I love and wish to marry."

Micaela was as amazed as Lord Crittendon, whose jaw literally dropped open. Hurriedly he clamped it shut again with a slight click. The angry flush remained on his face. "What kind of joke is this, Colonel? You were assigned to me, as I understand it, to aid me in any way I might desire. Now you claim to be in love with the young lady that I have selected for my own pleasures. Surely you were aware of Mr. Jacquard's arrangement?"

"But I was not aware that the lady selected was Mrs. Abbott—a widow of one of our gallant Yankee officers—with whom I had fallen in love and would have married except for our being parted due to unfortunate circumstances beyond our control. But now that I have found her again, I shall fight through hell and high water—resign my commission if necessary—to make her my own."

Micaela's incredulity grew. He would lie so rashly in a futile effort just to help her!

Lord Crittendon looked with suspicious eyes from one to the other, then suddenly burst into soft laughter. "Ah, young love. . . . Colonel, you have given the only possible answer that I could find acceptable. Whether your story is completely true or not doesn't matter. Your love for each other is apparent enough, and New Orleans, I've discovered, is a hotbed of most beautiful female blossoms from which I can find other charming creatures, I'm sure.

However, I believe you may have a problem in persuading Mr. Jacquard to let such a treasure slip out of his hands."

"That, Your Lordship, is a matter I intend to settle right away. I will appreciate it if you will accompany me when I explain the changed situation to Mr. Jacquard."

iii

Jacquard was livid with rage. Pace Schuyler had just finished explaining that with Lord Crittendon's consent, he intended to marry Micaela. The four of them had repaired to one of the private little rooms, intended for lovers, that were spaced along one side of the ballroom.

"You cannot!" Jacquard exploded. "Louisiana law forbids the marriage of a white person to an octoroon, and General Butler assures me that when military security is not involved, he will honor Southern law."

"In that case, I shall still take her under my protection until such time as I can take her up North and marry her.'

"She is already under my protection, monsieur. Micaela and I have a signed agreement—a contract that gives me complete control over her for as long as I wish."

Pace smiled wryly. "What you call a contract is in this case only another form of slavery."

Jacquard smiled thinly. "Slavery is still legal even under Federal law."

"It won't be for long. President Lincoln now has on his desk a preliminary copy of a proclamation which will banish slavery forever in this country."

"Monsieur, what might be or might not be in the future does not concern me at this moment. I, and I alone, shall decide what's best for Micaela's welfare."

"You made the decision to sell her favors to Lord Crittendon and since his lordship has agreed to relinquish his part of the transaction to me, I shall take over the obligation and pay you whatever sum has been charged and continue to pay the required amount for the time she remains with me."

Jacquard looked Pace up and down sneeringly. "I doubt that a mere army colonel could afford the fee."

Lord Crittendon laughed. "There you are in error, Mr. Jacquard. I happen to be well acquainted with the young man's father, who is one of the wealthiest merchants in New York. Pace is the only heir, and I can assure you he can afford the monies far more easily than I can."

"I can still refuse—"

"I doubt it—after I've explained matters to General Butler, who is also a close friend of my father's."

Jacquard glared at him for a moment, then shrugged. "Since you're willing to pay my high price for the whore—"

"Rotten bastard—!" Pace swung back a clenched fist. "How dare you insult the lady I love!"

Micaela caught his arm. "Pace—don't! He wants to provoke you to strike him so he can challenge you to a duel. He's an expert swordsman and marksman and would surely kill you."

"Kill me or not, I can't stand here and allow—"

Lord Crittendon quickly moved in front of him. "No, Pace, a fight will never do. It could bring to light my, uh, involvement, and be most embarrassing. If the Queen ever heard of it . . ."

Pace took a deep breath and stared coldly at Jacquard. "Out of deference to his lordship, I'll overlook your foul manners for the moment, but I won't forget. Now there is also the matter of Micaela's child. . . ."

"*My* child would be more correct. I am the father and have assumed the father's proprietary rights."

"He lies!" Micaela burst out bitterly. "He is *not* the father, but I have no way of proving it."

Pace glanced from Micaela to Jacquard. "For the present there may be nothing that can be done about it, but let me warn you, Jacquard—should anything hurtful befall the child, I will kill you!"

"If I don't kill you first!" Jacquard shot back.

"Gentlemen, gentlemen. . . ." Lord Crittendon frowned at both men. "There's no reason why all this can't be resolved amicably."

"Resolved it will be—but I doubt it will be amicable!" Scowling, Jacquard turned and strode out.

iv

In the back of a hired coach after leaving the ball, Micaela got her first chance to thank her benefactor:

"It was very kind of you to tell all those lies to help me, Pace, and I am very thankful."

"Lies? Like you, little lady, I do not lie. I meant every word of it."

"How can you love one you scarcely know?"

"I know all I need to know. I never expected to find a woman who not only knows how to be honest, and has great courage, but is also the most ravishing angel I have ever seen. Wouldn't I be a fool to let her slip away? If you will have me, I will marry you just as soon as I get you and your child out of this decadent state with its biased laws. That, little lady, is a proposal."

She felt another rush of tears and was grateful for the darkness that concealed them. Such weakness embarrassed her. She had always considered that crying was ridiculous, usually a form of self-pity, something to be tolerated only in children, senility or deepest bereavement but of late she seemed to have less and less control over such emotions.

Sensitive to her silence, he added hastily: "But I don't expect an answer yet. There's plenty of time to get used to the idea, and to know me better. . . ."

As the coach rolled on, she wondered why she couldn't respond at once to Pace's proposal, which she believed was sincere. He had done so much for her. She was saved, at least temporarily, from Jac's brutality, although she knew Jac's cunning could easily find a way to get her back

348

whenever he chose. Meanwhile, because of Rill, he had no worries about her running away. A new sense of guilt was growing in her, too, because Pace was paying such a dear price for her. For what? She knew she could not offer him the full love he apparently wanted—the image of Paul would always be between them, even if she only offered her body. And that he would certainly expect, at the very least. . . .

Pace Schuyler's quarters were on the upper floor of a fine old home that had been converted by its owner into comfortable apartments for the upper echelons of the Union officers who could afford the high rentals.

As he showed her into the larger of the two bedrooms, he said, "The bath is through that door if you'd care to wash. In the way of apparel, I regret that I have nothing to offer you but one of my nightshirts, which you'll find in the closet, but tomorrow I'll arrange to get you the clothing and personal effects you need."

She looked at the wide bed and knew that now the time had come to speak.

"Pace, it is only fair to tell you this. I am full of gratitude and much admire and respect you. I feel a great fondness for you and shall try to be everything you wish me to be—but I must be honest and say that I do not love you."

He broke into a gentle laugh. "Miracles I do not expect, my love. Never fear. I will teach you to love me." Then, noting her apprehensive glances at the bed, he added:

"But to avoid any misunderstandings, this is to be your bedroom. I will be sleeping in the smaller bedroom adjacent. I want you to be well rested and have all the time in the world to think things over before you make any decisions."

Book Seven

LINKUM'S ARMY MARCHES IN

"I, Abraham Lincoln, President of the United States of America, do proclaim that on the first day of January, 1863, all persons held as slaves within any State, or designated part of a State, the people whereof shall then be in rebellion against the United States, shall then be, thenceforward and forever, free; and the executive Government of the United States, including the military and naval authorities thereof, will recognize and maintain the freedom of such persons, and will do no act, or acts, to repress such persons, or any of them, in any efforts they may make for their actual freedom."
Lincoln's Emancipation Proclamation, 1863.

In 1863 conscription became necessary—a law favoring the rich, as they merely paid others to take their place. In the same year Negro troops for the first time were allowed to fight—an outgrowth of the Emancipation Proclamation.

In March of 1864 Grant was made general in chief of the Armies of the United States. He had changed. His kindly manner was gone; hard new animallike streaks were appearing in his nature. He lacked the brilliance of one of his Confederate opponents, but he always won. He won by refusing to admit defeat, even when defeated; by hammering on relentlessly regardless of losses, which by war's end were to reach 360,000 casualties.

The fighting men were changing, too, on both sides. War was losing its popularity. No longer was the ordinary man filled with rapture over the thought of bleeding and dying like a hero for the swollen profits of the industrialists. In the North the rich grew enormously richer, so powerful that they wrote their own laws for their own benefit, automatically getting rubber-stamp approval from Congress. The poor—the factory hands, seamstresses, clerks, the day laborers—grew poorer. Grew poorer and shed ever more tears for brothers, sons, or fathers dying in battle. In the South, inflation soared the price of coffee to $18.00 a pound; a bar of soap, $7.00; ladies' gloves, $33.00 a pair; a toothbrush, $8.00. A Confederate soldier's monthly pay of $18.00 in Confederate paper money was worth about ninety cents.

Meanwhile, the slaughter continued. . . .

One

Escape

i

The wheezy locomotive, spewing out black smoke and jets of white steam, rolled up alongside the loading dock. Coupled to it were three broken-down boxcars screeching along on unoiled wheels. Every inch of floor space in each car would be jammed with the latest batch of wounded Confederate soldiers.

Paul watched as his medical aides, both black and white, began unloading the casualties. The familiar dirge of moans and groans and wracking sobs rose above the chugging of the engine at rest. The engine would keep running, as it would only stay long enough to unload and then take on a new load of those sufficiently recuperated to return to their families or, in some cases, to service, but the majority of return passengers would be in flimsy wooden coffins or sewn in canvas shrouds.

In the more than two years since he had been at Mont-aven, Paul had seen thousands come and go. Without doubt he had saved hundreds of lives, but it was like shoveling against the tide, for the numbers kept increasing. With Christina Ashley's backing, he had trained crews of recuperated patients and slaves to cleanse wounds, apply bandages, change dressings, assist at operations. Dr. Stanberry had discreetly remained in the background, usually drunk, his main value being his contacts with the military to obtain medical supplies.

Paul's disgust and hatred of war burned in him like a banked fire. As a doctor he saw none of the "glory" of war, but only the horrors that were so carefully hidden from the civilian populace.

Millions being spent on devising and producing ever more efficient, ever more hideous ways of destroying life.

Only paltry thousands allowed for inadequate medical supplies and ill-trained doctors.

"It never gets easier to watch, does it, Paul?"

He glanced at Christina, who had moved up beside him. There was moistness in her green eyes.

"It only gets worse," he said. "In the beginning they had only the old smoothbore rifles and round balls to contend with. The old Springfields made a relatively clean wound. At long distance they barely pierced the skin. Now both sides are getting more and more of the new guns with rifled barrels, such as the Enfields and Rodmans—the bloodiest advance made in warfare since the invention of gunpowder. They shoot several times as far with far greater accuracy, and their soft-lead bullets splinter bone and tear flesh."

"I know, Paul, but thank God we've got you and the men you keep training to do the best that can possibly be done."

It was a tribute he got frequently from Christina, who long since, at the cost of considerable agony and round-the-clock help from Paul—with support from Cad Ganty—had overcome her drug addiction under Paul strict withdrawal therapy. Her health had much improve and the two had become fast friends.

Their thickening friendship, however, was not to th

liking of Cade Ganty, who often glowered at them from a distance when he saw them together.

"There's a pathetic example of what the rifled guns do—" Paul nodded toward a casualty being carried over the ramp to the loading platform. One glance told him that it was one of the intestinal wounds from a large soft-nosed bullet that was most invariably fatal. The dressings appeared to have been hastily stuffed against the wounded area and held in place by crude, bloodstained bandaging.

By the time such victims got to Paul, peritonitis had usually set in, too much blood would be lost, and there was absolutely nothing he could do to save them.

Someday, he knew, doctors would solve the riddle of how to give blood transfusions that would save lives. Most doctors still tried sheep's blood for transfusions with fatal results. Even those bold enough to try human blood rarely succeeded.

The irony of it was that rivers of blood drained off into the battlegrounds. A small fraction of it would be enough —if doctors could only learn to match the right blood to the right person—to save thousands of lives.

Paul walked over to the casualty in question for a closer look. He stopped suddenly, chilled. That face, so twisted with anguish, that familiar face—

"Etienne—!"

At his involuntary cry, the eyes of the man on the stretcher opened and stared at Paul. His voice came in hoarse gasps. "Paul—! Is it really—?" His head sank back, as if the expenditure of energy had been too much. His eyes closed.

Paul snapped at the stretcher bearers: "Get him to one of the operating tables as soon as possible. Get Cheeves, and hurry—!"

ii

Etienne's glazed eyes were fixed on Paul as his opened mouth gulped for air. The iridescent green wings of blowflies flashed in darting circles above him, drawn by the odors of blood and death. One alighted on a cheek, crawled alongside the aquiline nose, but Etienne appeared not to notice, or care. Numbness was setting in. The wet film giving a dull shine to his eyes came partly from the stupor of opium that Paul had given to alleviate his friend's pain; mostly it was an effect of the poison of peritonitis that was killing him. Paul had done all possible, to no avail. Etienne's life was seeping away fast.

His voice came in a hoarse whisper: ". . . wouldn't have married anyone as young as Narcisse, but your son needed a mother. . . ."

"Is Carson in good health?"

"Narcisse writes that he's well and happy."

Paul steeled himself to ask the question he most feared to ask: "Have you heard any news of Micaela?"

Etienne's eyes closed with pain. He seemed reluctant to speak. Then, "Sometimes it's better not to know certain things, Paul. . . ."

"Then you've heard something!"

"Only hearsay from friends. . . ."

"Tell me anyway, Etienne," he said gently. "I need to know. Hearsay or not."

The dying man waited until he had noisily sucked in another lungful of air. "They say she's living with a very rich Union officer in New Orleans . . . a Colonel Schuyler, and it is said—" His voice drifted off into silence and his eyes half-closed.

"And what else, Etienne?"

"Please, Paul. . . ." He made gulping sounds for more air. "Ask me no more. . . ."

Etienne died quietly several hours later.

iii

Throughout the afternoon and into the evening, Paul worked tirelessly. Cheeves tried to induce him to break of

356

for supper but Paul had no desire for food. Work was the best anodyne he knew for submerging the pains of bereavement and the anguish of his detonated dreams. His sustaining hope of ultimate reunion with Micaela had been shattered beyond repair.

But he still had Carson to think about. And Rill. Carson would be going on six, and he hadn't seen him since babyhood; Rill was about three and he had never seen her. He tried to visualize how each might look, but could not.

Darkness had arrived when he heard her voice near him:

"Paul, you can't go on like this! You've got to get some rest. You're just killing yourself!" She was wrapped in a green pelisse that complemented her eyes and accented her Titian hair.

"I'm afraid I'd just toss and turn tonight, so I might just as well put my wakefulness to good purpose."

"But then you'll be overtired tomorrow and be of little use to these men. Here, I've brought you something to help you sleep—" From beneath her robe she produced a small decanter and a brandy glass.

He looked at the glass, then at her earnest face, and smiled. "I guess you're right, Christina. But I won't go back to the cabin. I'll just nap for an hour or so on one of the mattresses in the supply room. The cognac will help."

A lantern was suspended above the door of the supply room, which was a boarded-off section at one end of the warehouse. Inside were kept maintenance supplies such as surplus blankets, sheets and the straw-stuffed canvas mattresses that the slaves had spent many days industriously sewing together. Any one of them placed on the floor would serve for his nap.

They stood in the open doorway under the yellow flare of lantern rays as she poured the brandy glass half full and raised it to his lips.

"Drink it, Paul, and have a good rest. . . ."

iv

. . . he was floating through darkest night, but a darkness filled with rich colors that swirled around him slowly as rising smoke. Colors that stained even the air he breathed, swelled in his lungs, made his head swim with giddy visions. . . .

The pulsing spurt of blood. . . .

The burning, molten gold of sun. . . .

Blood and red lips and red-gold hair. . . .

Somber blues merging into ice greens. . . .

And the blackness of Micaela's hair as she drifted out of the night.

Smiling, her perfect teeth a flash of whiteness.

In one hand the flash of a knife.

Floating closer. . . .

"Micaela," he called. "Micaela. . . ." He tried to rise. She floated down upon him, weightless, bringing the pressure of her naked breasts against his nakedness as he felt the knife sliding into his back. Painlessly. And her lips were crushing against his as the knife rose again and again, dripping crimson, but the kiss was so sweet . . . sweeter than honey. . . .

"Micaela . . ." he murmured.

And now, miraculously, she was beneath him, all her limbs spread open like the exotic petals of a rare blossom, then enfolding around him as they merged into oneness on a rising tide of ecstasy. . . .

"Micaela . . . Micaela—!"

He came awake in a rush as all the forces within him, all the frustrations, yearnings, hurts and hungers, came shuddering out of him in explosive climax.

Replaced by inexpressible joy.

It was no poisoned dream, but reality!

Her soft, warm body lay locked in his embrace, her lips breathing close to his, her cheeks damp. He raised up, the better to see her. A stray beam of moonlight through the tiny supply room window fell across the dark hair tumbled around the shadowed face, brought out the gleam of burnished copper.

"Christina! I don't understand how—"

"It was the opium I put in your brandy to make sure you'd get a good rest."

So that explained the weirdness, fevered colors and distortions of the dream.

"I stayed here in the darkness, thinking of many things I usually fear to think about," she went on. "You slept soundly for at least two hours, and I was about to leave when I heard you calling for Micaela. In your tone I could recognize your terrible need—because it is the same need I live with—so on impulse I lay down beside you and—"

The door crashed open. A glare of lantern light jounced over the floor. A voice bellowed:

"Christina—you in here? I heard voices—"

Christina had at once rolled away from the light, was hastily drawing her pelisse around her. Paul began rearranging his clothes.

Too late.

An animallike roar burst from Cade Ganty. The thumping of his peg leg was loud on the wooden floor as he rushed forward, halting only to put the lantern down so that his only arm was free to jerk a pistol from his belt.

"I'll kill you, you fuckin' bastid—!"

Christina sprang up, her pelisse still half open as she threw herself in front of Cade Ganty. "Cade—don't you dare!"

"Outta the way, Christina! Nothin's going to keep me from blastin' him to hell!"

"If you do, I'll have you executed before a firing squad!"

Cade snorted a harsh laugh. "For killin' a Yankee caught raping a Southern lady? They'd give me a medal!"

"No, Cade—you're the one who'd be shot or hanged for rape. . . ."

Astonishment was ludicrous on his face. "You're outta your head, Christina!"

"On the contrary, I'm more clearheaded than I have been in all those years since the time you first visited here as my husband's orderly. Remember, Cade? I'd just found out about my husband sneaking into a warehouse to lie with one of his black wenches. I was out of my head then, yes, hysterical, when you came and under the pretext of trying to comfort me, took advantage of me—"

"But-but that's the way I felt about you. I was in love with you since the first time I set eyes on you. I never would've dreamt of touchin' you except after I learnt how the general preferred black wenches to you—and if the truth be told, you sure didn't discourage me."

"Because I was out of my head at the time, not thinking straight at all! If I ever told the story to a military court, they'd call it rape. All your medals, your good record—everything would be stripped away. You'd be sentenced to an ignominious death and your name forever after held in contempt."

His voice dropped to hoarse pleading: "Why you doing this to me, Christina? Since the general's death, I've been protectin' you, worshiping the very ground you walk on. And you got to admit, not once have I tried to touch you."

"And I know why—!" Her voice rose to scathing fury. "The army surgeon who treated my husband told me, in confidence, what happened to you, Cade. Some of the canister shots that shattered your leg and arm also got you in the groin. Your male organs were so badly damaged that you're no longer capable—"

He gave a low moan. "No more, Christina—please—"

"You call it love," she went on relentlessly, "but the truth is that you've become a bitter, hating man because you can no longer give a woman physical love—and because you can't, you've been guarding me like a jailer all these years to make sure that no other man gives me such love either, even holding it over my head like black-mail, the fact that I once betrayed my husband with you—"

Paul, listening to all this with acute embarrassment, had been puzzling over why a lady of Christina's breeding would ever speak such intimate secrets that should never be heard by outsiders—except for a very compelling reason.

To distract the overwrought man's attention long enough to—

Paul leaped. In two strides he caught Ganty's arm and began twisting. Bellowing with rage, Cade resisted furiously. But muscular as he was, it was an unequal struggle. A final, vicious twist of the wrist brought a yowl of pain and the pistol clattered on the floor.

Christina snatched up the gun. "You can let him go now, Paul. And Cade, don't make a move to fight or I'll shoot."

Ganty's face was florid with baffled rage. "You mean you're siding with a damn Yankee against *me?*"

"I don't think of him as a Yankee, Cade, but as a kind, unselfish man whom I love very much." Her glance swerved toward Paul. "As for us, Paul, this is goodbye. Unfortunately, you'll have to leave Monthaven."

"But why?"

"I know Cade only too well. If you stay, he'll surely find a way to kill you at the first opportunity—either that or I'll have to kill him, and I don't want that on my conscience."

"But I'm needed here, Christina. All these hundreds of casualties—"

"We can manage. You've trained quite a few men as medical aides, and taught Cheeves to do minor surgery. He's already better at it than most doctors I've known. General Cooper is very pleased with what we're doing here and I think he'll try hard to get us another surgeon after you escape—"

"Escape!"

There's no choice, Paul. You'll have to leave tonight. Now. I can promise that no one will try to follow you before daylight, but after that I can't order Cade not to rent hounds and try to pick up your trail, as after all, you are a prisoner of war."

"He won't get far," Cade said sourly.

"It won't be easy, Paul, and it's full of danger, but I think it's the best chance. You can take a horse if you wish, but I don't advise it. The countryside is swarming with Confederate soldiers and you'd be too conspicuous riding in that Yankee uniform, which you must keep wearing. If you're caught that way, you'll only be taken prisoner again, but if you changed to other clothes you'd be shot as a spy. With luck you may run into Union troops in a day or two. Hurry now, and God bless you. . . ."

Paul stopped at his cabin only long enough to fill a small pack with a few personal items and the small amount of money he had. His medical kits, which would be too cumbersome, were left behind for Cheeves.

He had reached the last of the outbuildings when a heavy silhouette moved out from behind a tree and loomed in front of him. The figure approached slowly until Paul could see by the wide misshapen shoulders that it was Hunch. The black man's hand moved to his belt and a moment later the glimmer of moon shone on the blade of a knife.

Paul stood frozen with indecision. He knew he was no match for the hunchback, who despite his deformity was powerfully muscled and fast as a lynx.

Hunch was only a few feet away now, holding the knife in front of him—handle first.

"Yo'll need it, Yankeedoc. Dat swamp out dere full o' bad things."

Paul took the knife gratefully.

"Now yo' follow de moon smack ahaid to de swamp, den turn right along edge of de swamp till yo hit de stream an' wade up dat a few miles an' no hounds find yo' trail."

"Thanks, Hunch."

"Git runnin', Yankeedoc."

Two

Runaway

i

Awakening, Narcisse Duplessis Troyonne looked over at the broad-shouldered, hard muscularity of the body that was hogging more than half of the bed beside her and felt faintly nauseous. It had been another of those horrible nights, which, thank heaven, weren't too frequent. In his demanding, devouring assaults on her delicate body he was both brutal and insatiable. Before knowing him, never in her most shocking dreams had she ever envisioned that sexuality could be so hideously animalistic. Afterward she always felt limp, crushed, dirty. Sometimes she experienced arousal in response to his thundering passion, but that shamed her. He stirred in his sleep, rolling half on his back, and quickly she edged away to avoid the touch of his flesh. Léon Jacquard snored on.

He will awaken soon, she thought, noting that the slant of sun through the glass doors to the balcony indicated early forenoon. Hastily she rolled out of bed and scampered off to the dressing room. It was earlier than her wont, but to still be in bed when Léon opened his eyes would be at the risk of another arousal of his lust. Did the man never get enough?

At the same time, his very greed for her body gave her an exquisite sense of power. Looking into the great, gilt-framed mirror in her dressing room as she sat brushing her pale golden hair, she knew without conceit that she was a beautiful woman, still in the bloom of her youth. Yet Etienne had never shown any slightest desire to possess her body, in fact had not once shared her bed. Their marriage had been purely an arrangement: to provide a proper mother for Carson and a suitable mistress for Les Cyprès.

She had seized upon Etienne's physical indifference to her as sufficient justification for allowing Léon to share her bed. How could it be betrayal when that aspect of marriage was nothing that her husband either desired or required?

Thus she had also been able to rationalize as Etienne's own fault her inability to feel any real sense of loss or bereavement when news of his death had arrived two weeks ago.

Quite the contrary! When old Le Barone, Etienne's attorney, had come to discuss the terms of the will with her, she had been astonished and infuriated to discover that Etienne had left the bulk of his estate to his nephew, Carson, and to her a much smaller share that Etienne considered substantial enough for the scale of living to which she was accustomed. And she his own wife! She knew nothing of law, and perhaps the will could be disputed, but Léon had quickly pointed out a simpler way.

Adopt Carson as her own son!

Le Barone had agreed that it would be a wise step, and most beneficial for the lad. After all, Paul Abbott had for over two years been missing in action and had been declared legally dead. The child needed a parent's protection. Le Barone, not invulnerable to young female charms, which Narcisse exhibited to every possible advantage when in his presence along with an admirabl display of a widow's sorrowful damp eyes, even went beyond ethical bounds by slyly pointing out that young Carson was also the sole heir to Paul Abbott's rather considerable estate, including Les Cyprès. Without a loving mother's guidance during his formative years, cautioned the attorney, Carson might well turn into a wastrel and upon coming of age dissipate his fortune.

The adoption papers were now in the process of being drawn up.

It was concerning the adoption that Léon had come to visit her last night. It was connected with other matters of the greatest importance that he must discuss with her, he had told her on arrival. But after several brandies, which he had gulped down greedily, he was disinclined to talk, saying it would be better to wait until morning when his head was clear. His thoughts had shifted totally to his amatory interests, and none of her weak protests or postures of ladylike indignance had deterred him in the slightest from carrying her upstairs and throwing her on the bed. . . .

She was thinking about that now as she continued grooming herself, bright turquoise eyes continuously glued in self-fascination on her reflection. Once she had been skilled at fending off any male overtures verging on boldness, had always been the perfect lady. But war had turned the world topsy-turvy. Gentlemen were all but obsolete. She had no choice but to adapt. Now she allowed a vulgar, crass Léon Jacquard into her home and submitted to his unspeakable attentions as the high, but necessary, price she had to pay for benefits gained.

Part of the price she paid was being utterly ostracized by her Creole plantation neighbors. They had come to Etienne's funeral only out of regard for his memory, their attitudes clearly conveying their contempt for her. Doubtless they knew of the visits from Léon, whose reputation she knew to be unsavory. She knew very little about his business other than that some of it involved important Yankee officers and businessmen.

His high connections were among the benefits. Brutish Yankee troops were spreading through the South in increasing numbers. She had heard of many plantations being pillaged and burned. Léon had assured her that Les Cyprès would never be touched.

What were the important matters, she wondered, that he wished to discuss with her?

ii

Jacquard opened his eyes, stretched luxuriously, threw a glance at the empty space beside him. Snorted sourly. His mood was not of the best. Sexually he had been sated, but not satisfied. Remembering Narcisse's stiff, half-hearted submission, he grimaced. She would be worth little as a whore. Against his will, he thought of Micaela, bringing the usual pang of loss. It had been over two years—longer than he had intended—since he had lost her to Pace Schuyler.

But it wouldn't be much longer. Although General Butler had left New Orleans long ago, Jacquard still had top connections with the present military government. Through informants he knew that Colonel Schuyler had been ordered back to Washington. Thanks to his wealthy father, Schuyler had turned out to have great influence, or Jacquard would not have allowed him to keep Micaela this long—but his influence fell short of forcing Jacquard to give up the child, Rill, which he had attempted several times. Nor was it enough to induce Micaela to accompany him to Washington. Micaela would never leave without Rill.

Soon he would have her back, but first there were other important matters to conclude. . . .

Sitting up in bed, he bellowed, "Narcisse!"

She appeared in the doorway of the dressing room wrapped in a royal blue velvet robe. "Must you shout Léon? The servants will hear."

"Don't be such a prude. They know anyway. Com over here."

366

She looked at him apprehensively. "I have a terrible headache, Léon. Can't we wait until tonight?"

"You can save your headache for this evening, my dear. At the moment I just want to talk."

Obediently she came over and sat on one side of the bed, out of his reach.

"I won't beat about the bush. As we both already know, Paul Abbott's first wife willed everything to Abbott, and in the event of his death, all would go to their issue—Carson. Of course, now that you have adopted him, you have limited freedom to draw upon the income from such monies—every cent of which you will be held accountable for by penny-pinching Le Barone, you may be sure."

"Why are you telling me what I already know?"

"Partly to remind you that the pittance you will be receiving will never make you rich."

"I also have my inheritance from Etienne."

"Which was niggardly at best—and there's no guarantee even of that."

"What more guarantee do I need than the terms of a valid will?"

"What you fail to take into account is the greed of our Yankee conquerors, who are sure to win this war. The enormous expenses of war must be paid, and why should the victors pay when they don't have to? I predict they will close all our banks and confiscate whatever they want for war reparations—and then you will be an impoverished woman, my dear."

"*Non, non!*" she gasped.

"On the other hand," he went on, "it is within my power not only to safeguard everything you now have and will inherit, but to assure that you become a very rich woman."

Her eyes widened with intent interest. "But how?"

"Through my Yankee connections, my own monies are invested in ways that are completely safe, and so could yours be. But first, let's get on to the matter of Les Cyprès and the rest of the Abbott estate. Full ownership, protected by me, would satisfy your desires for riches, would it not?"

"*Mais naturellement!* But I don't understand—"

"Sometimes it is necessary to be blunt. I refer to the fact that if a fatal accident should befall Abbott's brat, you would automatically become the full owner."

"*Non, non*, Léon—you can't mean—!"

"You wouldn't have to know anything about it. I would make all the arrangements."

She was quiet, her face deathly pale as she gnawed on her lower lip nervously. Jacquard was amused. He could almost see her quick, shallow brain weighing the horror of the thought against her innate greed for wealth. Finally she spoke, evading his eyes:

"Is it a share of the money you want?"

He grinned. "Not money, my sweet. . . ."

She smiled and started taking off her robe.

Jacquard laughed. "Not that, either. I can contain my passion for a while longer. All I am asking from you is your hand in marriage."

"*Mais non*—" she gasped, but he saw at once it was not a rebuff—a tiny smile had instantly touched her lips. Again he imagined he could see the workings of her brain. She was well aware that he himself was rich, and could protect her fully from the conquering Yankees, and of course smugly believed he could scarcely wait for her favors in bed.

"Speak, woman—I am an impatient man!"

"Yes, Léon, yes. . . ." Her downcast eyes looked up at him with a false show of shyness as she added, "And then perhaps tonight you will return so we can celebrate?"

"No, my sweet. I will refrain from any more of that supreme pleasure until after we're married. Now go and complete your *toilette*. . . ."

He lay back, relaxed in the knowledge that he had taken another important step toward his ultimate dream— total ownership of Les Cyprès.

iii

Carson Dixon Abbott, five and a half, crept stealthily along
the balcony which skirted the second-story bedrooms. He
was practicing at sneaking up on Indians. Uncle Etienne
had told him many stories about the famous Indian scout
Kit Carson, after whom he had been named because they
were somehow related. Being a quiet, intense lad forced
by lack of playmates to find his own solitary amusements,
he spent much time daydreaming about Indians and fron-
tiersmen, and hoped to go West himself someday.

His present stealth, however, was mostly due to the
need to get past the windows of Aunt Narcisse's bedroom
without being seen so he could take the outside stairway
down into the garden and also avoid the alert eyes of his
mammy, who might otherwise force him to eat a hearty
breakfast as well as give his face a thorough scrubbing.
There was also the fear that he might encounter the
detested Monsieur Jacquard. He'd heard his voice in Aunt
Narcisse's bedroom last night, and then a lot of strange
sounds as if they were wrestling together—the sounds
they always made when Monsieur Jacquard came and did
those funny things with his aunt. He burned with curiosity
about it but could never imagine what they were doing.

Just as he was passing the windows, Monsieur bellowed
his aunt's name. Scared, he flattened himself on the
balcony, fearful that he had been spotted—and from
that point on was a terrified audience to every word
spoken inside.

Carson was a very intelligent lad who had begun
reading at the age of four, and he missed none of
Jacquard's implications:

". . . if a fatal accident should befall Abbott's brat—"

As soon as he dared, shaken and trembling, he wormed
the rest of the way past the windows to the stairway down.
Since Uncle Etienne's funeral, Carson had been

despondent, his grief only worsened when Aunt Narcisse had informed him that now she was his mother. At the time he had wanted to run away, but lacked the nerve.

Nerve was no longer in question. He would have to run to stay alive.

In the garden below one of the servants, Ammon, was at work trimming a hedge. He looked up in amusement as Carson scurried toward him.

"Why yo'uns in sich a hurry, Carse? Is de Injuns a-chasin' yo?"

Carson was good friends with all the blacks. They listened with tolerance to his braggings that his great uncle Kit Carson was the most feared Indian fighter in the West. In turn they told him their own kind of stories, a popular one of late being that "Linkum's" army was steadily marching toward them, and would arrive any day now to set them free. Carson was proud that his own father had been an officer in Linkum's army, until killed by Confederate soldiers. Except for Uncle Etienne, he hated all Confederate soldiers and had often wished he was old enough to fight against them.

"I was just playing that I was a scout for Linkum's army. Which way is it coming from?"

Ammon scratched his woolly head. "Ah 'spect dey's on'y one way it kin come fum, Carse—smack fum dat way—" He pointed straight north.

Carson looked long and hard in that direction until he had memorized every landmark in sight—tall trees, a hill, even the angle of the forenoon sun. After Ammon resumed work, he wandered off nonchalantly into the nearest cover of trees. Once out of sight, he began running.

Straight north—toward Linkum's army.

Three

The Moonshiners

i

It was late in the afternoon when Paul first heard the peculiar, bell-like musical sounds in the distance, which at first he took to be the bells of some nearby village. After listening for a while, it seemed that the sounds were rapidly coming closer, and only then did he realize they were the hounds. Back at Monthaven he had heard stories about the hounds kept by one of the neighboring plantation owners, who rented them out to slaveholders to catch runaways. Belled, because their great speed made it difficult to keep track of them, the dogs were said to be a cross between the foxhound and the larger deerhound. Their scent was extremely keen and when once on a trail were rarely thrown off. Recaptured slaves told fearful stories of how useless it was to try to escape them, and how they had to climb trees to keep from being torn apart.

So Cade Ganty had found his trail after all!

Following Hunch's directions, he had skirted through

the swamp, then wallowed up the middle of a meandering stream, sometimes sinking over his head in the greenish-scummed water. A few times he had a fright when a log on the bank turned out to be an alligator, or when a snake skimmed too close. But by the time he reached a rickety bridge over the stream, and had clambered up the trestles to the roadbed—which appeared to have enough daily traffic to obscure his scent—he had begun congratulating himself on covering his trail.

He had traveled by small roads and byways since, ducking among bordering trees or bushes whenever a wagon or horseman appeared. Having but scanty knowledge of the area geography, his plan was simply to follow a westerly direction toward the Mississippi. Sooner or later he would surely encounter Union troops.

But for the moment it was imperative to race for the nearest water, which was marked by a heavy line of trees bordering a stream ahead.

The stream was cold, but shallow. He began floundering up the middle of its winding course, encouraged by the thought that the dogs would be temporarily stymied by not knowing which way in the stream he had gone. In about fifteen minutes the stream started branching out in several directions. Blindly, he struck ahead in the branch swerving left. Another reprieve. He found small satisfaction in the thought that the dogs would go wild with frustration, trying to figure which stream he had chosen. The tinkling sounds could no longer be heard.

After another half mile or so on his watery course, he was stopped by the sound of chopping ahead. Screening himself as much as possible by dense thickets along the shoreline, he proceeded cautiously until he saw a Negro at work chopping down trees to make a clearing.

The black man looked up in sudden apprehension as Paul approached. His uniform now hung in rags and tatters. His hands and feet were cut and bleeding, and he was covered with mud from head to foot. The cuts and bruises that he had not felt when plunging through underbrush were now beginning to smart and ache.

The black man, who had been holding his ax in a

defensive manner, eyes bulging, suddenly let the ax drop back to his side.

"Dat a blue unifo'm yo' wearin', massa?"

"Yes—I'm an escaped prisoner of war—a Yankee."

"Praise de Lawd! Den yo' one'v Linkum's army!"

"Right now I'm being followed by hounds and I've got to find a way to keep them off my trail."

"Don' yo' worry, massa. I fool dem hounds—" Quickly the black man started dragging over sections of newly chopped logs and leafy branches, setting them in what appeared to be a trail toward the nearby woods.

"Massa, yo' step from de watah smack on dese logs an' branches an' keep walkin' on dem to whar ah leads yo'."

The makeshift corduroy footway, continuously extended by the Negro, ended beneath a large, low-branched tree with heavy foliage.

"Now reach up to dat limb over yo' haid," instructed the black man, "an' haul yo'self up an' climb to whar de branches hide yo'."

It took all of Paul's wearied strength to do as instructed. Meanwhile the black man was hastily gathering up armfuls of the branches and log sections, tossing them into the stream where all of his scent would be washed away.

"Now yo' jus' wait up deah till it be dark, an' I bring yo' sumpin' to eat. . . ."

ii

There was no further sign or sound of the hounds. With darkness, swarms of mosquitoes buzzed around him nastily, biting him again and again. Having once suffered from yellow fever, he had immunity to that, but malaria, which Paul was convinced was also mosquito-borne, was still a threat.

Sleep was impossible, but at least his empty belly was now filled with pork, corn bread and cold coffee brought by his black benefactor. Just before dawn he struck out again on his westerly course, gratefully keeping in mind the Negro's parting advice:

"Any time yo' git chased, or git hongry, jist look for de neares' nigger, an' he do all he kin fo' yo'."

For most of the day he trudged across fields, through woods and along small country roads without mishap. As twilight approached, while following a narrow woods road, he came upon a kind of clearing with a ditch partly full of muddy water leading to it. Beside the ditch was a queer-looking log hut and a scattering of large barrels lying around. The pungent odor of fermentation rising from the barrels told Paul what it was: an illegal distillery.

Not unfamiliar with the process of fermenting a mash of crushed fruit or grain before distillation, having known a family of moonshiners when he was a boy in Council Bluffs, Paul removed the bung from one of the barrels and leaned with an ear over the bunghole. The faint seething sound inside indicated it was working fine but probably had a few more days to go. At this phase it wouldn't be too strong.

Exhausted and thirsty as he was, he decided a bit of the weak liquor would be beneficial. Tilting the barrel until the cloudy liquid came sloshing out in spasmodic spurts, he caught it in cupped hands and greedily gulped down several handfuls. He tilted the barrel back in place, replaced the bung and stood up.

Unsteadily.

Waves of dizziness passed in front of his eyes. He felt now the burning of alcohol—far stronger than he had judged—in a shrunken stomach that had eaten only one meal in over two days. That on top of dead exhaustion. His head was fast hazing with drunkenness.

Wobbling over to a grassy spot about a dozen feet away, he sank to the ground, figuring it was as good a place as any. He lay back and within minutes was snoring

iii

A kick in the ribs jolted him awake.

"Git up with yore hands grabbin' air, mista!"

Paul clambered to his feet. His head throbbed with stabbing pain. He was surprised to see that dawn had come, which meant he'd had a long hard sleep, but he didn't feel rested. It was his first hangover.

An ancient Springfield-type cap-and-ball musket prodded him in the belly. It was held by a skinny, scraggly bearded man with a red face and a cud of tobacco in one cheek. He wore garments of homespun butternut and a felt slouch hat.

"Any varmint 'at would steal another man's likker oughter be shot daid!" he said, punctuating the indictment with a juicy squirt of brown tobacco juice at Paul's left boot.

"But sir, I only—"

"Git in the wagon, you Yankee bastuhd! You drive an' I'll say whar ter go. Now git a move on while ya still got a behind to set on!"

The wagon ride was over a bumpy road through some of the wildest-looking country Paul had ever seen. On all sides were thickets of black haw, wild plum, whortleberry, and above them towered trees so densely tangled with wild grape vines that scarcely any sun broke through.

In about five minutes they came in view of a cabin half-hidden amid a thorny locust grove. It had been haphazardly constructed of all varieties and sizes of grayed, sagging boards, some nailed in place, others held together with twisted wires or cord. The grounds around were a virtual jungle of weeds, rusted cans and bottles, a small garden of last year's dried cornstalks and a broken-down wagon so overgrown with thistles, tall grass and honeysuckle runners that it appeared to have taken root there many years ago.

A young woman clad in a garment of homespun cotton appeared in the doorway of the structure as Paul was climbing out of the wagon, the musket prodding his back.

"W'at's thet yer brungin' home, Pa?"

"It's a dam' Yankee I caught at the still." There was pride in his voice.

Another girl, similarly dressed, had crowded up behind the first. One had uncombed tresses the color of dirty rope; the other's hair was mouse brown. They approached timidly, eyeing Paul with great curiosity. Both were barefoot.

"Kin it talk, Pa?"

"Shet yer silly mouth, Ossie. 'Course it kin."

The girls came cautiously closer. "Whar's its horns, Pa?"

"Prob'ly hid under all 'at mud on its haid," said the other girl. "Pa, kin we-uns dump a bucket 'v water on its haid ter see w'at it looks like?"

"Dump all ya like. I want 'nough mud off thet uniform so's folks kin see plain it's a real live Yankee I captured."

The first bucketful sloshed refreshingly over his hair and down his face. Paul managed to catch some of it in cupped hands and get it down his parched throat.

"Why it hain't got no horns! It looks jest like a real hooman!"

"Bet it's got a tail, though," said Ossie. "All Yankees got tails." She advanced from behind, daringly poked at his rump and swiftly retreated, as if from a wild animal. "I didn't feel no tail." She giggled.

"You feeled fum the wrong side," said her sister. Both girls giggled.

"Stop yer danged foolery, Ossie! You, Hassie, git spry now, an' fix some eatin's fer this bastuhd. I want 'im in good shape when I take 'im in to the 'thorities."

The cabin consisted of but one room. Its rough board floor was littered with a miscellany of unidentifiable debris from having long been untouched by a broom. The only furnishings were a heavy table made of ax-hewn slabs, two equally rustic chairs and two sagging beds. At one end was a flat-topped iron cooking stove.

Taking a jug from a shelf, the bearded man seated himself at the table, placing the musket in front of him.

"Set down thar," he ordered Paul, indicating the other chair. He lifted the jug and took a long swig while eyeing Paul speculatively. The girls busied themselves at the stove.

"Heered down at Treadmill's Corners you Yankee bastuhds gettin' whupped bad. Cain't hardly feed yore men no more. Must be wuss'n we figgered fum the looksa the rags yore wearin'. Ain't fittin' fer hogs ter wear."

"I apologize for my appearance, but there were extenuating circumstances—"

"Listen to them hi-falutin' words comin' fum a scarecrow!" crowed Hassie from the stove. " 'Spect it's 'cause he's got them things on his shoulders. Thet's a high off'cer's uniform he's got on, Pa."

"Thet a fack?" said the father, eyeing Paul with new interest. "Is you an off'cer?"

"I'm a captain."

Both girls now stared at Paul. "Why, Pa—a cap'n's almost as 'portant as a gen'ral!"

"He thet 'portant," said Ossie, "bet they'd give a big reewa'd fer an'body thet ketched 'im. Yer oughter find out, Pa."

"Iffen they any reewa'd, I shore aim ter c'lect it. Trouble is, iffen I take 'im ter the sheriff, them fuckin' Treadmill boys, iffen they figger I got a captive wuth money, 'll try'n steal 'im away fum me an' c'lect the reewa'd fer 'hemselfs. Iffen I take 'im to the army post, that's a hull half-day's ride. Reckon I'll jes' set here fer a spell an' 'tudy out how it oughter be done." He took another swig 'rom the jug and began studying.

"Ya kin go ta the post without 'im, Pa, so nobody kin 'teal 'im fum ya. Then the soldiers kin give ya the money n' come 'ere to git 'im."

The father took another long swallow from the jug, 'till thinking hard.

"Cain't leave 'im alone here with jes' the two of yus."

377

"Wouldn't fuss us none, Pa. Jes' hogtie 'm an' leave us the gun. Ossie'n me kin shoot jes' as good as you."

After a couple more long swings, he set the jug down.

" 'Spect yer right. Hain't no sense luggin' 'im along an' risk gittin' 'im stole, an' I'm shore hankerin' ter c'lect thet reewa'd money."

iv

They fed him first, a substantial enough breakfast of chitterlings, fried mush and imitation coffee made from boiled chicory roots. Then, at the suggestion of Hassie, who seemed to be the older sister as well as the brains of the family, Paul was made to lie spread-eagled on the tabletop. Each arm was tied to one of the table legs, each ankle bound to one of the other two legs. Satisfied that the captive could sure never wiggle loose from such a heavy piece of furniture, the father took off.

Hardly was the father out of sight than the two girls began circling about the table, giggling, now and then poking at him lightly. Ossie had found a feather and tried tickling him along the cheeks and neck. Paul gritted his teeth and endured it in silence. Any protests, he knew, would only goad them on.

"He hain't even ticklish," Ossie said with a pout.

"Bet I know whar he's ticklish," said Hassie.

"I hain't gonna took off 'is boots jes' ter tickle 'im 'Sides, we'd hafta untie 'is laigs ter do thet."

"Didn't mean thet. Meant tickle 'is tail."

Ossie giggled. "Whyn't ya unbutton 'is pants, Hassie so's we kin look at it."

Paul felt bold fingers unfastening his trousers. Hassi was so possessed of giggling mirth and excitement tha he could feel the tremble in her fingers.

"Shucks, it's no bigger'n Pa's!"

"Wait'll I start ticklin' it with 'is feather 'n' ya'll see ho fast it grows."

378

Against his most determined efforts to ignore the unwanted but pleasurable stimulation of not only the feather but now the added butterfly caressings of female fingers, Paul felt the stiffening of his organ.

"Gawd," breathed Ossie, "I never seed Pa's git thet big!"

"Jes' lookin' at it makes me feel hot all over," breathed Hassie.

"Whyn't we-uns . . . you know . . . kinda have some fun with it. Pa wouldn't never know."

"Girls—please—"

"Y'see?" crowed Hassie. "He's beggin' fer it."

Ossie seemed hesitant. "What iffen he gives us babies? We-uns don't want no Yankee babies."

"He cain't give we-uns no babies when he's upside down like thet."

"Well . . . but you try it fust, Hassie."

"Fetch me a chair so's I kin git up thar."

Ossie eagerly fetched a chair and Hassie got on it, hauled her dress up to her waist—there was nothing beneath it but Hassie herself—then maneuvered herself up on the table over Paul and began lowering herself. She let out a squeal of delight.

"Hurry up, Hassie—lemme try it—"

"You gotta wait yer turn. I hain't hardly got started."

Making her connection, she began joggling up and down joyfully.

V

After the girls had taken their turns repeatedly, during which time seemed to stretch out eternally, Paul lay there humiliated and simmering with anger. Despite his efforts to resist, his organ had erupted with several orgasms.

But the girls' sexual greed wasn't sated. Ossie said hesitantly, "It'd be kinda nice ter try it jes' once with 'im the way Pa does it."

"We'd hafta cut 'im loose t' do thet."

"Only fer a spell. I could hol' the gun on 'im while yer doin' it, an' you hol' the gun while I'm doin' it—then we-uns could tie 'im up after."

"I git fust chance. You hol' the gun on 'im while I git 'im untied."

His bonds released, Paul sat up, feeling weak and dizzy. An appeal to the girls would be useless. The creatures were too carried away on the high tide of their innocent sensuality. But now that he was untied, and if he pretended to be sharing their joys, maybe—

"Now yer come ovah ter the bed with me, Yankee, hear? An' don' try nothin' funny or Ossie'll shoot a hole through yer."

At the bed, Hassie plumped herself down on her back and hauled up her skirt.

"Now come an' show me whut kinda man yer is, Yankee. . . ."

Paul lowered himself above the eager girl while Ossie moved closer to the left side of the bed to watch. He remained poised there a moment or two, gauging distances, the angle of the musket barrel—

"Whatcher waitin' fer, Yankee?"

In a sudden surge of all his strength and speed, he fell over Hassie, grasping her close as he swiftly rolled over to the right until Hassie was above him, tight against his chest as a shield against the gun.

"Don't shoot—" he warned, "or you'll kill your sister!"

A stream of choice cusswords burst from the girls as he worked himself off the bed holding the struggling Hassie in front of him.

"Lemmy sister go, hear!" screeched Ossie.

Paul had backed against the wall with his kicking, squirming captive.

"Not until you put that gun down. And quick! I'm going to start strangling Hassie right now, and if you don't put that gun down, she'll be dead in ten seconds."

Suiting his words, he brought both hands up to her neck and exerted pressure. Hassie's beginning screams choked off into gurgling. Her face started purpling.

380

Ossie dropped the gun on the bed and started sobbing.

Roughly shoving Hassie aside, Paul snatched up the gun and leveled it at the girls.

"Now we're going to play a new game. First, get your dresses off. . . ."

They stared at him, horrified. Paul's doctoring experiences had taught him that backwoods women, no matter how lewd—even professional tavern whores—were more shocked by complete nudity than by the vilest sin.

"Hurry, or I'll be forced to kill you both."

Sobbing, shamefaced, they divested themselves of their dresses, let them drop to the floor. They were fish-belly white where their rags had kept the sun off them. Sunburnt hands covered their breasts and private parts.

"Now outside—I'll be following with the gun."

"We cain't go outside!" whined Ossie. "Some'uns might see us."

"I'm sure you'd rather be seen naked alive than naked dead. Get going. . . ."

vi

About a mile down the woods road he came to a pleasant enough glade off to one side, into which he ordered the girls.

"Hassie, you sit at the base of that tree and put your arms around the trunk behind you. Ossie, you tie her wrists securely." He tossed her a section of the same rope that had been used to tie him to the table.

Sullenly, Ossie complied.

"Now Ossie, you come over and sit by this tree." Putting the gun down, he bound Ossie's wrists behind the tree in a similar manner. The girls had by now given up their tears and were glaring at him with the most scathing hatred.

"When Pa gits back, he's shore gonna kill ya, Yankee!"

"I hope he has the good sense to first give both of you the whupping you deserve."

"Is all Yankees such mean bastuhds? Ain't nobody but the lowdownest mean bastuhd ever lived 'd brung us 'ere nakkid whar the hull worl' kin peek at us."

Paul bowed. "My apologies, ladies. Try to understand it wasn't meanness, but necessity. With your clothes on, you'd go running to the nearest neighbors and get hounds on my trail before I could get very far. Now I have a fair chance. . . ."

With a final, cheery salute, he strode off carrying the gun.

Four

The Deserter

i

Shivering from the slashing rain, Carson stared out between the railings of the horsecar and wondered why the long troop train was coming to a creaking, screeching stop.

The cold rain had been falling steadily throughout the night and all morning, drenching him to the skin. His teeth chattered; his lips had turned blue. The small hands clenching the corral railing were reddened and stiff.

A bugle started wailing. A voice was shouting:

"Pile out, men, an' fall into marching formation!"

Somewhere from far away came a strange, muffled booming.

Rapidly the boy clambered up the wooden fence of the horsecar and down the other side. Jumping to the cinder railbed, he darted toward the cover of the nearest bushes along the tracks, unnoticed by the soldiers in butternut and gray who had begun piling out of the long line of open-doored boxcars.

For two days after running away, Carson had traveled on foot along roads, across fields and woods, stumbling through tangled underbrush, wading through swamps. Uncle Etienne had taught him the points of the compass in relation to the rising and setting of the sun, and he could identify the North Star after dark, so he was able to keep roughly in a northerly direction. Sometimes he wept when torn by brambles, or during the loneliness of night. His little belly rumbled with emptiness from having eaten nothing but an ear of dried corn stolen from a farmer's crib, and once he pulled up a peanut plant in a field and tried eating the raw, green peanuts, but the taste was so horrible he had to spit them out. At times he wondered if he should go back home, but always the thought was more frightening than going ahead.

Yesterday he had come into a small town where a troop train was stopped to take on water. Seeing the open doors of the boxcars crowded with Confederate soldiers, he guessed that they were headed north to fight Yankees. Without much trouble he had clambered into one of the horsecars. Soon it began to rain. For the entire night and half the next day he had remained standing in the soaking rain against the railing, afraid to lie down for fear of being trampled by the milling horses.

And now hiding in the bushes near the railroad tracks his heart was beating with fierce excitement. The distant thunder of big guns was continuous.

Linkum's army!

Boldly he darted out of the bushes and began running toward those booming sounds.

ii

Paying little attention to the whine of bullets overhead unknowing of the danger, he nimbly darted in and out among the trees, around bushes. There were zipping sounds through the foliage. Leaves and twigs came falling here and there as if plucked by a strong wind. He scampered across fields, down and up gullies, over hillocks. He saw men in butternut lying in the wet grass, behind trees, everywhere. Often they shouted, but their words, muffled under the steady drizzle, rattle of musketry and heavy crash of cannon, were indistinguishable. Thick black clouds of smoke, mingled with puffs of blue, hung low over the ground, stinging his eyes, making him cough. He kept running.

Coming out of a copse of woods onto a grassy slope, the noise got even louder. On a far hillside, endless puffs of blue smoke kept popping into the air. Across from them on the opposite hillside was a long trench with men's heads and rifles sticking out, also puffing up smoke and pounding away like hammers on empty barrels. Running around the top edge of the slope to get around the trench, he came upon a seething whirlpool of men battling each other with bayonets, rifle butts, knives, fists. Jeers of triumph, screams of pain. Big whooshing sounds went overhead, shrieking like banshees. Everywhere were the stinging clouds of smoke. And bodies. The ground was littered with them.

He tried to avoid the bodies by going around or stepping over, but once he accidentally stepped on the face of a man he thought was dead. The resulting howl of pain sent Carson racing away so he couldn't be blamed. Another time he passed a man sitting against a tree holding his rifle, his face forward on his chest. He stopped a moment, thinking to ask the direction to Linkum's army, then saw that half of the man's face was shot away, just a gory mess, and he couldn't talk. He hurried on.

Now he was reaching a section of battlefield that was quieter. Still, he saw men everywhere, most of them in all sorts of strange unmoving positions on the ground; a few crawled or dragged themselves along.

He walked gingerly among them, sometimes slipping in pools of blood, trying hard not to step on any of them because it was scary when a body he thought was dead let out a groan. Most of those who could move were trying to get down a ravine to a stream at the bottom. He started down the slope, walking even more carefully because here the ground was thicker with bodies who had tried to reach the stream but couldn't make it. Ahead he saw a row of men lying on their bellies along the stream with heads in the water drinking. Some of them, he noted, had their whole heads under water and couldn't seem to get enough. How could they hold their breath that long? The water, red as wine, didn't look like anything he'd want to drink.

Halfway down the slope he was startled by a voice calling from behind:

"Son, son—!"

Turning, he saw a man on hands and knees staring at him. He was white-haired, scrawny; blood dripped steadily down the side of his face, from out of his mouth.

"Son—don't you recognize your old daddy?" The voice was weird, sepulchral.

Carson's heart thudded in a frenzy of fright. No, this couldn't be his daddy! Uncle Etienne had said he was very handsome. Besides, he was already dead. He backed away fearfully. The man was crawling after him. The voice croaked:

"Johnny . . . my little Johnny . . . oh come an' see your old daddy while I'm still breathing. . . ."

Carson backed away faster, stumbled over a body, fell splashing on his back into the stream. He sat up, spitting out a mouthful of bloody water. The man scrabbling after him was at the water's edge.

"Johnny, Johnny . . ." he croaked piteously as he crawled out into the water among the dead bodies. "Don't run away from your daddy. . . ." He crawled with an extra spurt of effort, then suddenly seemed to collapse, fell face down into the stream.

Carson stared at the reddish water flowing over the man's neck. Could it really be his father, and he'd just forgotten his real name? There was a stinging sensation behind his eyeballs. He floundered over and with a great sense of horror and distaste forced himself to grasp the man's torso and struggle with it until he managed to turn it over.

The shiny wet eyes stared with a fixed expression—staring not at him but at eternity.

A quivering started up Carson's spine, up his throat, and then he started bawling.

iii

Private Orrin Oakes of the Confederate army rubbed his groggy, bloodshot eyes and wondered if it was only a dream when he saw the boy. . . .

The fact was, until a moment ago he *had* been dreaming about his own small son and his wife at home while sitting back against a tree resting. When the fighting had shifted off to the left, he'd made no attempt to go along with the handful of men still left in his company. Instead, he'd lain flat on the ground pretending he was dead. Not from cowardice—he had nearly four years of hard fighting behind him to prove that—but because those long years of blood, killing, near starving, freezing and forced marches in shoes with the soles worn through had just plumb worn out another kind of soul inside his chest. He was just plain too sick and disgusted with being a poor man who couldn't afford any slaves of his own fighting his ass off for the rich, and nothing could ever make him push his exhausted body and spirit another step.

A paragraph in the last letter from his wife was part of the sickness:

". . . Seems like everybody's trying to rob and make big profits off us poor folks. They ask five dollars for a loaf of bread and sixteen dollars for a pound of butter—and us without a cent in the house! I don't want to worry you none but we got nothing left to eat but a little meal. I don't want you to stop fighting them Yankees, but try to get off and come home and fix us up with some food, and then you can go back. . . ."

That had been six months ago. He'd written back that the captain refused him permission to go home, and he couldn't send money because they hadn't been paid in several months. She'd never answered that letter, or others he'd sent since.

He rubbed his eyes again to make sure it wasn't some kind of crazy trick they were playing on him, instead of a real boy out there walking among the dead bodies, delicate, kind of, to avoid stepping on them. It couldn't be! How could a kid of no more than maybe five or six ever get out here in the middle of where all the fighting had been going on?

Wearily, Oakes got to his feet and walked toward the lad, called:

"Hey, young feller—what're you doin' way out here?"

The boy's wide gray eyes darted a glance at him, not frightened, but suspicious. He had been crying, Oakes noted, and his clothes, though in tatters, were plainly of an expensive quality. "I'm just walking," he said defensively.

"Walkin'? Oh I kin see that all right—you think I'm blind or somethin'? How'd you git past all them guns an' bullets is what I want to know."

The boy regarded him with hostility. "I already told you. I just walked. Sometimes I ran."

Oakes was stumped. The kid couldn't be lying—he sure didn't fly here, and no one in his right mind would ever bring a kid to a battlefield.

"Walked, you say," Oakes said in exasperation. "Why in thunder'd you ever want to walk out here?"

"I'm looking for Linkum's army."

Oakes was suddenly stricken with an overwhelming sense of sorrow. Now he understood. The little tyke had been scared daft, didn't know half what he was doing or saying. It was the way some old folks got and had to be humored, as though you really believed them.

Slinging his rifle over one shoulder by its strap, he took the boy's hand.

"Come with me, son. I'll help you look. . . ."

Five

Through a Sea of Mud

i

A dripping sky, heavy with more rain to come, hung over the small band of marchers like a gray shroud. They were stragglers, the ragtag remnants of a Union battalion of foot soldiers who had been cut off from the main body of their comrades by accident or apathy during a furious, bloody engagement, and now they were lost. For two days they had been trudging through mud and rain, sticking mostly to the swamps to avoid rebels because their numbers were few, and their will to fight was gone. Last night they had slept, or tried to, without tents or blankets in oozing mud, too exhausted to worry about water moccasins or alligators. Now they marched at a slow, slogging pace, boots sucking deep in mud. They were less like soldiers than a disorganized band of outcasts. Their beards were long and filthy, their blue uniforms in tatters, faces expressionless as they bent under the weight of their rifles. They marched without plan or resolution, by habit only, held together simply by the primal trait of survival and the human need for company. Their minds, nearly as blank as detonated shells, were concerned only with thoughts of food and reaching some indefinite goal—they didn't know where—that seemed an eternity away.

Joreen was one of them. How she had gotten separated from her company in the last sprawling battle, she didn't know. Or care much. She had been enmeshed in the nightmare of war for so long, had killed so many men, that nothing seemed to matter anymore.

Nothing but her undying hatred for rebels. It was rebels who had robbed and murdered her father, raped her, killed her brother. The scars still burned in her like acid.

Following the days when she had been a proud recruit in the cavalry—from which she'd fled after the terrible incident with Lieutenant Verlandigham—she had run across a regiment of Union infantry. The commander, badly in need of a horse, had paid her well enough for Thunder and welcomed her into the infantry.

With good reason. It was just prior to the battle of Antietam, where she soon found herself in the thick of more slaughter and bloodshed than she could have imagined. One cornfield near a little Dunker church had been mowed down as cleanly as if by a giant scythe, leaving Union bodies piled high in the windrows. Somehow she had survived.

After that, the Wilderness Campaign. Another bloodbath. Crawling through tangles of brush and vines so thick you couldn't see your enemy until he was a dozen feet away. Fighting eyeball to eyeball while bullets slashed overhead like a continuous, horizontal hailstorm.

Then other battles. And others. She'd lost count. While comrades fell around her, miraculously she was still alive. But it was not pure luck. She was a seasoned veteran, had quickly learned the first rule of keeping her behind down, had a natural instinct for always seeking the lowest ground level, safe from raking enemy fire. She was a sharp-eyed crack shot.

No longer did she worry about her masquerade as

man. Uniforms were never changed; bathing, except for a few face washings, was rare; the informality of the battlefront made other needs for privacy a simple matter. Because of her formidable fighting reputation, even her lack of a beard drew no gibes.

The once gentle, sensitive young woman had slowly transformed into something almost subhuman—a fighting machine whose only objective was to survive and kill more rebels.

They plodded on. One of the men had begun wobbling, finally stopped.

"Can't go no farther," he said. "Reckon I'll just sit 'ere an' rest fer a spell. . . ." He staggered off to one side and slumped down in the mud on his back to sleep—or die. The other men kept going, not bothering to waste more than a glance on him. Two others had already dropped by the wayside.

After another timeless interlude, the distant boom of cannon rolled through the murk. Of a common accord, all the men stopped to listen. Some thought they heard rifle fire.

"If that's where the fightin' is," said one man, "I'm going in the other direction."

"What the hell are you?" said another. "A goddamn deserter?"

"Call it what you want. I done my share. Nobody gives a piss about it either, except me. I'm fed up to my goddamn ears with killin' an' dodgin' bullets." As if to emphasize his words, he threw down his rifle.

After a few awestruck moments, another spoke up: "By God, I'm with 'im! They kin hang me if they want, but I'm not fightin' anymore."

Other voices joined in agreement. Rifles began dropping.

"All right, men," said the second speaker, "but use your God-given brains. We don't have to go where the fightin' is. We can just set here, or go anywhere we want, but pick up your goddamn rifles. If our colonel finds us, or we find him, do you want to go home as deserters or heroes?"

As the men reluctantly started picking up their rifles, Joreen drew away from the group and turned a face of fury on them.

"You snivelin' cowards!" she spat at them. "Maybe you'll live to go home as big heroes, an' maybe you won't, but if you do, I can promise you one thing: in your own hearts to the end of your days, you'll never be able to hide from what you really are—the scum of the army!"

With that she swung around and strode away—in the direction of the firing.

ii

The rain had ceased and so had the distant firing, but Joreen kept walking. Through a deathly stillness of carnage. Bodies, wrecked vehicles everywhere. She paused to look at a horse hitched to a wagon that had been shot while struggling to haul its burden out of a mudhole; the beast was still upright, frozen in action on lowered haunches, bent front legs stiff and straining, neck arched down with its nose buried deep in the mud. She felt a rush of sympathy for the innocent beast far deeper than anything she felt for the human dead littering the ground in every direction, all of them in butternut or gray. Some were beginning to stink. Apparently the Federals had picked up their own dead before going on. Maybe, she thought, the rebels had been running too fast to bother, or they'd run out of burial squads.

She saw a flash of movement ahead and automatically ducked down, rifle on the ready. By golly, there was one of them they'd missed! He didn't see her because he was facing away, walking along just below the lip of an incline so that only the upper half of him showed. His uniform or what was left of it, was of the homespun, butternut dyed material worn by the poorest rebels.

With ease she could have picked him off at that eas\

range of about a hundred yards and got him square through the head, but she'd never shot a man from behind.

Crouched low, she raced on ahead, parallel to the direction he was moving in, until she found a good spot to hide. When he came close enough, she stepped out into full view of the astonished man with her rifle aimed at him.

"All right, you danged reb—say your prayers!"

He just stared at her for a moment, then shrugged tiredly and let his rifle slide to the ground. "You got the drop on me. Go ahead an' shoot."

She noticed the boy then, who had been hiding behind the reb.

"What're you doin' with that kid?"

"Hain't none of your damn business. You goin' t' shoot or ain't you?"

She wondered too why she hadn't shot when she had him dead to rights like this. "Fair is fair. I'll put my gun down; then you can grab yours an' I'll grab mine, an' the quickest one wins."

"I ain't takin' favors from any damned Yankee."

"You danged mulehead! I can't just shoot down a fool too ornery to fight back!"

"In that case, I'll just mosey along. Come on, boy. . . ." He started away holding the lad's hand, and after a few steps stopped to grin back at her.

"What's the matter, Yankee? You too yaller to kill me?"

She started after him, rifle still pointed at him. "I decided I'm takin' you prisoner instead."

"Thet so? Then you better count on takin' me pris'ner in the wrong direction, 'cause I jest decided either you kill me or I'm haided home."

Fuming and exasperated with his stubbornness, she fell in a few steps behind him. She should have killed him right off, she knew, because after seeing him up close it was too late. There wasn't anything mean in those plain blue eyes or in that dumb yokel face with the mess of uncombed reddish hair hanging around it. And the way he held the boy's hand showed he had something good about him.

What the danged hell was she going to do with him?

iii

They walked in constrained silence. She tried to ease it by speaking to the boy, who walked beside the rebel.

"What's your name, little boy?"

"Carson Abbott."

"Where are your folks, Carson?"

"Dead."

"Where've you been livin'?"

Carson just shook his head, tight-lipped.

"What's wrong with him?" she asked the man. "Don't he ever talk more than that?"

"Reckon he's just choosy about the kind he talks to."

They weren't much better company than the dead, she thought resentfully, glancing at the pitiful bodies strewn along the way. Most of the corpses wore uniforms so ragged as to only half cover them. She could see the soles of some of their shoes; all had big holes in them; some had no soles at all. Out of spite, she said:

"You rebs sure don't dress good."

"We don't put on our good clothes for killing hogs."

"You're a sore trial, reb! I sure hope we come across a Federal patrol soon, so I can turn you over to get took to a prison camp where you belong."

Another few minutes of silence, then: "Better keep hopin', Yank. I see soldiers up yonder."

She squinted her eyes ahead. "They don't look like Federals to me."

He grinned at her. "They hain't. Them's Confederates. Hand me your rifle—"

"In a pig's eye! I'll fight the whole shebang of them first!"

394

"Don't be such a damn fool, Yank. I got to have your rifle so's I can pretend you're *my* pris'ner. Or else—"

"Else what?"

"Else they'll take you pris'ner, an' the kid away from me, an' put me back to fightin'. Now give me your rifle—quick!"

Dumbly she handed him the rifle, thinking herself the stupidest fool that ever lived, but she saw no other way out of it except a bloody fight she would surely lose, or being taken prisoner anyway.

As they neared the group of rebels, she saw that they had a wagon into which they were loading the dead. Just a burial squad. One of them hailed their comrade:

"See ya got yerself a fuckin' Yankee pris'ner. Whar ya takin' 'im?"

"Back to my outfit."

"Who's the young 'un?"

"Hell, he's one of their new recruits. They's scrapin' the bottom of the barrel so hard up North, they plumb ran outta uniforms an' rifles to give 'em."

The burial squad guffawed.

They trudged on. When they had gone far enough past the other rebels, Joreen's ex-prisoner turned and thrust the gun at her. "Here's your fuckin' rifle back."

She took it gravely. "I didn't figure you to give it back."

"Us Confederates always keep our word."

iv

By late afternoon she still hadn't made up her mind what to do with him. She was making no objections to his leading the way, and they had not encountered any Union troops. By this time they were cutting through what once must have been beautiful farm country, but now was the most desolated country she had ever seen or could possibly imagine.

Nearly all of the small farmhouses, barns and shacks

had been burned to the ground. Fields too had been ravaged by fire; cornfields stripped of every ear; fruit trees robbed of their fruit. In the wild, blind rage of the Yankee conquerors, some of the orchards had been chopped down, for no earthly good that could accrue to the victors. A few scrawny horses and mules wandered about forlornly seeking forage, but almost every vestige of grass was gone and even leaves on lower branches of still existing trees had already been eaten. Everywhere was gloom, fallen pride, hunger, deathly stillness.

The rebel stood hands on hips, eyes cold blue fire, gazing about.

"It's that bloodthirsty Sherman's hordes that done it!" he finally burst out. "The rottenest, dirtiest low-down fighters in the whole war!"

"They're only fightin' back same as you godderned rebels started it!" she shot back. "If you'd seen how they robbed my dad's farm, then killed him an'—"

"It's you goddamn Yankees made us fight, tryin' to tell us what to do an' how to do it!"

"That's a thunderin' lie! You and your consarned slave owners forced the fight on us. We only got in it to free the slaves an' get 'em treated like regular human beings."

"You ain't got 'nuff sense in yore head to fill a pinhead, Yank! I don't even own a slave—never did. I like niggers an' I'll let 'em eat at my table anytime, long's they come in the back door, but you damned Yankees are too stupid to know niggers got to be kept in their place or they'll walk all over you."

"Stop that kinda talk, reb! You're just as bad as the big slave owners, talkin' cruel about the Negroes, an' tryin' to blame us for startin' a fight that you're to blame for."

"Damn you, Yank! Say another word and I'll—"

Joreen threw her rifle aside and danced back with fists up. "Start tryin', you lunkhead reb!"

"If you weren't such a little squirt—!"

Joreen started forward, fists outthrust. The rebel backed away.

"Lookee here, Yank—I ain't a-lookin' for a fight tha hain't fair. You're hardly more'n half my size—"

She flew at him, fists flying like windmills. He thrust out one arm and held her back while he drew back a mighty fist. "You're strainin' my patience, Yank—!"

At that moment Carson rushed between them, tried to shove them apart.

"Don't fight," he pleaded.

"Git away from here, kid! You might git hurt."

"But you can't fight when *both* of you are right."

The rebel glared down at the boy. "You takin' a damn Yank's side against *me?* Sayin' he's as right as I am—!"

"Well, you both talked like you thought the other one was stupid, and you both are."

"*Stupid?* Listen, I don't take no sass from any young snip—!"

"Reb—*you* listen for a while," said Joreen. "Don't you realize the boy is talking like a grown-up? An *educated* grown-up?"

"Mebby he can talk fancy, but that part about stupid really riles me."

"I didn't mean *that* kind of stupid," said Carson. "I meant the same as about my own father and my Uncle Etienne. They loved each other like brothers, but my father joined the Union army and Uncle Etienne joined the Confederates. Both got killed—" Tears started forming in the boy's eyes.

There was an abashed silence. The rebel spoke:

"Guess the little tyke's brighter'n we are, Yank. Iffen you want to forgit what I said—even though I was plumb right—I'll forgit all the lies you said."

She took a deep breath. "I guess you mean right, reb, even though you say it all wrong. I'm willin' to admit all rebels aren't like the kind that murdered my father if you'll admit all Yankees aren't like some of the scum in Sherman's army."

The rebel scratched his head. "I reckon that's about right. We got trash on both sides."

"Now that we got one thing agreed, I'd like to ask you a favor. You stop calling me Yank an' I'll stop callin' you reb."

"Gotta call each other somethin'."

"You gotta name, haven't you?"

"Reckon I have."

"Mine's Jory Jones. What's yours?"

"Oakes."

"Oakes what?"

"Orrin Oakes."

"All right, Orrin, let's make one more agreement. Let's promise never to fight again, no matter what."

"I'll have to think on that for a spell. No man's a man if he cain't fight."

"I just meant fightin' between you an' me."

He grinned. "Guess that's an easy promise to make, seein' as I'm the biggest of the two."

"To make a promise stick, you got to shake on it."

He thrust out a big, muscular hand and gripped hers firmly. It made her feel more like a captive than the captor.

Six

End of the Masquerade

i

Two days later, in late afternoon, they saw a curving strip of green ahead that turned out to be a fresh clear stream about twenty feet across.

Orrin was delighted. "Wherever there's good water, there's bound to be good houses close by. We'll just mosey along the stream till we find one. Mebby Sherman overlooked one or two. . . ."

For the next hour they followed the stream. Apparently Sherman's raiders hadn't overlooked much. They passed a railroad trestle bridge that had been dynamited and was now caved into the stream. Most of the iron rails had been pried loose from their wooden ties and turned into what were called "Sherman's hairpins"—the rails having been held over a furiously hot fire until soft enough to bend into useless shapes around the trunk of a tree.

But the wildlife, fortunately, had not abandoned their watery sanctuary. Frequently they heard the flurry of wings as ducks took off from the stream. Rabbits or small deer went bounding along the banks. Orrin took Joreen's rifle and shot two ducks, which he strung to his belt with the comment, "At least we'll have solid food for dinner."

Shortly after they saw ahead the impressive outlines of a two-storied plantation about a hundred yards back from the stream.

ii

The mansion, grander than any that Joreen had ever seen, had been turned into a sight to sicken anyone. Several of the front columns that supported the gallery had collapsed, half blocking off the entrance. Scattered over the lawn were the relics of vandalism: Wedgwood china smashed to chips, shattered glassware, fine furniture axed to pieces for firewood. Piles of ancient books had been burned, only the brass clasps which held them together still evident. Cast-iron cooking pots were strewn about. Inside were even worse signs of devastation: a clavichord ripped apart until its musical brass wires were sticking up all over like unruly long whiskers, a chandelier hanging lopsided, twisted askew with most of its prisms broken as if the vandals had made beauty a special target for their vengeance. Lamps had been smashed, their shards still littering Oriental carpets; squares of faded color on the wallpaper gave evidence that once paintings had hung there. In many places the plaster had cracked or fallen off from shelling, and a big gaping hole at least twenty feet across in one section of the ceiling showed where a shell must have exploded. Beautiful old mahogany tables, their surfaces now marred and scratched, were filthy with remnants of food that must have been scavenged from the larder. Fine damask draperies had been torn; everything of remote use or beauty had been destroyed. All was in a shambles.

Sickened, Joreen tugged Orrin's arm. "I take back

everythin' I said about rebels. They sure ain't any worse than the damn Yankees who did this!"

Orrin's voice was gruff: "I promised not to git het up about it with you, an' I'm so afeard I'll explode, why'n't you go an' drum up some firewood while I git the ducks cleaned. We'll cook 'em in that big fireplace."

She headed for the stream to search for dry branches, and coming in view of the crystal-clear water had a sudden overwhelming desire to bathe. The sight of the brutal destruction in the mansion had left her feeling as dirtied inside as the mud and filth that caked her face, uniform and every part of her body. She hadn't washed in weeks.

She went several hundred feet downstream and amid a thicket removed her garments—*ughhhhh!* They too needed a scrubbing!

Wading into the astringent chill of water, she let out a sigh of content. It was so refreshing—luxury beyond belief! Going into deeper water that covered her breasts, she vigorously scrubbed her body, yearning for soap but doing the best she could by rubbing away caked dirt. Repeatedly she ducked her head under water, massaging her scalp to get out all the dirt and stickiness.

Feeling cleansed and invigorated she returned to her clothes and hastily as possible put on the filthy garments, wishing she could take the time to wash them too, but she feared that Orrin might wonder why she was gone so long and come down to investigate. Quickly she gathered up an armful of dried sticks and branches and hurried back.

He at once noticed the difference. He frowned. "So you went to wash up," he said in a peeved way. "Couldn't recognize you right off with all that filth off your face. Hell, you don't hardly look old enough to be in the army." He paused. "Anyway, it ain't fair leavin' me here to do all the work while you go out to swim."

She looked at the two ducks on the table all plucked of their feathers but their innards not yet removed. Apparently he had found firewood for there were crackling flames in the fireplace.

"I'm sorry, Orrin. Look—you go take a swim while I finish cleanin' the ducks an' get 'em over roastin'. Take

Carson with you an' watch him good 'cause the stream's fulla deep holes."

"You damn right that's what I'm goinna do," he said a bit sullenly. "An' don't 'spect me back in a hurry. When I go for a swim, I like to *swim*." He crooked a finger at Carson. "Come along, Carse. . . ."

Deftly she finished cleaning the ducks and got them on the spit, placing them high over the heat of the fire. It would take at least an hour to cook them, she judged, and until the fire built up more heat they wouldn't require much turning. There was time to look around. Something about the grand mansion, wrecked as it was, had cast a sort of hypnotic spell over her. What must it have been like, she thought wistfully, to have been born in a mansion of this sort and raised in the rich life it suggested. Dormant yearnings in her were coming to life. The urge to explore became overpowering.

iii

Destruction on the second floor was just as bad. Old four-poster beds were wrecked, mattresses ripped open, feathers scattered around as if from a whirlwind. Shards of smashed mirrors glittered on the carpets.

But somehow they had overlooked the attic. She found a broken but still usable ladder leading up to a trap door in the ceiling and climbed up, pushing the trap door aside. A gaping hole in the roof admitted light, revealing several trunks, piles of books, tables, various pieces of furniture covered with dust cloths and along one wall a row of closets.

She peeked in a closet. It smelled of dried lavender and was filled with dresses of the richest fabrics she had ever seen. Timidly she reached out and ran fingers over some of them. Her heart sped. She had never before touched silks, satins, velvets. She had never owned dresses of anything but cotton or muslin, and worn them but rarely.

Mostly she had worn the same kind of boys' clothes that her brother had worn.

A huge French mirror leaning sideways against a wall suddenly caught her attention because of her moving reflection, which showed only her ragged, muddied uniform up to the knees. Out of sheer curiosity, for she hadn't seen her face in a mirror for nearly three years, she struggled with the mirror to set it upright, stepped back to look at herself. Was appalled.

How ratty she looked! A wild tangle of still-wet blond hair, a smallish face with mouth open and staring eyes she scarcely remembered, a dreadfully torn and filthy uniform. She stuck her tongue out at the image.

A sudden urge came over her. Back to the closet she went and began pawing through the dresses. They were all so gorgeous! Finally she selected one of pale green, pulled it out and held it in front of her. It looked to be a good enough fit.

Looking around guiltily, she quickly got off her filthy clothes and horrible boots. She had no undergarments but that didn't matter. All she wanted was to see what she looked like in a dress—a *real* dress.

With some difficulty she got it pulled down over her head, straightened it out around her body. The waistline was narrow, but so was her own waist. The fit was quite good. It took all her dexterity to get the back hooked up. Then, barefoot, she tiptoed over to the mirror.

The first glance startled her—almost as if she'd intruded on some rich young lady. Flushed with both embarrassment and pleasure, she stepped forward for a closer inspection. It was incredible! Except for the wild, uncombed hair, she wouldn't have known herself. She'd never worn anything but loosely fitting men's things or shapeless cheap gowns—never before anything that so brought out her femininity.

Pleased, she began prancing back and forth in front of the mirror, her fascinated eyes glued to her reflection. It was hypnotic, but something was missing. Shoes, of course! Remembering all the fine ladies' shoes she had seen in the closet, she raced back and found several pairs with heels

—something she'd never worn—and flopping down on the floor, man-style, put on a pair. They were a bit tight but looked so elegant.

Clambering up, she minced back to the mirror in the unaccustomed heels and was even more enamored of herself. Everything but that impossible hair! Automatically her hands went up to try and comb it with her fingers into some semblance of order.

When the voice barked out, she was so startled she almost fell. Whirling about, she saw Orrin's head thrust above the hatchway trap door opening, gawking at her in disbelief.

"What in thunderation!" Clumsily he climbed the rest of the way up, not once taking his goggling eyes off her. She backed away, feeling humiliated and strangely naked.

"So you're one of them kind—?" he said, his jaw half dropped open. "I heered there's some like that in the army—"

He broke off as his eyes became riveted on one spot. The gown was very low-cut—only half covering her breasts. In the three years that she had been in the army, despite her most valiant efforts to repress them, those breasts had continued to develop. He stared at the firm mounds that were peeping above the edge of the gown.

"By God and by Jesus," said Orrin.

iv

They feasted ravenously on the roast ducks, but in subdued silence. Joreen had kept the dress on because it had given her an opportunity to wash her uniform, which was now drying by the fireplace. Orrin couldn't seem to resist stealing frequent glances at her, and even Carson looked at her with greater interest.

"You look a little like my Aunt Narcisse," the boy said at one point. "Only nicer."

Neither she nor Orrin had been able to get Carson t

404

divulge anything about his background, so now her curiosity was piqued. "Oh, so you have an Aunt Narcisse. Did you live with her?"

"Yes."

"Where was that?"

"At Les Cyprès."

"Never heard of any town named that," said Orrin.

"It's not a town. It's a plantation."

"Plantation? You mean with a big house an' everything, like this one?"

Carson glanced around. "A little like this, only bigger, and nothing in it is broken up like it is here."

Joreen and Orrin looked at each other in surprise.

"Your Aunt Narcisse must be a very rich woman to own a plantation like that."

"Oh, she doesn't own it. I do."

Orrin, seated behind Carson, caught Joreen's eye and tapped his head, making circular little motions with a finger. Joreen wasn't so sure. Carson's soiled and torn clothes were plainly of fine quality, and the way he could speak better than she or Orrin could only mean the kind of education she expected rich kids got.

"Where is this Lay Saypress plantation?" she asked.

"It's pronounced Les Cyprèss" he corrected politely. "But I won't tell you where it is."

Orrin scowled his annoyance. "What ya mean, you won't tell us?"

"I'm afraid if I tell you, you might want to send me back there."

"What's wrong with that?"

"Aunt Narcisse wants to kill me so she can have the plantation for herself."

Again Orrin caught Joreen's eye and made the same circular motions with a finger near his head.

But Joreen was troubled. What if the boy was telling the truth? Orrin obviously didn't believe him because he thought the poor lad's brain had been affected by fright and hardships. Just as obviously his greater interest at the moment was in her. The way he kept looking at her, his eyes seeming to be gobbling at the area of her low-cut gown, sometimes sent strange, prickling sensations up her spine.

His changed attitude became more apparent when she rose and automatically began picking up the remains of the meal and cracked plates she'd found in the scullery to eat on. Orrin was quick to jump up and help. And when she started out to get more wood for the dying fire, he stopped her.

"Now you just set there, Jory. It's a man's job to git the wood."

"Stop being so godderned polite toward me, Orrin. It ain't natural!"

"Natural or not, iffen I'd known you was a female right off I first saw you, I'd sure have treated you different."

She looked down at the gown. "It's this dress, ain't it, that makes you treat me different?"

"Well, you sure look mighty pretty in it."

"But what's inside it ain't any different than it ever was, Orrin. I'm just a soldier with the mud washed off—and wearin' a dress. You got no call to start treatin' me any different than you have all along."

"What you mean I got no call? I know how to treat a female. I was brung up right. You're the one had no call ever to go dressin' like a soldier an' carryin' a gun in the first place. Females is supposed to stay home an' wear dresses."

"If you don't stop actin' toward me like I'm a lady, I'm going to take this dress off right away an' put my uniform back on!"

"You keep that dress on! I'm not lettin' you catch a bad cold in that wet uniform."

"You try to stop me, I'll swop you one!"

"No lady ever swops at a man."

"Well, I ain't no lady, an' don't you forget it."

He shrugged, now pretending indifference. "Suit your self if you don't mind lookin' like something the hound been chewin' on." With feigned nonchalance, he added "Anyway, it's gittin' late. We might just as well sta lookin' for a room to sleep in."

She looked at him suspiciously. "You can go find a room for yourself. Me, I'll sleep somewhere else."

"But you just got through tellin' me you ain't any different than you ever was, an' we been sleeping side by side all this time."

"Not in the same bed we hain't!"

"I never said the same bed. I just wanta be close so I can protect you."

"I don't need protecting!"

"In that dress you do, an' as a man it's my duty to be close where I can watch over you."

"I never needed anybody to watch over me, and I ain't any different now—it's *you* who're different, Orrin. I know how men's minds work. And I ain't about to sleep in the same room with a man who knows I'm a lady."

"You just said you weren't a lady."

"I got a right to be a lady or not a lady whenever I please. Right now I'm going to find my own room and you can go find your own place for you an' Carson."

She got up and pranced away, unable to resist swinging her hips. Something about the dress had induced the urge.

Behind her she heard Orrin saying in a low voice to Carson: "My Gawd, can you b'lieve this? Or am I jest dreamin'?"

V

For two days they traveled, hiking long weary hours. She had put her uniform back on, against Orrin's objections. He wanted her to at least take the dress and shoes along as something she was entitled to, considering what she had lost because of the war. When she said she didn't think it was right, he wrapped them in a little pack anyway and took it along slung over a shoulder.

They had long since dropped the pretense of one being the captor and the other a captive, but it had given Orrin an idea for keeping them together.

"If we run across any Yankees, you take the gun an' say I'm your pris'ner, an' I'll take the gun and say the same if we meet Confederates." Still, she knew they would have to part sooner or later. She was reluctant to think about it.

She soon learned that wearing her old uniform didn't alter Orrin's new attitude toward her. In his eyes she still seemed to be wearing a dress. Whenever they forded a stream, he was quick to come and steady her with his arm, always looking for small things to do that a man did for a lady. At times it was so comical, Joreen wanted to laugh, but didn't because it would hurt his feelings. He couldn't seem to remember that she'd lived a hard life among hard men, sleeping on the ground, shooting, killing and out-fighting men. At all times it seemed as if he were trying to prove that because he was the strongest, she needed him for protection.

In a way, she was beginning to enjoy it.

On the second night after leaving the plantation, he made the move she was expecting. It was a lovely, warm moonlit night and after Carson was asleep, he moved over closer and stealthily put his arms around her, tried to draw her close.

"Don't you try any of that funny stuff with me!" she hissed at him, pushing him away firmly.

He was so embarrassed, she felt sorry for him but didn't want to show it because it might encourage him to try again. Living among men had sure taught her what was on their minds most of the time, and she wasn't allowing any of that stuff.

"And you a married man!" she added stingingly. "You oughta be ashamed."

"Heck, it's been nigh two years since I seen Stella, an she never was much for lovin'. Man gits lonely, he hankers to hold a female close, an' I got to figgerin' mebby you liked me."

"I do like you, Orrin, but I'm not lettin' anybody do anything like that."

He grinned ruefully. "Well, I guess you really *are* lady, but right now I sure wish the heck you wasn't."

Sinking back into sleep, she had to admit to herself that she was getting fonder of him every day that passed. He had such a good heart, and unexpected tenderness. Earlier that day when he'd noticed Carson limping because the thin soles of his sandals were shredded to bits, he'd called a halt until he could find a dead soldier whose boots were in relatively good repair. With a knife he'd cut off sections of the sides and patiently cut them into new soles that he bound to the sandals with leather laces from the dead man's boots.

Yes, she was liking him more and more—too much, considering he was still a damn rebel. The fact was that at times she almost felt happy again, a feeling she hadn't experienced since her father was murdered.

But that other deep sadness—the unknown fate of her twin brother, Jody—still lay heavy in her heart. Hardly a day passed but she wondered if it was possible that he might still be alive.

Seven

"This Soldier Is a Female!"

i

"Soldier—halt!"

At the sharp command, Private Jody McNally of the 2th Illinois Infantry Regiment stopped and looked round to see if the order was meant for him. He had just returned from patrol duty with six of his comrades who ad been separating to return to their tents, but now alted.

"Yes, I mean *you*, soldier—!" The officer pointed a nger at Jody as he approached. He walked with a slight mp. It was the new lieutenant who had arrived yesterday serve as an aide to the general. It was said that once had been in the cavalry but due to a strange wound in e crotch could no longer ride and thus had been transrred to a foot regiment.

The lieutenant, a handsome young man in a spotless iform, stopped a few feet in front of him. His bright blue eyes had widened in astonishment and his lips were twisted with anger.

"You—!" he spat out. "My God, I never expected to see *you* again!"

At Jody's look of mystification, he stormed on:

"Come on there, Jones—don't pretend you don't know who I am!"

"Jones? Why sir, that ain't my name nohow—"

"Rotten little liar—!" The lieutenant limped forward and caught him roughly by the shoulder, shook him. "Maybe Jones isn't your real name—I guessed that when you were under my command—but your face is so branded in my memory—the eyes, the nose, lips, hair, even the ears—that I could pick you out of a thousand men. I ought to shoot you on the spot, you bloodthirsty little scoundrel. Instead, I'm going to have you hanged!"

He turned toward a sergeant who was standing nearby, listening with mouth agape. "Sergeant, put this man under immediate arrest!"

ii

Seated behind his field desk in the command tent, the general skimmed a glance from Jody to the angry-faced lieutenant.

"Lieutenant Verlandigham, this is a most serious charge. You claim that Private McNally is the one who once attacked you, wounding you grievously, after which he turned traitor during battle and vanished?"

"Yes sir. It's the same person—I would bet my life on that! Private Jones—an alias, of course—deserted our company during a battle, directly after wounding me. was captured by Confederates, and later paroled in prisoner exchange after I had recovered somewhat from my wound. I have been looking for this scoundrel ever since."

The general leaned back in his camp chair, glanced

412

his adjutant with arched eyebrows, then back at the lieutenant.

"Your allegations are hardly in accord with our information, Lieutenant. Private McNally is known to have been wounded at Shiloh, later spent several months in a field hospital recovering. After that he served under Colonel Crandall in several major battles, including Gettysburg. We are unaware that he ever served in the cavalry, so you probably have the wrong man. Without more proof—"

"But sir, I *do* have proof—irrefutable proof! Obviously this person is a skilled liar who has stolen another soldier's good name as a way of hiding from the heinous crime, but fortunately I have the facts to prove my charge."

The general sighed. "And what is your proof?"

The lieutenant assumed a smug smile of triumph.

"Simply that this soldier is a *female*, sir. A sex-crazed female who joined the service only to avail herself whenever possible of all our loyal young men, who of course cover up for her in exchange for her sexual favors."

Jody, suddenly understanding, felt a startled thrill race up his back. After recovery in the field hospital, he had been furloughed for a visit home—there to be shocked by the discovery that his father was dead, the farmhouse burned down by rebel raiders, his twin sister missing. Instantly he knew what must have happened: the fiery-tempered, tomboy Joreen would of course have dressed as a boy and enlisted in the cavalry! And the lieutenant looked like the kind who would have tried to get funny with a young soldier.

The general could not help smiling. "Private McNally, are you perchance a female?"

"No sir, I surely hain't no female!"

"Well, just to conclusively satisfy all present on that matter, you will please unbuckle your trousers and pull them down."

Jody flushed. "Sir, do you mean—here? Now?"

"Exactly. We're all men here . . . I think."

With great embarrassment Jody lowered his pants. His underwear had long since rotted through and hung in shreds. His private parts were clearly evident.

The general chuckled. "If this is your idea of a female, Lieutenant, I'll concede that the Lord dealt you a bad hand."

The dismayed lieutenant's face was red. He made a groaning sound. "Oh God, but I could have sworn—"

The general looked at him in a kindly way. "It happens now and then to certain high-strung types, Lieutenant. With exposure to warfare they sometimes lose their grip on reality. I'm afraid I'll have to order you put under restraint and removed to a hospital specializing in mental disorders."

"But General—"

The general turned to his adjutant. "Major, see that my order is put into effect at once." Then he grinned at Jody.

"It's all right, soldier. You can pull your pants up now."

Elation had replaced Jody's embarrassment as he hauled his pants up.

He was sure now that Joreen had to be alive, and that someday, somewhere, he would find her.

iii

They had made a pact to stick together until they reached Orrin's home. And now, almost there, Orrin seemed to get gloomier with every step. Joreen's mood too was increasingly somber with the dismal knowledge of their imminent parting.

Orrin's glumness was not totally because they would soon be separating. For days he had been saying that he could feel it in his bones that something was wrong at home. If not, why hadn't Stella written in over six months?

When they finally came in view of his place—a neat but humble cabin set back against a row of pines—the sense of foreboding suddenly intensified. Orrin's face grew rigid with apprehension.

"The curtains is drawn, an' there's weeds all over the

414

yard. Stella was always finicky about them weeds. . . ." He broke into a run.

Joreen and Carson lagged behind. Apparently the door was unlocked, as Orrin had gone right in.

After a few minutes, Carson tugged at her hand. "Come on, Jory . . . what are we waiting for? Don't you want to meet his family?"

They found him in the living room of the small, three-room cabin. He was seated at a table, staring vacantly into space.

"Is something wrong, Orrin?"

"There hain't no sign that anybody's lived here for months."

"Maybe she left to live with friends or relatives."

"Hain't got no relatives, either of us, an' I don't know no friends that could afford to feed a coupla more mouths."

There was a timid knocking on the back door. Orrin rose tiredly, went over and opened the door. Joreen caught a glimpse of a black face.

"Jus' seed yo' come home, Mista Oakes, an' figgered ah should come ovah an' tell what done happen. . . ."

Orrin opened the door wider. "Come in, Ishmael. I'm sure anxious to find out where my family's gone."

Ishmael's eyes widened momentarily at sight of Joreen's Yankee uniform, but after that he studiously avoided looking at her.

"Miz Oakes git feelin' poorly an' skinny as a beanpole. My woman done offer ter share our eatin's, but Miz Oakes, reck she too proud ter eat nigger eatin's. She git weak an' en she'n de li'l un git tooken by de fever. . . ."

A low wail started in Orrin's throat. "You mean dey—?"

"Dey daid, Mista Oakes. Squire Hawkins come down n' us bury dem by de barn unner de big apple tree. My oman clean up in heah, an' us been keepin' watch on de ouse. . . ."

Orrin was no longer listening. He had buried his face in s hands in an effort to hold back the great sobs that came

415

choking out. After a minute or two he turned in the general direction of the front door, and never had she seen a face so stricken with pain—and rage—as he blindly began shaking his fist at the world in general.

"Goddamn you, Jeff Davis—" he roared, "I hope ya burn forever in the hellfires! An' that goes for all yer goddamn cabinet an' Congress an' all the ass-lickin' pol'ticians, an' yer goddamn army—all the guns an' marches an' drums an' bugles an' mules an' flags an' slavery an' the whole fuckin' Confederacy that kilt my family—!"

Joreen caught his arm, shook him. "Orrin, Orrin—please—"

He turned blurry, reddened eyes toward her, shamed. "Guess I plumb lost my haid there for a moment."

"I understand, Orrin."

He went over to a rough board closet and from a top shelf hauled down an old blanket. He turned. "Cain't stay here tonight, Jory . . . too many memories. You an' Carson take the bedrooms. I'll bunk down in the barn. . . ."

iv

Joreen sloshed around in the big copper tub, luxuriating in her first real bath in three years. Carson, bone-tired from his many days of hardship, was sound asleep in the smaller bedroom, but Joreen, unable to sleep, had decided on a bath the moment she had found the tub in a closet. The water had come from the kitchen pump and had been heated over the wood stove in buckets. She had even found a thin bar of soap, and towels.

Despite the sensuous pleasure of the warm water, her heart was still heavy with concern for Orrin. She was sure that he, too, would be unable to sleep.

Thoroughly scrubbed and rinsed, she stood up in the tub and began drying herself with a towel. She looked at her uniform hanging over the back of a chair and shud dered at the thought of putting it on again. She was beginning to hate the sight of it, but had nothing else to wear.

At that moment she saw the package containing the fine gown that Orrin had insisted on bringing from the plantation manse. She smiled.

Five minutes later she was smiling at her reflection in the small bedroom mirror as she worked vigorously at combing out her damp hair. The mirror was not large enough to show any more than her face and the upper part of her gown, enough to reassure herself that it might help take Orrin's mind off his tragedy.

She'd never promised that she was always going to be a lady!

It was almost dark when she ventured into the barn. She thought she heard a muffled sobbing from up in the hayloft, and suddenly she felt deeply ashamed. She knew that men, even when seized by unassuageable grief, thought it unmanly to shed tears, and he would only be embarrassed to know that she had heard. Her eyes moistened with a welling of compassion. He was so alone in his grief, so much like a lost child in need of comforting.

She padded to the hayloft ladder and softly ascended, unmindful of the bite of the hard wooden rungs against her bare feet. In the dimness she saw him curled on the blanket spread over the hay.

Awkwardly she crossed over to the blanket, each step sinking deep into the soft hay, and knelt down beside him. He turned heavily.

"That you, Jory?"

She didn't answer at first. She had come to him in the dark, thinking to offer comforting words, but what good could words do? He had been suddenly shorn of everything of any real importance in his world—his wife and child—and nothing could help him now but human warmth and closeness. Filled with an overwhelming tenderness, she quickly lay down beside him and pulled his head close to the hollow of her neck and shoulder. He was quivering uncontrollably.

"There's no need to talk," she whispered shakily as her

own tears ran down her cheeks. "Just try to remember that everything heals. . . ."

He buried his head between her breasts, like a child clinging intensely, and with trembling hands she held him tight. Even then she had a prescience of boundaries, defenses, all of her own fears of men melting away. Some of the terrible, fractional violence of death had long filled her with secret terrors, as it had him, and she had no power to turn away his blind, groping need for her now, for she was just as much in need of him.

Then his arms were strong and warm around her, clinging to her in a surge of gratitude, and she knew in that instant, without really thinking about it, that it was only natural and right that she would yield to him whatever she could. Her own arms clasped around his hard back and she could sense that the pain was easing from his heart, that she was helping to banish the dreadful darkness of death from his body under the pulsing inflow of new life.

And soon, for the first time in her life she felt the exhilarating strangeness of passion ignite within. She felt his hands fumbling at her gown, and without shame she helped him undo the fastenings and remove it until she was naked and warm in his arms.

Quite suddenly, in the depth of her body, she began to experience a most wondrous feeling glowing into life from where before she had known nothing but blind, wistful yearnings.

She was unaware of her own short wild cries as the rapture built to a crescendo.

Book Eight

GLORY,
HALLELUJAH!

"Glory, hallelujah, glory, hallelujah! Dis is de year of de jubilee, sure 'nuff. Bless God, bless God. I never 'spected to see dis day."
Slave witnessing approach of Union soldiers, 1865.

One

Lay Dis Body Down

Weary and dispirited, Paul stumbled through the darkness. Tonight there was no moon, but enough stars were visible so that he knew the narrow road he was following led approximately in a southerly direction. He had taken to traveling mostly at night because it was safer; daylight travel exposed him to too many close calls. Farmers, their wives or children were quick to grab their guns and take potshots at any Union straggler, or set their hounds on him. Darkness, however, increased the difficulty of finding food. His stomach was rumbling with emptiness and the keyed-upness of extreme exhaustion had started his ears ringing. At times the ringing seemed to take the form of rhythmic singing . . . growing louder. . . .

He stopped abruptly. It *was* singing—many voices raised in song, and not too far away. At this time of night! The voices seemed too numerous to be anything but troops, though it hardly seemed likely that either rebel or Federal troops would be feeling exuberant enough to be singing when they could just as well be sleeping. Slaves?

The singing did have the deep, melodious rhythm of Negro spirituals. But what slave owner would allow his blacks to gather and sing so late at night?

He proceeded faster. If they were blacks, it could mean food, shelter, protection. He could now begin to make out some of the words:

> "I walk in de moonlight,
> I walk in de starlight—
> LAY DIS BODY DOWN. . . ."

Definitely they were Negroes. He hurried on. The rich voices were soaring into another verse:

> "I'll walk in de graveyard,
> I'll walk troo de graveyard
> TO LAY DIS BODY DOWN.
> I go to de judgment in de evening of de day
> WHEN I LAY DIS BODY DOWN. . . ."

He came upon them in a glade a few hundred feet off the road and was astonished to see they were Union troops after all, gathered around a blazing campfire.

His astonishment was even greater when he came close enough to see that all the faces were black. It was his first inkling that blacks had entered the war and were allowed to wear uniforms.

The singing died down as Paul's ragged figure came into view. A black sergeant detached himself from the group. "Kin I he'p you, Cap'n, suh," he said, instantly noting the insignia on Paul's uniform.

"I'd like to speak to your commanding officer."

"The kunnel's in his tent, suh. Yo' wait heah while I go fetch 'im."

Waiting, it came to Paul that his big black giant friend, Zambullah, who had always yearned so mightily to become a soldier to fight against the slaveholders, given the opportunity would have been among the first to enlist. It was unlikely that there would be many Negro regiments. There was just a possibility—

Paul turned to one of the Negroes. "Do you happen to know of a soldier named Zambullah?"

The man's face split into a grin. "Yo' mean de Zam dat stan' way dis high?" He held a hand far over his head.

"That's the one!"

"Why, ever'body knows Big Zam. He in one de udder battalions."

The sergeant was back. "Heah Kunnel Westland, Cap'n. . . ."

Colonel Westland, a somewhat rotund, balding man with an amiable face, thrust out a hand for Paul to shake.

"Looks like you're a bit the worse for wear, Captain. Come back to my tent and I'll see if we can fix you up with a little food and coffee. . . ."

About an hour later, after a kingly repast of hardtack and dried beef washed down with coffee, and after Paul had finished telling the colonel some of the events that had brought him to his present situation, he got around to asking about his friend Zambullah.

The colonel chuckled. "So you know Big Zam? He's gotten to be quite a legendary hero among all our black troops. Yes, he's in one of my battalions. A sergeant. Fiercest fighter I've ever known. There isn't a Negro soldier who wouldn't follow him through hell. And by the way, I don't mind admitting this war has changed my opinion about the Negroes. Don't let anybody tell you they can't fight. These men are wildcats. If we'd been smart enough to enlist them in the beginning, I warrant you the war would have ended before now."

"Where did Zam enlist?"

"Fact is, he never did rightly enlist. One of our picketing patrols came across him in rags, with a rifle he'd picked up on the battlefield, peppering away at a Confederate skirmishing party. They brought him back and fed him. When he found out that we were headed for Louisiana, which is just where he wanted to go, he asked to join us. I was glad to have him. We found a tailor in one of the villages who sewed him up a uniform, and you never saw a more delighted man."

"Colonel, I have a request to make. Zambullah's reason

for wanting to go to Louisiana is, I believe, very similar to my own. It would be most beneficial for both of us and most greatly appreciated, if you would release him on furlough to accompany me for the rest of the way."

The colonel looked thoughtful. "To tell the truth, I have no right to keep him against his wishes, since he was never properly inducted, so I'll send for him and if he wants to go with you, you've got your man. . . ."

Two

"I Take These Women. . . ."

i

Ensconced on her favorite seat, a velvet-covered stool in front of the great French mirror above her dressing table, Narcisse Duplessis Troyonne Jacquard smiled compla-cently at the reflected flash of a huge diamond ring on the third finger of her left hand as she primped at her hair. Beside it was another ring of gold set with a dozen smaller diamonds. Both were larger and far costlier than the rings she had received from Etienne, but of course she real-zed Léon Jacquard was a far wealthier man. The wedding, a small secret one attended only by a few of Jacquard's New Orleans friends, had taken place at Les Cyprès a fortnight ago.

The secrecy of the wedding, also the fact that the honey-moon had to be postponed until a more propitious time, had flawed her happiness somewhat. But Léon had ex-plained that these were touchy times and he feared to subject her to nasty repercussions from the Creoles if it became commonly known that so soon after her husband's death she had married a man who had carried on business dealings with the Yankees. It was all perfectly legal, he assured her, and it was the same in any war when businessmen on both sides were bold and astute enough to seize upon opportunities of mutual benefit that would not only swell their financial holdings but establish them as the backbone of the country who would be needed to help rebuild it after the war ended.

The deferred honeymoon, he told her, was one of the cruel necessities of war, due to the delicate complexity of his many military-related activities that night and day required all of his attention.

So much of his attention, she thought bitterly, that she didn't see him for days on end. Most of his time was spent in New Orleans, or in supervision of the remodeling being done on his manse, Les Colonnades, which he would not permit her to see until the work was finished. It was not so much that she missed his sexual demands—they often frightened her—but they made her feel *so* desirable.

Still, it always pacified her to remember how much she had gained—one of the richest husbands in the state, and so clever at making more money. When she turned all her money and the inheritance from Etienne over to Léon for investment, he had assured her that he would double, if not quadruple, it within the year. Not many women were so fortunate these days.

There came an unduly hard rapping on the dressing room door, followed by Aimée's excited voice. "Oh Missy Narcisse! Massa's back—!"

Narcisse was surprised. Léon had specifically said he couldn't possibly come today as he would be too busy at Les Colonnades.

"Well, why doesn't he come up?" she said sharply.

"Oh it not Marse *Jacquard*, missy! It be Marse Abbott who down dere!"

Narcisse sat as if petrified. "Impossible! Your old Marse Abbott is dead."

"He not daid! He de same as he usta be, 'cept for de Yankee unifo'm."

426

She felt a chill slither down her spine as she reached for her notepaper and a pen and rapidly scrawled out:

> *Léon—*
> *Paul Abbott is NOT dead! He has returned and is here now. Hurry!*
> *Narcisse*

Sealing the note in an envelope, she handed it to Aimée. "Tell Ammon to take one of the fastest horses and deliver this to Monsieur Jacquard at Les Colonnades immediately!"

"Yes, missy."

"And tell Monsieur Abbott that I shall be down presently."

Hastily, she completed her *toilette*, heart thudding with apprehension. If the person downstairs was *really* Abbott, much of her world would come tumbling down! But thank God for Léon. He would know how to handle it.

Putting on her practiced social smile, she swept regally toward the grand staircase, prepared to receive Abbott with her most iced civility.

ii

With a magnificent diamond in each ear and tears as large and brilliant in each eye, Micaela listened to the sonorous words of the priest:

". . . and I now pronounce you man and wife. . . ."

Then as Jacquard bent to kiss her, purely as a matter of custom, it was all she could do to keep from bursting into tears. But there were tears enough elsewhere in the room from the house servants, who were standing back watching.

While Jacquard was slipping money to the priest in an envelope and paying off the two witnesses, who promptly departed, she sank into a chair thinking, *So it has finally come to this. . . .*

The end of her long reprieve from Jac's tyranny had come with jolting suddenness. Pace Schuyler had been ordered back to Washington, effective immediately. Life with him had been tranquil and relatively happy. He had fervently declared his love for her and begged her to return to Washington with him and become his wife, promising that in Washington he would be able to hire the best lawyers and get the help of powerful congressmen in the recovery of her child.

Micaela had no choice but to refuse. Although she had grown very fond of Pace, she did not love him and felt it would be most unfair to him to marry him. More important, she would not leave without Rill.

The tears of their parting were scarcely dried on her cheeks when Jac reappeared. He had, as she well knew, kept her under close surveillance.

But it was a changed Jac. His manner was gentle, kind, apologetic.

"You were wise not to run off with Schuyler," he told her, "and you shall be rewarded. . . ."

"Rewarded for wishing to stay near my child?"

"For giving me an opportunity to make amends, my sweet. The truth is, I have had much time to think about how much I have made you suffer. I am more deeply ashamed and regretful than I can ever express in words. My most fervent wish now is to do all possible to make you happy."

"But that's so easy! All you need do is return my child."

"And you shall have your child back. But first you must understand the reasons for my actions. I am an impetuous man. I have a rash heart that often prompts me to actions beyond my control, and which later I regret. The terrible things I have done to hurt you were only because of my jealousies growing out of my great love for you."

"I would like to believe that, Jac."

"Then I am prepared to prove my words with acts. I wish you to marry me."

"Marry you—!" she gasped.

"What greater proof can I give of my sincerity? I wish you to share my life and my wealth. It is the only condition by which you can have your Rill back, for I too have come to love the child and could not bear to part with her. With you as my wife, you can be assured that Rill will receive a proper upbringing, the finest of educations, and be endowed with a fortune when she grows up."

For Rill's sake, Micaela had accepted.

"Of course it will be necessary," he had added later, "that our marriage be kept secret until after the war, when it will no longer matter what our Creole neighbors think. . . ."

And now it was done. She was Mrs. Léon Jacquard, mistress of Les Colonnades.

The priest was gone; the servants had returned to their various duties. She was alone with Jac.

"Though the cruel necessities of war force us to postpone a proper honeymoon, my love," Jac said with a touch of sarcasm in his smile, "we can at least enjoy some of the perquisites of marriage. I will ring for a servant and have champagne sent up to our bedchamber."

He started for the bellpull, but at that moment his elderly manservant entered. " 'Scuse me, massa, but heah a 'portant message jus' come fo' you—"

Jacquard snatched the envelope from the man's hand, tore it open. As he read, his face darkened with fury. Quickly he stuffed the note in a pocket and strode over to a cabinet, taking out a pistol. First checking it for ammunition, he thrust it under his belt, where it was hidden by his frock coat.

"What's wrong, Jac?"

"An urgent matter has come up that must be attended to promptly, but have no fear, I shall be back in an hour or two."

After he went out and was shouting for a groom to get his horse saddled, Aurora hurried into the room. The black girl had accompanied Micaela to Les Colonnades as her personal maid and to care for both of the children. Her face was both frightened and excited.

"Miz Micaela! Marse Paul come home!"

Shock pierced her like a knife. "What are you saying, Aurora! It can't be true!"

"It do be true! Ammon brung de message fo' Marse Jacquard. He say he seed Marse Paul wid 'is own eyes! Marse Jacquard goin' now to kill 'im!"

Micaela wasted not a moment. "Aurora, tell the groom to saddle me a horse while I get changed into a riding habit—!"

As she rushed up the stairs, a silent prayer was on her lips: *Dear God, don't let me be too late. . . .*

Three

Drums

i

It was a changed Paul Abbott who sat in a great Empire chair in the living room of Les Cyprès facing the extraordinarily beautiful Narcisse. Zambullah, who had accompanied Paul to the plantation and who was now waiting outside in the slave quarters, had told Paul the whole story of the kidnapping. Thus one great weight had lifted from Paul's spirits—but only to be replaced by another. He understood now the cruel duress Micaela had been under, how she had been forced to do Jacquard's bidding to save her child.

The new blow was to learn that his son Carson had disappeared. Narcisse had gone to great lengths, spending at least a half hour relating to him how Carson was believed to have wandered off into the swamp. Searching parties had combed the area in all directions for many days, turning up not a single clue. Meanwhile, refreshments had been served.

"I can well understand how very painful it is for you to hear such sad news about your son, Monsieur Abbott, for I too loved him so dearly that I had adopted him as my own son."

"But madam—how could you adopt a child whose father is still alive?"

Narcisse showed surprise. "Are you not aware, monsieur, that you were believed to be dead?"

It was Paul's turn to be surprised. So Micaela also would have been under the impression that he was dead!

"It is the first that I have heard of my demise," he said wryly.

"This is all so confusing," she said slowly, the fingers of one hand toying delicately with the large diamond on her other hand. "As the wife of Etienne, and as the adoptive mother of Carson, I had become accustomed to viewing Les Cyprès as my own home."

"I don't want to cause you any hardship, but I believe it would be more appropriate if you made suitable arrangements to move to another home, at your convenience."

"I much fear that my husband's thoughts on the matter differ from yours. . . ." As she spoke, her eyes frequently slid past him as if fearing to look directly at his face. Why was she so nervous, he wondered. Was her mind addled?

"But Mrs. Troyonne, your husband is dead."

"I am no longer Mrs. Troyonne. I have remarried. My present husband is Léon Jacquard."

Jacquard! His worst enemy! Apparently his astonishment showed on his face, for there was a tiny, taunting smile on her lips as she went on:

"Yes, we were married only two weeks ago. He is now handling all my plantation matters, so I could not move from here without his approval."

"Madam, aren't you overlooking the obvious fact that I am very much alive, and as the sole owner of Les Cyprès—"

From behind, a familiar male voice intruded:

"But that, monsieur, is a mere statistical error that can very easily be corrected—"

432

Paul whirled in his chair just in time to see the barrel of the gun descending. It crashed down on his skull amid a turbulence of bright lights that quickly sliced off into utter blackness. . . .

ii

Jacquard's face was exultant as he looked down at his enemy, slumped unconscious in the chair. He brought his pistol up, took aim—

"*Non*, Léon—*non*—!" Narcisse swiftly rose from her chair and went to push the pistol aside. "There is no need for it—!"

He faced her with a smile that was more of a snarl. "Don't you realize that if he lives you will lose Les Cyprès, everything?"

"Does it matter that much, Léon? After all, you are already a wealthy man."

"Only a fool rejects an opportunity for greater riches."

"But the risk—"

"What risk? Nobody knows he is here."

"The servants know."

"Hah! Niggers? Their words mean nothing."

"But you can't do it here—not in my home!"

"What's a little blood? The niggers can clean it up."

Narcisse stared at him as if seeing a stranger. For the first time it occurred to her that he might be a little mad. She had in fact gone through many tormented nightmarish nights because of Carson, because of her implied assent that the child should be disposed of. God would surely punish her! The thought was something she had been able to tolerate, blinded by the rich rewards, because it was nothing she had to witness, or even know about, something she could easily put out of her thoughts.

But this—murder in front of her own eyes!

"I won't permit it, Léon!" she said more firmly. "You

may take him away—into the swamp if you wish—but I am no longer a party to the deed."

He sneered. "Yet you seem willing enough to share the profits—"

He turned toward the gallery at the sound of approaching hoofs. Narcisse's nervous glance followed. Who could it be? She was not expecting guests.

"Ammon!" she called. "See who is arriving on horseback!"

In a few moments Ammon hurried in.

"It be Miz Micaela, missy. . . ."

Jacquard cursed. "She must have found out about Abbott—"

"How could she know?" Narcisse, having no knowledge of Micaela now living at Les Colonnades, was undisturbed. Her confidence was flowing back. She felt more than a match for any other woman. "And even if she does suspect, we can always deny that Abbott is here." To Ammon she called out a sharp order:

"Carry Monsieur Abbott into a closet at once!" She felt no need to explain matters to Ammon. He was the perfect servant. Unquestioning, absolutely loyal. He adored her. He would lay down his life for her.

"Yes, missy. . . ." The muscular Negro picked up Paul and carried him away.

Jacquard laughed harshly. "I too will remove myself from sight. Micaela will talk more freely without my presence, and it is imperative that I find out how much she knows. If too much, my plans will have to be radically changed. . . ."

iii

Micaela had become aware of the drums as she rode:

> *Toom-ti-ti-toom—*
> *Toom-ti-ti-toom—*

The voodoo drums! What was their message now, she wondered? Many slaveholders forbade their blacks to practice the cult of voodooism, which was universal among all slaves, but usually they permitted the drums. Drums were the black man's newspaper, as mystifying to whites as they were speedy. By some exotic cadence of beats and timing too subtle for white ears, messages could be transmitted and understood by all black listeners. The vibrations carried for miles, were picked up by other drums. They were said to be faster than telegraph. Whites were often amazed to discover that their blacks usually knew of happenings before they did.

Perhaps they were announcing that Marse Abbott was back, she thought with elation.

As she neared Les Cyprès, the intensity of the drums increased:

> BOOM-BOOM-BOOM—
> Tum-ti-ti-tum—
> Tum-ti-ti-tum—
> BOOM-BOOM-BOOM—

Dismounting at Les Cyprès, she saw Jacquard's horse tied to a hitching post. Praying that she was not too late, she hurried to the wide front door of the manor.

Ammon admitted her, his hooded eyes giving no indication that he knew her.

Narcisse greeted her with chilled aloofness.

"And what, may I ask, is the reason for this intrusion?" she said as her glance skimmed over Micaela from head to foot in a most insulting manner.

"I came to see my husband."

Narcisse's eyebrows arched. "I know nothing about your husband, whoever he may be."

"I refer to Paul Abbott."

Again the arched eyebrows. "It is common knowledge that Paul Abbott is dead."

She's a poor liar, Micaela thought angrily. "Then I wish to speak to Monsieur Jacquard."

"He is not here."

What devilry are they up to? she wondered. *Not only is she lying, but she's snubbing me in Paul's own home, which is my home too.*

"In that case I shall wait for him. . . ." Deliberately she walked past Narcisse to the big Empire chair and gracefully seated herself.

"You are most insolent! You are not an invited guest—!"

"Do I need to be? If Paul Abbott is truly dead, as you say, then as his widow I am the owner of Les Cyprès."

"What an outrage! You are but an octoroon! Because of your black blood, your marriage to Paul Abbott is not valid, and thus you have no claim whatsoever on his property."

"We were married in the North, where such marriages are valid."

"But this is Louisiana. I will no longer listen to such nonsense. I am ordering you to leave!"

"Not until I speak to Monsieur Jacquard. I know he is here because his horse is tethered outside."

"His horse, you say—?" Narcisse was now fairly screeching in anger. "I will have you know that my husband and his horse are not one and the same!"

Micaela's eyes widened. "Your husband? You and Jac—?"

Narcisse raised her aristocratic head high; her bright turquoise eyes hardened. "It is something we did not wish to advertise, but for the likes of you it matters not. Yes, we were married a fortnight ago—"

Micaela suddenly began laughing, almost hysterically.

"It amuses you, yes? Please spare me the sarcasm of informing me that you were once his mistress, as that I already know."

"I would not be crass, madame. I merely wish to fling back in your face your own words that Louisiana forbids marriage between a white and a *gens de couleur*. Did Monsieur Jacquard forget to tell you that he, like me, also has black blood coursing in his veins?"

Narcisse's face went white. "Y-you're lying!"

"Am I? Ask the voodoo priestess, Momselle Delphine,

who was once a maid to Jacquard's quadroon mother in Haiti. Ask any of the slaves from Haiti."

"*Non, non*—!" Narcisse gasped in horror.

"To further enlighten you," Micaela went on coolly, "I have also been honored by becoming the bride of our mutual husband—only about an hour ago. See my new rings?" She held up her left hand. "Are they as pretty as yours?"

Narcisse gaped at the rings. They were even more magnificent than her own.

"It cannot be—!" she cried.

Jacquard stepped into view wearing a sardonic smile.

"I fear it is, my love. Unfortunately you found out sooner than I had hoped, but now that the cat is out of the bag—"

"You monster!" Narcisse hissed at him.

"No melodramatics, please. Have some sympathy for my plight. I am now burdened with two lovely wives, and obviously, since I cannot legally keep both of them, one of you must go."

"Have no worries about that!" Narcisse snapped at him. "Since our marriage wasn't legal in the first place—thank God!—I'll be most happy if you keep your octoroon and I never have to see you again!"

"Ah, but now you have put your finger on the very problem I must solve. Micaela, you understand, is now my legal wife, and cannot by law be made to testify against her husband, but since you are not my wife and know far too much, you are the one I must eliminate—"

Narcisse looked at him aghast. "Léon! Surely you can't mean—"

"I mean precisely that, my dear. Be realistic. When it comes to a choice between losing ultimate ownership of Les Cyprès, or assuring the silence of one who stands in my way, which do you think I would choose?"

Listening, Micaela was appalled. Jac had to be insane!

"Jac, you are wrong—!" she cried. "Legally I am no more your wife than is Narcisse. I know now that our marriage is not valid because Paul is still alive!" Playing her cards like an expert, she threw the bait in front of Narcisse. "Is that not true, madame?"

Narcisse grasped at the straw eagerly. "Yes, yes—it is true! Your Paul is still alive!"

Jacquard laughed. "But that is the very linchpin of the problem—and can easily be solved with a single bullet."

A voice came from just inside the main entry:

"That may not be quite so easy, Mr. Jacquard—"

Joy at first soared in Micaela when she saw the two men in Yankee uniforms. The huge one holding a rifle was Zambullah. The other—

Then she saw the flash of movement as Jac whipped out a pistol.

"Paul—!" she shrieked. "Watch out!"

Zambullah threw himself in front of Paul just at the moment of the explosive report. The black man pitched forward on the floor, his rifle sliding over the carpet.

"Rotten bastard—!" Paul started toward Jacquard. Jacquard tossed aside his empty gun. A knife appeared in one hand. His teeth shone in a smile as he sprang at Paul.

Micaela watched in horror. It was all happening too fast to follow.

Ammon had come in and rushed forward to snatch up the rifle. Zambullah, blood staining his uniform, was trying to rise. Paul was grappling with Jac, one hand gripped on the wrist of the hand holding the knife. Both men's faces were contorted from a muscular impasse: the one striving to hold back the knife, the other straining to plunge it into his opponent. The knife was slowly gaining way. She could see now that Paul was not himself; his face was thinner, he had lost weight. Plainly his strength had been too drained by hardships to be a match for Jac's.

"Ahhh—!" Jacquard's voice was like a groan of triumph. "This is the supreme moment of pleasure I have been looking forward to all of these—"

The crack of a pistol cut off his words, and simultaneously a little red hole appeared in his chest. It began dribbling crimson. The knife slipped from a lax hand; his body slumped downward like a loose bag of grain. His unbelieving eyes rolled toward Micaela and the smok-

438

ing little pearl-handled pistol in her hand. He let out a forlorn wail.

"Micaela—" he gasped weakly. "How could you? Did you not know that I have always . . . loved you? As a beast loves, yes . . . but the only way I know . . . how to love. . . ." Choking sounds issued from his throat and now his eyes rolled heavenward. "Holy Mother, forgive me!"

Micaela dropped the gun and began weeping as Jac sank back dead on the carpet.

But Narcisse had spiraled into another kind of emotion; her voice rose hysterically:

"Ammon—shoot them—both of them! They have murdered Monsieur Jacquard!"

Ammon shook his head stolidly. "No, I no do dat."

"I'm *ordering* you!" she screamed. "Kill them and then I can say they were trying to murder me and you were only defending me. Kill them and I will make you rich and set you free. I promise!"

Ammon looked at her with a lugubrious smile.

"I already free, woman. Hear dem drums? Fo' de past hour dey been tellin' us de war's ovah. Gen'ral Lee done surrender to Linkum's army. . . ."

Narcisse burst into tears. "Now I've lost everything. . . ." she wailed.

Paul looked up from where he and Micaela were bent over Zambullah. "Not everything. I think you will find that since the Union has won the war, your marriage to Jacquard may be recognized as valid—in which case you will be a very rich woman."

"B-but then the whole world would find out that I married a husband with black blood!"

"My deepest sympathies, madam. I am truly sorry for you. . . ." Paul turned his attention back to Zambullah.

"It's a minor shoulder wound," he told Micaela. "After treatment, it will heal quickly."

Micaela's wet eyes searched his face. "But what about he wounds I have given you, my darling? Will they ever eal?"

"Knowing the truth has already healed them," he said.

if we say scripts are trademark, you own me and I own
us. I'm your partner. — — — partner, and it's the
same if we need Confederates. — — — they would
have to part, sooner or — later. — — — — — —

Epilogue

Paul and Micaela were at breakfast when Ammon rushed in waving an envelope in one hand.

"Mistuh Abbott," he said in great excitement, "de steamboat jus' brung me a letter—fust I ebber got'n ma hull life. I 'preciate it if yo' read it fo' me!"

Paul read it aloud:

Dear friend Ammon,

This letter is being wrote by my new mother to let you know I am well and happy. I wanted you to know becuz you are my best friend. I only run away becuz I heard my aunt Narseese and monsoor Jackard say they was going to kill me to get Lay Saypree all for themselfs. If my father was alive he sure would fix them good!

My new parents are my good friends, Joreen and Orrin Oakes, who just got married. They are going West in a big wagon to look for Joreen's brother and maybe build a ranch. They are taking me with them so I'll get to see lots of Indians. I hope you didn't worry too much about me.

Sincerely, your friend,
Carson Dixon Abbott

Paul put the letter down.

"I'm afraid," he said slowly, "that I can never rest or be happy in the knowledge that my fatherless, homeless son is wandering around somewhere in the West—even with the kind strangers who have taken him in. I shall have to begin a search for him. You and Rill stay here at Les Cyprès. Zambullah and Aurora will look after you. Of course I'll write, and return as soon as possible."

"*Non!*" Micaela's tone was most vehement. "Never again will I let you get far away from me! From now on wherever you go, Rill and I will go too." She rose from the table.

"Come—let's start packing. . . ."

John Updike

W0123-W

☐ TOO FAR TO GO	24002-9	$2.25
☐ THE CENTAUR	23974-8	$1.95
☐ COUPLES	24023-1	$2.50
☐ MARRY ME	23369-3	$1.95
☐ A MONTH OF SUNDAYS	C2701	$1.95
☐ THE MUSIC SCHOOL	23279-4	$1.75
☐ PICKED-UP PIECES	23363-4	$2.50
☐ PIGEON FEATHERS	23951-9	$1.95
☐ THE POORHOUSE FAIR	23314-6	$1.50
☐ RABBIT REDUX	23247-6	$1.95
☐ RABBIT, RUN	24031-2	$2.25
☐ OF THE FARM	30822-7	$1.50

DONALD HAMILTON Matt Helm Series

Isaac Asimov

Isaac Bashevis Singer

Winner of the 1978 Nobel Prize
for Literature

HOSHA	23997-7	$2.50
HORT FRIDAY	24068-1	$2.50
ASSIONS	24067-3	$2.50
CROWN OF FEATHERS	23465-7	$2.50
NEMIES: A LOVE STORY	24065-7	$2.50
HE FAMILY MOSKAT	24066-5	$2.95

FREE
Fawcett Books Listing

There is Romance, Mystery, Suspense, and Adventure waiting for you inside the Fawcett Books Order Form. And it's yours to browse through and use to get all the books you've been wanting . . . but possibly couldn't find in your bookstore.

This easy-to-use order form is divided into categories and contains over 1500 titles by your favorite authors.

So don't delay—take advantage of this special opportunity to increase your reading pleasure.

Just send us your name and address and 35¢ (to help defray postage and handling costs).

FAWCETT BOOKS GROUP
P.O. Box C730, 524 Myrtle Ave., Pratt Station, Brooklyn, N.Y. 11205

Name_____
(please print)

Address_____
City_____ State_____ Zip_____

Do you know someone who enjoys books? Just give us their names and addresses and we'll send them an order form too!

Name_____
Address_____
City_____ State_____ Zip_____

Name_____
Address_____
City_____ State_____ Zip_____